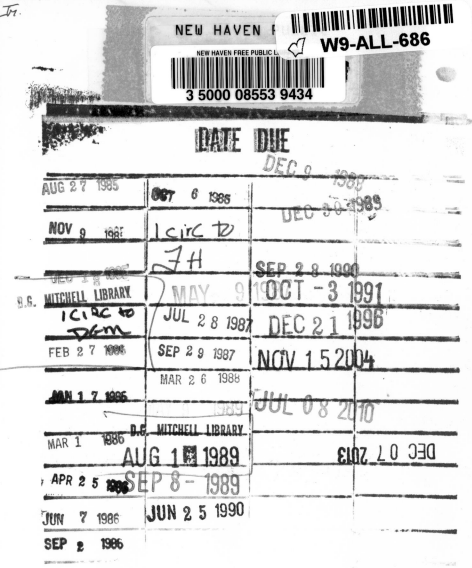

Books by Max Allan Collins

NOVELS:

Bait Money
Blood Money
The Broker
The Broker's Wife
The Dealer
The Slasher
Fly Paper
Hush Money
Hard Cash
Scratch Fever
The Baby Blue Rip-Off
No Cure for Death
True Detective
Kill Your Darlings
True Crime

NONFICTION:

One Lonely Knight: Mickey Spillane's Mike Hammer
    (with James L. Traylor)
Jim Thompson: The Killers Inside Him
    (with Ed Gorman)

EDITOR:

Tomorrow I Die (Mickey Spillane collection)
Mike Hammer: The Comic Strip (two volumes)

COMIC STRIP COLLECTIONS:

Dick Tracy Meets Angeltop (with Rick Fletcher)
Dick Tracy Meets the Punks (with Rick Fletcher)
The Files of Ms. Tree (with Terry Beatty)

MAX
ALLAN
COLLINS

St. Martin's Press
New York

Although the historical events in this novel are
portrayed more or less accurately (as much as the
passage of time, and contradictory source material, will
allow), fact, speculation and fiction are freely mixed,
here; historical personages exist side by side with
composite characters and wholly fictional ones—all of
whom act and speak at the author's whim.

Library of Congress Cataloging in Publication Data

Collins, Max Allan.
   True crime.

   I. Title.
PS3553.04753T68   1984   813'.54   84-18338
ISBN 0-312-82045-3

First Edition

10 9 8 7 6 5 4 3 2 1

*For my son Nate
a real heller*

"Let's do it."
—Cole Porter

"Let's do it."
—Gary Gilmore

CHICAGO, 1934

1
THE TRAVELING SALESMAN
JULY 13, 1934–JULY 23, 1934

SALLY RAND AT THE WORLD'S FAIR

Somebody had to burst Sally Rand's bubble.

And I was elected. I was, after all, the guy she'd hired to find out the truth about the self-professed oil millionaire from Oklahoma who'd proposed to her last Saturday night, after a month of flowers and gifts and nights on the town—though Christ knows where Sally found the time for the old boy, what with her various shows at the Paramount Club, the Chicago Theater and of course here at the Streets of Paris, at the world's fair.

Sally had *made* the world's fair, you see, or at least that's what her press agent had led everybody but Chicago to believe. Story was the poor old Century of Progress Exhibition was a dismal flop till Sally dropped her pants and climbed behind her ostrich plumes, at which point the fair's turnstiles began spinning like the city fathers in their graves.

Only that was a press agent's dream; the fair was its own dream-come-true, and help from Sally Rand was appreciated, but hardly crucial. Chicago had watched through the fall, winter and spring as the art-deco spires rose from eighty-six acres along the lake, and by summer the city was eager to leave hard times temporarily behind to enter the City of Tomorrow. The turnstiles were spinning from the fair's first morning, and Sally was only one of a small army of exotic dancers who helped fan the latter-day Chicago fire.

Because there was more than naked women to see at the fair. Like silk stockings being woven, and a Gutenberg Bible (and the press it had been printed on); like the Silver Streak streamliner; and an auto-mobile assembly line; and something called television. You could even see a million dollars (at the Federal Building, under armed guard) or a million dollars worth of diamonds (at the General Exhibits building, similarly guarded). And kids of all ages could wonder at Sinclair Oil's plaster dinosaurs, and the Seminole village where real, live Indians wrestled real, live alligators. And you could see *Time* and *Fortune* magazine covers two stories high, and a thermometer nineteen stories higher than that. You could see a lot more than just Sally Rand in the nude.

Not that there was anything wrong with seeing Sally Rand in the nude. I'd seen her show last year, the first year of the fair, and she by damn *didn't* have anything on under there but her. The boys hadn't been lying! And I understood this year she'd traded her plumes in for a big transparent balloon, a bubble she called it, and was nuder than ever.

I supposed most healthy male Chicagoans had made it out to Sally's show during the opening week of the fair. But this was my first time this summer to the Century of Progress, though it had been open over a month already—because I'd had my fill of the place the summer before.

Like a lot of people in Chicago, for me the 1933 fair had meant work. Thousands of jobs had bee created by the Dawes brothers— Rufus T., president of the fair, and his older brother General Charles G., former vice-president of the United States (under Coolidge), thought by many to be the real brains behind the Century of Progress. Say what you will about the Dawes brothers; dismiss them as businessmen/bankers whose efforts were self-serving, if you like. But they saw to it that a lot of dough got pumped into the Windy City.

Hotels were packed (and the hotels could use it—most of 'em were verging on bankruptcy before the fair) and restaurants and theaters did booming business, as did the newly reopened nightclubs and taverns (or at least newly openly reopened) after beer became legal in April of '33 , during the fair's first summer. Prohibition gasped its last dry gasp (Repeal was only months away); and the Century of Progress—awash in beer as it was, thanks to the Capone/Nitti Outfit, who were willing to sell people suds even if it *was* legal—became a celebration of a better, wetter, tomorrow.

Of course, many—probably most—of the fairgoers were from out of town; and amid all those solid citizens from the farms and villages of the Midwest were pickpockets from everywhere else. And that's where I came in.

Me. Nathan Heller. A private operative, but formerly a plain-clothes dick on the pickpocket detail. Having that background, I'd been hired to coach the pith-helmeted private police force working the fairgrounds in the fine art of the dip. Or should I say, the fine art of spotting and nabbing ther dip. And I'd done some supervising throughout the summer and fall, until the close of the fair in November. The job had paid a pretty penny.

I'd been hired by General Dawes himself, not because I was such a stalwart citizen, but because I had him over a barrel. That's another story, which has been told elsewhere; for the purposes of this narrative, it's enough to say that once General Dawes had repaid what he felt was a debt owed me, he saw fit not to hire me back when the Century of Progress was held over for a second year.

That, and a few other unpleasant experiences on these fairgrounds, had kept me away this summer, thus far. Now, as I strolled the fair on this sultry July afternoon, the walkway brimming with women in bright print dresses and floppy hats and men in shirt sleeves and straw boaters and kids in short pants and smiles, I felt a sense of nostalgia for the place, I'd spent time here with a woman I loved. Still loved.

But she was in Hollywood, both literally and figuratively, and I was in Chicago, underfed and underworked. Sally Rand was the first client I'd had in two months, outside of the ongoing work I did for a retail credit firm, checking credit ratings and investigating insurance claims. The A-I Detective Agency (me) had had a good first year; unfortunately, it (I) was deep into its second year, and subsisting mostly on the dwindling proceeds of the first.

If Mr. Roosevelt was leading the country out of the Depression, he was starting somewhere other than Chicago—or anyway, somewhere other than the corner of Van Buren and Plymouth.

So now here I was again, feeling faintly ridiculous in my lightweight white suit and wide-brimmed Panama hat (souvenirs of a Florida job last year), wandering the avenues of the City of Tomorrow, in the shadow of the twin Eiffel-like towers of the fair's famed Sky Ride, where "rocket cars" skimmed above the flat surfaces and pastel colors of the modernistic pavilions. One of the towers was nicknamed Amos, and the other Andy, but I never could remember which was which. (Except on the radio.) I hopped a double-decker bus, took a wicker seat on the upper open deck, where you could feel a lake breeze cut through the heat; that felt good, but being here at the fair again felt odd. It was like I was my own ghost, somehow; haunting myself. I got off at the Streets of Paris, which you entered through a big blue-and-white-and-red facade designed to look like a steamship.

Inside, the narrow "streets" were patrolled by phony gendarmes, a

temporary world of sidewalk cafés with striped awnings and little
round tables under big colorful umbrellas, and stalls where you could
buy Parisian hats (by a North Side milliner) and charcoal sketches of
yourself (by a Tower Town art student in a beret and paste-on mustache), along walkways prowled by chestnut vendors, strolling trou-
badors and flower girls. (No wildly careening taxicabs or whores,
however.) The flat surfaces of flimsy exterior walls were covered with
startling bright posters, and an outdoor "Lido" swimming pool
boasted free floor shows of bathing beauties every bit as lovely as
Miss Rand.

But Miss Rand was a star, now (she'd made a movie in Hollywood
with George Raft, since her success here last summer), and she had
her own revue in the Café de la Paix, with dancing girls and the
works. She had a matinee coming up in half an hour, so I went in and
dropped her name and a tuxedoed waiter whose French extended to,
"This way, mon sewer," sat me at a postage-stamp table, near ringside.

The place was nearly full, couples mostly, the men trying to hide
anticipatory smiles, the women pretending to be embarrassed, when
irritated (if curious) was more like it. Meanwhile, overhead fans kept
the place cool—overhead fans and beer.

The show took place on the dance floor, behind which the tuxedoed orchestra was seated in tiers on a stage; there was no seating to
the right or left of the polished floor, which extended to draped areas
on either side. I was halfway into a second beer when the orchestra
began playing something vaguely Parisian and the lights dimmed and
the dance floor filled up with blond show girls in filmy dresses, moving around trailing gauzy cloth like untalented but well-endowed
Isadora Duncans.

After a while the show girls went away, the lighting went blue, and
Sally came gliding on, in a clinging white gown, long blond tresses
swaying, accompanied by her big bubble, which she guided, though
it seemed to have a mind of its own, The orchestra, who kept their
eyes on their music despite the rear view they were getting, played
Beethoven's *Moonlight Sonata*, while the gown seemed to accidentally slip, and expose a breast. Then it slipped again, and pretty soon
it slipped entirely. This was seen in gratefully accepted glimpses, as
she moved behind and to either side of the bubble as she bounced
and directed it, but as the orchestra eased into a Brahms waltz, the
glimpses became more generous, and as the blue light dimmed no-

ticeably, Sally stepped from behind the bubble, nude as a gr , smiling, Godiva-like hair almost glowing, hands arched in a combination of grace and pride.

When I entered her dressing room backstage, she was sitting before her lightbulb-surrounded mirror combing out her medium-length light brown hair; the long blond hair—a wig—was on the head of a dressmaker's dummy nearby. She wore a silky blue robe and had a bobby pin in her teeth.

"Heller!" she said, looking at me in the mirror. "I saw you, ringside. How'd you like the show?"

"I liked it fine. I've always liked classical music."

She put the hairbrush down and the bobby pin too and turned and looked at me; her wide, red pretty smile seemed sincere. She had the longest eyelashes I ever saw on a woman (or a man, for that matter) and they seemed to be real. Her eyes were the same color blue as her robe.

"Culture lover, huh?" she said. "Take off your hat, and pull up a chair. I like your white suit."

I took off my hat, pulled up a chair. "I feel like an ice-cream man."

"The ice-cream man cometh, huh? What did you find out for me?"

A little fan—an electric one, not the kind Sally hid behind—was whirring on a table over to the left, turning in a little half-circle, blowing streamers in the air.

"Your sugar daddy may be a gold digger."

She looked disappointed, but only mildly. "Oh?"

"He's in oil, all right. He owns a gas station."

"The lying little weasel."

"These are hard times; he used to own a dozen of 'em, all over Oklahoma. He may have been worth a little dough, once. Hell, he still is. A little dough."

"But he doesn't make two grand a week like yours truly."

"Ouch," I said. "Don't say that to a man you're paying ten bucks a day and expenses."

"Maybe you're in the wrong business."

"I've been told that before. But so far nobody's offered me two grand to prance around in my birthday suit."

She smiled wryly and leaned forward, folded her hands; her silky blue robe fell open, just a little. One well-formed, large but not-too-large breast was half-exposed. I crossed my legs.

"You might look pretty good in your birthday suit," she ventured.

I shook my head, grinned. "Not two grand worth."

She lit a cigarette. "You want one of these?"

"No thanks. Not a habit I ever picked up."

She shrugged. "They say it's good for you. Anyway, Heller, why haven't you made a pass at me?"

I didn't see that coming, so it took me a moment before I could reply.

"You're a client," I managed. "It wouldn't be ethical."

"Ethical? In Chicago? I think I've made it plain I find you attractive. And there's worse-looking women in town than Sally Rand."

"So I hear."

She blew a smoke ring. "Are you afraid of me?"

"Why, 'cause you're a star? I met famous people before."

"Did you ever sleep with any?"

"Just Capone. He snores."

She laughed; it was high-pitched, very feminine. But there was a core of strength in the little dame, no question.

"So my millionaire's a faker, huh? Easy come, easy go. I guess I didn't want to quit show business, anyway." She sighed and turned back to the mirror. "How old are you, Heller?"

"Twenty-eight."

Her electric fan whirred; streamers tickled the air.

"I'm almost thirty," she said. "How long can I take my clothes off for a living?"

"From the looks of you, a good long time."

She *had* been around, though, even if it didn't show. She'd been a cigarette girl and a chorus girl, a dancer in a Gus Edwards Revue, an extra in the silents, a Hollywood Wampus Baby Star, which led to a contract with De Mille, though when sound came in she was dropped. She was a has-been of twenty-eight when she made her overnight success after fourteen years in show business by dressing as Lady Godiva for a Fine Arts Ball at the Congress Hotel on the eve of the world's fair.

Now she was peeking out from behind fans and bubbles, when she wasn't in and out of court—which of course created the publicity that kept her hot.

"My real name is Helen, you know," she said. "Helen Beck. But very few people still call me Helen."

"Would you like me to?"

"I'm thinking about it." She began brushing her hair. Her other

hair, the blond wig on the dressmaker's dummy, was blowing a bit in
the electric fan's breeze. "Do you know where I got my name?"

"Off a Rand McNally map?"

"You've read the newspaper stories, then."

"Who hasn't? You're better known than the First Lady."

"And a damn sight better looking."

"Yeah, but so am I."

She turned and smiled and looked at me. "Why are you still here?"
She said this with no nastiness.

"I don't know."

"Are you thinking about making a pass at me?"

"Maybe."

"What changed your mind?"

"You're not a client, anymore."

"Does that make it kosher?"

"It could."

She stood and the robe slipped to her waist. Her breasts were very
beautiful. She was powdered white, for the stage; talcum powder.
She smelled good; she smelled like a great big baby.

I went over and kissed her.

It was a nice kiss, but something was missing. She looked up at me
with those long lashes and sad blue eyes.

"What is it, Nate? What's wrong?"

"Nothing," I said, moving back. "Maybe I better go."

"It's that actress of yours."

"You—you know about her?"

"I know a lot of things. She left you. Went to Hollywood. You don't
owe her anything."

"We still write."

"Do her letters keep you warm at night?"

"Not particularly. But in this weather, who needs it?"

"Maybe you do. Come and kiss me again."

I thought about it a second, then did.

It was better this time.

"You need a new girl," she said, and enfolded me in her arms.

"Maybe I need a new actress," I said into her neck. Her sweet,
talcum-smelling neck.

She pushed me away, gently, keeping me within her arms. Her
eyes, her smile, were knowing and yet gentle, very gentle.

"I'm just a Missouri farm girl," she said. "Scratch most any actress, and that's what you'll find. We're not special. Just playing at being special."

"Shush, Helen."

The floor was wooden but her silk robe was cushion enough.

Now all I needed was another client.

He was waiting outside my office door, hat in hand.

My office was at the dead end of a hall on the fourth floor of the building on the corner of Van Buren and Plymouth, just a stone's throw from the exclusive Standard Club. But don't get the wrong idea: it was also just a healthy spit away from a couple of flophouses. Chicago's an open-minded place—bums and bankers, whores and debutantes, crooks and cops. There's room for everybody, here. Just don't ask me to sort out who goes in what slot.

The building my office was in was full of marginal businesses and second-rate doctors and third-rate lawyers and possibly one first-rate detective who deserved better. So if anybody shlepped up three flights and stood outside my office, he was either a bill collector, a process server or a potential client. Walking down the corridor, the wood-and-mostly-glass walls of offices on either side of me like a tank I was a fish in, I studied this bird and tried to sort out *his* slot.

He was a pale blond man with a darker blond mustache, immaculately groomed in a tailored brown suit with a yellow-and-brown bow tie. The hat in his hand was straw, with a chocolate band; he had a thin, rather pointed nose and eyes the color of slate behind wire glasses. He looked rather harmless, and from the way he stood, head bowed a bit, he seemed shy, even a little timid. Which either made him a client, or a process server. Process servers study looking timid, you know.

On the chance that he might be a client, however, I did not turn around, but kept walking; approached him.

"Mr. Heller?" he said. He smiled tentatively; the skin of his face pulled tight over his cheeks. Like he'd never smiled before. Even tentatively.

"That's right," I said, and he stood to one side as I unlocked the pebbled-glass door.

"I'd like to inquire about your services," he said.

I smiled and made a gracious gesture with one hand. "I'd like you to," I said, and he nodded, and stepped inside.

Mine was a good-size office, but there was no outer waiting area, just one big room, with cream-color plaster walls. A big scarred oak desk was opposite the door, and behind the desk were windows, several of which I immediately opened to let a little air in. Out the windows was a view of the El. There was also a brown leather couch with tears repaired with brown tape, a wooden filing cabinet, a hat tree and, against the right wall as you came in, a big brown cabinet.

"Is that a Murphy bed?" my potential client asked.

I got him a chair and he sat across from my desk, which I got back behind and said, "Yes. We're like Pinkerton's. We never close."

He shrugged. Seemed embarrassed to have brought it up. "I just . . . wondered. You just don't often see a Murphy bed in an office."

"I live here," I said, taking my suitcoat off and tossing it on the desk, loosening my tie, rolling up my sleeves. It was hot, and, unlike Sally Rand, I had no fan. "If you'd like to take your coat off, be my guest. Make yourself at home."

He waved that off, despite a faint beading of sweat along his forehead, but did place his hat on the edge of my desk, saying, almost incredulously, "You *live* here?"

"I try not to advertise it, because it doesn't impress my other clients any more than it's impressing you. But I have an arrangement with the landlord to live in the office in exchange for rent. I'm a night watchman of sorts."

"I see." He folded his arms, crossed his legs; tried to hide his second thoughts about hiring me.

"Times are hard," I said.

He looked at me blankly.

"It's been in all the papers," I said.

"Oh. Yes. Of course. I . . . I'm not bothered by your lack of . . ."

"Of a secretary. Of associates. Of decent furniture. I'm relieved."

He smiled again, a little nervous twitch of a smile; his face was tight as a mask. "I'm not a wealthy man, myself. I probably couldn't afford someone like . . . Pinkerton's or Hargraves. What are your rates, Mr. Heller?"

"Ten dollars a day and expenses."

He nodded, stroked his mustache, adjusted the way his glasses were sitting on his nose.

"Is that too high for you?" I asked. "I assure you I'm fully qualified.
I was on the police force here for a number of years. . . ."

He twitched his smile again. "I won't hold that against you, Mr.
Heller."

Where this flash of humor—however slight—came from, I hadn't
the faintest idea; but a brief sparkle in the slate eyes disappeared as
quickly as it came, and he said, "I have full confidence in you, Mr.
Heller."

That stopped me.

"Why?" I said.

That stopped him.

"Well . . . let's just say you were recommended by an attorney."

"Who would your attorney be?"

"I, uh, didn't say it was *my* attorney, Mr. Heller."

"If I was referred to you by an attorney, I'd like to know who it
was."

"Is that important?"

"If I haven't heard of him, I'm going to start wondering what this is
about. Excuse me, but one thing I can't allow my clients to be is
evasive with me. I can't do honest work for you if you won't be honest with me. Fair enough?"

"Louis Piquett," he said, softly.

"Louis Piquett," I said.

I didn't know what to make of that. I *had* done a job for Piquett
once—through him, I'd performed a service for a certain underworld
figure. Much of Piquett's practice was criminal law, so it was natural
he'd have connections with both mob and local government (the line
between which was often a fine one).

Piquett had a large, and apparently mostly aboveboard, practice;
he was, after all, a former city prosecutor—though admittedly that
had been in the especially corrupt administration of Big Bill
Thompson (a onetime law partner of his). That his client list included
a who's who of bank robbers and gangsters—among them Leo Brothers, the accused slayer of Jake Lingle—only made him "colorful" in
Chicago terms.

"Okay," I said, still a little thrown. "That's a reference I can accept.
How do you know Piquett?"

"He's the attorney my employers recommended."

"Who are your employers?"

"I'd rather not involve them—they're a grain sales and service company, out of Gary." He cleared his throat, and added, "Indiana?" as if I might not know where Gary was.

Well, this at least made sense; a grain company might have had business with the mob, back in the recent bootlegging past, which could lead them to Piquett. That seemed innocent enough. And so did my client.

I took out a yellow pad from a left-hand drawer. Began scrawling some notes in pencil.

"Why don't we start with your name," I said.

"Howard," he said. "John Howard."

"All right, Mr. Howard. What is it I can do for you?"

He uncrossed his legs; put his hands on his knees. "This is hard for me . . ."

"Just regard me as you would your attorney, Mr. Howard. Whatever you say, it'll be confidential. Anything embarrassing, or illegal . . . that'll stay within these walls. Between us. And whatever problem you're having, it's nothing I haven't dealt with before, believe me. Like a doctor, I've seen a lot of different kinds of illnesses."

"I think my wife is cheating on me."

Imagine that.

"Go on," I said.

"I'm a salesman. Traveling salesman. Selling to feed and grain stores in a two-state area. That keeps me on the road much of the time. Weeks at a time, at times."

"I see."

"And Polly . . . well, Polly's always been a little free-spirited. Very independent."

"How long have you been married?"

"Just over a year. A few months ago, I got this new territory—it was a big opportunity for me, how could I pass it up? Only it meant . . . being gone for longer stretches of time than before. And, well, she didn't seem to mind. I guess I wish she would have minded. Then last week I found out she's been working at a café. Took the job without even telling me. I confronted her about it, asked her why, why on earth she was doing this, didn't I make good money, didn't I do right by her, and she said she was just bored—and that 'a girl can use a little money of her own.'"

"Do you have any children, Mr. Howard?"

"No. None. Not yet. I hope to . . ."

"I see. Is it so wrong for her to have a job, a little something to keep her busy?"

"I suppose not."

"Extra money, in times like these, is that anything to be angry over?"

"Perhaps not . . ."

"Wouldn't some husbands be grateful for the extra income?"

"Possibly . . ."

"If that's all the more reason you have to be suspicious, I'd have to advise you—much as I hate to lose a prospective client—to leave well enough alone."

Outside, the El rumbled, rattled; he glanced at it, like the world passing him by. I waited for the noise to go away before getting back into this—with the open windows, there was no other choice.

Then, when silence filled the room again, he looked at me and said, "She should have told me."

"Told you what?"

"That she was working! She should have asked me."

"Asked your permission, you mean?"

"Well of course! I'm—I'm the *husband*, aren't I?"

"Somebody's got to wear the pants," I said, keeping the sarcasm to myself, I hoped.

"That's not the most disturbing part."

"Tell me what is."

He looked away from me, as if he couldn't bear to make this admission and eye contact at the same time. "She's working under her maiden name. Hamilton. Not her married name."

That seemed curious, but not necessarily sinister.

"She's just asserting her independence," I said.

"But she's a married woman!"

"Married women have a right to an identity of their own. Or anyway that's what a lot of 'em think."

He spoke barely moving his lips. "She may be asserting more than just her independence."

"You think she's seeing other men, then?"

"That's what I'd like you to find out."

"You have no other reason to believe this other than your wife using her maiden name to get a job."

"There's another reason."

"Well?"

He sighed, heavily; looked out at the El. "It's personal."

"Getting cuckolded is personal, Mr. Howard. Convince me I wouldn't be wasting your money by taking on this job."

"It's the way she is . . . way she acts . . . in bed."

"Cold, you mean?"

He looked at me, the slate eyes very sad. "Not at all. Just the reverse."

"What's wrong with that?" I should have this guy's problems.

"She's doing things I didn't teach her."

"Oh. Maybe she's imaginative, or has a girlfriend who's been around who shared some secrets."

"Or read a sexual manual. Or was more experienced before our marriage than she at first let on. Yes, I've thought of those things. But she's trying too *hard*, in bed; it's as if—as if she's trying to allay any suspicions I might have. Besides. A husband *senses* when a wife has been unfaithful, don't you know that?"

Actually, I knew the opposite to be true in many cases; but why argue with money?

"I'll be glad to look into this, Mr. Howard. For one reason only— to ease your mind. I'm inclined to think your wife will come out of this smelling like a rose."

"I pray you're right, Mr. Heller."

He gave me the particulars—the address of the café, 1209½ West Wilson Avenue, which was in the neighborhood known as Uptown, so called because that was where the El ended; and their apartment, in the Malden Plaza Hotel, a few blocks from where she was working. He also gave me a snapshot of her, a pretty, apple-cheeked girl who seemed innocence personified.

I gave him some particulars, too—assured him that I would shadow his wife without her knowing; that if I did find she had a lover or lovers, I would make no direct confrontation. That sort of embarrassment, that sort of complication, he pointedly did not want. I assured him that his wife—and any lover—would not know I was there. That was my job.

He didn't want photos; he wasn't looking for evidence for a divorce case.

"I just want the truth, Mr. Heller."

"That's a scarce commodity, Mr. Howard," I said. "And this *is* Chicago . . ."

I asked him for a twenty-five-dollar retainer and he stood and drew five tens from a fairly well-stuffed wallet.

"Since I'll be on the road, and you won't be able to reach me," he said, spreading the five bills on my desktop like a poker hand, "I'd prefer to pay you for a full week's work, now."

I managed not to stutter. "Fine. If I need to go beyond a week. . . ?"

"Do it. I'll be in touch soon."

With a final tight mirthless smile, he extended his hand and I stood behind the desk and shook it.

"I appreciate your help, Mr. Heller."

"I hope I *can* be of help, by proving to you you've a good, loyal, loving little wife at home."

"I pray so," he said. "I pray so."

Then he was gone, and I put his money in my pocket, and wondered where I'd seen the pretty, apple-cheeked girl in the snapshot before.

UPTOWN

I started the job the following Monday, which was the day the heat wave really started taking itself seriously. At 7:00 A.M. I caught the El—Uptown was six miles north of the Loop—and already it was sweltering; every man on the train was in his shirt sleeves, with suit-coat over arm or left the hell home. The only men I saw that day with their coats on were the old gents sitting on benches in front of the El station, where I got off at Wilson and Broadway; they seemed to be unchanging fixtures of the landscape, a part of the ornate, carved-stone station, like the marble arch with the clock in its grillwork belly that hovered above the front entryway.

The terra-cotta El station—patterned, so they said, after New York's Grand Central—was typical of the Uptown district's naïvely grandiose opinion of itself. Though few of the buildings were taller than three stories—the exceptions being a couple of hotels and a few high-rise apartment houses and the occasional office building—Uptown fancied itself a miniature Loop, and with some justification. The gingerbread on the buildings bore the influence of that other Chicago world's fair, the Columbian Exposition of '93, where the hodgepodge beaux arts style of pseduo-European/classical architecture reigned; and in Uptown to this day a fairlike atmosphere prevailed. There were movie palaces like the Riviera, dance halls like the Aragon, specialty shops, department stores, banks, drugstores, delis, tearooms; restaurants from Russian to Polish to Greek, as well as chop suey joints and a Swedish cafeteria.

In this blistering weather, however, the beaches of Lake Michigan, the eastern border of Uptown, would be doing more business than the businesses—with the possible exception of the orange juice huts and ice-cream parlors. And the bars and cafés, offering something cool to drink, wouldn't be faring poorly, either.

The Howard girl's café was a block from the station—a sign protruded over the sidewalk proclaiming it the s & s SANDWICH SHOP— in a three-story building with apartments above. Since its address had a "½" in it, I'd expected a hole-in-the-wall greasy spoon; but as I walked by, glancing in the window, I saw a long counter and floor space to the tune of eight or ten tables, and a trio of waitresses, one of which was the apple-cheeked pretty Polly.

That's all I saw, because I was glancing, and I walked across the street to a four-story residential hotel called the Wilson Arms. The bottom floor was a bar, and the check-in desk was at the top of the second floor. The place was no competition for the Edgewater Beach, but it was no flophouse either. I paid for three nights—which set me back as many dollars—and rented an electric fan for one day. At twenty-five cents, the fan was highway robbery; after all, I knew store clerks who were making only a nickel an hour, these days, and glad for it. But it was hot, and I had a fifty-buck retainer to play with, and Chicago was unfair even when there wasn't a depression.

So I sat in a small room on the second floor by the open window, the fan on a table not far from me, blades clicking on the wire mesh as they whirled around, attempting to cool me. I had pulled up an easy chair and was as comfortable as possible, my tie loosened, my shirt unbuttoned.

Down on the street, as morning headed toward noon, the sidewalks were filled with men in shirt sleeves and girls in light summery dresses. The dresses clung sweatily to the girls, which in many cases made for pleasant viewing; the equally sticky shirts of the men, with their underarm sweat circles, didn't. There weren't many school-age kids around—they were at the beaches, mostly—but matronly gals in shade hats and tent dresses prowled the sidewalks, carrying shopping bags, looking cross and wishing they were younger and weighed less. I wished I could grant them their wish.

In this heat nobody but working stiffs stayed indoors. Even in cool weather, though, there'd have been plenty of activity on this street. Broadway and Wilson was the heart of Uptown's considerable commercial district; parked autos lined either side of the street, and cabs prowled constantly by, often finding takers.

Polly's café was doing a brisk business, as people headed in for Cokes and lemonades. Cooling off was the priority of the day. College boys (or anyway college-age boys) sat on little stoops in doorways, or leaned against lampposts, often nibbling at ice-cream cones that threatened to melt down their arms, or drinking orange juice out of paper cups that gave them citrus mustaches. The boys were watching the girls in the summery, sweat-clinging dresses, the little rats. Shame on 'em.

Hard times seemed not to have hit Uptown as hard as some parts of the city; but there were, now and then, reminders: several men wearing homemade sandwich signs wandered by, asking in bold hand letters: WANTED—A DECENT JOB. Then something personally descriptive, like FAMILY MAN, 43. In smaller letters beneath were printed job résumés, including phone numbers and addresses.

From down the street I heard Louis Armstrong, faintly; I craned my head out the window. There was a shoeshine parlor down there, on Polly's side of the street; the colored boys in their undershirts and wide pants were singing along with the Victrola, mimicking Satchmo, as they whapped the cloths across their customer's hot feet. They even danced a little. But just a little. In this heat I was surprised they could sing. Jazz does wonders.

Buttoning my shirt, snugging my tie, I went down to the bar and bought a bottle of cold beer and back up to the room and spent an hour drinking it; the last swig was warm as spit. By now there'd been any number of men going in the sandwich shop alone who might have been Polly's boyfriend; but no one had stayed longer than it would take to have a Coke or anyway a sandwich. Polly was working the tables, and I caught a glimpse of her occasionally in the café window, taking an order at, or clearing, one of the front tables. Nothing seemed to be going on in Polly's life today except waitressing.

She still seemed familiar to me. And I still hadn't placed her.

By 2:00 P.M. my stomach was making noise, so I went down on the street and gave one of the college-age boys half a buck to go across the street and buy me a ham-and-cheese sandwich at Polly's café. He didn't ask why I didn't want to cross the street myself; he just went for the sandwich, brought it to me in a paper bag five minutes later, and earned the quarter's change. Maybe now he'd go rent himself an electric fan.

The sandwich was okay, the bread was fresh at least, but another beer from the bar downstairs to wash it down was better. Afternoon came, and the heat let up a bit; down to the mid-nineties. Customers, many of them male, and unaccompanied, went into the café; but none stayed long enough to rate even a suspicious glimmer.

By 7:00 P.M., I'd had five beers and as many trips to the hall john. The beers had taken no inebriating toll on me, spread out over the eleven or so hours I'd been here. But they—and the clicking bladed fan—had kept me awake, and alive. Evening was on its way—though it was still sunny out; who the hell's idea was this daylight savings time crap, anyway?—and a reprieve from the communal hot seat would soon be in Chicago's grasp.

Shortly after seven, Polly Howard (or Hamilton, as she was calling herself here) stepped out of the café, wearing a pink-and-white print dress with a bow in front. She must've changed out of her waitress uniform in the back. Despite having worked a twelve-hour shift in unbearable heat, she looked rather fresh, her reddish-brown hair bouncing above her shoulders as she looked side to side, a small purse in her hands held like a fig leaf in front of her.

Since she seemed to be waiting for someone, someone who might be about to pick her up, I hurried out of the room and down the stairs and then slowed to a saunter to find an inconspicuous spot on the street, to continue watch. I wandered up to the corner and picked up a *Daily News* from the stand; making like I was reading as I walked, I could see Polly standing there, patiently, waiting for her ride. Men and boys walking by gave her the eye, but got nothing back for their trouble.

Maybe Polly *was* faithful to her traveling-salesman hubby.

A cab pulled up and a man got out.

He was a handsome, dapper-looking dark-haired man with a pencil mustache and gold-rim glasses and a tailored gray suit, suitcoat slung over his arm. He was hatless. Not tall. Not short.

The cab stayed in place, motor purring as the man held the door open for Polly and she flashed him a smile that said her husband was in a lot of trouble.

He got in after her, and the cab pulled away, east on Wilson.

A second later I flagged the next eastbound cab and climbed in back and leaned forward and pointed.

"Follow that car," I said.

The red taillights of the Yellow cab up ahead of my Checker were soon headed south, down Broadway; when we cut over on Diversey, toward the lake, it was obvious we were headed for the Loop. The guy in the gold-rim glasses and mustache must've wanted to impress pretty Polly, because they could've almost fallen onto the El, as close to the Wilson Avenue Station as her café was. And here he was cabbing it downtown. Throwing his—and my—money around.

That fifty-buck retainer was looking smaller and smaller.

When they got out in front of the Morrison Hotel on Madison, just a few blocks from my office—which I'd vacated to be closer to Polly, remember—I really began to resent the way the guy was spending my money. The Morrison had a traveler's lounge where I freshened up each day, thanks to an arrangement the landlord of my building had made for me. Being led here was like following your wife and her boyfriend to your own house. Somehow I was beginning to feel as much a sucker as my poor traveling-salesman client.

Well, Polly and her pal probably weren't here for the mattress—there were a few thousand less conspicuous places in the city for a one-nighter than a hotel in the heart of the Loop—so they had to be here for the nightlife.

Which irked me, because the Uptown area—which they'd fled by cab—was, at night, the North Side's Great White Way. A hodge-podge of nightclubs and restaurants, to be sure, with its share of sleazy joints, but also ritzy ones and everything between. Why come to the Loop? Except to impress a dame and blow your money. And mine.

My cab went on by as the mustached man, his arm gently around the beaming Polly's shoulder, went in the main entrance. I paid the cabbie around the corner—a buck for the ride and a dime tip—got out, made a note of the expense in my little notebook, and went around to the Clark Street entrance.

The Morrison lobby was plush, lots of gray marble and dark wood

Still, there was no mistaking her.

"Nate, you bum," a familiar tenor voice said. "You're supposed to be working!"

I touched a napkin to my mouth and smiled up at my friend Barney Ross, who was wearing a tux he looked uncomfortable in and had a good-looking redheaded girl on his arm, which made a more comfortable fit.

"I am working," I said softly. "Why don't you and your lovely friend fill these two empty chairs before you blow my cover?"

Barney's bulldog-cute face made an embarrassed smirk and the puppy-dog brown eyes rolled, and he pulled a chair out for his lady and sat down between us and shrugged and said, "So tonight I'm a shlemiel. I'll pick up the check."

"Thanks, but no thanks. I got a client who'll pick it up."

His grin turned lopsided. "Gee, that's white of you, Nate. I think I'll have lobster."

"I'm not that white, chum. I don't pick up checks for rich guys, even when I'm getting expenses."

The redhead smiled at hearing Barney called "rich," but it embarrassed him.

"Rich, smich," he said. "A few years, I'll be out of work and borrowing from you."

"Keep playing the ponies and you may be right."

Barney's only vice was gambling; that, and being a soft touch for his old West Side pals. We'd grown up together on Maxwell Street, when I'd been his family's *Shabbes goy* (my father was a Jew, but nonpracticing; my late mother's Catholicism never caught on with me, either). By the time I was a teenager, I was living in Douglas Park, but I'd come back Sundays to Maxwell Street where Barney and I worked together—Barney as a "puller," a barker in front of the store who often physically yanked prospective buyers off the street and inside; and me taking over from there, with the sales pitch. A couple of roughnecks, but Barney was rougher, a scrappy little street fighter who'd had to fend for himself and his family since he was a kid of thirteen. That was when thieves shot Barney's father in the Rasofsky's hole-in-the-wall dairy, and killed him.

By the way, in case you didn't recognize the name, Barney Ross grew up to be another kind of fighter, namely the lightweight champion of the world. And just this past May he'd taken the legendary Jimmy McLarnin in NYC for the welterweight crown, as well.

and stuffed furniture and bronze lamps and a ceiling that went
heaven, which by Chicago standards is a couple of stories. At
fancy marble-and-bronze check-in there was no sign of Polly and
boyfriend. I had a good idea where they were.

A marble staircase led down to the Terrace Garden, a big shiny a
deco dine-and-dance spot the before-and-after theater crowd ha
made popular. We were in the "during" mode at the moment, wher
theater was concerned; but the place was still doing nice business
Great to see so many people had money to spread around in times
like these—too bad I wasn't one of them.

Polly and friend were seated at one of the round tables in the circular, terraced dining area that surrounded the sunken dance floor,
where even now Guy Lombardo and his Royal Canadians played
their bouncy, mellow brand of hokum while couples in evening attire—white coats for the men, low-cut formals for the ladies—
mingled with real people, a certain number of world's fair tourists
among them, who met the dress code (ties for men, no slacks for
women) but would never make the society page. Part of the reason
business here was so brisk was the pleasant, even icy feel of the air
conditioning. A man could get used to not drowning in his own
sweat, given half a chance.

The food here was first-rate, but not cheap; I talked it over with my
stomach and decided to take a table, despite being uncomfortable
about calling attention to myself by dining alone—this was a couples
crowd, almost exclusively, and I should probably just go stand at the
bar. But what the hell. I ordered the boiled brisket of beef with
horseradish sauce, made a mental notation of the expense (not wanting to take out my little notebook), and sipped some rum while I
waited for my meal, watching Polly and her friend holding hands
across their table, on the other side of the room from me, seated on
the terrace level just above the dance floor, just as I was.

Polly was animated and constantly smiling; it was a nice smile, but
it tried a little too hard. He seemed taken with her, but was more
reserved: she seemed to be doing most of the talking. They had cock-
tails—gin fizzes, it looked like—and took in a dance before their
main course arrived. They danced right by me, at one point, and
that's when I recognized Polly.

She, however, didn't recognize me; or didn't seem to, when I just
barely glanced at them, between bites of brisket, over the little white
fence that separated us, as they floated by.

"This is Pearl," he said, gesturing to the attractive redhead. "The gal I been telling you about."

I reached a hand across the table and took hers, shook it; her hand was smooth and warm and she had a nice smile. Her eyes were big and blue, and her nose was a little big. It looked good on her, though. She had a low-cut blue velvet formal on; her bosom was milky white and there was plenty of it.

"So you're Barney's private detective friend," she said.

I put a finger to my lips in a shush gesture. "Let's make that our little secret, for the time being."

Barney put an arm around her shoulder and said, sotto voce, "Like he said before, he's working. He's tailing somebody or something. Mum's the word."

She crinkled her chin in an embarrassed, attractively earthy little smile. "Sorry."

"S'okay," I said, smiling back. "Let me get you something from the bar . . ." I started to wave for a waiter.

"Thanks, Nate, but no," Barney said. "I'm in training, remember?"

"But Pearl's not. Are you, Pearl? And have you eaten yet?"

They admitted they hadn't, and I insisted they join me.

"A man alone at a place like this sticks out like a sore thumb," I explained. "Stick around and make me look legit."

They ordered—Pearl asked for a Pink Lady, and both of them had the baked finnan haddie à la Moir—and Barney said, "Pearl's in from New York through the weekend, Nate."

"That's terrific."

"I, uh . . . wanted her to meet Ma, and my brothers and my sis."

"This sounds serious."

Barney almost blushed; Pearl just smiled.

"Be true to this guy, Pearl," I said, "or someday you might have somebody like me following you around."

Barney leaned forward conspiratorially. "Is that what this is about?"

I nodded. "That pretty apple-cheeked lass and the mustached gent across the way are, well, naughty. Or so it would seem."

"His wife your client?" Barney asked.

"Her husband," I said.

He shook his head. "Dirty business you're in."

"Beats having some guy bash your head in."

He smiled a little, cocked his head. "If you're trying to describe the way I make *my* living, let me remind you a couple things. First, I make my living by having some guy *try* to bash my head in—no-body's quite got the job done yet. And second, my work pays better than yours."

I took a last bite of brisket. "Yeah, but you can't eat on the job."

Pearl was watching us closely, and seemed to have figured out that Barney and me needling each other was just a sign of how deep our friendship ran.

"Incident'ly," he said, "Pearl's got her own room, here. Just wanted you to know, before you got any ideas."

"Barney, with you everything's got to be kosher," I said. "Person-ally, I enjoy being a fallen angel."

"You're getting your religions mixed up, Nate."

"It's the Irish in me."

Barney lived in a suite here in the Morrison; and the hotel had even converted a portion of one of their exercise rooms in the trav-eler's lounge into a mini-gym—good public relations, having a champ on the premises, accessible to the people.

Pearl, trying to fathom what must've seemed at times to be psychic communication between Barney and me, said, "How did you know Nate was supposed to be working tonight?"

Barney looked for a way to say it, but I said it for him.

"Barney's my landlord," I said. "Has he taken you to his 'Barney Ross Cocktail Lounge' yet?"

"Not yet," she said.

"It's about the only investment he's made that doesn't have four legs. Anyway, he owns the whole building, in case he hasn't men-tioned it, and my office is there. In exchange for rent, I stay there at night and keep an eye on the premises. On nights my work takes me away from the building, I call the landlord, to warn him his night watchman's not going to be around."

"Which is seldom," Barney said, as if defending his generosity to Pearl, who looked at him with a warm glow that had admiration in it as well as love. I hoped it would last. I hoped they would never have some sorry son of a bitch like me following either one of them around.

Their food came, and I asked Barney about his next fight.

"Not till September," he said.

"McLarnin again?"

With visible discomfort, he said, "McLarnin again. Fair's fair—gotta give him another shot at it."

I'd seen that fight, and while Barney won by a wide margin, he'd taken some hard shots from McLarnin, who was a powerhouse hitter, particularly his short right cross, which had sent many a good man into dreamland. McLarnin was heavier than Barney, but not slow. The rematch would be no picnic.

"I'll have some tune-up bouts between now and then," he shrugged. "No title defenses, though."

Across the way Polly and her date were heading down to dance some more; Lombardo was doing a version of "Pennies from Heaven" that would've made a marshmallow sick to its stomach.

"Don't you just love that," Pearl said, looking out at the dance floor.

"The music, you mean?" I asked.

"Of course! What else?"

"The finnan haddie?"

She turned to Barney. "Make an honest woman out of me. Dance with me."

"Sure," he said. "Soon as I finish my fish."

Pearl had already finished her fish, so she took the opportunity to go to the powder room. Shortly thereafter, Polly and her mustached friend glided by. Barney caught a glimpse of them, as he put a final bite of fish into his mouth, and his eyes narrowed.

"Where do I know that girl from?" he said.

"You recognize her, too, huh?"

"I don't know. She looks kinda familiar."

"Remember a few months ago when we were doing Uptown, one night?"

He winced. "You mean that night I went off training, a little."

"Yeah. You went off training a little, like some guys fall off buildings a little."

"Just don't tell Winch and Pian."

Winch and Pian were Barney's managers, who were stricter than a Catholic upbringing.

"I won't tell your ma, either. Particularly not where you know that girl from."

"Oh, shit," he said, as it came to him.

"That's right," I said. "That bar on Halsted? I knew the gal who ran the place, she was from East Chicago? Remember?"

East Chicago wasn't a part of Chicago; it was in Indiana nearby. Nearby enough that my work took me there from time to time.

Barney glanced around to see if Pearl was coming back yet.

"We didn't go upstairs with those girls, did we?" he said.

"We started to," I said. "We were both pretty drunk."

"God, if the reporters had got hold of that. I got a reputation."

"The reporters wouldn't print anything to darken your sickeningly pure name, you little shmuck. You passed out and Anna—that's the gal that ran the place—laid you out on a bed. By yourself."

He nodded, sort of remembering it.

"What about you, Nate?"

"Me?" I said. "I was drunk, too. But I went upstairs with one of the girls."

Polly glided by in her man's arms.

"That one?" he said.

I nodded.

"Oh boy," Barney said.

Pearl came back, and she and Barney went down for a dance. Across the way, the girl in pink and white and the man in the gold-rim glasses and mustache were getting up to go.

Shortly after, so did I.

They took a cab again; gritting my teeth, I followed in one, too. The expenses were chipping away at my fifty-buck retainer; and my conscience, or that tattered thing that flapped in the wind of my brain where my conscience used to be, chipped at my concentration.

I didn't know which confused me more: that my traveling-salesman client's bride was a prostitute—possibly an ex-prostitute, giving her the benefit of the doubt—or that I'd screwed her once.

And, as I recalled, drunk or not, liked it.

5

Back in Uptown, the cab let Polly and her boyfriend off at the corner of Wilson and Malden, and they walked half a block to the Malden Plaza, a four-story residential hotel. It seemed a newer, more modest building than its neighbors, with their terra-cotta trimming and elaborate porches; this building had only some halfhearted gingerbread along the roof and over the entryway, was set back from the sidewalk without a porch, and seemed to have been squeezed in between the two more elaborate apartment buildings on its either side, on what might have been a mutual yard between them, by a landlord whose greed outdistanced his aesthetics.

Gray suitcoat still slung over his arm, Polly's dapper Dan opened the front door for her and they stepped inside.

My cab went on by, and I got out a block down, near Saint Boniface Cemetery. Malden was an odd little street—existing a scant four blocks, connecting two cemeteries; the other one, Graceland Cemetery, was full of famous dead Chicagoans, in their fancy tombs—George Pullman was in a lead-lined casket under concrete and steel, to keep pissed-off union types from seeing him without an appointment, presumably. I walked down the little street, with death at its either end, coat slung over my shoulder, thinking about how my traveling-salesman client was likely to react when he heard about his wife.

It was a hot night, tolerable only when you thought back to the day, and a few people were still sitting out on porches, on the stairs, cooling off as best they could. Now and then people would look in the direction of the lake, wondering where the breeze was.

But it was ten-thirty, and a lot of people were in bed by now—possibly including Polly and her guest—and it wasn't hard for me to find an empty stoop approximately across from the place, to sit on and seem like just another neighborhood joe trying to beat the heat.

I couldn't stay here all night, though; if I'd brought my car up here instead of taking the El, I could've parked on the street and most likely got away with maintaining a watch. But an all-night stakeout wasn't practical here. Sooner or later somebody—a cop possibly— would question my presence. I'd have to make my stay a short one.

From the look of the building, the flats within were probably single rooms. This was the address my client had given me for his and his wife's home; so this was where they lived together, when he wasn't on the road—meaning he must not've been making much, hawking his feed and grain. He'd said he made "good money," but that's a vague term. Just because his wallet seemed fairly fat didn't mean anything—it could've been his life savings. Probably that fifty-buck retainer cut him deep.

Of course they hadn't been married long; he'd said he just landed a new territory, so maybe they planned moving up in the world soon. Nothing wrong with the neighborhood (if you didn't mind ceme- teries—and dead neighbors seldom keep you up at night with their loud parties). But this was the least classy building on Malden. Then, who was I to talk, a guy who slept in his office.

Half an hour dragged by. There were lights on in some of the windows, but most were dark; all were open. It wasn't good weather to keep the windows shut. It wasn't good weather period. I felt like I was wearing the heat; like it was something I had on. Something heavy.

Heavy like the guilt that had settled over me for having fucked pretty Polly one drunken night in a room over the bar on the corner of Willow and Halsted. And feeling guilty was stupid, as well as pointless: How was I supposed to know the little prostie would quit the business, and marry some poor putz who thought she was just a waitress or something? A pathetic chump who would then, thanks to God's sick sense of humor, hire me to ascertain his bride's virtue? A hardworking salt-of-the-earth salesman who wondered why his wife seemed to know things in bed that he hadn't taught her. . . .

I wondered if Polly really *had* quit hustling. Maybe dapper Dan wasn't a boyfriend—maybe he was a john. Maybe, like her waitress job, this was something she was up to while her hubby was on the road, something designed to fight her boredom and keep her wearing nice clothes and build a nest egg to help move 'em both into a nicer apartment.

And if she *was* hustling, should I tell the husband?

Of course I should. I wasn't paid to decide whether or not the information I turned up was good for my client's health; if my client paid for me finding out certain information, he deserved to get it. And brother was he going to get it.

Maybe this was innocent; maybe they were in there having tea and milk. Polly wasn't necessarily over there boffing that guy in the glasses. Right. He probably took 'em off first.

What the hell. I already had enough to tell my client what he didn't want to know. I could get up off this stoop and walk over to the Wilson Avenue El and go back to the office and get a good night's sleep, and to hell with traveling salesmen and traveling salesmen's wives and guys that boffed traveling salesmen's wives.

At that point, after having been in there an hour, the dapper Dan came out of the building and walked up to Wilson Avenue and hailed a cab.

I hailed one, too.

Followed him to a nice three-story apartment building, a big brick place that probably had flats running to six and eight rooms. It was on Pine Grove Avenue, near the lake, near Lincoln Park. Dapper Dan had dough—more dough than a traveling salesman, that was for sure.

He went in, and my cabbie drove on.

I had him drop me at the El station. I'd planned to stay overnight at the room I'd rented, at the Wilson Arms, but now I couldn't see any point in it. I did figure to give my client some more of my time, tomorrow, but I also figured to follow Polly around in my car, to hell with this cab noise.

So I didn't return to Uptown till near seven the next night. I spent the day in Evanston investigating an insurance claim; why sit in that little hotel room, looking out the window at Polly's sandwich shop? It wasn't going anywhere. And neither would she, till after work.

My '29 Chevy coupe with me in it was parked down the street when she came out of the S & S just after seven, wearing a light blue dress and a darker blue hat that fit snug to her head, and waited for her boyfriend to show up. That's the way it seemed, at least: her behavior today was no different than yesterday.

Neither was dapper Dan's.

With one exception: while he arrived in a cab again, he shooed it on, and they walked arm in arm, east on Wilson. He looked jaunty, with a straw boater and a white shirt with dark pinstripes and a blue tie and pale yellow slacks.

I got out of the car and shadowed them.

They walked under the El and across to a waffle shop on Sheridan.

It was a small place, but at this point I figured I could risk them making me. After all, I'd pretty well established what was going on here; I'd already earned my client's money—did it really matter whether Dan was her boyfriend, or just another john? Either way, she was fucking somebody who wasn't her husband, and that's all I'd been paid to find out. But for some reason, which I cloaked in giving my client his money's worth, I couldn't let go of this just yet.

They sat at a table; I sat at the counter. We all had waffles and bacon. We all had coffee.

Then we all went to the picture show. *Viva Villa* with Wallace Beery, which was playing at Balaban and Katz's Uptown on Broadway. We didn't sit together. And I didn't get spotted. There were better than four thousand seats in the Uptown, all of them full; there wasn't an air-cooled movie palace in town that wasn't doing land-office business, and the cavernous, opulent Uptown, with its sculptures and murals and gold drapes, was no exception.

I almost lost Polly and Dan, when the show was over; the fancy lobby was mobbed, and I had just squeezed out onto the street when I saw them pull away in a Checker cab. I caught the next cab and fell in behind them.

Tonight, they went to his place, that fancy apartment house near the lake; maybe her room in the Malden Plaza was too cramped. Maybe she had a Murphy bed; speaking from experience, I can say that making whoopee in a Murphy bed'll do till the real thing comes along—but Dan probably had six or seven rooms in his flat, one of which was no doubt a room with a bed in it that didn't fall down out of a box or the wall.

It was too ritzy a neighborhood to risk my sitting-on-the-stoop ruse, so I stayed in the cab and headed back to her place, the Malden Plaza. There I took my position on a stoop opposite and waited for Polly to come home. After two hours, I decided she probably wasn't going to.

So I walked over to the Wilson Arms and finally used that bed I'd paid for.

The S & S opened at six-thirty, so I wandered across the street at seven. I'd made a decision—in my sleep apparently, because there it was in my brain when I crawled out of the sack: I was going to talk to Polly.

I didn't know what I was going to say—certainly not that I was a private detective checking up on her for her husband. Still, I felt the need to talk to her. To see if I could get her side of the story. Maybe even give her a break.

Or not.

I wasn't sure. I just felt I somehow owed her this much. Possibly because I couldn't remember paying her for that night over the bar on Halsted.

I took a counter seat and a pretty brunette with a cap of curls and blue eyes came up to take my order. I asked for scrambled eggs and bacon and orange juice, and while I waited for them, I glanced around, looking for Polly. There were only two waitresses here today—the girl behind the counter, and a poor harried thing with blond hair and too many tables.

When the brunette waitress delivered my juice, I said to her, "You're shorthanded this morning."

"I'll say," the brunette smirked. "Our other girl called in sick today."

"Polly, you mean?"

"Yeah. I don't remember you eating here before—"

"Sure. Bunch of times."

"If it'd been at the counter, I'd remember you."

She went away and I sipped the juice. Pretty soon she placed the eggs and bacon in front of me.

"Toast doesn't come with it," she said, "but I can get you some."

"Please."

When she delivered a little plate of toast, I said, "I know you're busy, but I wondered if I could ask you something."

She smirked again, but it was pleasant. "Make it quick."

"Does Polly have a steady boyfriend?"

"Yeah. For the past few weeks she has."

"Funny," I said. "I thought she was a married gal."

The waitress shrugged. "She was," she said.

"Was?"

"Yeah. Excuse me, I got customers."

"Uh, sure. I'm sorry."

She came back a little later and asked me if I wanted coffee.

I said yes, and she poured me some, black.

"I don't have a boyfriend," she said.

I found a smile for her. "That's hard to believe. What did you mean, Polly *was* married?"

"What do you think? She's divorced. Has been for two or three months. Why don't you stop back when we're not so busy and we'll get acquainted?"

ANNA

6

The woman who ran the tavern on the corner of Willow and Halsted wasn't around, but the apron behind the bar traded me his boss lady's home address for a buck. You can't buy that kind of loyalty—unless you have a buck.

She lived about a mile north of the bar, at 2420 North Halsted, on the second floor of a big graystone three-flat. The ground-floor was unlocked; I climbed the stairs and knocked on her door. She answered on the third knock, just barely cracking open the door, peering out at me with one large dark eye, startlingly dark against the white sliver of her face.

"Who are you, and what do you want?" she said. She had a low, melodious voice, and a Garbo-like middle-European accent.

"I'm Nate Heller," I said, taking off my hat. "The detective. Remember?"

The dark eye narrowed.

"We met over in East Chicago, a couple times. And I was in your bar not so long ago. With Barney Ross?"

The dark eye widened and what little I could see of her red-rouged mouth seemed to smile.

Then the door opened and Anna, a big dark-haired handsome woman in her early forties in a gray tailored suit with white frills at the neck, gestured for me to come in.

I did, and she took my hat and placed it on a small table in the entryway.

"Mr. Heller," she said, smiling, but politely. Shrewdly? Cautiously. "What brings you here? And how did you locate me? I've only lived in this apartment a few weeks."

"I'm a former Chicago cop, Anna," I said, pleasantly. "I know all about bribing people."

Her smile was reserved yet genuinely amused; she gestured again. "Come," she said. "Sit."

She showed me into a big living room where a thick carpet and dark expensive furniture bespoke money. And why not? There was always dough to be had when you ran a bar—particularly when you had B-girls and rooms upstairs.

"America's treating you good, Anna," I said, seated on a well-stuffed sofa, glancing around.

"I've been good to it," Anna said, seated primly in a chair nearby. It was warm in here, though not stifling; there was no electric fan, but the front windows were open. Anna seemed not to notice the heat. A little yellow bird in a standing cage was sitting silently nearby, taking the heat less well than Anna; too damn hot to chirp.

For a Romanian immigrant—probably an illegal one—Anna was doing very well indeed. She had to be: she was operating in Paddy Bauler's ward, the forty-third, where nothing came free.

"You wouldn't be fronting for somebody, would you, Anna?"

Her smile faded, but she wasn't exactly frowning. "That's a little forward, Mr. Heller, for a guest who hasn't announced his intentions."

She had that oddly formal, calculated manner of speaking of someone who's learned English as a second language; I found it kind of charming—and somehow unsettling.

"You're right," I said. "It's none of my business what your business arrangements are. Say, do you own this building?"

My impertinence got another genuine smile out of her; her teeth were very white. And, unlike Anna, not first generation.

"I might," she said. "It was my understanding you were no longer with the police—"

"I'm not," I shrugged. "But I'm still a cop. Just because you go private, that doesn't take the cop out of you."

"It was also my understanding that you weren't on friendly terms with the police."

I shrugged again. "We try to stay out of each other's way. I still have friends on the pickpocket detail. But you can't testify against cops and not make some other cops not like you."

"Even if the officers you testified against were guilty."

"Every cop I know is guilty. But suppose the force was a bunch of lilies and all I did was pull a couple weeds . . . I'd still be seen as a squealer."

Anna smiled like a wry sphinx. "The world of crime, the world of law. Two sides of the same coin."

"A double-headed coin at that."

"The last time we met you didn't strike me as a philosopher."

I shook my head. "I probably struck you as a drunk who wanted to get next to one of your girls."

"As I recall, you succeeded."

"Right. Which is sort of why I'm here . . ."

"Sort of?"

"How well do you know Polly Hamilton?"

"Is there some reason why I should answer that question?"

"Is there some reason why you shouldn't?"

She thought about it.

"I could insult you and offer you money, Anna," I said, making a show of looking around the joint, "but I hate giving money to people who're doing so much better than me."

Anna's smile shifted gears to madonna-like. "I won't ask you for any money, Mr. Heller. I will ask if you'd like some tea, or coffee? Or something stronger?"

"How about something cool—ice water?"

"Fine."

She rose and left the room; I thought I heard something off to the right. Like somebody moving around in the next room. There were six or eight rooms in this flat, at least. From the sound I heard, maybe she was taking in boarders. Or maybe some of her girls were staying here with her.

She returned with ice water for me and coffee for her; she didn't seem to feel the heat, despite her almost wintery apparel.

"What's your interest in Polly, Mr. Heller?"

"It has to do with a job I'm on. Nothing criminal, I assure you; Polly's not in any trouble. Not . . . legal trouble."

"What other kind is there?"

"Oh, well—there's man trouble."

"I've heard of that," she allowed, sipping her coffee.

"Is Polly married, Anna?"

"She was. To a policeman in East Chicago."

"A policeman?"

Anna nodded. "She met him when she was working for me."

"At the Kostur Hotel?" That was where Anna ran her brothel, in Gary; there'd been an infamous speakeasy and gambling casino in the basement, called The Bucket of Blood. Shootings and stabbings were commonplace, though Anna was known to run a clean, straight house upstairs.

"Yes," Anna admitted. "At the Kostur."

"That'd be a few years ago. Polly looks pretty young to have worked for you at the Kostur, what, eight years ago?"

"She looked even younger then."

"I bet she did. How'd she happen to meet a policeman?"

Now Anna *really* smiled. "However could a girl meet a policeman in a brothel?"

"Sorry. That was dumb. So she married a policeman."

"Yes."

"And it didn't last."

"It didn't last."

"Could you describe him for me?"

"Why? Mr. Heller, you're really overstepping—"

"Please. Humor me. There's no harm in it."

She sighed. "He's a tall man, rather lean. Brown hair, with a bald spot. Not unpleasant to look at."

That didn't sound like my client.

I hadn't taken the brunette waitress back at the S & S too seriously when she said Polly was divorced; after all, my client had told me his wife was working under her maiden name, and—particularly if she was running around on him and possibly even hustling—she very well might not be spreading around the fact that she was married.

I tried again. "Her husband's name wouldn't have been Howard, would it?"

"No," Anna said. "Keele. Roy Keele."

"And they were divorced only a few months ago?"

"That's right."

My client had told me he and Polly had been married over a year. So much for the notion that my traveling salesman might be her second husband, on the rebound from Keele.

"Tell me," I said. "Has she had any steady boyfriends?"

"Yes," Anna said, nodding. "Several. Lately, one who calls himself . . ." And she paused here, as if what followed would be significant. ". . . Jimmy Lawrence. Says he works at the Board of Trade."

"Gold-rim glasses, pencil mustache, kind of medium build? Nice dresser?"

She kept nodding, seeming suddenly vaguely troubled. "That's him."

"Who before that?"

She touched a finger to her cheek, thinking. "I believe—I'm not sure, mind you—I believe it was a traveling salesman."

That was more like it. Now I could begin to make sense of this.

"Was his name Howard? John Howard?"

"I don't know. I never knew his name. Why don't you ask Polly?"

"That would be awkward, at least at this point. The traveling salesman, is he a blond man, also with wire glasses and mustache?"

"Why, yes."

"Physically a bit similar to this Jimmy Lawrence?"

"I suppose. Why?"

"Nothing. I had a client who lied to me, is all. A man who said he was a husband when he was really just a jilted boyfriend. Who was afraid no self-respecting private detective would take on his case, if he weren't the girl's spouse."

"He doesn't sound like he's from Chicago."

"No," I said. "He just passes through here, obviously."

I stood.

"Thank you, Anna. And thanks for the ice water."

"Are you going to talk to Polly?"

"No."

"Why not?"

"Why? I've finished the job I was hired to do. And I've answered the questions that had my curiosity up. You needn't show me out, and thanks again. . . ."

She reached out and touched my hand; her touch was warm, her hand was trembling. Trembling! This cool cucumber was trembling. . . .

"Why, Anna," I said. "What's wrong?"

"Nothing," she said, her face impassive, but her hand still trembling against mine. "Please—sit down. I'd like to talk to you. I need to talk to someone, and . . . you would do nicely. You're almost a policeman, after all."

I sat down.

Her dark eyes seemed very soft, then, and compelling; this big attractive woman had the ability to seem strong one moment, vulnerable the next—like many madams, she'd got out of hustling herself early enough to hold onto her looks; but had hustled long enough to remember how to push a man's buttons.

Leaning forward in her chair, hands folded in her lap, she said, "You spent a night with Polly once."

"In a manner of speaking. I was drunk, and I hadn't been with a woman in a long time . . . I'd had some of that *other* kind of trouble—woman trouble. You've heard of that."

My effort to lighten this conversation wasn't having much effect: Anna's ready smile was nowhere to be seen.

"She liked you," Anna said.

"I wouldn't go that far," I said.

"She said she did. And you, maybe you liked her, a little?"

"I liked her in the sack, Anna, to be blunt, but that's as far as it went. I was drunk, remember? And if you do remember, you're one up on me."

Her face looked pale and tragic, the dark eyes hooded, the red mouth a thin line. "I thought you might be interested in . . . helping her."

"Well . . . sure. I guess. Anna, I've been shadowing her for a couple of days, and she hasn't recognized me, even up close. We're not bosom buddies."

"But you'd help her, if you could. You'd help anybody in trouble."

"Not really. But make your pitch. You've got my curiosity back up, if that's what you're after."

She stood and paced; whether for dramatic effect, or out of actual nervousness, I didn't know. I still don't.

She stopped and said, "Polly may be in dangerous company."

"How so?"

"This Jimmy Lawrence. She brought him here. For dinner. Polly, and several of the other girls, are more than just employees to me— they're family. And I often invite them here. Have Romanian specialties, which I cook myself. I'm famous for my culinary arts, for my dinner parties."

"I'm convinced. But you've drifted off the point, Anna."

She paced some more, then sat down next to me; put a hand on my knee. She smelled good—face powder and exotic perfume. She might have been as much as fifteen years older than me, and I was very much aware that she had been in the cold-blooded sex business for decades, that she'd been a hustler then and a madam now; nevertheless, she had a sultry sensuality that made me uneasy.

"My son Steve and his girl, they've gone out with them. Several times."

"Gone out with who?"

"Polly. Polly and her boyfriend Lawrence."

"So?"

"Do you know how much danger they're in?"

"Who's in? What danger?"

"My son Steve! And his girl. They're just kids. In their twenties."

"So am I, Anna, and your point eludes me."

"Do you know what the other girls at the sandwich shop call Lawrence, behind his back?"

"I haven't a clue."

"Dilly."

"Oh. What's that stand for? Has he got a pickle in his pocket, or what?"

"No," Anna Sage said. "They think he looks like Dillinger."

DILLINGER

7

I drove over to Pine Grove Avenue and parked just across and down from the ritzy digs where Polly Hamilton's boyfriend lived. Since she had called in sick today, Polly might well be in there with Jimmy Lawrence right now; bedridden, probably. I hoped the poor girl got to feeling better. . . .

I sat in my shirt sleeves on the rider's side with the windows rolled down; I could actually feel something passing for a lake breeze. In front of me was this morning's *Herald and Examiner*: "a paper for people who think," according to Mr. Hearst. Well, maybe he was right—I wasn't reading, but I was thinking.

Thinking about Anna Sage, and her contention that Polly Hamilton's male companion Jimmy Lawrence was really one John H. Dillinger.

"Didn't you notice the resemblance?" she'd asked.

No, I'd said; but, yeah, I guessed he looked a little like Dillinger.

So did a lot of people. Every few days, these last months, there'd be another story about a "Dillinger double" who'd been picked up by the police, somewhere in the Midwest. One poor guy in St. Paul had been arrested five times and was on his way to the local police station to try to work out this mistaken-identity problem for good when he was arrested again; he wasn't sprung till they'd taken his fingerprints and compared them with Dillinger's.

Less than a month ago, another unwitting Dillinger double had strolled out of the lobby of the Uptown Theater—where Polly and her beau and yours truly had seen *Viva Villa* last night—and faced six riot squads of Chicago cops, who advised him not to move or they'd blow his head off.

And just this past Sunday an insurance salesman in Columbus, Ohio, had got off a plane from a business trip to Indianapolis only to be greeted by a dozen shotgun-bearing cops who had received "positive identification" of his being Dillinger from the manager of the hotel where he'd stayed the night before. Whether the guy sold life insurance or not, the papers hadn't said.

A sort of Dillinger fever gripped the country, and had ever since the bandit's year-long spree of bank robberies came to a bloody head a few months ago, at the Little Bohemia Lodge in upper Wisconsin, when the feds'd had Dillinger trapped and managed only to kill a civilian or two, and capture a few of the gang's molls, while Dillinger, "Baby Face" Nelson and crew slipped out the back door.

How this "public enemy" (a phrase borrowed by the feds from Chicago, where the Crime Commission had coined it for Al Capone) became a household word in one short year had more to do with the style the outlaw brought to his robberies than the robberies themselves. The outline of his legend was already known to every man, woman and child in the country—including this kid.

Given a twenty-year sentence by a hanging judge for his first, relatively minor offense, twenty-year-old Johnny Dillinger had gone from his father's farm to the reformatory and on to jail, spending nine years going to school under the tutelage of the likes of Harry Pierpont, Homer Van Meter and John Hamilton—experienced, hardened criminals all, skilled in the art of robbing banks.

When Johnny was paroled, following a petition seeking his release to help work on his father's farm (signed by the man Dillinger had robbed as well as the now-repentant judge), he immediately began robbing banks and stores to raise money to finance a jailbreak, to get Pierpont, Van Meter, Hamilton and six other of his buddies out of the state prison at Michigan City. He smuggled several guns into the prison in a barrel of thread sent to the prison's shirt factory; the nine Dillinger pals escaped just in time to bust John himself out of the jail at Lima, Ohio. Seems he'd been captured while visiting pretty Mary Longnaker, one of his numerous girls. The press loved Johnny and his pretty girls.

They loved Johnny, period. Because when he robbed his banks, he leapt over bank railings, flirted with the ladies and was courteous to the men. When somebody got shot, Johnny never was the one to do the shooting; and he regretted such violence—such as when Pierpont shot the sheriff during the Lima crash-out, and Johnny paused to kneel by the dying man, whom he'd grown fond of during his incarceration, saying sadly to Pierpont, "Did you have to do that?"

The public loved that; they loved it when he allowed the depositers unlucky enough to be in the bank being robbed to hold onto their dough—he wanted only the "bank's money." And when he busted out of the Crown Point, Indiana, jail using a wooden gun he'd carved and then darkened with shoe polish (so the story went), the common man said, "Nice going, Johnny—you showed 'em, Johnny!"

The common man liked identifying with John Dillinger, and why not? He had the common man's face. Oh, perhaps a shade on the handsome side, at least for a bank robber; and his photos often showed him with a wry smile worthy of a picture-show heavy. But he had the kind of face you passed in the street and didn't think twice about.

Unless a sort of national hysteria was under way, as in these past three or four months, when "positive identifications" of Dillinger would be reported in, say, Massachusetts and Ohio—on the same day.

So when Anna saw a Dillinger resemblance in Polly's dapper Dan, I was momentarily caught off guard, but not bowled over. Dillinger was on everybody's mind, in every paper's headlines; like this one I was pretending to read—DILLINGER SEEN IN FLORIDA—and the one Jimmy Lawrence had been reading a few nights ago in Anna's flat. So she said.

It had gone like this: Anna had prepared a Romanian specialty for Lawrence, Polly, Anna's out-of-work son Steve and his girl, whose name Anna didn't mention. They'd eaten in the kitchen, next to several open windows, which helped with the heat. After dinner, the women cleared the table and began doing the dishes; there was talk of playing pinochle later. Conversation lagged—too damn hot for chatter. Still, despite the heat, Lawrence lit up a cigar—a big, fat expensive one. And he began to read the paper.

After a while he said, "Well—they've got me in St. Paul today," and laughed.

Then he got up and went out on the back stairs to smoke some more, and get some air. Anna stopped polishing a dish long enough to look at the front page of the paper Lawrence had been reading; the face of John Dillinger stared at her, from a photo.

I had said to her, on hearing this tale, "How can he be Dillinger? He looks a *little* like Dillinger. Sure. But not just like Dillinger."

Hadn't I heard about plastic surgery? Gangsters go underground and get plastic surgery these days, she said. Like she was talking about the latest dance step.

Still, it was hard to dismiss Anna's opinion. This was not the hys-

terical reaction of a harried housewife in Duluth, on her way to the
bank with this week's hard-earned deposit in hand, who spotted a
man who looked like that John Dillinger and ran immediately to the
station house. No. Anna had been around; she'd been dealing with
crooks and crooked cops since I was in knee pants. If she thought this
guy might be Dillinger, well . . . this guy might be Dillinger.

And if he was, maybe I'd do something about it. After all, the
reward money was hovering at around twenty thousand dollars, half
of it federal, half of it from half a dozen states in the "crime corridor"
of the Midwest, where Dillinger had been harvesting banks for over a
year now.

Only I couldn't go to the cops. I was persona non grata with too
many of the boys in blue for that. And the head of the special Dillinger Squad—forty officers strong—was none other than Capt. John
Stege (rhymes with "leggy"), who would rather shoot me than give
me the time of day.

Stege was a rarity in Chicago—an honest cop; he was one of half a
dozen individuals credited with being "the guy that got Capone" (my
friend Eliot Ness was another) and, in a way, Stege was as worthy of
that credit as the next guy (Eliot included). Stege had fought Capone's Outfit all through the twenties and it was his raid on Capone's
Cicero joints that brought forth the ledgers that allowed the feds to
put together the income tax evasion rap that finally sent the Big Fellow to Atlanta.

But Stege'd had his share of bad press, too. He'd lost his job as
chief of the Detective Bureau over the Jake Lingle case; he'd looked
dirty, guilty by association, because he was thick with the police commissioner, who in turn had been thick with reporter Lingle, who'd
been thick with Capone and company. This all came out after Lingle
was murdered in the subway tunnel under Michigan Avenue.

I'd been involved in that case; specifically, I'd been a traffic cop on
Michigan Avenue, and had pursued, and failed to catch, the fleeing
killer. I'd been a star witness at the trial. I'd lied, of course, to help
put away the scapegoat the Outfit had given the D.A.'s office to sat-
isfy the public and the press. And had gone on to be a plainclothes
cop, as part of my good-conduct reward.

It was then that my father, an idealistic old union man who hated
the cops and hated me becoming one, blew his brains out with my
gun. But that's another story.

Stege, like my father, smelled a bad apple when young Nate Heller traded his uniform, and his integrity, in for plain clothes. He—and a lot of people on the force—pegged me as a kid on the make, willing to go along with just about anything. That led to my being pulled in by two real sweethearts named Lang and Miller—the late Mayor Cermak's chief bagmen and bodyguards (this was before Cermak was late, of course)—on an attempt on Frank Nitti's life.

That was when I left the force to go private; but eventually I had to testify about the Nitti hit, and—since Mayor Cermak had since been killed in Miami by a Sicilian assassin named Zangara—I felt under no obligation to lie. Maybe I was trying to make it up to my old man and his Bughouse Square idealism. Or maybe I was trying to make it up to me. But I told the truth on the stand—a novelty around these parts—and made Lang and Miller, and the late mayor, look very bad.

Stege, though a tough, straight cop by Chicago (or any) standards, had a blind spot: he didn't like even a crooked cop getting a public bath. And I was an ex-cop who'd publicly bathed not only two Chicago police sergeants, but Mayor Cermak as well.

And Stege had been a Cermak crony. The story went that shortly after Cermak was elected, Stege had been transferred to the South Wabash station, in the heart of Bronzeville, to "raise hell with the Policy racket"—and in the process the captain put about two hundred colored prisoners in jail per day, in cells so crammed they couldn't sit. The Negro politicians had bitched to Cermak, at first, then finally begged: What did Cermak want from them, to get Stege out of their district?

"Become Democrats," Cermak said.

And they did.

Stege would've done anything for Anton J. Cermak, and I had dirtied His Honor's posthumous honor. The last time I'd seen Stege—at City Hall, where I'd come to testify in one of the subsequent Lang–Miller proceedings—I'd nodded to the stocky, white-haired copper, saying, "Good afternoon, Captain."

And Stege had said, "Go straight to hell, you lying son of a bitch, and don't come back."

Hal Davis of the *Daily News* had heard our exchange, and, cleaning it up a bit, added it as color in his coverage of the trial. Now whenever I talked to my few remaining friends on the force, the first thing I heard was, "Shall I say hello to Captain Stege for you, Heller?" Followed by smug laughter.

No, I wouldn't be able to go to Captain Stege with this; of course, if Jimmy Lawrence *did* turn out to be Dillinger, and I gave him to Stege, maybe I'd be off the captain's shit list.

But if Jimmy Lawrence turned out to be just another Dillinger double, I'd probably find myself tied up in a little room in the back of some station house somewhere doing the rubber-hose rhumba.

Around dusk a Yellow cab pulled up in front of the apartment house, but on my side of the street, facing south. I leaned back and dropped my hat down over my face—mostly—and made like I was snoozing. A few minutes later Jimmy Lawrence and Polly Hamilton, arm in arm, came out the front and got in the back of the cab. I waited thirty seconds, crawled over in the driver's seat, turned the key in the ignition and pushed the starter and pulled out after them.

The Yellow cut over to Halsted and before I knew it the scenery was looking familiar.

The cab stopped in front of a big graystone three-flat and waited as Jimmy Lawrence got out to hold the door open for Anna Sage, who came out of her apartment building in a smart blue dress and a broad-brimmed white hat.

I followed them to the Marbro Theater on the West Side.

We all saw *You're Telling Me* with W. C. Fields.

It was funny.

8

The next morning around ten I walked over to the Banker's Building on the corner of Clark and Adams and took an elevator up to the nineteenth floor, where the feds kept house. The chief agent of the Chicago branch of the Division of Investigation was Melvin Purvis, but I hoped to speak to Sam Cowley.

Cowley I'd never met, but my friend Eliot Ness—who until about a year ago had been the top fed where crime-busting in Chicago was concerned—had spoken highly of him. Purvis, whom I'd met once or twice but didn't really know, was another kettle of fish; Eliot had contempt for the man—though I had to keep in mind that Ness and Purvis were enough alike that a little professional jealousy on Eliot's part was not to be ruled out.

After all, Purvis, a Justice Department special agent, entered the Chicago picture about the time Eliot, a Treasury Department man, was being phased out, his Prohibition Unit going gradually out of business when Repeal came along (beer was legal first, so the Prohibition Unit limped along well into '33). Purvis was the guy who'd get to go after the outlaws like Dillinger, while former gangbuster Ness was being shuffled offstage, being turned into a mere "revenooer." Even now Eliot was chasing moonshiners around the hills of Ohio, Kentucky and Tennessee.

But from what I'd observed—admittedly from a distance, reading about him in the papers, listening to my pals on the pickpocket detail gossip—Purvis was a fuck-up. His biggest claim to fame was tackling the "terrible Touhys," a gang of suburban bootleggers who'd been too minor for Eliot to mess with, though they'd somehow managed to keep Capone off their home turf of Des Plaines. Post-Repeal, the Touhys were *really* not worth messing with—but last year Purvis had charged Roger Touhy with the hundred grand kidnapping of William Hamm, the Hamm's Beer baron. It didn't make sense; Touhy was well fixed and moving into legit concerns. Maybe Touhy's motive was

Greetings from Headquarters
Melvin Purvis

MELVIN PURVIS

supposed to be envy—since Hamm was back in the brewing business legally.

Purvis proudly told the press he had an "ironclad case," an opinion the jury didn't share. Even before Touhy was cleared, underworld word was the Karpis–Barker gang had pulled the Hamm snatch; if Purvis was any kind of investigator he'd have heard that too—*I* heard it, and I wasn't anywhere near the case.

Almost immediately, Purvis hit Touhy with another kidnapping charge—that of Jake "The Barber" Factor, no less, a notorious if slick international con man with Capone ties. Everybody in town knew that Factor was just looking to avoid extradition to England, that he'd kidnapped himself (with a little help from his Capone connections) and framed Touhy.

Everybody but Purvis, apparently; he'd bought it—and managed to sell it to a jury, this time, because poor old Roger "The Terrible" was doing ninety-nine years at Joliet. And no sooner had the prison doors shut than Frank Nitti—at the helm of the Capone Outfit— waltzed into Des Plaines.

Purvis had come off looking good in the press, however, though the Little Bohemia episode, last April, had finally caught "Little Mel" with his pants down. (I heard Purvis didn't like being called Little Mel to his face, but that's how everybody referred to him behind his back.)

Purvis had had a tip that Dillinger and his gang were holed up in the Little Bohemia Lodge way at the top of Wisconsin. He and a couple handfuls of other agents piled into three little planes and flew to Rhinelander, where they connected with Division of Investigation agents from St. Paul. The hastily assembled task force commandeered some local cars and drove another near-fifty miles over snow-covered secondary roads. Two of the four cars broke down along the way, and by the time the sixteen agents reached Little Bohemia, half of them were riding the running boards, chattering with cold.

They approached the lodge on foot, moving through the pines, flashlights in hand. As the agents reached the lodge, which was brightly lit, three men exited the front door and went quickly to a coupe in the nearby parking area, and Purvis ordered his men to open fire. One of the three men was killed instantly; the other two were wounded.

Purvis and his agents had just killed a Civilian Conservation Corps worker and wounded a CCC cook and a gas-station attendant. Meanwhile, John Dillinger, among others, having seen the flashlights, had gone out the back way. Baby Face Nelson stopped long enough to shoot up some feds. And hours later Purvis collared some of the gang's molls, who'd been huddling in the basement with the lodge's staff, while the feds had pummeled the place with machine-gun fire.

This time the press had Purvis for supper. There were demands for his resignation aplenty, but his boss J. Edgar Hoover had made a show of standing behind his boy—at the same time bringing reliable, methodical Sam Cowley in to take charge of the Dillinger case. . . .

There was no secretary or receptionist in an outer office, at the Chicago field office of the Division of Investigation. There was no outer office. It was just a big open room full of desks, without any partitions. Agents were scurrying around with papers in hands, going from desk to desk conferring with their brethren, and the typewriters clicking and phones ringing and electric fans whirring mixed with street sounds coming from open windows, making a cacophony that had to be talked over.

One of the agents, seated at a desk near the door, looked up from a typewriter with irritation; apparently being close to the door got him stuck with receptionist-type duties.

"Can I help you?" he said sharply. He had a smooth rosy-cheeked face and light blond hair and, like everybody in the room, had his coat off but his tie snugged at his collar. He looked like he didn't shave yet.

"I'd like to see Sam Cowley," I said.

"If you're with the press, you should know by now that all reporters are barred till further notice from this office."

"I'm not from the press. I'd like to see Sam Cowley."

"The inspector's out of the office," he said, crisp as dark toast. All these guys looked like college kids. Which they were—attorneys and accountants who, in better times, might be earning some real dough in private practice.

"When will he back?"

The rosy-cheeked agent had already looked away from me and back at what he was typing.

"Tomorrow," he said, not looking at me. Typing.

I put my hand on the typewriter, on the platen, and kept it from turning; he looked up at me with round outraged eyes.

"I pay your salary, junior," I said. "Let's have a little service, here. And some respect while you're at it."

He sighed and smiled, just a little. "You're right. My apologies. It's hot."

"Yeah. Ever since Little Bohemia."

His smile faded momentarily, then returned; just a ghost of a smile, but it was there.

"You'll have to speak to Chief Purvis, if this can't wait till tomorrow. If it's about John Dillinger, that is."

"How did you know it was about Dillinger?"

"You asked for Cowley. Dillinger's his only case. And the only other guy that works on Dillinger is Chief Purvis."

"Every crank call you get, every little tip—"

"Goes straight to Cowley and Purvis. Separate copies to each desk."

"Interesting. Could you tell me where Chief Purvis' office is?"

"This is the only office we have, mister. And that's Chief Purvis back by the window, in the corner."

I should've spotted him before, but he was so small he was blocked. He was the only man in the room wearing his suitcoat, a smartly tailored light gray. The only difference between his desk and anybody else's was that it was slightly bigger and glass-topped. And by an open window, where something approaching air was wafting in, along with street noise.

I walked down a path between the desks and Purvis looked up from his work and in a rather high-pitched Southern drawl said, "You're Nathan Heller, aren't you? Sit down."

I had to admit (to myself) I was impressed; we'd only met once— Eliot had tersely introduced us and we shook hands—and had nodded at each other another time in the Federal Building, in a manner that didn't necessarily mean we were acquainted and/or recognized one another.

Like the guy Polly Hamilton was dating, Melvin Purvis was a dapper little man. He was only a couple years older than me, but still the oldest man in the room. He pushed aside a report he was reading, closing the file folder and smiling at me. His hair was brown with a stray lock dangling onto his forehead, his face heart-shaped with pointed, chiseled features, like a ventriloquist's dummy. The eyes in that wooden face, however, were sharp and dark.

"I'm surprised you remember me," I said.

"Ness introduced us. He doesn't think much of me. That's all right. I don't think much of him. No offense meant."

"None taken."

"I just find your friend Ness, well—I find his penchant for press agentry a little much."

I resisted the urge to tell Little Mel that the thing he and Eliot had most in common was that particular penchant.

Instead, I said, "Some positive press wouldn't hurt *you*, right now, would it?"

He smiled on one side of his face; it made a dimple bigger than Shirley Temple's.

"I can't blame you for that crack," he said. The Southern accent seemed soothing on this hot day. I wondered if Purvis being from the South had given him the ability to take heat like this in stride, sitting there in his coat like that.

"You're undoubtedly a busy man, Mr. Heller," he said, without sarcasm. He seemed to have some of that Southern politeness, too; he seemed honestly to be a gentleman. "Why are you here?"

"I may have seen Dillinger."

He arched an eyebrow. "I hear that from a lot of people—most of them aren't trained detectives, however. You wouldn't make a statement like that lightly, now, would you, Mr. Heller?"

"No I wouldn't. I'd like to ask you something, though."

"What is it?"

"After the affair at Little Bohemia, I heard Will Rogers say on the radio that he figured the feds would eventually shoot John Dillinger—if he could manage to get himself in the middle of some innocent bystanders."

To his credit, Purvis only smiled. And on both sides of his face, this time. "I heard him say that, too. What's your point?"

"It's just that I read in the papers that the Justice Department has admitted it'd prefer its agents shoot Dillinger on sight rather than risk another gun battle. That both your boss Hoover and his boss the attorney general have said, 'Shoot to kill, then count to ten,' where Dillinger's concerned."

Purvis was leaning on his elbows, his hands clasped together prayerlike; he smiled impishly and shrugged.

"That's what I figured," I said. I stood up.

"Where are you off to, Mr. Heller?"

"I don't feel confident enough that this individual is Dillinger to give you specifics of where you might find him. There've been too many people who look like Dillinger lately almost get their heads shot off by overeager lawmen. I don't think I want to be part of that."

"And you think I'm capable of that?"

"I think you want a dead Dillinger awful bad."

"Sit down, Mr. Heller."

I just stood there.

"Please," he said. He gestured with an open hand. "Sit down."

I did.

"Your concern is noted," he said. "Perhaps justified. The Little Bohemia debacle has served to make yours truly look a little trigger-happy. That I admit. But consider this: if I shoot the wrong man, if I shoot an innocent bystander, I'll find myself the next day back in South Carolina mowin' my daddy's yard."

"I doubt that," I said, charmed a little in spite of myself. "You're a lawyer, and that daddy you mentioned is rich, I hear."

"You hear right. That just means he has a bigger yard for me to mow. Times are a little hard to be hangin' out a shingle. I need this job, Mr. Heller. Can I call you Nathan?"

"Nate."

"Call me Melvin, if you would. I need this job. I don't need to mess it up—not any further. Little Bohemia was the last mistake I can afford to make."

"So if I give you this information, you won't fuck it up."

He didn't flinch at the harshness of that; he just shrugged again. "I'll try not. Who can say? Public enemies don't tell you when or where they're going to be, or what they're going to do. A crystal ball is not part of a special agent's government issue."

"Who said it was?"

"You did, Nate. You asked me, in effect, to guarantee that if you give me some information, I won't . . . foul up. Correct? How can I guarantee you anything, other than I'll give it my best shot?"

The guy was sincere—he had a touch of Southern bullshit, and a streak of pomposity—but he was for real.

"I don't know," I said, glancing around the room at the young agents scurrying about, going no place. "I don't know if these college boys can cut the mustard."

"Nate," Purvis said, leaning forward, looking like a puppet come to life. "The division has found it infinitely more sensible to teach intelligent men to be manhunters than to try teaching manhunters to be intelligent."

"Don't make me sick."

"I notice you didn't go to the police with this—"

"No, I didn't go to the cops. The head of their Dillinger detail isn't fond of me."

"Ah. Captain Stege. Seems to me I heard that you and he weren't close. But even without Stege, I wonder if you'd go to Chicago's finest—a corrupt, lazy, unskilled bunch of louts, as we both know. My people, however, have gone to school. For which you deride them, but they've gone to school, and not just college. They've learned to photograph fingerprints and where to look for them. They've learned how to use a microscope. They've learned the science of ballistics. They learned how to shoot every weapon, from a pistol to a machine gun. Nate, the criminal mind is clever—but the scientific mind is *always* its superior."

"Let me ask you something."

"Of course."

"Tell me the inside story on the Kansas City Massacre."

At Union Station in Kansas City, federal and local officers ushered gangster Frank "Jelly" Nash from a train to a car that would take him to Leavenworth. Just as they'd piled into the car at Union Station, a big man with a tommy gun showed up, quickly joined by two other gunmen, and all three sprayed the car with bullets, killing four lawmen, and Nash.

Purvis cocked his head back. "It's one of the two events that gave the Justice Department the punitive power it has today. The other, naturally, being the Lindbergh kidnapping."

"I see."

"When I became a special agent, I was limited in the cases I could investigate. My duties were largely . . . inquisitorial. I couldn't even make an arrest. When I ran down my man, I was compelled by law to call in a local policeman or a U.S. marshal to snap on the bracelets."

"And the Kansas City Massacre changed all that."

"Yes. It, and the Lindbergh tragedy. The public revulsion that followed the Kansas City Massacre, particularly, got us more money, more men and better backing—and better laws. The heavy artillery we needed to meet the hoodlums on their own battleground and take 'em for a cleanin'." He stopped, realizing he was lecturing, falling into one of his standard spiels for the press, probably; he seemed a little chagrined, but also seemed to catch that I was leading him on. "But why am I telling you all this? You're on the fringes of law enforcement yourself—surely you already know it."

"And have you nabbed those responsible for the Kansas City Massacre?"

Purvis shifted in his seat; his confidence was suddenly undercut by an apparent nervousness. "One of the men, Verne Miller, was found dead in a ditch."

"A Syndicate hit."

"Apparently."

"Why, do you suppose?"

"For botching the job. For killing the man they were there to rescue."

"Nash, you mean."

"Certainly. And for killing police officers and federal agents. For bringing the heat down on the lawless."

"That last I can buy."

"What *don't* you buy?"

"Nash was the target. Because he knew too much. Surely you know that."

"Don't be ridiculous."

"All right, Melvin. Have it your way. Nash wasn't the target; he just got accidentally machine-gunned. Who else are you looking for, in connection with the massacre?"

"Well, the other two killers, of course—'Pretty Boy' Floyd and Adam Richetti."

"What if I said that was a load of hooey. That Floyd and Richetti weren't there."

His thin lips pursed. "I'd say you were mistaken."

I shook my head, smiled humorlessly. "Well, I hear they weren't there."

"You're mistaken." And finally some sarcasm crept into the drawl: "Unless your sources of information are better than mine."

"Melvin, some things you can't find out looking through a microscope." I rose. "I'll see you later."

"Sit down, Heller. Sit down!"

I didn't.

I said, "I may have seen Dillinger. I'm going to check into it a little more. You see, the guy who may be Dillinger is hanging around with a client of mine's girlfriend. And if you and your college boys get her killed, my client's going to be unhappy with me. So I'm going to take it nice and easy on this one. I'll get back to you."

The muscles in his jaw were pulsing. "Is that your final decision, Mr. Heller?"

"Yeah. Yeah, it is. And don't bother having any of these Harold Teens try to tail me . . . you and your boys have been embarrassed enough lately."

His jaw muscles still jumping, he said, "There's reward money in this, Heller."

"I know there is. I mean no offense, Purvis. I'll be back in touch."

"Soon?"

"Soon."

With Cowley, I thought.

And left.

9

I spent the afternoon tailing Lawrence and Polly for what I assured myself was one last time. Around noon I'd driven back to the apartment house on Pine Grove, near the lake, and, with suitcoat and hat off and tie loosened, had just got settled in on the rider's side with my newspaper when a Checker cab pulled up, and Lawrence and Polly came out and got in. Lawrence was in shirt sleeves and bow tie and straw hat and yellow slacks; and Polly was in a yellow dress and matching hat. They looked like an advert for butter.

I followed 'em to North Lincoln Avenue—just a block or so from Anna's—and they got out of the cab. As I drove by I saw that, not ten feet away from them, two uniformed cops were standing on the corner, talking. Lawrence didn't even glance their way. A squad car went by just after I parked, and it swung around to pick up one of the cops, and Lawrence and Polly, strolling along now, didn't seem to notice or care. If this Lawrence *was* Dillinger, he was one cool customer.

But apparently not so cool, on this blistering day, to be able to resist the strawberry sundaes he and Polly ate, in lieu of lunch, at the soda fountain next to Biograph Billards. Here they split up, with Polly beaming at him and giving him a peck on the cheek; off she went, presumably to shop—North Lincoln being a nifty little shopping area.

I stayed with Lawrence. I hung a loose tail on him—if this really was Dillinger, he'd be picking up on me any time now, unless I was very careful. After all, he might be armed—though I didn't see how: he had no coat on, and there was no gun bulge in any of the pockets of his yellow slacks.

Whoever he was, he got his hair cut at the Biograph Barber Shop; and then went across to the Biograph Theater and in the door just to the right of the marquee. Visiting his bookmaker, no doubt—there'd been a bookie joint operating in the loft over that theater for years.

A few minutes later he came out and walked down the street to a

SGT. MARTIN ZARKOVICH

haberdashery, the Ward Mitchell Company, where he bought a striped shirt. This I'd glimpsed through the storefront window, and was on my way across the street, to maintain my tail at a distance, and almost missed it when Lawrence came out of the store and bumped into a beat cop who was walking by, swinging his stick.

Lawrence dropped his package, and the bull helped him pick it up and they smiled and nodded to each other and walked on.

The hell with it, I thought, and went to my car and headed back to the Loop. That flatfoot sure didn't think Lawrence was Dillinger, and Lawrence didn't exactly wet his pants on bumping into the law, either. Hell with it.

By four that afternoon I was sitting in a booth in Barney Ross' Cocktail Lounge, having a beer. Ceiling fans whirred overhead and, with the beer, made the heat almost seem to go away. It was a long, narrow, dark room with a bar against one long wall, a small dance floor at the far end, a few tables by the dance floor, and booths lining the walls. There were framed photos of fighters everywhere, and not just Barney—King Levinsky, Jackie Fields, Benny Leonard, among others. Barney himself was rarely around the place, these days—too public a figure for it, and Pian and Winch, his mother-hen managers, didn't like him owning a bar, let alone hanging around in one. Barney had a wholesome reputation going for him, and counted plenty of kids among his fans, so him lending his name to the place was bad enough, much less actually being there.

And he was busy. Not just with the fight game, but speaking at civic functions (hearing a Barney Ross speech was a pleasure I'd somehow managed to avoid) and generally being Chicago's favorite son.

So when Barney surprised me and walked up to the booth, I asked him for his autograph and he told me where to go and grinned and sat across from me, and watched with envy as I drank my beer.

"Where's Pearl?" I asked him.

"State Street."

Like Polly, Pearl had gone shopping.

"How's that case coming?" he asked me.

"Private dicks don't work on cases. Lawyers work on cases. Sherlock Holmes works on cases."

"Oh, yeah? So what are you working on?"

"A job. At least I was."

"Oh. The one from the other night."

"Yeah. Right."

"You wrap it up, or what?"

"What. I'm thinking about tossing in the towel on this one."

"Happens to the best of us," he shrugged, waving for his bar-tender, an ex-heavyweight named Buddy Gold, to come over. He asked Buddy to bring him a glass of soda water.

"I did what my client paid me to," I said. Adding, "Even though he lied to me."

"Doesn't sound to me like you tossed in the towel."

"This has gone past the job itself into something else. Something maybe worth serious dough—but I'm not sure I want any part of it."

"Why not?"

"I'd be the finger man. A guy'd probably die because of me."

Barney studied me close, to see if I was leading him around the bend.

I said, "A wanted man, you understand. A bad guy. But he would probably die."

He knew I was serious now. He said, "Nate, uh . . ."

"What?"

"Why don't you take a pass on this one—whatever it is."

"That's good advice."

"You don't need the grief, mentally." He said mentally like mently.

"I know."

"You still carrying the gun?"

He meant the automatic that my father had killed himself with.

"I don't carry it often. But I still got it."

"It's what you carry when you feel you need to carry a gun, though."

"Yeah. Sure."

His soda water came; he sipped it; smiled.

"Good," he said.

I smiled at him. I knew what he meant.

A big tall man in a natty dark suit and a gray snap-brim hat was asking a question of Buddy Gold at the bar. Buddy pointed over to us, and the man—a dark, handsome guy in his late thirties—ambled over.

"Another fan," Barney muttered under his breath.

"I don't think so," I said.

"Mr. Heller," the man said, nodding to me. "I don't believe we've met. But I'm—"

"I know who are, Sergeant Zarkovich," I said. "No, we haven't met, exactly, but you were pointed out to me several times in East Chicago. This is Barney Ross. Join us, if you like."

He smiled; it was a winning smile. I'd have liked him immediately if I hadn't known him to be the crookedest cop in East Chicago. Which was going some.

He said, "I recognized you, of course, Mr. Ross," and he tipped his hat, "and it's a real honor to meet you. I saw you take Canzoneri. I won a half a C, thanks to you."

The big man was still standing there, so Barney, smiling back at him, said, "Thanks. Do join us, why don't you?"

"No, thanks. And I apologize for busting in. I just wondered if I could have a little of Mr. Heller's time . . . in private . . . when you two men are through talking. I can wait over at the bar. . . ."

He was smooth, I had to give him that. But seeing him here was giving me a sick feeling.

He was the cop in East Chicago who the madams paid off every month; he was the bagman, the collector, who Anna Sage would've had dealings with. Would've, hell—that was where I'd seen him, where he'd been pointed out to me—in East Chicago, at the Kostur Hotel.

"Don't be silly," Barney said, "join us—have a beer on the management."

"Well, okay," Zarkovich said, his smile turning shy. Aw shucks, the bagman said.

He scooted in on Barney's side, dwarfing the champ.

"I knew you had Canzoneri," he told Barney. "I wasn't worried a second."

"You were the only one, then," Barney said. "That was too close to call. They didn't even consider me champ in NYC, till I beat their boy on his home ground."

"And gave him a good licking."

Barney made an embarrassed face; but he enjoyed the attention. He was a good guy, but he was human.

"Tried like hell to knock him out," Barney said, almost apologetically. "Son of a gun just wouldn't go down."

"Look, Zarkovich," I said, leaving off the "Sergeant." Annoyed with all this small talk. "If you got business with me, let's go upstairs to my office."

Barney seemed offended by my lack of manners. "Nate, come on—
I'm the one who insisted he join us."

Zarkovich half-stood. "I apologize for intruding."

Barney really was embarrassed now, put a hand on Zarkovich's
arm, stopping him. "You're not intruding. Let me get you that
beer—"

I slid out of the booth and stood. "I'd just like to get business out of
the way, first. We'll be back down later, Barney. We'll both let you
buy us a beer—if you'll be around awhile."

Barney's face settled into a distrustful mask. "Uh, sure, Nate. I'm
just waiting for Pearl to get back with what's left of my money. I'll be
here half an hour or so at least."

Zarkovich thanked Barney for his hospitality and followed me out
onto the street, in the shadow of the El, where we went in the door
between the cocktail lounge and the pawnshop and up the stairs to
my office, where I unlocked the door and ushered him in. We hadn't
said a word on the way.

I opened a window and got back behind my desk and Zarkovich
stood till I gestured for him to sit, in one of the chairs opposite me.
He took off his hat, and I invited him to take off his suitcoat; he
smiled politely and, despite the heat, declined.

"I thought we should talk," he said.

"I wonder what about."

"You seem to be ahead of me, Mr. Heller."

"Let's drop the 'mister' horseshit, okay, Zarkovich? Anna Sage still
owns two houses in East Chicago, so you're here today collecting
from her, right?"

His handsome face was impassive.

I went on. "Only this trip Anna happened to tell you a story, and it
interested you. A story about a man one of her girls has been seeing."

He nodded.

"What Anna told you was she thinks the man might be somebody
famous," I said.

He nodded.

"Now I wonder who that somebody famous might be. The Dionne
Quints? Charlie McCarthy? John Dillinger?"

He had big hands; he clasped them together and then cracked his
knuckles. It sounded like the Saint Valentine's Day Massacre.

He said, "Your remarks don't amuse me, Heller."

"They were for my own benefit. It's my office, after all. What the hell."

"This is a serious business, you know."

"No. Do tell."

"You're just a penny-ante private cop who used to be a penny-ante Chicago cop, Heller. You're nothing special. You were on the take like everybody else."

"You're repeating yourself. You already said I was a Chicago cop."

"Funny. Just don't be so high and mighty. Some graft comes my way, all right? I don't deny it. That doesn't make me a bad cop. If times weren't so hard, I—"

"Wouldn't be wearing a hundred-dollar suit and a ten-dollar tie? I don't care if you're a grifter, Zarkovich. If you weren't, you'd be unnatural, a saint or something. And I wouldn't feel comfortable around you."

"You feel comfortable around me, do you?"

"Yeah. I'm at home. I know where you've been and where you're going."

"I could say the same thing about you. Mind if I smoke?"

"I don't care if you burn."

Zarkovich gave me a little twitch of a smile and took out a silver cigarette case, selected a cigarette and inserted it in a black holder, and lit up.

"How did your meeting with Purvis go?" he asked.

If that was supposed to throw me, well, I felt steady enough. I didn't like the idea that I'd been tailed and hadn't picked up on it; but I didn't bust out crying.

I said, "I told him I might have seen Dillinger. But I didn't go any further than that."

He nodded, the cigarette holder at a jaunty, FDR angle. "Wise. Waiting to talk to Cowley?"

"Yeah. Maybe. If I talk to anybody."

"Why wouldn't you?"

"Maybe there's nothing to talk about; Jimmy Lawrence takes an awful lot of taxicabs for a Board of Trade clerk, but that isn't illegal."

"You have your doubts he's Dillinger?"

"Hell yes. If this guy is Dillinger, he's the brazenest, coolest lad I've ever come across. He goes to public places all over the city, day and night; he bumps into cops without blinking; wears snappy clothes—this is a whole new way of lyin' low. And he's apparently unarmed . . . he doesn't even look like Dillinger, exactly."

Zarkovich nodded knowingly, smiled the same way. "Plastic surgery. Good enough to give him a sense of confidence. To go out in public and be an everyday joe. But it's a false sense of security. Anna recognized him, for one."

"So she says."

"So does he. He admitted to her last night he was Dillinger."

"What?"

"Call her," he said, pointing to my phone. "Ask her yourself."

"Why would he admit that?"

"He trusts Anna. She can be warm and motherly, you know."

"I bet."

"She's been nice to him and, as a madam, she seems trustworthy from his point of view . . . fellow underworld denizen and such like. And Anna's been known to, uh . . . rent space out to fellas on the run."

"I see. And now Anna wants to sell Mr. Dillinger out."

"What's to sell out? He isn't one of her roomers; he's got his own place, doesn't he? On Pine Grove Avenue?"

I nodded.

"Is it Anna's fault the guy confided in her?"

"Zarkovich, what's this got to do with me?"

He drew on the cigarette holder. "I'd like you to talk to Purvis again—or Cowley. I'd like you to arrange for one or both of them to meet with Anna."

"Why doesn't Anna approach them herself?"

"With her criminal record, she could use an intermediary."

"Why don't you do it?"

He made a sweeping, magnanimous hand gesture. "I could. In fact, I was going to suggest we go together. You could report what you've observed; and I would say Mrs. Sage, an old friend from East Chicago, contacted me about Dillinger, and put us in touch."

"Why don't you just leave me out of it?"

He shrugged. "Just trying to be fair. Can't see the point in working against each other. There's plenty of money in this for all concerned, Heller. At least twenty grand, to split four ways."

"Four?"

"Besides you and I, and Anna, there's my immediate superior, Captain O'Neill. He's in town today, too."

"He always accompany you to pick up collection money from madams?"

"Heller, we were in town following up leads on the Dillinger case. We had a tip our man was in Chicago, on the North Side."

"From Anna?"

"No. From a gambler I know, a Croatian. But never mind that. When I talked to Anna yesterday—not long after she'd talked to you—I realized our man was within our grasp. We have a vested interest in Mr. Dillinger in Indiana, you know."

"Besides the twenty-thousand-dollar reward money, you mean."

"Of course. Dillinger's an embarrassment to Indiana—a native son gone wrong."

"Is Leach in on this?"

Captain Matt Leach was the Indiana state cop who had devoted his entire career, of late, to tracking down Dillinger. A publicity seeker who made Purvis and Ness seem modest by comparison, Leach was hated by a lot of cops, but he was known to be a tireless, even obsessive pursuer of Dillinger.

"No," Zarkovich said tersely. "He's not involved. This is East Chicago business."

"A minute ago you said Dillinger was Indiana business."

"Specifically, East Chicago."

"Why?"

"He killed a cop there."

"Oh. That's the one killing they have him for."

"That's right. He killed a cop on his way out the door of the First National Bank, killed him with a machine gun. And there were plenty of witnesses."

"And you knew this man, this cop Dillinger killed."

"Yes—a fine man, who left a widow and children."

"So you'd like to get Dillinger."

"Yes."

"You want to be in on the kill."

"You might say that."

"As opposed to the capture."

"Heller, do you really think Dillinger could be taken alive?"

"Why not? He's been caught plenty of times before."

"But he knows this time he won't get away; there wouldn't be any repeat of the Crown Point disaster—no female sheriffs or shoe-polish guns."

"Maybe you're right. I don't know. In any case I don't think I'm interested."

"Suit yourself. You're not planning to talk to Cowley, then? Or Purvis, again?"

"No. But if you want revenge for that East Chicago cop, then Purvis is the man to see. He'll shoot first and ask questions later, all right."

Zarkovich stood and put his hat on, smiled wryly, cigarette holder still in his mouth. "I've dealt with Purvis before. A very excitable boy. He's just too young for the job."

"His 'men' are even younger."

"I know. The boy's bungled every job he was ever sent on; he should never have been put in charge of things. It's a good thing . . . never mind."

"It's a good thing the East Chicago police are around this time to help him out?"

"Yes," Zarkovich smiled. "Exactly."

I stood behind my desk. "Just out of curiosity, Sergeant—what are you going to do?"

"Try to arrange a deal in Anna Sage's behalf."

"What kind of deal?"

"Anna's got some problems with the immigration people. She thinks maybe these government men could swing things her way, if she helps out with Dillinger."

"Maybe they could. I take it you won't be going to the Chicago cops, then."

"Hell, no! Would you?"

"Stege is a good man."

"That's funny, coming from you."

"Just because he doesn't like me doesn't mean I don't respect him. He's honest and tough. You'd be much better off with him than Purvis."

"Thanks for the opinion, Heller. You're out, then?"

"I'm out."

"That doesn't make much sense to me, you know."

"Just as long as it makes sense to me," I said.

He shrugged and left. The topic of going back down to have a mutual beer with Barney never came up.

But I went down and joined Barney, who asked me why I was so rude to Zarkovich.

I explained that he was a bagman for East Indiana politicos.

"And he's got ties to the Capone crowd," I said. "Not just because the brothels are Syndicate controlled, either. He was up on a federal conspiracy charge about four years ago. He sided with the Capone faction in a gang war that involved some local East Chicago hoods. He got off, 'cause his politico pals clouted him off. But that is one dirty cop, my friend."

"He seemed okay."

"He's slick, and he's smart. But once he stepped into this picture, an odor turned up. A fishy one."

"So you're getting out of this case," Barney said. "Or is that 'job'?"

"I don't know what it is," I said.

But I didn't answer the rest of Barney's question, because I wasn't sure if I really was out of the Jimmy Lawrence–Polly Hamilton case. Job.

I drove over to Anna Sage's three-flat and parked down the street and sat on the rider's side and pretended to read the *Trib* while I watched. One of the things I was watching for was Zarkovich. I didn't see him.

Around seven-thirty a Checker pulled up and Jimmy Lawrence, with Anna on one arm and Polly on the other, came out of the three-flat, got in the cab, and headed for the Loop.

I followed them, and guess where they went?

Down to the lakefront, to the fair.

Where they caught Sally Rand's show at the Streets of Paris.

10

"That was nice," Sally Rand said, lighting a cigarette, sitting up in bed with a silk sheet draped across her breasts, "but somehow I don't think your heart was in it."

I propped the pillow up behind me and sat up myself. "I thought my heart was in it," I shrugged.

"That wasn't your heart, sweets. But I'll settle." She stroked the side of my face with the back of a gentle, long-nailed hand; the nails felt cool. The whole world felt cool, up here in her air-conditioned suite atop the Drake. "What's on your mind, Heller? What's going on behind those brown eyes?"

"Not much."

"You want to get some shut-eye? It's pretty late." The radium hand of the little round chrome clock on her white nightstand glowed half-heartedly in the near dark. What light there was in the room came in the windows; she had the shades up, curtains back, and the light from Lake Shore Drive and the Gold Coast and winking boats on the lake came in and bathed us like a cool blue breeze.

"Sleep if you like, Helen."

I was still calling her Helen; at least in bed I was. She seemed to like it. Being called Helen, I mean. And the rest of it, too, I guess.

She stabbed the cigarette out prematurely in a round glass tray on her nightstand. Then turned back to me, leaned on an elbow and smirked. "Most men in this burg would give up one of the family jewels for a night with Sally Rand. And you somehow don't seem too thrilled."

"It's not you. Really."

"It's something else."

"Yeah. Something else. You get some sleep. I'll just put on my clothes and head back to my place."

"The hell you will! You'll spend the night, whether you want to or not, Heller. I'll be damned if I'll put up with any hit-and-run driving through this joint."

I half-smiled at her. "I didn't mean it like that. I just figured I was lousy company. I'm tickled pink to be sharing a bed with Sally Rand—even if I do happen to know she's really Helen Beck from Missouri."

She hit me with a pillow.

Then she flicked on the nightstand lamp. It was a translucent glass tube with a silver base, and the light it gave off glowed; it made her, and the room, look like a soft-focus photograph. She leaned forward, pretty breasts swaying, and kissed me on the mouth for about thirty seconds, then kissed me again, just a smack.

"Let's get up," she said, "and I'll fix you a midnight snack."

"It's after midnight."

"Don't quibble."

"I don't have any pajamas. Will you take offense if I get dressed?"

"Yes. Eat in your underwear. I won't tell anybody."

She got up, her body as graceful and supple moving across her bedroom as onstage; she slipped into a white silk kimono, belted it, and waited for me to climb out of bed and follow her. Which I did.

She led me out through the living room, its soft plush carpet soothing my toes. The room was something out of Hollywood, running to modern, rounded furniture—sofa, divan, chairs, all soft-looking and covered in a sort of sun-bleached gunnysack. Everything was white (except for occasional blond wood) right down to the marble fireplace over which hung an airbrushed painting of orchids. On her way to the kitchen, she stopped to turn on a lamp on the blond end table by the sofa, a lamp that looked like her: a silver nude holding a round piece of frosted glass, like a flat bubble, behind which a pale little light gave off a minimal glow.

Earlier, before tumbling into bed, we'd sat in this living room, having martinis—a drink I hate, but when Sally Rand offers you martinis in her white art-deco suite before going off to bed with you, you can afford to suffer a little—and leafing through her big scrapbook of show biz clippings and such. There were stills of her in a silent called *Paris at Midnight* (she was wearing her natural light brown hair publicly in 1926) and another called *Golf Widows* (but by '28 was blond); and some on-the-set shots with De Mille, as well as some publicity photos from her Orpheum circuit act, "Sally and Her Boys." Then the huge front-page spread of her Lady Godvia entrance at the Fine Arts Ball, and the many court appearances her nude dancing earned her (she was given a year in jail, but won an appeal before serving a day) and several pamphlets complaining about her act circulated by "anti-indecency leagues" (anti-indeceny being a lot like pro-decency, I would imagine) and a few stills from the movie she'd made not long ago, with George Raft. I mentioned to her that I knew Raft, and she said, "Small world," and left it at that. Never name-drop with celebrities.

Now, in the white, modern compact kitchen, where mosaic white tiles chilled my feet, she scrambled some eggs and put me to work squeezing some oranges; she made some American fries, too, and toast, and we sat in the big modern living room, the one little lamp on, the city lights coming through a wall of windows, with the plates on our laps and our feet up on an ottoman.

"Where'd you learn to cook like this?" I said.

"Back on the farm. And I'm a bachelor girl pushing thirty, Heller. If I can't cook by now, I won't ever learn."

"You can cook," I confirmed. "Why don't you give up show business and marry me? I'd let you cook like this all the time. Hell, I make good money. It only takes me a year or so to make what you make in a week."

She made a crinkly closed-mouth smile, while she dealt with a bite of breakfast. Then she said, "If that's a serious proposal, I'll give it some thought. But you might as well know I'll never give up show business. You have to take me and my fans, too."

"Which fans are those? Feathered, or men with their mouths open?"

"Fans in general. You don't disapprove of what I do, do you?"

"No," I said, meaning it. "It's harmless. And you're good at what you do. I admire that. It's really very lovely, your act."

"Thanks, Nate," she said. Nibbling on a corner of toast. Eyes sparkling. Corners of her mouth upturned. "I could go for you in a big way. I really could."

"I bet you say that to all the boys."

Her smile faded; she wasn't mad or anything, just all of a sudden serious. She put a soft, warm hand on my bare arm.

"You're 'all the boys,' Nate. I'm no floozy."

"I didn't mean to suggest . . ."

"I know you didn't. But you got a right to think I sleep around. Any man who had me on my dressing room floor's got a right to think I might be a trifle . . . promiscuous. But I'm not. You're the first man

up here in a long time. That 'oil millionaire' you checked up on for
me, he only dreamed of getting up here."

"You mean you never cooked him breakfast?"

"Not an egg. Got me?"

"I gotcha."

"Good. Just 'cause I take my pants off to make a buck doesn't make
me a . . ."

"No it doesn't. And if I implied that, shame on me."

She leaned over and gave me a buttery kiss, buttery from the toast.

"Thanks, Nate."

"It's okay, Helen."

She smiled at that; she had a rather wide smile, too wide by some
men's standards, but I thought it was her best feature.

I figured we'd shut the book on this subject, but she went on,
looking off distractedly toward the windows and the lights of the Gold
Coast. "It's just that I wasn't raised to entertain men in my rooms. I
was raised to believe in virtue triumphant, honesty prevailing . . .
the old homilies, the old values. They don't hold up in the real world
too well, though, do they, Nate?"

"Not in Chicago they don't."

"Not anywhere. Not in these times. Not since the Crash. How can
a man who's been at his job thirty years suddenly not *have* a job?
How can it be that businesses that have been around for generations
suddenly *aren't* anymore? I had friends jump out of windows, Nate.
With accuracy."

"Things are getting better, Helen. A little."

"I don't know. Maybe I'm just feeling guilty."

"Why?"

"For being a bad girl and taking off my pants to make a buck. It
isn't what my daddy wanted out of me, and it isn't what I wanted out
of me, either. I wanted to be a ballerina. I wanted to be an artist. An
actress."

"A girl's gotta eat."

"Yeah, I know," she said, eating a last bite of American fries. She
chewed somberly, swallowed and said, "Maybe I feel guilty 'cause I
get thousands of dollars for strutting around with my pants off, while
men with families are getting peanuts for working in a factory or
something. Or getting nothing at all, 'cause they can't even find a
factory to work in. It just isn't right."

"Why don't you give all your money to the poor, then?"

"Don't be silly! I can't feed the world! I'm not *that* well off, I . . . you're needling me, aren't you? That was the point you were making."

I shrugged, smiled, chewed.

"I don't know, Nate. I eat caviar, and people a few blocks away are in soup kitchens; I wear mink, and pregnant women in Hoovervilles are wearing rags. I pay five hundred bucks a month to sublet this fancy-ass flat from a fag who's in Florida, and over in Little Italy, not a mile from here, families are living in basements for six bucks a month. How do you expect me not to choke on my success a little?"

I sipped my orange juice. "Pay your taxes. Find a church to give some money to. That's a start. Support some charities, if you like. But don't climb on the cross. It's hard to hold those fans with your hands nailed like that."

She smiled crookedly. "There'd be too many lechers like you trying to climb up there with me."

"That's the ticket," I said. "These are sad times, Helen. Your heart can break every time you walk down the street, if you let it. And there isn't much you can do in this life but your job, if you're lucky enough to have one, the best you know how. And try not to hurt too many people along the way. And maybe buy an apple from a guy on a street corner, once in a while, even if you don't like apples."

She studied me; she had a pale, beautiful look, right then, that I can see before me now.

"You're okay, Heller," she said. "This town hasn't got the best of you yet."

I laughed a little. "Oh yes it has. Many times."

"Here I been bellyaching about my silly concerns, and it's you who's been so troubled and preoccupied all night. What's going on with you, Heller? And why exactly did you show up unannounced at one of my shows, on a Thursday night? Last I heard from you, you planned to come by on Friday. . . ."

"I was just anxious to see you."

"Horseflop. What's eating you? Come on, Heller, spill!"

I sighed, thought it over.

Then I said, "Can you keep something to yourself, even if it's pretty hot stuff?"

She blinked, shrugged. "Sure."

"You got newspaper pals, and I—"

"This won't be in any of the boys' columns, I promise you."

"I know it won't. This is front-page stuff, Helen. Ben Hecht would come back to cover this."

"Now you *gotta* tell me."

I told her.

I gave her chapter and verse on the events of the week, from my traveling-salesman client to the guy who seemed to be Dillinger.

"I know I ought to walk away from this," I said, "but I feel a sort of . . . I don't know, responsibility for Polly Hamilton. Not 'cause I . . . slept with her once. That was nothing—it was just business. But my client hired me to follow her, and that's business of another stripe. Now, I know he hired me to see if she was cheating on him—he didn't pay me to be her bodyguard or anything. But he clearly cares about her, and here I am, leading her into a potentially dangerous situation. Potentially, hell—she's going to be in the middle of a goddamn shooting gallery."

"You really think the federal men will just start blasting away at Dillinger, then."

"Hell yes. And I'm not even sure the guy's really Dillinger. I feel a certain responsibility for putting that poor bastard's head on the block, too—and even if it *is* Dillinger, I'm not crazy about setting him up for an execution. That's a job for a judge and jury."

"If you feel this way, why don't you just warn Polly Hamilton? Get her out of there?"

I shook my head. "She hasn't left the guy's side in days; she's shacking up with him, for Christ's sake. I can't warn her without warning him."

"Maybe you should. Warn him, I mean."

"Maybe I should. But what if he *is* Dillinger? If I go near him, I might get my head shot off. Or if he just lams, and the feds get wind I warned him, suddenly I'm an accomplice or accessory or something. Obstructing justice, that's called. Shit. I should just walk away from this one. I really should."

"That's what you told this Zarkovich guy—that you wanted no more part of this."

"You bet. When I found out that son of a bitch was involved, I *knew* I wanted to jump ship."

"You say he's a smooth character, though."

"Very. A real ladies' man, too. They call him the 'Police Sheik,' back in Indiana."

"What's his relationship with this Anna person . . . Anna, what was it?"

"Sage. Well, like I said, he's a bagman. He picked up money from her and other madams to pass along to the big boys, keeping some for himself."

"Do you trust Anna Sage?"

"Not particularly."

"But you don't suspect her of anything, either."

"No."

"You don't think maybe she talked to this Zarkovich *before* she talked to you?"

"I suppose that's possible . . . but why would she talk to me about her suspicions, if she'd already talked to Zarkovich?"

"I been in show business since I was about nine. And I can tell you from experience, things are rarely as they seem."

"I don't get you."

"This whole thing seems . . . orchestrated, somehow. Don't you think?"

I didn't answer.

"You were led to Jimmy Lawrence. By your traveling-salesman client—who you have no way of contacting, right?"

I nodded.

"In fact, you can't even check up on the guy. The only address you have is that flat in Uptown where Polly Hamilton lives."

I nodded again. "And since they aren't married, that's not really his address. Right. I hadn't thought of that."

"Did he tell you what company he worked for?"

I shook my head. "Just a feed and grain company. No name."

"So you can't check up on him."

"I can't check up on him. Well—he said the firm was out of Gary. That would be a start."

"So this client, who lied to you, leads you to Polly Hamilton and Jimmy Lawrence. Now, Polly Hamilton knew you through Anna Sage, so if Polly was in on this—just bear with me, Heller—if she was in on this, she could well assume you'd check up on her with—or try to warn her through—Anna Sage."

I started nodding again. "And Anna Sage fed me the Dillinger story."

"And Anna Sage led Zarkovich to you."

"No denying that much."

"Maybe you're being used to set this guy up—whether he is or isn't Dillinger."

"But why? A simple anonymous phone call would do the trick just as well—they could call the cops or the feds and say, 'I think I saw Dillinger at such and such,' and accomplish the same thing."

"I can't explain it, Heller. You're the detective. You've got to figure the motives out. Me—I just know theater when I see it."

We took the dishes out to the kitchen, and soon she was snoring peacefully beside me while I lay with wide-open eyes staring into how smart she was.

COWLEY

11

I spent the next morning, Friday, sitting in my office running phone checks on the credit ratings of half a dozen would-be borrowers. This I was doing for the Retail Credit Company in Jackson Park, the single account that was keeping me afloat these days. The thought of a piece of the Dillinger reward money coming my way hung in the hot air in front of me, like laundry on a line.

Just around noon, when I was thinking about going downstairs to the deli for a pastrami sandwich, a big moonfaced man of about thirty-five in a gray hat and a gray suit and a gray tie came in. His complexion was a little gray, too—that hot ball of sun that had been baking Chicago for days upon end hadn't got to him yet, it would seem.

"Mr. Heller," he said, taking off his hat. His dark brown hair was longer on top than on its graying sides.

"Yes?" I said, half-rising.

"I'm Sam Cowley. With the Division of Investigation." He moved forward with a tight, somber expression and extended a hand. I rose the rest of the way to take it, then motioned for him to have a seat.

"Mind if I take off my coat?" he asked. Apparently the sun *had* got to him a bit.

I said sure. Since I wasn't wearing a coat myself, this piece of protocol struck me as excessive, but sincere—unlike smoothie Zarkovich, who used manners and charm as devices, Cowley was just a big heavyset guy who seemed a little awkward having to deal with people.

Or at least with me.

"I understand you spoke with Chief Purvis yesterday," he said. He had slipped the coat on the back of the chair. I'd misjudged him and the sun: the sweat circles on his shirt, under his arms, were like moons. They complemented his round face.

"I spoke with Chief Purvis," I confirmed.

"He informs me you feel you may have seen John Dillinger."

"That's right."

He moved his hat around in his hands, fingers on the brim like he was drying a plate. "We could use any information you might care to give us."

"I've . . . reconsidered."

"How so?"

I chose my words carefully. "I now feel I was hasty. I've had second thoughts about the likelihood that the man I saw was John Dillinger."

Cowley made a small shrugging gesture with his head. "There have been some misidentifications. I can understand your caution."

"Your associate Mr. Purvis—Chief Purvis—strikes me as a little too hot to trot, where Dillinger's concerned. I'm afraid he'd shoot Aunt Jemima if you pointed at her and said, 'There's Johnny.'"

I thought I saw the faintest trace of a smile appear on Cowley's lips, but he buried it. Said, "Chief Purvis is not alone on this investigation."

"I know. Your boss Hoover sent you in to be a steadying influence. I read the papers."

Cowley stirred in his chair. "That—that wasn't in the papers, not in that manner."

"I can read between the lines. Your boss seems real public-relations conscious to me. He couldn't fire Purvis after Little Bohemia without making the division look bad; so he sent for you."

Cowley waved a big deliberate paw in the air, said, "Be that as it may—I can assure you, any information you relay to our office—to *me*—will not be treated lightly, will not be acted upon rashly."

He was choosing his words carefully, too. I leaned back in my chair; studied him. I instinctively liked this man. He was a big, shy bear who could be trusted. He struck me as competent, as well. But I was still afraid that his competence would only be canceled out by Purvis' incompetence.

"I'm looking after a client's interests," I said. "And I don't think my client's interests would be best served by my getting further involved in this matter."

Cowley's face turned stern and he pointed a finger at me as thick as a twenty-five-cent cigar. "If you're aiding and abetting a fugitive, Mr. Heller, you can't hide behind the cloak of your profession. You're not a lawyer. Just a private operator. You'll go to jail."

"Inspector Cowley," I said, with what I hoped was a peacemaking smile, "I'm not harboring a fugitive. My client is not John Dillinger. He happens to be a traveling salesman and a law-'biding citizen. Whose girlfriend happens to be seeing another man, on the sly."

Cowley nodded thoughtfully. "The man who may be Dillinger."

I pointed at him this time. "That's a good way to put it. A man who *may* be Dillinger. And to be frank, if I had to bet on it, I'm not so sure I wouldn't bet against."

Cowley lifted his shoulders and eased them back down. It was about as demonstrative as he got. "Why not clear it up by leading us to this man? We can talk with him, find out who he is, clear this all up."

I shook my head and kept shaking it. "My client's girlfriend has been at this man's side day and night for at least a week. If I lead you to him, how can I be assured your overeager associate won't lay down a tommy-gun welcome for this 'man who might be Dillinger'—a welcome Nervous Purvis is likely to extend to my client's girl, as well?"

He didn't blink at my rather arch brand of sarcasm. He just said, "Maybe you can best prevent that by being involved yourself."

"I don't see it that way."

"Are you still shadowing this man?"

"No."

"Why not?"

"I've ascertained what I need to, where my client's concerned. I've fulfilled my responsibilities. And besides, maybe you've actually got somebody in that officeful of college boys who might succeed in shadowing *me*. Though I sincerely doubt it."

Cowley looked at me blankly; then the corners of his mouth turned up, barely perceptibly, and he said, "I doubt it, too."

An El train rushed by and we just sat and listened to it.

Then Cowley said, "We've had contact from someone else who has a line on Dillinger."

"That's interesting."

"Someone who's seen him on the North Side."

"Oh?"

"Yes. Someone with a police agency. An out-of-state agency."

"Really."

"East Chicago, Indiana, as a matter of fact."

"No kidding."

"A Sergeant Martin Zarkovich and his captain, a man named . . . it escapes me . . ."

"O'Neill," I said.

Cowley, feigning surprise, said, "You know of them?"

"I know Zarkovich. I don't believe I've met O'Neill, but I've heard of him."

"Do you have an opinion of, uh, the East Chicago police?"

"Generally, or specifically?"

"Either. Both."

"Generally, corrupt. Specifically, Zarkovich."

He smiled a little and leaned forward in his seat. He held the hat in one hand, now, and seemed to be offering it to me.

He said, "Then you know why we can use a corroborating source. As a matter of fact, if I could handle this through you entirely, I'd feel more comfortable. So would Chief Purvis."

That surprised me. "Really?" I asked. "What makes me such a sterling character?"

"Being compared to Zarkovich," Cowley said, deadpan.

That made me smile. "You're going to have to go with Zarkovich. He's a cop. Why don't you bring Stege in, while you're at it?"

Cowley didn't answer at first. "There's little love lost between our office and the Chicago police. Precious little mutual respect or cooperation."

"I take it this state of affairs predates your coming aboard."

"I haven't been here long, Mr. Heller. You know that. Just since April. But it doesn't take very long to realize the Chicago police are lacking in certain respects."

"So instead you deal with East Chicago? Look, there *are* a few good Chicago cops around—and Stege is one of 'em. I know, I know—you've heard he doesn't think much of me. Granted. But you could do with him in your corner, on this one, believe me."

Cowley rose. He wasn't leaving: he was just restless. Quietly so. He went over to one of the windows and looked out at the El. Without looking at me, he said, "I hear you're an honest man, Mr. Heller."

"More or less," I said.

He smiled, again without looking at me. "That's high marks in Chicago. We, uh . . . have a mutual friend, you know."

"I know."

Eliot Ness.

"So," Cowley continued, "if I say some things off the record, you'll keep them there."

"I'm not a reporter."

"If a reporter asked you." He looked over at me sharply. "Or even a judge."

I nodded.

He walked back and stood by the chair. Said, "Zarkovich and O'Neill have made some conditions. One of them is that Stege and the Chicago police not be involved in Dillinger's . . . capture."

"Why do you pause before the word 'capture'?"

He hesitated. "It has to do with another of their conditions."

"I see. Have you agreed to these various conditions?"

"Not yet. That's where you come in, Mr. Heller. Why not help the federal government avoid having to rub up against something as dirty as the East Chicago police? Why not tell us what you know, and keep us from having to deal with the likes of Zarkovich and O'Neill?"

I didn't say anything.

"Well," Cowley said, with an air of finality, "think it over. But think quickly. Because this is liable to come together quickly."

"And go down the same way?"

He nodded slowly. He put on his coat, his hat. "Your help would be appreciated. By tomorrow, say."

"I'll be thinking it over."

"Why don't you contact your client, if you're worried about getting his girlfriend involved."

"I'm afraid I have no way of contacting him. He's on the road, and said he'd check back in with me. He hasn't, yet."

Cowley shrugged. "You're a detective. How did he get in touch with you?"

Through a referral from a lawyer. Specifically, Louis Piquett. Piquett!

"Say, Inspector. You're obviously more up on the Dillinger case than I am. What lawyer was it Dillinger contacted to come up to Crown Point and defend him, right before he broke out last year?"

"It was February of *this* year," Cowley said. "And I'm surprised at you, Mr. Heller—you said you read the papers, and the papers played up Dillinger's hiring such a colorful 'mouthpiece.'"

And I—like you—knew what he'd say next.

"Louis Piquett, of course," Cowley said, and nodded to me, and left.

LOUIS PIQUETT

12

They call LaSalle Street the Wall Street of the West. Whatever, it's a concrete valley where money and power live—if there's a difference. Between Randolph and Washington streets, well before its claustrophobic canyon dead-ends at the Board of Trade Building, LaSalle in an act of sacrifice before the great god graft devotes an entire city block to City Hall, a modern whitestone monolith with classical airs. Money and power reside there, as well.

But tucked away in the skyscrapers along LaSalle, above the giant banks and brokerages, are small offices where men who are not financial wizards nor politicans but who find their way toward money and power, just the same, also reside. Men like attorney Louis Phillip Piquett.

On the west corner of Washington and LaSalle, a sleek gold-brick skyscraper was where Piquett kept his office. He was on the twenty-fifth floor. Looking down on City Hall.

Going up in the elevator was like riding in an oven; it was just me, the uniformed operator and a couple of guys in business suits. I was in a business suit, too. We were basting in our own sweat. This was LaSalle Street, however, and one of the few places in the city where shirt sleeves were not the heat-wave order of the day. I suppose when you're on your way to an air-conditioned office, you can afford roughing it.

Piquett's office was air-conditioned, beyond its pebbled-glass-and-wood facade, and brother did it feel good. The waiting room was surprisingly modern, for such an old-fashioned mouthpiece, with a white wall-to-wall carpet and black leather chairs with chrome arms along the glass-and-wood walls; there were several doors leading off the reception area, all of which said PRIVATE in black letters. A disturbingly pretty secretary at a big black desk, her head a cap of blond curls, gave me a sharp businesslike look, letting me know her chorus-girl beauty may have got her the job, but she was here to work, by God. She was, in fact, typing at the moment, sitting sideways at her desk working at a typewriter on a stand. She had black-frame glasses she maybe didn't need and a white mannish blouse and said, "Yes?"

"I'm Nathan Heller," I said. "Would you tell Mr. Piquett I'm here to see him?"

"Have you an appointment?"

"No."

"I'm afraid Mr. Piquett's a busy man."

The office wasn't exactly jumping: we two were alone in the reception area, and there were no sounds from behind the doors marked PRIVATE.

"Just let him know I'm here, would you?" I said, and smiled politely, letting her know her chorus-girl beauty didn't interest me particularly, which I could tell bothered her. She was the sort who resented you for noticing she was pretty but if you didn't, resented you for that. I sat down. She knocked on Piquett's door and went in and in a minute or so came out looking vaguely confused, then covered it quickly with that businesslike manner.

"He'll see you," she said, and I started to rise, but she motioned me back. "It'll be a few minutes."

And she returned to her typing.

I sat and read one of the handful of magazines on a small glass-and-chrome table between two of the chairs; a *Saturday Evening Post* from the second week of January. Between the air conditioning and pictures of kids building snowmen, I was ready to find myself a pair of snowshoes.

The frosty receptionist answered the phone on her desk and it was an inner-office call; she glanced up at me disinterestedly and said, "You can go on in, now."

I'd been waiting half an hour.

Piquett was seated behind his desk, paperwork spread out across it unconvincingly. He'd kept me waiting on purpose; why, I didn't know. But one thing was for sure: Piquett wasn't a paperwork-style lawyer.

He'd never been to law school; he studied the law books while working as a bartender and waiter. That much was well known by the public at large, who viewed him as a colorful character. Lesser known was Piquett's stint as a hanger-on at police precinct houses, carrying messages to lawyers and bail bondsmen, as sort of an apprentice ambulance chaser. Ward heelers and politicians, as well as various underworld characters, were valuable connections made in those days by the would-be lawyer (rumor had it he tried out for the bar a dozen times before passing). And working as a waiter and bartender in road-houses and, later, in various Loop and North Side restaurants and taverns enabled Piquett to make some good, lasting friendships.

One of which, you would think, was the friendship between Piquett and Heller, the way the stocky little man stood and smiled and flung his hand out toward me. I shook it, and he gestured for me to sit in a chair opposite him, and I did, but he remained standing.

For a small man, he cut an impressive figure. Even on this warm day (albeit in an air-cooled office), he wore a three-piece suit, though nothing fancy; the vest and gray-speckled tie were for respectability, but the slightly worn look of the suit was for Clarence Darrow mock-humility.

"It's good to see you again," he said, with a disarming half-smile. His features were crowded toward the center of his chubby face—bright eyes, bulbous nose, tiny mouth; dark circles under the bright eyes gave him an intensity, and the effect was at once boyish and fatherly. His most striking feature, however, was his hair: a three-inch-high salt-and-pepper pompadour rose in startled waves, as if he'd stuck his finger in a socket.

"Nice to see you, too, Counselor," I said, smiling faintly. The only time I'd ever seen him had been in court, in the Lingle murder case. I'd been testifying for the prosecution; he'd been the defense lawyer. Still, we'd been on the same team. Both of us were helping railroad a Syndicate patsy named Leo Brothers, Piquett's client, who'd been chosen by the Capone crowd to take the rap.

"What brings you here, Mr. Heller?" He sat.

"I wanted to thank you for referring one of your clients to me. I sure can use the business."

He brushed a hand over the pompadour and it did a little dance. "I don't remember having recommended your services, Mr. Heller. Although I may have. You did reliable work for me, and my client, last year."

All my dealings with Piquett on that job had been via intermediary or phone.

"But you don't specifically remember recommending me to anyone?"

He shrugged, smiled like a pixie. "Sorry. I'd love to be of help. And I'll certainly keep you in mind, for future referrals. I do, however, have a permanent investigator on staff."

"I see. Do you know a John Howard?"

Piquett thought, then slowly shook his head. "Can't say as I do."

"He's a traveling salesman."

Piquett shook his head slowly, no.

"Works for a feed and grain company. Whose bosses gave him your name."

Piquett shook his head slowly, no.

I described my client; Piquett shook his head.

"This isn't good," I said.

"Why is that?"

"I appear to have been used to set somebody up."

"How so?"

"Mr. Piquett, my guess is that you already know the answer to that question."

His round face took on a cherubic innocence that would've fooled most any jury.

He said, "I really don't know what you mean, Mr. Heller."

"You don't."

"I do not. I haven't the slightest idea what point you're trying to make."

"Well, I'm no orator. That's not my line. I'm just a detective who doesn't like being played the fool."

"No one does, Mr. Heller."

"I understand you're representing John Dillinger these days."

With a tiny smile, Piquett said, "That's correct."

"The first time I ran into you, you were defending Leo Brothers—a man accused of killing Jake Lingle . . . a friend of yours. In fact you were one of the last to see Jake Lingle alive. And yet you defended the man accused of killing him."

"Everyone deserves representation under the law, Mr. Heller. That's the American way."

"And on that job I did last year for you—your client was Al Capone."

A small noncommittal shrug. "Yes."

"And now you're representing John Dillinger. Don't you *ever* represent anybody who isn't a gangster or a thief?"

Hands folded on his desk, he smiled like a child and said, "They're the only ones who have money these days, Mr. Heller."

"What I don't get is why you're helping set up your own client.

The reward money's substantial, but Dillinger himself ought to be pretty well fixed by now. . . ."

Piquett stopped smiling. "If you're implying that my client, Mr. Dillinger, is in some danger at the moment, that's hardly news. Every lawman in the country is gunning for him. But I would hardly betray my own client, Mr. Heller. And if you have knowledge of any . . . conspiracy to do him harm, why, I'd be grateful for details."

"You're a slick one, I'll give you that."

"You flatter me, Mr. Heller."

"Do I. Let me tell you something, Piquett—I got off the force and into private business because I was sick and tired of being pulled into this scam and that one. I got good and fed up with being up to my butt in graft and bullshit. And I didn't—and don't—like being played a patsy, particularly where setting somebody up for a kill is concerned. So I'm not taking kindly to being pulled into this set up, whatever the hell it's really about."

"I thought you said you weren't an orator, Mr. Heller."

"I'm not. But whoever decided to use me in this one made a bad mistake. Because I'm pulling the rug out from under this whole damn deal. Got it?"

"I haven't the faintest notion of what you're talking about."

"Do you know Anna Sage?"

"I'm afraid I don't."

"Martin Zarkovich?"

"Not familiar with the name."

"Polly Hamilton? Jimmy Lawrence?"

"No . . . no . . ."

"I see. You're going to play it cute and innocent. Fine. And that traveling salesman who came to me just *happened* to use your name. . . ."

Piquett stood, glanced out the window, down at City Hall; then moved around from behind his desk and sat on the edge of it. With a patient smile and a run of his hand over the salt-and-pepper pompadour, he said, "Mr. Heller, I am a public figure. Just because someone walks into your office and invokes the name Piquett, that doesn't make Piquett a part of *anything*."

That actually was pretty convincing; I tried not to show it in my face.

But he caught it. And went on: "Futhermore, I may very well have

mentioned you as a reliable investigator to several people, who may
have passed your name along to this Howard fellow. Yes, it seems to
me I *have* mentioned your name to several other lawyers and a
number of other professional people as well. . . ."

Now he'd gone too far; I knew he was faking.

I said, "Why don't you tell me what's really going on? Maybe if you
cut me in, I'll play along. Otherwise, I'm liable to blow off the whole
deal."

Hands folded over his vested belly, he sat perched like a lep-
rechaun and said, "What deal?"

I stood. "Think about it, Louie."

"About what?"

I was going out the door, when he called out, "Always nice to see
you, Mr. Heller. Drop by anytime."

The secretary-receptionist gave me an icy look and I walked out of
the office, wondering if I should talk to Captain Stege about this, or
maybe try to get through to Cowley—he'd seemed anxious enough to
hear my story. Purvis I wanted to avoid at all costs; he was just too
damn eager to bag his man.

The elevator ride was just as stifling going down, and in fact after
the air-cooled comfort of Piquett's office seemed even worse. The
elevator operator didn't smell so good.

I slipped out of my coat, when I got outside, LaSalle Street or no,
and slung it over my shoulder.

That was when two big guys in suits and ties and hats came up to
me and smiled. They looked like they could play catch with a Ford.
They both nodded to me.

But only one of them spoke.

He said, "Mr. Nitti would like to see you. Just walk along with us,
okay, Heller?"

13

It wasn't much of a walk to the Capri Restaurant on North Clark Street. Just a block up. Like Piquett's office, the Capri was close to City Hall, and its large, smoky, air-cooled dining room—the walls paneled in an unfinished oak, the booths covered in brown leather— was crowded with judges, city officials, attorneys, theatrical folk, strictly male. A few of them were heavies: in a booth nearby, Jake Arvey was animated as he chewed Pat Nash's ear, while Nash seemed more intent on chewing his corned beef and cabbage. I thought I saw Rudy Vallee sitting at a table back in the far left corner, chatting over steaks and chops with a couple of men I didn't recognize, theatrical agents or producers I supposed.

But I didn't see Frank Nitti, even though it was widely known that he owned the Capri and held court here.

My two burly escorts escorted me politely to the left, through a glass door into a little tiled waiting area by an elevator. One of the pair, a guy with smile dimples so deep they stood out when he wasn't smiling, pushed the button for the elevator. It came down and the cage door was opened from within by an elevator operator wearing a suit and tie and a bulge under his left arm.

"Better pat him down," the elevator operator said.

The other escort, a guy without smile dimples but with several facial moles, said, "He don't have his coat on, fer crissakes. Where's he gonna keep a gun?"

As he was saying this, the other guy was patting me down. I didn't have a gun. Or a knife or a bomb. Just my car keys and a money clip with ten bucks, a five and five ones. These he had me remove from my pockets, however, and examined them and handed them back, laughing a little at the money clip, smile dimples deepening.

"Sure rolling in dough, ain't ya, dick," he said, cheerfully.

He was too big to banter with.

So I said, "Right," and stepped inside the elevator. They followed me.

NITTI

We went to the third floor, where the two guys got off first. The elevator didn't go back down; the elevator operator with the suit and the gun bulge stepped out and joined us. We were in an anteroom paneled in that same unfinished oak; the walls were barren.

Opposite the elevator there were double doors, which smile-dimples pushed through; he came back a moment later and, holding the door open for me, gestured with a thumb.

"Mr. Nitti'll see you now," he said.

I went in, and my escorts didn't.

I was alone in a big dining room—cloth-covered tables and along the left wall a banquet table, the walls that same scarified oak— alone, that is, with Frank Nitti.

He sat, by himself, at a table for four at the far right of the room, his back to the corner. He was eating. He looked up from his plate and smiled on one side of his face and waved me over with a hand with a fork in it and looked back at his food.

There was no carpet on the parquet floor and my shoes made small echoes as I weaved through the well-spaced-apart tables back to the corner table, where Nitti glanced up again, half-rose, and nodded to a chair across from him. I sat.

I hadn't seen him in about a year. He looked skinny and quite a bit older; he'd shaved his mustache off. Still, he was a roughly handsome man, with flecks of scar here and there on his face, notably his lower lip. His hair was slicked back and parted at the left. A former barber, he was always immaculately groomed. His suit was black, his shirt too; his tie was white, with a ruby stickpin.

He was eating what looked to be boiled beef with some small skinned potatoes and some sliced carrots. He was drinking milk.

He must've noticed me looking at this less-than-lavish lunch, because he grimaced and said, "Goddamn ulcers. Can you believe it? And this is one of the better meals I had lately."

"Hardly pays to own a restaurant," I said.

He smiled a little. "Yeah. Maybe I oughta find another line of work."

I didn't say anything; I was nervous. Nitti seemed to like me, but he was an intimidating figure, albeit a short one.

"Heller," he said, "you look older."

"You look about the same, Frank."

"Bullshit. I aged ten years since those bastards shot me last year. If you hadn't been there and made 'em call an ambulance, I'd be with the angels right now."

"The angels, Frank?"

He shrugged elaborately. "I'm a good Catholic. Are you a Jew, Heller? You look more like a Mick."

"I'm both and neither. I never been to church in my life, except your occasional wedding and funeral."

He pointed his finger at me, and gave me a scolding look. "That ain't good. Take my advice, kid—get some goddamn religion. You ain't gonna live forever."

"Should I take that as a threat, Frank?"

His smile returned; the ruby on his tie winked at me. "No. Just advice. I like you, kid. You did me a favor. I don't take that lightly."

"You returned the favor. We're even."

"Maybe. But I like you. You know that."

"Well, uh, that's good to know."

"I got respect for you. You got, whaddya call it, integrity. Not too many people got that, you know."

I figured he held this opinion because I'd quit the force after Mayor Cermak's two police bodyguards had taken me along, unawares, into what turned out to be an assassination attempt on Nitti's life.

"And you got balls," he said, picking at one of the potatoes with his fork. "You're smart and honest—though not so honest as to be a problem—and you got integrity. So that's why I like you."

I risked a wisecrack. "This is starting to sound like a testimonial," I said. "Maybe we should move over to the banquet table, and invite those guys who brought me up here to join us."

He tolerated that, even smiled again, then frowned and quickly said, "They didn't get nasty, did they? I told 'em you were to be my willin' guest. Nothin' nasty."

"They weren't nasty, Frank. But they didn't have to be. Where'd you get those guys, Lincoln Park Zoo?"

He drank some milk and this time when he smiled he had a milk mustache, which he wiped off with a thick hand on which rested a gold ring that must've weighed half a pound.

"Healthy-looking boys, ain't they?" he said. "I beefed up my security after the Cermak hit."

I didn't know if he was referring to the attempt on his life by Cermak's two cops, or the subsequent assassination of Mayor Cermak in Miami last summer, which he'd directed. And I didn't ask.

"Would you like something to eat?" he asked, gesturing to the empty place in front of me.

Actually, I hadn't eaten all day. But somehow I didn't have much of an appetite, and declined.

"You're wondering why I asked you up here," he said.

"I think I know, Frank."

He looked up from his boiled beef, with an almost pop-eyed look. "Really?"

"Well, let's just say that I've figured out that Piquett kept me waiting in his office for half an hour so he could call you and you could send some people over."

Nitti didn't confirm or deny that.

He just said, "You're involved in something. And I'm sorry as hell about it."

He cut his beef with the side of his fork, leaving a pause for me to fill, but I couldn't find anything to fill it with.

He ate a bite, and went on. "This thing that's about to go down, I'm on top of it—it's happening with my approval, even my guidance. But I'm an executive, kid. I don't handle the detail shit, you know?"

"I can understand that, Frank."

"I didn't know they were going to pull you into this. And if I'd known, I'd have stopped 'em."

"Who, Frank?"

"Don't ask questions, kid. Just listen." He paused to see if I was going to pay heed, and I was.

"I want you to get out of this," he said. "And stay out. Just let things take their course."

He ate his boiled beef.

"Is that all, Frank?" I said.

"Sure. You wanna go, go ahead. It was good to see you again."

He'd been very careful in choosing his words—everything vague, all references couched in euphemism.

"Frank, we are talking about setting John Dillinger up, aren't we?"

He shrugged, chewed, watched me with eyes that warned me not to go too far.

I went ahead anyway. Just a step at a time.

"It makes sense that you and your associates might like to be rid of

a guy like this," I said. Carefully. "Having the likes of Dillinger in
town—and he seems always, eventually, to come back to Chicago to
hide out—stirs up all kinds of heat. Local *and* federal."

Nitti nodded, chewing.

I shook my head sympathetically. "Cops and feds can't put out the
dragnet for Dillinger and his ilk without disrupting your Outfit's activities, of various kinds, in the process. Public outcry over gangsters
like Dillinger leads to mass arrests—which your people get caught up
in. Dillinger's bringing down too damn much heat on the Outfit."

Nitti narrowed his eyes and said, "Last December three of my best
people were killed. It was a raid on a flat on Farwell Avenue by
Stege's Dillinger Squad; those trigger-happy sons of bitches mistook
my guys for Dillinger and two of his pals. Shot 'em dead. Didn't
know they had the wrong men till they took their fingerprints, hours
later." Disgusted, Nitti sipped his milk. "It's gotta end."

"Is that what's happening?" I asked. "You're putting an end to Dillinger?"

"Be careful what questions you ask me, kid—I might answer 'em."

"That fed Cowley came to see me today."

Nitti said nothing; pushed his plate away from him. There was still
some food left, but he'd had all of it he could stomach.

I said, "I got the feeling he'd cut a deal with Zarkovich, agreeing to
shoot Dillinger down. Rather than take him in."

Nitti patted his mouth with a napkin.

"So it's not enough for Dillinger to be captured," I said. "He's got
to buy it. He's got to die."

Nitti cleared his throat. "Let me tell you something, kid. For a
long time these fuckin' outlaws could get away with what they're
doing. They were like stagecoach and train robbers in the Old West;
fact is, most of 'em are dumb Okies who think they're Jesse James.
And they got away with it, for a while. 'Cause all they needed was
fast flivvers and lots of back roads and plenty of hideouts. And they
weaved all across the country, and the law couldn't even cross state
lines to chase 'em. They had a sweet little thing going. Long-term,
however, it stunk. Which is why only suckers—farmers, dumb Okies
like that—got in that business. But they had their time, I'll give 'em
that. Only their time is over."

He sipped some milk. He seemed to be through with his speech,
but I nudged him on. Carefully.

"You mean their time's over, because of the feds," I said. "Because now the feds *can* chase 'em across state lines."

Nitti nodded, shrugged. "That's it, that's a big part of it. The rewards on their heads'll smoke 'em all out eventually, too. But times are changing. You can only get away with that shoot-'em-up bullshit for so long."

"You mean you can't get away with too many Saint Valentine's Day Massacres."

"No. And you can't shoot too many Jake Lingles. The public likes to make a hero out of somebody like Al or Dillinger, for a while. But when things get too bloody, when the headlines get too nasty, the public turns on you."

"Frank, these outlaws—your Outfit's had dealings with 'em over the years. . . ."

"Where'd you hear that?"

"I hear things. I'm awake."

"That's a nice way to be, awake. You ought to hold onto that thought."

I said nothing.

Then for some reason he continued. "Yeah, Al had a soft spot for that kind, particularly the bank robbers. Don't ask me why. The suburbs, Cicero, Maywood, Melrose Park, they were always welcome there, where Al was concerned. There were always thieves hiding out there."

"For a fee?"

"Nothin's free, kid."

"I'd guess a certain amount of fencing of goods and hot money by such thieves might also be handled through the Outfit."

"Easy, kid."

"And the guns those guys use, machine guns particularly, and explosives, they got to come from somewhere. And sometimes, like any small business, they'd need seed money, short-term loans. And Outfit sources are the natural place for both. . . ."

Nitti was shaking his head, but not by way of denial. He said, "You better button it right there, kid." Not mad; just fatherly advice.

I buttoned up.

Then Nitti couldn't keep from saying: "It's just better for some people to be dead, kid."

He'd opened the door, so I took a breath and went on through.

"Well, uh, if somebody wanted Dillinger dead, why wouldn't somebody just kill him? Why go to such elaborate lengths to have the feds do the job?"

Nitti's mouth etched itself into an enigmatic little smile.

Then he said, "You're operating here out of curiosity, Heller. Nothing else. No client. Just curiosity. And you know what happened to the goddamn cat."

I knew.

"You played a part in this thing," Nitti said. "Like I said, if I'd known they was planning to suck you in, I'd have stopped it. Only they did suck you in. Well, you played your role, now get offstage, go home. Stay out of it, and stay the hell out of the way."

"What if Cowley or Stege or Purvis come around?"

"Why don't you just report what you know to be true, and leave it go at that, in such event."

"You mean, tell them about tailing Polly Hamilton and Jimmy Lawrence, and that Anna Sage says Lawrence is Dillinger."

"Yeah. It starts and ends with that."

"And I just stand by and let the poor shmuck get killed."

He raised a finger in a cautionary fashion. "I'm not saying *anybody's* going to get killed. But what skin off your ass is it if some fuckin' Hoosier outlaw gets what he's gonna get someday anyway?"

"Frank," I said, "when I bitched about Cermak's boys hitting you, the same argument was advanced. That Nitti was a guy who was going to meet a bullet one of these days anyway, so what the hell."

He gestured with two open hands. "I'm a restaurant owner. Restaurant owners don't get shot, not unless maybe some goddamn outlaw comes in and robs the till."

"I don't like being a part of this."

"Good," Nitti said. "Don't be." He reached in his right pants pocket and took out a money clip. The thickness of bills included a fifty on top, which he peeled off, then he peeled off another fifty. He smoothed them on the tablecloth before me; the two bills were spread out in front of me like supper. Like a six-course meal.

"I want to be your client," Nitti said.

"You do?"

"Yeah, kid. That's a hundred-dollar retainer. I want your services between now and Monday. I got something I want you to do for me till then."

"What's that, Frank?"

"Sleep," he said. "Go home and sleep. Till Monday."

I swallowed.

Then I took the money, because I didn't dare not take it. Added it to the five and five ones on my own clip.

"This meeting between us, it never happened. *Capeesh?*"

"*Capeesh,*" I said.

"This is hard for you, ain't it, kid?"

"Yes," I said.

"I like you. I really do."

And he did. He cared about me. The way you like and care about a character in a radio serial you follow. But if a streetcar ran me over in tomorrow's episode, he wouldn't lose any sleep that night.

"Is it okay if I go now, Frank?"

"Sure, kid. You don't have to ask my permission to do things. You're your own man. That's what I like about you. Now, go."

I went.

RANDOLPH AND STATE; DEARBORN, A BLOCK DOWN

14

At my office that afternoon I couldn't resist checking one last thing out. Frank Nitti or no, there was something I had to follow through on. In the bottom of my pine four-drawer file I had several out-of-town phone books, as well as two Chicago cross-directories (numbers first; addresses first). I took out the Gary, Indiana, book and looked in the Yellow Pages. There were six grain companies. I called the personnel departments of each; it took all the rest of the afternoon, and talking to two or three people each place, which ran my phone bill up, but I did it. And John Howard didn't work for any of them.

Not that I'd expected him to. It was obvious, now, that my traveling-salesman client was a con artist hired to rope me into the play Zarkovich and Nitti were putting on. I felt like a chump. And with good reason: I was a chump.

I took the money clip out of my pocket, peeled off the two fifties Nitti had given me. A braver man would've tossed them in Nitti's face. He'd also be a dumber man, and possibly a deader one. Maybe if I had the integrity Nitti was talking about, I'd turn the bills into confetti and toss them out my office window; or give 'em to the first down-and-outer on the street I ran across. But I needed a new suit, so I went out and bought one. The rest of the money could go for luxuries. Like eating and the phone bill.

Some of Nitti's money I decided to blow on Barney Ross and his girl Pearl. I called him over at the Morrison and he said he and Pearl were planning to go out for a bite, but had no special plans. So I drove over and picked 'em up and took Pearl and her smart green dress and Barney and his blue bow tie to my favorite restaurant in the city, Pete's Steaks.

Pete's was on Dearborn, just north of Randolph. Pretty redheaded Pearl, on Barney's arm, tried to hide her surprise as we approached the place; the neon sign that hung above the awning had a few vowels burned out, so that it read P T 'S STE KS, and looking in the window all you could see was an ordinary white-tile, one-arm joint. But then we went inside, and back to the rear of the place and up the steps to the air-cooled dining room, where framed autographed celebrity photos (including one from Barney, signed to Bill and Marie Botham, the owners—I never did find out who Pete was) rode the walls of the long, narrow dining-car-like room.

As soon as Pearl started spotting celebrities (Eddie Cantor and George Jessel were at a table together and, at another, second time today, Rudy Vallee) she brightened. The place catered to the show biz crowd, press agents, song boosters, chorines, vaudevillians, with a good number of newspapermen tossed in in the bargain. Doc Dwyer of the *Examiner*, Hal Davis of the *News*, and Jim Doherty of the *Trib* were here tonight, and probably some others I didn't recognize.

Our table conversation ran to small talk—Barney had taken Pearl to the fair today, including Sally Rand's matinee, which Pearl found "shameless," but sort of giggled when she said it—and I mostly just listened. But Barney was watching me close; he knew I was in a black mood. He also knew I'd called and invited him and Pearl out to try to shake that mood, and that I wasn't being particularly successful.

The steaks arrived and helped distract me. Thick and tender and juicy, with melted butter and a side concoction of cottage fries, radishes, green onions, peas and sliced Bermuda onions that spilled onto the steak. I'd eaten nothing today except a bagel at the deli under my office, when I'd got back from Nitti's; it'd been all I could make myself eat. But I was ravenous, now, and I attacked the rare steak like an enemy. Pearl, fortunately, didn't notice my rotten table manners; she was too caught up in her own Pete's Special. Barney, though, continued to eye me.

A minor sportswriter from the *Times*, whose name I didn't remember, buttonholed Barney on the way out, and I stood and talked to Pearl at the top of the stairs.

"You're a very special friend to Barney," she said.

"He's a special friend to me."

"When you're in Barney's position, the friends you had before you got famous are the important ones, you know."

"Are you going to marry him, Pearl?"

"If he asks me."

"He will."

She gave me a pretty smile, and I managed to give one back to her. A smile, that is. I doubt it was pretty.

I drove them back to the Morrison, and let them out, but Barney leaned in the window on the rider's side before I pulled away.

"Are you going to be all right, Nate?"

"Sure."

"You want I should drop up tonight, and we can talk?"

"No. It's okay. You only got tonight and tomorrow night before Pearl goes home. Spend your time with *her*, you bum."

"You sure, Nate?"

"Sure I'm sure—now, go be with your girl!"

"Thanks for supper, Nate."

I smiled and waved and pulled away.

Pete's special steak, good as it was, was grinding in my stomach. I passed some gas and it smelled the way I felt.

There was a place in the alley behind the building where Barney let me park my Chevy. I'd been lucky—no vandals or thieves had had at it yet. During the winter, it was hell to start 'er up, on the really cold days; but on the really cold days I tried to work out of my office, anyway. A telephone's a detective's best tool, after all; and I was like anybody born and brought up in Chicago—I was more comfortable riding the Els and streetcars, and didn't use the car much, really.

I stopped in Barney's Cocktail Lounge for a beer, thinking about how you used to go into the place through the corner deli. The cocktail lounge had been a blind pig, a bar that seemed to be closed down and boarded up but was actually wide open, like Chicago. Somehow I missed sitting by the boarded-up windows. It had felt safe, secure, snug, somehow. I rarely took one of the window booths, these days. Tonight I sat along the wall.

After the beer, I had some rum. Just enough to settle my stomach. The warmth moved through my belly in a soothing wave. I felt better. I had a little more rum. Not too much. Sally was going to stop by this evening, after her show. She said she wanted to see how the other half lived, and I guessed it was time she found out, Murphy bed and all. But the least I could do was greet her soberly.

I sat there, sipping the rum, and felt so goddamn depressed I could cry. I got out of there before I did.

I walked up the stairs to my floor and down the hall and worked the key in the lock and stepped in and a fist sunk in my stomach and bounced off my spine. I fell on my knees and puked. Heard the door shut behind me.

"Did you get any on you?" a hushed voice said.

He meant me puking.

"Yeah, shit." An arm wiped itself off on my back; I was still doubled over, retching, but nothing was coming out, now. A mulligan stew of steak, potatoes, radishes, peas and onions shimmered before me. It smelled foul and a little like rum.

A hand grabbed the small of one my arms and dragged me away from the pool of puke. So they wouldn't get any more on them.

I looked up. The office was dark, just some neon glow coming in and making orange pulsing shadows on the craggy indistinct face under the fedora before me. The other guy was behind me, hooking his arms through mine, pulling me back, though I remained on my knees. The craggy-faced guy with neon on his face had something in his hand, something like a piece of tube only limp. It drooped, like a big phallus.

He raised his arm, quickly, and the thing in his hand swished. Then it swished again as he curved it across my chest.

A rubber hose.

"Fuck!" I said.

The arms behind my arms pulled back. "Take it like a man," a voice said. Kind of a whiny, upper-register voice. "Take your goddamn medicine."

The guy in front of me hit me about the body with the rubber pipe, my chest, my stomach, my arms, my shoulders. Not my face.

Then the guy behind me pulled me up, stood me up on shaky legs, and the neon-faced guy worked over my legs.

I took it like a man. Like any man would. I cried my fucking eyes out.

All I could hear was their breathing and the swish of the hose and my own whimpering. This went on forever—for three minutes at least—and then I heard something else.

A voice.

Barney's.

"Nate," he said, "are you in there?"

"Barney!" I yelled.

I looked over and he was peeking in the door and night vision and what little light there was allowed him to finally make out what was going on and he moved across the room and pulled the guy off my back and I could hear him belt the guy back there while I found the strength to smack the guy with the rubber hose in the mush with a fist on the end of an arm that had gone numb from pain anyway. He swung the hose and I took the blow on my forearm, but moved the hose and his arm out of the way while I butted him in the face with my head.

The sound of him landing on his ass was music. There was still an orange neon glow on his face, but bright red mingled there as well. I must've broke his fucking nose. I went to kick him in the balls and he grabbed my foot and threw me into my desk. The desk slid, banged up against the wall by the windows and the phone and desk lamp tumbled off and landed noisily and, holding his bleeding nose, the guy headed unsurely for the door. His panicked friend had Barney in a clinch, using his size to squeeze Barney and keep from getting hit anymore.

The bleeding guy was to the doorway, when he turned and said, "Toss him!" to his friend, and his friend threw Barney over at me and we were in a pile together. Barney's guy slipped in my puke on the way out and took a fall on his face, then picked himself up and was gone. I would've laughed, if I hadn't had the sense of humor beat out of me.

Barney got up slowly and shook himself—he'd taken a hard knock against the desk—and started to go after them, but by that time the sound of their feet slapping down the corridor had disappeared. He went to the window and looked down.

"Damn!" he said. "Someone's out front with a car for 'em! There they go . . . damn!"

Shaking his head, he walked over and switched on the light by the door. I was still sprawled against the desk like a rag doll. Barney looked a little mussed up, still wearing his suit and bow tie, though the bow tie was sideways, now. I probably looked like shit.

He bent over me, touched the side of my face gently. "You look like shit."

I tried to smile. Couldn't.

"I was worried about you, Nate. Thought I'd better check in and see how you were doing. I guess I found out."

I said something. Not a word. A sound.

"Nate, I'm going to put the Murphy bed down and get you stretched out on it so you can take it easy."

I made a sound. Affirmative sound.

Then he was setting me gently down on top of the blankets on the Murphy bed. The overhead light was in my eyes and I winced at it, turned my head. He went over and quickly moved the desk back in place, picked up the phone, and the desk lamp, which he turned on.

"*Something* isn't broken, anyway," he said, with a little smile.

He went over and turned off the overhead light. Then into my washroom over by the door and dampened a washcloth and cooled my face with it. My face was the only place they hadn't hit me, but the cloth felt good just the same.

"There's a doc in residence at the Morrison," he said. "I'll call him and get him over here."

I tried to swallow; my mouth felt like cotton.

He was over at the phone when I managed to say, "No."

He looked back puzzled, then came over and sat on the edge of the bed. "No doc?"

"No broken bones," I said. "Just gonna be sore . . ."

"I think you should see a doc."

"Tomorrow."

He didn't like that, but he didn't press. "You want the cops?" he said.

"That *was* cops."

"Cops?"

"Rubber hose. Cops. East Chicago, I think."

"You want some Chicago cops?"

"They'd . . . just thank the East Chicago boys."

He smiled sadly. "What was it you said about your job? That it beat having people bash your head in?"

"Didn't lay a . . . glove on my head."

"No more talk. Get some rest."

He went over to the washroom and got a towel and cleaned up the puke. He was on the floor doing that, in fact, when Sally showed up.

"What the hell is going on here?" she demanded. She had a white dress on. She seemed angry. And afraid.

Barney told her.

I passed out about then. When I woke up she and Barney were helping me out of bed and then out of my office and down the hall and even, God help us, down the steps. She seemed almost as strong as Barney. An athlete, too. Dancer.

Then they were putting me in the back of a cab.

I heard Barney say to her, "Are you going to be all right?"

"Fine. I'll call you tomorrow."

Sally got in, told the cabbie, "The Drake," and we were moving.
"What. . . ?" I said.

"You're staying with me at my place, tonight," she said. "No one's
going to hurt you there."

I went to sleep in her arms; my last conscious thought was how
nice she smelled. Talcom powder . . .

15

A bell was ringing.

I opened my eyes slowly. The round chrome clock on Sally Rand's nightstand said it was four-oh-seven. Sun streamed in through sheer curtains. I was bathed in sunshine and pain.

The bell kept ringing.

I managed to sit up, but it took a while. The pain was general. Everything from the neck down ached. A long slow dull ache. I'd been sleeping since late morning. I'd been awake for a few hours early this morning, I remembered; Sally had fed me some breakfast and some aspirin. She'd given me some aspirin the night before as well, she said, but I didn't remember that. And I'd been awake awhile mid-morning, too: a doctor had come 'round—Barney's doing—and recommended more aspirin. And sleep. And I'd slept.

The bell kept ringing. In a brilliant intuitive flash—even battered I was still a detective—I realized it was a doorbell.

I swung my legs over to the side of the bed. Lowered them to the floor. The pain became specific. My eyes teared, but I didn't wipe them dry. I didn't want to make the effort because my arms hurt worse than my legs. I looked down at my legs and they were splotched with black-and-blue bruises of various sizes—from as small as a dime to as large as a saucer, though they were oblong dimes and saucers. I was in my shorts, I noticed, and my undershirt. My arms had odd-shaped bruises, too. No small ones, though. Large black-and-blue patches, strips of black and blue from the rubber hose.

The bell kept ringing.

I stood. My legs started to buckle but I forced myself not to fall; if I fell, I wouldn't be able to get up, and that would hurt even worse than standing. Moving across the soft carpet with the slow pathetic urgency of a very elderly man walking toward a bathroom that he has little chance of reaching in time, I found my way into the living room and, eventually, to the front door of the suite.

Facing the white door, the bell louder here (but I was used to it by

now—in fact, I couldn't remember a time when that bell wasn't ringing), I decided to see if I could speak.

"Who?" I said. It didn't hurt much to talk. I didn't have a head-
ache; the aspirin had done that much for me.

"Inspector Cowley, Mr. Heller. Sam Cowley. Could I speak to
you?"

There was a night-latch, which I left in place, as I cracked the door
open.

"Mr. Heller? Could I come in?" His round, somber, earnest face
under the gray hat was damp with sweat.

"Another hot day?" I asked.

A tiny smile creased his face. "Hottest yet."

"Another good reason for me to stay inside."

"Could I come in?"

"That putz Purvis with you?"

"No. Nobody's with me. Nobody knows I'm here."

"I know you're here."

"Nobody at the office."

I let him in.

The pain turned general again. A neck-to-toe ache. It felt like a
cross between the flu and having fallen off a building.

Cowley took off his hat; he had on the same gray suit as before, and
the same gray complexion. He wiped his face with a hanky, put it
away, looked me over and shook his head slowly.

"My God," he said. "You took a hell of a beating, didn't you?"

"They wouldn't serve me at a lunch counter down South, would
they?"

"Your friend Mr. Ross told me you took a beating, but I didn't
imagine . . ."

"That's how you found me? Through Barney?"

He nodded. "When I couldn't reach you at your office this morning, I called around. Ross wouldn't tell me where you were on the
phone. So I went and saw him in person and he finally consented."

"He's a good judge of character."

"Does that mean you don't mind seeing me?"

"No. I don't mind. I wanted to talk to you anyway, and it's better
for my health if you come to me. There are people who wouldn't
appreciate my going to see you."

"The people who did this to you?"

"Among others. Could we sit down? Or would you prefer to wait till I collapse?"

Looking genuinely concerned, he said, "Oh, hell, I'm sorry—you need some help?"

"No. Just let me take it at my own pace. Let's sit in the kitchen. It's through there. . . ."

In the small white modern kitchen, there was coffee on the stove. Bless Sally's heart. She'd be doing her matinee about now. Dancing with a bubble.

I sat at the table while Cowley, at my direction, poured us some coffee. He put a cup in front of me and sat and sipped his own.

With a disgusted look, he said, "I know the aftermath of a rubber-hose session when I see one."

"Well, you're a cop. You've probably administered a few."

He didn't take offense; he didn't even deny it. "Never to an inno-cent man."

I laughed, and it hurt. "I been called a lot of things, but innocent?"

Cowley's laugh was short and gruff, like he didn't do it much. "More or less innocent, then. Was it cops?"

"Yeah. East Chicago boys, if I'm not mistaken."

"Zarkovich and O'Neill?"

"Not personally. Zarkovich was behind it, I'm sure. Did he bring any men to town with him?"

The disgusted expression returned as he nodded. "A contingency of four, not counting him and his captain."

"I didn't get a very good look at the bastards who did this to me, but with that small a field to choose from, I might get lucky."

"What was this about, Heller?"

I sighed. It hurt. "They wanted me out of commission. They weren't trying to kill me or anything. Just hurt me bad enough to put me on the sidelines for a few days. Take me out of the action." I sipped the coffee. It was hot, black, bitter; I liked it. "I'd served my purpose."

"Which was?"

"To finger Dillinger for them. Specifically, to contact you guys. The feds."

Cowley did a slow burn, like Edgar Kennedy. "Would you mind telling me the rest of it, in your view? I think I know most of it. But I'd like to hear your thoughts."

"First, why don't you tell what's been going down on your end, where Mr. Dillinger's concerned?"

He thought about that, then said, with finality and formality, "A few hours ago, in the lobby of my hotel—the Great Northern on Dearborn, to be exact—Melvin Purvis and I met with Martin Zarkovich." It was like he was writing his field report. "We've set up a meeting with Anna Sage. For tonight."

"And she's going to give you Dillinger."

"Apparently, yes."

I thought about giving him Jimmy Lawrence's Park Grove address. I thought about Frank Nitti telling me to stay in bed. I thought about the rubber hose swishing in the air.

I said, "I'm going to tell you what I think is going on here. It's my best educated guess. And it's just between you and me. Agreed?"

He nodded.

I told him, briefly, about the traveling salesman who'd come to me. About tailing Polly Hamilton and Jimmy Lawrence. About Anna Sage. Everything that led up to my seeing Purvis.

"And contacting Purvis was my function in this," I said. "A private detective working on a domestic case who just happens to stumble onto Dillinger. Much better than an East Chicago cop like Zarkovich making first contact—the corruption on the East Chicago force makes the Chicago cops look like priests. You guys knew of Zarkovich's reputation, and wouldn't have liked the smell of this, if he'd initiated it. Yesterday you said straight out you'd rather deal with me than him, and that you liked the idea of having me—honest ol' me—as an independent, outside, corroborating source."

Cowley was nodding again, slowly. "No doubt about it. You gave the Dillinger story credibility."

"Agreed. Now, anybody else in my shoes would've gone to Captain Stege, rather than Purvis. Stege has a solid name in this town, whereas Purvis's been a joke since Little Bohemia. But my past differences with Stege—well known to just about everybody—made it easy to predict I wouldn't go to him with the information. And if I had, I'd probably got tossed out on my ass."

"You sound as if you think there's a . . . conspiracy, here. That somebody consciously selected you for this. To put all this in motion."

"Yes."

"Who?"

"I don't know who selected me for my role. Piquett, probably. But it's obvious who gave the go-ahead for the overall plan."

"*Who?*"

I told him about my meeting with Nitti.

"If the Outfit wants Dillinger dead," Cowley said, "why not just kill him, if they know where's he hiding?"

"Well, they've obviously known that from the start. Nothing happens on the North Side that Frank Nitti doesn't know about. And Dillinger's hidden out on the North Side any number of times, over the course of a year."

"Which would mean . . ."

"Which would mean he did so with Nitti's knowledge—and, most likely, blessing."

"You think Dillinger is connected to the Outfit, then."

I shrugged. It hurt. "Only loosely. Only in the ways I outlined to Nitti. Baby Face Nelson is a former Capone torpedo, remember. They aren't in the same organization, but they're members of the same club."

"Make your point."

"Nitti made it: 'It's better for some people to be dead.' Dillinger's at the end of his string. But he's got a reputation for not shooting it out with the cops, and after all his jailbreaks, security next time'll be tight. Johnny won't be doing any more crashing out."

"Then it's a simple case of 'he knows too much.'"

I nodded. It hurt. "That's why they wanted Purvis in on it. Because Purvis would agree to something Stege never would: to shoot Dillinger on sight. After all, your boss Hoover gave the go-ahead on that. Fuck capture. Kill him."

Cowley looked bleakly into his coffee.

"It's Syndicate all the way, Cowley. Anna Sage is a madam—and the Syndicate always has a piece of every brothel in any city of any size at all. Zarkovich has connections to the Capone crowd going back ten years, and is a bagman between the brothels and various crooks, some of 'em political, some of 'em Syndicate. Louis Piquett is in the Syndicate's pocket, enough so to betray his own client, it would seem. Do I have to spell it out for you? Frank Nitti has set you up to kill Dillinger for him."

Cowley's face seemed impassive, but there was anger in his eyes.

In his voice, too: "Why, damnit? *Why don't they just kill him them-selves?*"

"Why send a man when you can get a boy to do the job?"

"Don't be cute."

I gestured with one hand. It hurt. "That's Nitti's style. It's the Cermak kill all over again. The world thinks a 'demented bricklayer' tried to kill FDR in Miami last year, and 'accidentally' killed the mayor of Chicago instead. But you and I know that Cermak and Nitti were blood enemies, and little Joe Zangara was a one-man Sicilian suicide squad, sent to take His Honor out. Which he did."

Cowley said nothing; his face looked like it was made out of gray putty.

"Don't stir up the heat, that's Nitti's motto. He learned the lesson early on that Capone learned too late—he learned how nervous the public gets when you go around having massacres on Saint Valen-tine's Day. So let a would-be presidential assassin 'miss' and shoot 'Ten Percent' Tony Cermak instead. So let Melvin Purvis, G-man, courageously blow off John Dillinger's head and make the kind of headlines the public'll eat up."

"You've made your point."

"Not to mention how Dillinger's outlaw cronies might react to one of their own being murdered by the mob; who needs a bloody shoot-ing war breaking out with the likes of Baby Face Nelson and the Barker boys? That's a battle Nitti could obviously win, but at a high cost—lives of his men, bad publicity—why bother risking it?"

"Enough, Heller."

"Face it, Cowley. You're being used."

"Stop it."

"Well, actually, it's Purvis they're using. He's dependable. After all, Capone and Nitti used him to put Roger Touhy in Joliet, al-ready."

"Touhy was guilty."

"Of a lot of things, but not the kidnapping you guys prosecuted him for."

"I disagree."

"It's a free country, Cowley. You're like the rest of us—operating of your own free will. It's not like you're a puppet or anything."

"You're not funny."

"I know. But the way the Syndicate manipulates you feds is pretty

funny. Do you really think Jelly Nash was 'accidentally' shot at the
Kansas City Massacre? Sure—him and Mayor Cermak. Innocent vic-
tims."

"You're full of crap on a lot of this, Heller. You really are."

"Maybe. But not on Dillinger. I'm on the money, there."

Cowley's coffee cup was empty; he held it by the china handle and
tapped it nervously on the table. "Maybe you are. But it doesn't
make any difference."

"It doesn't?"

Cowley shook his head slowly. "Dillinger is public enemy number
one. He has to be stopped. And where the information comes from
that helps us stop him—whoever it is behind the scenes helping us
get him—doesn't matter. What matters, when you're going after
someone like Dillinger, is getting him. Nothing else."

"I see. You don't mind owing a debt of gratitude to Frank Nitti."

"I don't know that I do."

"You heard what I said . . ."

Cowley grimaced. "Yes, and it makes a lot of sense. It just might
be true. But it doesn't matter."

"Because Dillinger has caused your Division of Investigation so
much grief, given you so much embarrassment, that you have to get
him, whatever it costs."

Cowley, with sadness in his eyes, said, "That's exactly right."

That's when I decided not to give him Jimmy Lawrence's address.
That's when I decided not to play, anymore. To do what Nitti wanted
me to. To do what the East Chicago boys wanted me to. Stay home.
Stay in bed.

"Thanks for the coffee," Cowley said. He rose. "I'll find my way
out."

He went out into the living room but then, suddenly, he was back
in the doorway. With a small smile as inscrutable as a Chinaman's, he
said, "You just may be surprised how this turns out."

"Why's that, Cowley?"

"Purvis won't be alone. I'll be there, too, when we get Dillinger.
And I'm not trigger-happy. And I'm also not inclined to keep deals
with crooked cops who insist on me shooting the man they finger for
me."

I smiled. It hurt. "You think you can take Dillinger alive?"

"I'm going to try. If Frank Nitti wants him dead, then Mr. Dillinger's a man who may have some things I'd like to hear."

He tipped his hat and was gone.

I wondered if I should have given him Lawrence's address after all. Why bother? I'd been paid one hundred dollars by Frank Nitti to go to bed; and two East Chicago cops had given me some rubber-hose incentive to do just that. Cowley was on his way to meet with Anna Sage. She could tell him Lawrence's address. She could get her blood money, and her free pass with the immigration department. Let her do it.

I had other things to do.

Like hurt.

16

I opened my eyes, one at a time. Sun was filtering in through sheer curtains. I was under the covers in Sally Rand's bed in her air-cooled apartment; Sally was on top of the covers next to me, in white lounging pajamas, a pillow propped behind her as she smoked and read a magazine. *Vanity Fair.* This was, if memory served, Sunday; and she didn't do a matinee on Sunday; local bluenoses wouldn't let her get away with it.

I sat up in bed, slowly.

"Good morning," Sally said, with a sideways glance and a wry little smile.

"Is that what it is? Morning, I mean?"

"For the next few minutes."

"It's almost noon?"

"Almost noon. How do you feel?"

"Different than yesterday."

"Oh? How so?"

"Today my head hurts too."

Her smile was a smart-aleck curve. "You shouldn't have drunk all that rum last night."

"It was your idea."

"No, it wasn't. You sent me out for it."

"I did?"

"Yes—I merely suggested alcohol as an anesthetic. And you were too fussy to settle for something civilized, like gin. You made me go out and get rum."

"I'm a sick boy. I deserve to be pampered."

"And you deserve that hangover, too." She put the cigarette out in the tray on her nightstand, flopped the magazine on her lap. "How else do you feel?"

I rotated my shoulders; lifted my legs. "About the same. Maybe a little better."

She threw back the sheets.

"Well," she said, "you seem to be changing color. For what it's worth."

The black-and-blue splotches on my legs had turned purple, with patches of yellow spreading within them. My skin looked like a suit in poor taste.

"Why don't you go take a shower?" she said. "I'll get some brunch going. . . ."

I took her advice; cold first, then hot. I did feel better. I still ached, but it didn't hurt just to breathe. Except for my head. Maybe that was it—maybe the hangover was distraction enough to make me forget the other aches. I got out of the shower and toweled off—and it didn't hurt any worse than having somebody tear off one of my fingernails—and found a little can of tooth powder on the counter by the sink with a brand-new toothbrush. Brushing my teeth made me feel vaguely human again, and I wrapped a fresh towel around my middle and plodded back into the bedroom.

The new suit I'd bought with Nitti's money was laid out there for me; also a shirt I'd bought, a hat, and socks and underwear, not new, but clean. I hadn't brought any of this with me, so it looked like my friends had been taking care of me. I got into the underwear and pants and shirt and went to the kitchen, where she was making brunch. Scrambled eggs again, or actually an omelet with some diced vegetables and cheese. It reminded me a little of the side dish at Pete's Steaks and I felt my stomach go queasy. But then I was all right, and I wouldn't have said anything to her even if I wasn't.

I took a seat at the table and she glanced over with a maternal smile. "Barney brought some of your things over," she said.

"I don't have many friends," I said, "but I got the right friends."

"You count me among them?"

"You and Barney are at the head of the list, today. If Barney hadn't come in when those guys were dancing with me, I might be in traction right now." I laughed, and it only hurt a little. "They didn't exactly expect a world's champion fighter to come to my rescue. The guy he lit into must have a swollen puss about now."

"He really took care of 'em, huh?"

"He did all right for a lightweight. Anyway, it sent them running fast enough."

"You know who they were?"

"Not their names. But they were East Chicago cops."

"Cops?"

"Yeah—say, have you seen the papers today, been listening to the radio?"

She shrugged, stirring the eggs. "I have the Sunday *Trib* in the other room, if it's the funnies you're after."

"I don't follow the funnies. What about the radio?"

"I had the radio on, earlier. Why?"

"What's in the news?"

"The heat. Real muggy out there today. It's one hundred one point three degrees, last tally I heard. Seventeen died of heat prostration yesterday, and half a dozen more reported today already."

"Nice to be inside where it's cool."

"Why'd you ask? It's not the heat you're interested in."

"I thought there'd be something else in the headlines."

"What?"

"Dillinger captured."

She looked away from the pan she was cooking in to give me a wide-eyed, disturbed look.

"Nate—why don't you find another way to make a living?"

"I considered nude ballet with a bubble, but it's been taken."

She crinkled her mouth and chin in mock-anger. "You're dodging the issue. You're an intelligent, capable man. Why do you sit in that shabby little office, doing shabby little work? Not to mention dangerous."

I shrugged. Didn't hurt much. Half a fingernail being torn off. I said, "My work isn't usually dangerous. Don't be deceived into thinking exciting things like these happen to me every week. Hard to believe as it may be, I never been worked over with a rubber hose before."

She had turned away from me; she was easing the omelet out of the pan onto a plate. "A lot of people go through life without ever being 'worked over' with a rubber hose at all."

"Think what they missed."

She put the omelet down in front of me, with a side plate of toast. "You like some cottage fries with that?"

"No. This'll be fine."

"Coffee?"

"Orange juice'd be better."

"I already squeezed some." She got a small white pitcher out of a small white icebox and poured me a large clear glass, turning it orange. I sipped it and it tasted good; the feel of the pulp in my mouth was nice. The hangover seemed to be fading.

Just the same I said, "And a side order of aspirin?"

She smiled and nodded. "Comin' right up." The aspirin was on the kitchen counter; I took two with the last swallows of the orange juice.

Then she sat by me and said, her expression almost somber, "I wouldn't like to see anything happen to you."

"I wouldn't like to see anything happen to you, either."

"You live in your office, Nate. I saw it. You sleep in a Murphy bed."

"I know guys who sleep in parks."

"Don't try to shame me—I'm no snob, you know that. I just know a real waste when I see one."

"A real waste."

"Yes. A waste of a mind, potentially of a life."

"This omelet is very good. Sure you don't want to give up show biz and marry me?"

She laughed, sadly. "You're hopeless."

"That's what they tell me. Look, Sally—Helen—I only have one trade. It's all I'm trained for, it's all I know. And I really do have plans to live somewhere besides my office someday. I'll have a good-size agency with operatives working under me, and a nice big office with a pretty secretary to fool around with while my wife raises little Nates and Helens at home." That made her smile, not sadly. "It's a shabby little office, because I'm just starting out, and this is the god-damn *Depression*, okay?"

"Okay, Nate. I won't press. Maybe it's none of my business."

I touched her hand. "It's your business. You're my friend. That gives you the right to stick your nose in, at least till I ask you not to."

Impish smile. "Friend, huh? You sleep with all your friends?"

I managed to do an exaggerated shrug and not pass out. "Just you and Barney," I said.

"You're looking for another beating, Heller."

"I promise I'm not. This omelet *is* good. Are you sure there was nothing about Dillinger in the papers or on the radio?"

"Of course I'm sure. If John Dillinger had been captured, it'd be all over the place. Wouldn't it?"

I nodded. Not much pain. "It should've took place last night. They were meeting with Anna Sage—she would've given them the address or otherwise led the feds to him. . . ."

"Dillinger, you mean."

"Yes. I don't understand why it didn't happen."

"Maybe something went wrong."

"Maybe," I said, and stood. "Mind if I use your phone?"

Not liking it, she said, "Not at all."

In the living room, I sat in an overstuffed round-looking chair by the window and dialed the phone, a white candlestick type she kept on a low coffee table. The curtains were back and I glanced out as I waited for the call to go through. Down where Lake Shore Drive curved around the front of the Drake, people on Oak Street Beach and the surrounding park formed a blanket of flesh, staring out at the ironic blue lake, where sailboats and yachts taunted them. The boats were keeping away from the shoreline, though; just beyond the bobbing heads of more casual bathers a pathway was being maintained for those single-minded souls competing in the *Herald and Examiner* fifteen-mile marathon swim.

From the phone a young male voice said, "Division of Investigation, Hart speaking."

I could hear something of a hubbub in the background.

"I'd like to speak to Inspector Cowley."

"Inspector Cowley's tied up. Can I help you?"

"Tell Cowley Nathan Heller's on the line."

"Sir, we're busy here, could you—"

"Tell Cowley Nathan Heller's on the line."

There was a pause while he thought it over, then a sigh, and another pause while he fetched Cowley.

"Mr. Heller," Cowley said, "let's keep this short. Now what can I do for you?"

"Sounds to me like you've got a rather full house for a Sunday afternoon."

"Twenty or thirty people, and it's rather frantic; now what do you want?"

"What happened last night?"

"I didn't think you were planning to be involved in this matter any further, at this stage of the game."

"Why don't you tell me what happened last night, Cowley?"

"If it's the reward you're after, I may be able to arrange a partial—"

"Fuck the reward, and fuck you, Cowley!"

There was a long silence.

Then Cowley said, "We met with Anna Sage last night. She promised to deliver Dillinger to us today. That's all."

"That's all? Why didn't she give him to you last night?"

"She didn't expect to see him again till today. She and Polly Hamilton and Dillinger have a date of sorts to go to the movies together. At the Marbro. The features change today, you know."

"This is stupid—Anna Sage knows where Dillinger's been staying . . . it's a swanky place on Pine Grove."

"*You* know where he's been staying?"

"Yes." I gave him the address. I could hear his pencil scribbling it frantically down.

"Why didn't you tell me this before, Heller?"

"It's like I been telling you—I didn't want to finger the guy because I wasn't sure he really was Dillinger. I was afraid you guys might blast some poor civilian into Kingdom Come because he had two arms and legs and eyes, just like Johnny."

"Well, this is Dillinger all right."

"You won't get any argument from me on that score. Otherwise I don't know why Frank Nitti would want him dead."

Cowley didn't like being reminded of Nitti's role in this; I could tell from the silence over the wire.

Then he said, "We're waiting for a call from Mrs. Sage, any minute now, at which point we'll go to the Marbro. There are continuous showings all day, and since this plan is in motion already, and we haven't the manpower to spare for a spur-of-the-moment effort, we won't be following up on this address, not at this time."

"Use your own judgment."

"Our plan of action for the Marbro is well under way. We sent agents over yesterday evening and we've made maps covering exits and entrances, alleys and fire escapes, and surrounding streets. We're ready to put the plan into play when Mrs. Sage calls."

"Why don't you just go over to Pine Grove and see if Johnny's home? Or why not just move into Anna Sage's apartment till he shows up?"

Silence for a moment; embarrassed silence, I thought.

"Heller, uh . . . this is Chief Purvis' plan and, uh, Mr. Hoover has approved it. I'll make them both aware of the Pine Grove situation, and perhaps they'll act on it. But I believe we'll be following through with the Purvis plan. . . ."

"*What* plan?"

"We'll have agents on the fire exits and on either side of the front entrance. Chief Purvis will be on one side, Zarkovich on the other."

That sounded like a cross fire to me.

"Why them?" I said. "I thought you told me *you* were going to see to it that Dillinger was captured, not shot."

"Heller, last night when we met with Mrs. Sage, it was under what you might call cloak-and-dagger conditions. We picked her up on the North Side, drove a ways to a secluded spot along the lake, and I was with Captain O'Neill in one car, while Chief Purvis and Sergeant Zarkovich—and Mrs. Sage—were in the other."

"What does that have to do with my question?"

"Simply that only Chief Purvis and Sergeant Zarkovich know Mrs. Sage well enough to recognize her . . . I wasn't in the car with her."

"Oh, for Christ's sake. Have you considered the crowd you're going to be dealing with at that theater? With this heat wave, everybody and his duck is going to the movies to cool off! If you have to shoot it out, you're not going to get just Dillinger—you'll probably bag a grandmother and a ten-year-old or two."

"Heller, I'm going to be there, and I'll control the situation myself. You have my word on that."

"I'm not your goddamn conscience, Cowley. Do what you want."

"Mr. Heller. If you'll excuse me . . . I have to attend a briefing."

"What, is Little Mel going to explain how he plans to fuck up even worse than Little Bohemia?"

"I don't appreciate your language, Mr. Heller. It so happens I'm a good Mormon—"

"I don't care if you're a bad one. Melvin Purvis is a fuck-up in any religion."

Cowley cleared his throat. "Sergeant Zarkovich is about to give us a detailed description of Dillinger, now that his appearance has been altered by plastic surgery."

"Maybe Zarkovich can have his *own* plastic surgeons explain that: those 'doctors' from East Chicago who operated on me with a rubber hose."

Short pause. "I don't believe that to be true."

"Sure you do."

"I've got to go, Heller. Are you, uh, feeling any better?"

"A little, thanks."

"Get some rest, why don't you? Leave the police work to us."

"Speaking of police work, how the hell did you get Captain Stege to go along with this cockeyed plan?"

Silence again.

"Cowley?"

"We see no reason to involve the Chicago police."

"No reason to involve the Chicago police? In the capture of John Dillinger, in Chicago? Novel approach, Cowley. How'd you arrive at this?"

"Too many crooked cops," he said, and didn't sound too convinced himself. "Don't want somebody on the inside to tip Dillinger off."

"Oh, don't worry about that, Cowley."

"Why not?"

"If he heard about your plan, he wouldn't believe it."

Silence; then a grunt.

I grunted back and hung up.

I felt Sally's cool hand on my shoulder and I glanced back at her.

"It's going to happen tonight?" she said.

"I think so."

"And it's really Dillinger?"

"It's really Dillinger."

"Come to bed."

"I don't know if I can sleep anymore."

"Who said anything about sleep?"

Well, I was definitely feeling better; but the effort was enough to tire me out, and I fell asleep again. By the time I woke it was getting dark out.

"What time is it?"

Sally, rousing herself beside me, looked over at her clock. "A little after six."

"I'm sleeping my life away."

"You're just recuperating. Nothing to feel guilty about."

"Who's feeling guilty? Say, don't you have a show tonight?"

"Yeah—gotta leave in an hour or so."

I threw the covers off. "Let's go in the other room and listen to the radio till then."

We sat in the living room and listened to WGN, which was broadcast out of this very hotel; Wayne King the Waltz King bored us till the news came on. The hot spell, and the deaths by heat prostration, was the big story.

"When did you change your mind?" Sally said.

"About what?"

"This guy not being Dillinger. Didn't you think it *wasn't* Dillinger, at first?"

I shrugged. "I just wasn't sure. He looked a little like Dillinger. But not exactly like him."

"Then why do you now think this *is* Dillinger?"

"Because Frank Nitti wants him dead."

"I thought you said Dillinger and the Boys were friendly."

"Well, they used to be, before Dillinger's fun and games started bringing the heat down on 'em."

"Would they kill a friend?"

"Anytime, sugar."

"But why would his own *lawyer* betray him?"

"Piquett? Money. Fear of reprisal from his other, more powerful client . . . those Boys you mentioned."

"It seems to me the lawyer and the Boys might try to find a way to get rid of Dillinger without killing him. Like shipping him off to Mexico or something."

"No, honey, he's just too famous for that. As long as he's alive, they'd keep looking for . . ."

I thought a minute.

Sally said, "Something wrong?"

I said, "Don't you get tired of being smarter than me?" and got up. Went back into the bedroom and dressed.

She stood in the doorway and watched me. She was still in the lounging pajamas, and lounged against the door.

"What did I say?" she asked.

"You said this guy might not be Dillinger," I said.

"And?"

"And he might not be."

I kissed her on the cheek and left, moving faster than the pain.

17

A large homemade map of the Marbro Theater and its surrounding area, grease pencil on butcher paper, was pinned to the wall behind Cowley's desk, which was in the opposite corner from Purvis' currently empty one. A dozen or so agents in shirt sleeves and shoulder holsters were milling around the big open office, some of them sitting on the edges of desks, many of them smoking, the electric fans pushing the smoke around. Windows were open to let smoke out and let the cool night air in, only there wasn't any cool air, just night. The college-boy agents had been here most of the day, waiting for Anna Sage to call.

I pulled up a chair, tossed my hat on the desk. My suitcoat, which I'd been lugging over my shoulder, I draped across my lap. "No call yet?"

Cowley's gray face lifted from the cup of coffee he'd been staring into; his expression was one of frustration, but his eyes were just plain weary. He was in shirt sleeves and striped tie and shoulder holster.

"Worse than that," he said. "She did call."

"Hell! When?"

"A little after five."

"What's happened since then?"

He swallowed some coffee. "Nothing much yet. We had to send somebody over to the Biograph."

"The Biograph? Why?"

Heavy sigh. "When she called she said Dillinger was there, at her apartment, and that they'd be leaving in five minutes—for either the Marbro or the Biograph. She wasn't sure which."

"Shit. The Biograph. That's some wild card to get played this late in the game. What did you do?"

He told me. He'd quickly sent two men to the Biograph on the North Side to reconnoiter; they'd returned with notes on entrances and exits. A special agent had accompanied Zarkovich to the Marbro;

and Purvis and another agent were staking out the Biograph. Each pair was to have one of its men phone in every few minutes with a report.

That had been an hour and a half ago.

"That's a long five minutes," I said, "especially if they're going to the Biograph, walking from Anna's apartment—the theater's just around the corner from there, you know."

"I know," Cowley said glumly.

"Looks like it's not going down tonight."

"Looks like."

"Just as well."

"Why?"

"I've had some second thoughts about whether Jimmy Lawrence is really Dillinger."

Cowley sighed again and looked upward, as if he would've thrown his arms in the air, if he'd had the energy. "You're not going into *that* old song and dance again. What does it take to convince you, Heller?"

"Quite a bit, before I go pulling a trigger on a guy."

"We're not pulling a trigger on anybody—not unless he forces us to. And if it isn't Dillinger, we'll straighten it out after we've made the collar."

"I thought you were going to supervise this yourself and make sure nobody got trigger-happy. Being a trained detective, I can tell right away you're here sitting at a desk."

He patted the air with his free hand, as he sipped his coffee. "I *will* supervise the capture. Don't worry about that. When they spot Dillinger, I'll be called and go straight to whichever theater it is."

"They won't take him as they see him go in?"

"Probably not."

"*Probably* not?"

"With only two men at each site, we'd prefer to wait till our entire contingent has converged on the one correct theater."

"Then what? Take him after he's inside the dark theater?"

"Possibly. But only if there's an open seat behind him and we could grab him from behind."

I shook my head. "Not in this heat. There isn't an empty seat in any air-cooled movie house in town, tonight."

Cowley shrugged with his eyebrows. "Then we take him when he comes out."

"Anna and Polly are with him?"

"The Sage woman and Miss Hamilton, yes."

"Is Polly in on it?"

"We've been dealing with Mrs. Sage."

"You mean Purvis has. You haven't even met her."

He scratched the side of his head, where it went from brown to gray. Didn't look at me. "That's right. But it's not pertinent."

"I think you should be very careful, if this does fall into place tonight. Particularly if you're planning to let the East Chicago boys come along. *Will* they be a part of your 'contingent'? All six of 'em?"

Stone-faced, Cowley just looked at me; then, slowly, reluctantly, he nodded.

I said, "Zarkovich is at the Marbro, I know. The rest of them, where are they now?"

Sarcasm etched itself into the corners of his eyes. "In our conference room down the hall, with some of my men, having sandwiches. Why, is there somebody you'd like to talk to?"

"Your conference room," I said, my aches and pains suddenly coming back to me. "They ought to be comfortable, there. Isn't that where you guys do your own rubber-hose work, and hang guys out the window till they talk and such?"

Cowley didn't like that. But he just said, "That's not the way we do things. Maybe it's different in East Chicago."

"So I hear. Anyway, be careful tonight, if you decide to go to the movies. Because the Outfit may be providing you with a fall guy for the main feature."

"A fall guy."

"A patsy. A ringer."

He made a dry disgusted *tch-tch* sound. "And you think that would fool us. You think we could be fooled."

"Well, Purvis could. He has been before."

"Don't start again, Heller . . ."

I shrugged elaborately, and it only hurt a little. "Hey, it's your job on the line, not mine. Just don't forget that you're following through on something put in motion by Dillinger's *own lawyer.*"

He swatted at the air with one thick hand, like my thoughts were flies. "That doesn't mean anything. Piquett just double-crossed him, is all."

"Maybe. Or maybe you're falling in line with Piquett and doing Dillinger a favor."

"What kind of favor?"

"Getting him declared dead."

Cowley, not a man given to smirks, smirked. "And what does John Dillinger do, once he's 'dead'? Disappear in thin air?"

"With the accumulated loot from his various bank jobs, sure. He could buy a fucking island."

Cowley winced at "fucking." He just didn't like that kind of language; I knew he didn't—that's why I said it. Anything, to light a match under his Mormon butt.

"You're a good man, Cowley," I said. "Don't get taken in."

"Your confidence in me is an inspiration, Heller."

The phone on his desk jangled and he grabbed it, the weariness in his face replaced with urgency.

Then his face fell, while at the same time he sat erect, as he said crisply, "No, sir. No developments . . . yes sir, immediately, sir . . . yes, sir, I quite agree. We'd reached that conclusion ourselves . . . yes, sir."

He hung up.

"Hoover?" I said.

Cowley nodded. "He's been calling every few minutes. From his home in Washington, D.C. Pacing his library, I gather."

"This is a make-or-break moment for you guys."

"Yes, and Hoover knows it. He was just vetoing the notion of taking Dillinger within the theater, by the way. He wants no gunplay in a crowded auditorium."

"It occurs to me this sudden possible switch from the Marbro to the Biograph is a trifle suspicious."

"Oh, really," he said, with flat, almost disinterested skepticism. "Why is that."

"It allows you to plan for one theater all day, and then pulls the rug out from under you at the last minute . . . besides scattering your forces between the two locations."

Cowley counted on his fingers, as if explaining to a child. "First of all, we'll have time to converge on whichever theater it is, before we take him, and that includes the two men currently covering whichever theater proves to have been a false alarm. Second, your suspicions only hold true if they go to the second theater, the Biograph, because we've had ample opportunity to scout the Marbro."

"What's playing?"

That threw him. "What?"

"What pictures are playing?"

Cowley rolled his eyes. "I haven't the foggiest."

"You got a Sunday paper up here?"

He sighed heavily, called one of the college boys over. Told him to get me the movie listings from one of the Sunday papers. The college boy did, looking like a kid playing guns with that .38 slung heavily under his arm.

I spread the paper open on Cowley's desk and pointed to the Marbro listing. "See what's opening today? *Little Miss Marker*. Shirley Temple. Now look at the Biograph." I pointed there. "*Manhattan Melodrama*. A gangster picture."

Cowley tried to act like he didn't get my point, but he did.

I told him anyway. "Whether it's Dillinger or not, my guess is he's going to the Biograph. The other's a kid's picture, and they'd have to go to the West Side, something like nine miles, to see it. Of course if he's the kind of guy who'd rather sleep with Shirley Temple than Myrna Loy, my thinking here could be all wet."

The sexual allusion to Miss Temple didn't sit well with the good Mormon Cowley. He looked irritated. And he looked weary again. Particularly with me. "I don't think you have business here, Mr. Heller. Why don't you leave this to the government?"

"Good idea," I said. "I'm in the mood for some relaxation, anyway."

I stood up; put on my hat. Slung my suitcoat over my shoulder casually.

"Think I'll take in a show," I said, smiled, and let him do his Edgar Kennedy slow burn behind me.

The theater marquee was pulsing with little white bulbs in sockets, lined in rows and curlicues above and around the name on the front, *Essaness*, in cursive letters, and below, boldly in block letters:

BIOGRAPH

On either side of the marquee, more rows of bulbs in sockets called attention to the featured attraction:

"MANHATTAN
MELODRAMA"
with
CLARK GABLE and
WILLIAM POWELL

Below the marquee a dark blue banner with light blue letters hung; on the sides, under the featured attraction billing, it said ICED FRESH AIR; and in front it said

C O O L E D
BY REFRIGERATION

The promise of cool air, as much as Clark Gable (and William Powell and Myrna Loy), accounted for the steady stream of people going in the theater. It was now 8:00 P.M. and the next show would start at 8:30. Couples, families and the occasional single man or woman approached the Biograph box office, a central glass booth, bought their tickets and went in to wait in the cool lobby and buy some popcorn and Coca-Cola.

Otherwise there wasn't much activity on the street. The muggy night—overseen by an unreal, orange-tinted sky that seemed just as Hollywood as the Biograph marquee—was untouched by a lake

breeze. Occasional traffic found its way down Lincoln Avenue, but no cool air. Not unless it slipped out of the doors opening and closing as people went in and out of the Biograph.

There were a few people around. Folks living in second-story apartments above shops along the street had their windows open and many were leaning out, wondering where the hell Chicago's famous lake wind had gone to. The tavern next to the theater was open, Goetz's Country Club, and a soda fountain down the block, and a few other places. None of the shops, outside of those selling orange juice or ice cream or the like, was open. Some younger people, in their teens and twenties, were out wandering, window-shopping, boys in shirt sleeves, girls in light summery dresses. Sometimes they were paired off, but more often a trio or quartet of girls giggled along, often followed by a similar number of swaggering boys. Even the heat couldn't put a stop to mating rites. If anything it encouraged them.

Oh, and I was there. Having gone high-hat by cabbing it from the Drake to the Banker's Building, I hoofed it from the latter to my office, where I got my Chevy and headed for the North Side, specifically Lincoln Avenue. I had thought about going up to my office for my automatic; but that seemed to be asking for trouble. There would be too many people at the Biograph tonight with guns without my adding to the arsenal.

I'd parked on the same side of the street as the Biograph, just to the right of the mouth of an alley. The marquee was glowing just down the street; between me and it was a grocery store, on the alley corner, and past that the tavern next to the theater. As I got out of my car, it occurred to me that just a few blocks down was the garage where the Saint Valentine's Day Massacre had taken place. Small world.

I fell behind a family, father and mother and a boy of about ten and a girl of about eight—on a summer, non-school night, and in heat like this, parents taking their kids out this late wasn't unusual—and was just passing the Goetz Country Club tavern when I noticed an ostentatious-looking car, a gray-and-black Pierce Arrow, parked along the curb. I looked down through the open window.

Melvin Purvis was behind the wheel.

He was lighting a cigarette with a hand that was shaking; just a little, but shaking. He wore a jaunty straw hat and blue sports coat. He looked like he should have a debutante next to him. Instead he had in the rider's seat one of those college-boy agents from the

Banker's Building, who was now looking at me with wide, somehow frightened eyes.

I held my palms up and out, chest-high, and smiled a little.

Looking past his college-boy companion and out at me, Purvis, cigarette lit now, frowned like a housewife whose cake just fell, and motioned at me. I went around on his side and leaned against the car and smiled in at him.

"Hello, Melvin," I said.

"What the hell are you doing here, Heller?" He squeezed off each word, his Southern accent vanished. His speech pattern reminded me of Walter Winchell's, at least at that moment it did.

"Just thought I should check in with you, since I was in the neighborhood," I said cheerfully. "Just for the record, I'm not Dillinger."

His mouth fell open a little and his eyes glowed like the tip of his cigarette, which dangled from his mouth forgotten.

"I just thought I should point that out," I said. "I'm in no mood to get shot."

"You're interfering with a government job, Heller. Get lost."

"It's a free country, Melvin. I thought I might take in the show."

He glanced over at his companion and his Southern drawl suddenly replaced the clipped Winchell tone. "Agent Brown," he said, "why don't you accompany Mr. Heller from the premises."

I leaned in and stared right into Purvis' startled face and smiled; I could smell Sen-Sen on his breath. "Send him on out. I never broke a government agent's arm before."

"Are you threatening—"

"Promising. Promising a scene bigger than any that ever played that movie house. Want to risk blowing your stakeout over that?"

He bit the words off: "Go to the movie then. Go to hell."

I shrugged. "I wouldn't mind standing out here and watching the parade of humanity go by. A detective can always learn something by studying people, you know."

He looked over at Agent Brown. "Get in the back seat." Brown did that, and Purvis looked at me; his face looked more than ever like the chiseled kisser of a ventriloquist's dummy—when he spoke, I was almost surprised my lips didn't move. He said, "Get in on the rider's side, Heller. If you're going to be around, at least you can be under my watchful eye."

"I know I'll sleep better tonight for it," I said.

He jerked with this thumb. "Go around and get in."

I did.

"Nice car, Melvin," I said.

"Shut up and don't bother me." He was intently studying each passerby. His technique was as subtle as a guy in the front row at a State Street burlesque house.

"Say, uh . . . Melvin?"

Without looking at me, he snapped, "What?"

"You're going to burn yourself."

Then he looked at the cigarette in his fingers, burned down to the point where it would soon sizzle against his skin, and nervously jumped, flicked it out the window.

"Melvin," I said, suddenly feeling a little sorry for him. "Calm down. Take it easy."

He looked at me expecting sarcasm, didn't see any, sighed a little, nodded, and kept looking. He was wearing, in addition to that navy-blue sports jacket with white buttons, white slacks and white shoes. He had a white hanky in his sports jacket pocket; the initials MHP showed. He was as immaculately groomed as Frank Nitti, albeit in an Ivy League manner foreign to Al Capone's successor.

But he was sweating like a wop; that much they had in common.

He glanced at me, and, in a peacemaking gesture, said, "Would you like a cigarette?"

"No thanks."

It was 8:15 now. Agent Brown got out to use the phone in the tavern to call Cowley and report no sign yet of John Dillinger.

"Melvin?"

"Yes?"

"I stopped by the Banker's Building."

He nodded. "Cowley mentioned it when we called in, a while back."

"Did he say I might stop by?"

He nodded again. "Advised we keep an eye out for you."

"Did he tell you anything else?"

"No."

"While you're watching the folks pass by, mind if I tell you a little story?"

"I suppose not."

And I told him how Frank Nitti had, in collaboration with Louis Piquett and Anna Sage and Sgt. Martin Zarkovich, put a man they *called* Dillinger on the spot. Set him up for execution.

Purvis was remarkably calm as I told him this.

"Much of what you say seems reasonable," he said. "And, in truth, Sam Cowley did run some of this by me the other day. He admitted to me that his reaction to your . . . suppositions . . . was that we didn't care *where* we got help in capturing this felon. I personally don't believe the end justifies the means; but neither do I think one can work this side of the street without stepping in something occasionally."

I didn't know what to say to that; so I didn't.

Purvis continued, all the while watching people stroll up to the Biograph box office to buy tickets. "What I don't understand is your implication that the man we're stalking tonight may not actually be Dillinger."

"I'm not saying that's the case," I said. "Just a possibility. Frank Nitti's pulled scams like this before."

"It would be outrageous for Nitti and Piquett and company to *dream* they could get away with such a thing. I can't believe they'd try."

"You can protect yourself, in any event."

He looked away from the people on the street, momentarily, and his eyes met mine. "How?"

"Don't shoot Jimmy Lawrence tonight; and don't let anyone else do it, either."

His mouth made a tiny twitch and his eyes flickered and he looked back at the street, where people continued to approach the box office.

"Melvin," I said. "What's wrong? What aren't you telling me?"

Brown wasn't back yet from phoning in to Cowley. Purvis glanced toward the tavern to make sure he wasn't on his way back yet; and then, with an exaggerated air of confidentiality, he said, "I will admit something to you . . . Sergeant Zarkovich and Captain O'Neill—neither sterling examples of law enforcement, I'll grant you—took me to one side this afternoon." He paused; puffed his latest cigarette.

"And?"

He exhaled. "He—Zarkovich, that is—told me that he wanted to go up to Dillinger, after the movie was over, and . . . blow his brains out, from behind."

"I'm not surprised."

"I was. I told them I'd put up with no such thing—but they were of the opinion that, having brought Anna Sage to us, the least we could do for them is allow them to 'finish him off.' Naturally I refused."

"Naturally."

"So I want you to know I'm not taking what you've said lightly, Heller. There will be no gunplay, unless initiated by the suspect. But if Dillinger offers any resistance, each man will be for himself. It will be up to each individual to do whatever he thinks necessary to protect himself in taking this man."

"But that's only if Lawrence, or Dillinger or whoever he is, pulls a gun."

Purvis nodded curtly. "There will be no executions under my aegis."

Well, that sounded good and it sounded fancy, but I wasn't convinced. Oh, Purvis was not a bad man; he was a little pompous, and he was certainly in over his head. But he wasn't stupid, and he wasn't a coward—his being nervous like this didn't make him a coward, just human. Still, I remembered the dead civilians at Little Bohemia, which took place under his "aegis," too. And I had the feeling he— and even good Mormon Cowley—had not really vetoed the Zarkovich plan to blow Dillinger's brains out. Nor did I think Zarkovich's plan had been first proposed this afternoon; clearly it had been a part of the package since before a troubled Cowley first turned up at my office, Friday.

I was afraid that Melvin felt he could contain both Lawrence/Dillinger, *and* Zarkovich. That he could control the situation. He'd had to humor Zarkovich, because Zarkovich was his contact man with Anna Sage; he needed to keep the East Chicago cop happy. But, like Frank Buck, he intended to bring 'em back alive.

And I just didn't think Melvin was up to the job.

Brown came back.

He said, "Inspector Cowley says call every fifteen minutes instead of five, from now on."

"I take it," Purvis said, "there's no sign of our man at the Marbro?"

"None," Brown said.

"If he shows up anywhere," I said, "it'll be here. We're just around the corner from Anna's."

"I know," Purvis snapped. "Damn. Where *are* they? It's been almost four hours. . . ."

Brown said, "I think the inspector's on the verge of giving up the ghost."

I said, "I think they're playing with you. Getting you worn out and frazzled. I think it *will* happen. Tonight."

"So do I," Purvis whispered, wide-eyed, and he pointed.

A man in a straw hat, gold-rimmed glasses, a striped white shirt, gray tie and gray pants walked along flanked by two attractive women. One of the women, walking along on the outside, was Polly Hamilton. She was wearing a tan skirt, white blouse and white open-toe sandals; she was beaming, and looked pretty as a summer's day— or anyway, night.

The other woman arm in arm with Jimmy Lawrence, walking on the inside, also smiling but more restrainedly, was heavier set but still attractive, and wore a white hat and a two-piece burnt-orange bouclé suit. When the lights of the marquee hit her, Anna Sage's dress seemed almost to glow, and seemed more red than orange.

Blood red.

19

By five minutes after nine, the rest of the agents had arrived. They parked their cars along North Lincoln Avenue and its side streets and took their positions. Melvin Purvis stood in the recessed area at the right of the box office, near a display case of stills from *Manhattan Melodrama*. Three more agents were staggered along the street, starting at the left of the box office and continuing on down by Biograph Billiards—though it seemed unlikely the Anna Sage party would head that direction upon exiting the theater, her apartment being the opposite way. Milling about the front of the theater were five men; a couple of them I figured to be East Chicago cops. A couple more agents hovered around the tavern that was next to the theater, a couple more in front of the grocery that was next to the tavern, on the corner by the alley; and seven men were stationed in the alley itself—including three who climbed a fire escape there, to get a bead on their man from above should he flee down the alley. And that did make sense, as the alley was a shortcut to Anna Sage's.

Just on the other side of the alley, near where I'd parked my coupe, was a man I'd never met, but who was pointed out to me as Capt. Tim O'Neill of East Chicago. A dissipated-looking old copper with black-rimmed glasses and a pockmarked puss.

I viewed this from across the street, where Cowley held down a command post under a streetlamp; several other agents roamed Lincoln Avenue, on this side of the street, among them lady-killer Zarkovich, dressed tonight in a natty black suit and a straw hat, smoking an occasional cigarette in the black holder.

Cowley wasn't pleased to see me.

"Stay on this side of the street," he said, pointing a thick finger at me.

"That's fine with me," I said. I was the only one of these men not wearing his suitcoat. "I'm unarmed. I'm not interested in Wild West shows."

Cowley slammed a fist into his hand. "This isn't going to be any damn Wild West show! Understood?"

"Understood," I said. "I just hope this cavalry you got riding circles around the fort understands, too."

With quiet exasperation, Cowley made a motion with two hands like an umpire calling a guy "safe"—only that wasn't Cowley's meaning, in my case. He said, "Just stay out of the way. And stay out of this."

"He isn't armed, you know."

"What?"

"I saw him go in. He doesn't have a coat on. If he's got a gun, it's up his ass."

"I don't like that kind of talk. You're crude, Mr. Heller."

"It's a rough old world, ain't it." I walked away and leaned up against the side of a building, by a barber pole.

Zarkovich, between smokes, wandered up to me; he was just tall enough to be able to look down on. me, and I'm six foot. He said, "Warm night, Heller."

"Getting warmer all the time."

He had his hands in his pockets; his gold watch chain was showing. He smiled broadly but didn't show any teeth. Rocked gently on his heels. Said, "I thought you were out of this."

"Someday I'll get you and your friends alone and demonstrate the superiority of a piece of lead pipe over a similar length of rubber hose."

His smile drifted to one side of his face. "Whatever could you mean?"

I didn't say anything. I wasn't smiling.

He said, "I overheard Cowley giving you some advice. About staying back, and staying out. That's good advice. Why not take it?"

"I probably will. I figure you'd like nothing more than for me to catch a stray bullet."

"Oh, there's a few things in this life I'd like more than that." He nodded to himself, as if trying to list them mentally; it was a short list. "A few," he added, then wandered down and sat in a car parked opposite where his buddy O'Neill was standing by the alley. Occasionally he smoked a cigarette in the black holder.

Across the way, standing by the glass case of movie stills, Purvis was fiddling with a cigar, but not lighting it. Lighting it was supposed to be his signal for recognizing Dillinger.

He claimed he'd recognized Lawrence as Dillinger immediately, when Lawrence walked by arm in arm with Anna and Polly. He'd said to me, and Agent Brown in the back seat, "That's him. One glimpse tells me everything I need to know."

"It does?" I asked him.

"It does," he said. "I've studied every available picture of John Dillinger. You couldn't miss it, if you'd studied that face as much as I have. Just looking at the back of his head I can tell it's him. . . ."

At this point Dillinger had been buying three tickets from the girl in the box-office window, while Anna and Polly chatted, waiting.

"How many pictures of the back of Dillinger's head *are* there?" I asked Purvis, but he didn't bother answering.

Shortly after Dillinger held the door open for his ladies and went in, so had Purvis. And so had I. He sent Brown to telephone Cowley, and asked me—actually asked *me*—to help him check out the theater. We'd bought tickets from the girl in the glass booth (no one at the theater had been alerted to the stakeout) and went on into the lobby, where the cool air and the smell of popcorn greeted us. There were a few people at the concession stand—Lawrence/Dillinger not among them, nor either of his ladies. We went into the auditorium, one of us on either aisle, and I began to wish I had brought my gun. The air in here was cooler than the lobby, almost cold. It was very dark. The heads of theater patrons were craned up looking at the silver screen where Mickey Mouse danced with some farm animals and spoke in a squeaky voice that reminded me a little of Purvis.

Virtually every seat in the house was taken.

We met in the lobby.

"Did you spot 'em?" he asked me.

"No. You?"

He shook his head. "I'd hoped to find them, *and* three empty seats behind 'em."

"You know what people in hell want."

He nodded. "I wouldn't mind some, either," he said, and he went to a drinking fountain and gulped several mouthfuls. When he was done I did the same. Then we headed back out to the hot street, and waited for the reinforcements to arrive.

That was the last active role I'd been asked to play here thus far, and would likely remain so.

Now the street seemed filled with men in hats and suitcoats, when before the majority of pedestrians and motorists were in shirt sleeves and, if any hat, caps. The agents stood out like a battalion of sore thumbs. I watched the girl in the box-office window, a pretty little blonde barely out of her teens. She looked scared.

I ambled up to Cowley.

Without looking at me, he said, "What do you want?"

I said, "The girl in the box office is getting spooked. Why don't you let her in on it."

"Mind your own business, Heller."

"She thinks you're a bunch of hoods, probably. And where the East Chicago boys are concerned, she's not far wrong. Anyway, she probably thinks she's about to be robbed. Several theaters have been robbed, these past few months, you know."

"I wouldn't know. That isn't a federal offense."

"Nice to know you guys stay so on top of things. Best of luck in all your future endeavors, Cowley." I faded back to my spot by the barber pole.

In a few minutes I saw the girl in her glass booth furtively talking to a man in a white shirt and a bow tie and a mustache: the manager, no doubt. He was nodding, and then rushed off. None of the feds picked up on it.

Within five minutes a blue sedan with CHICAGO POLICE DEPARTMENT in white letters on the sides pulled up; there were two cops inside. Neither had their blue coats on—because of the scorching heat, the cops had been allowed to work out of uniform this week, just wearing their caps and blue pants with blue blouses with badges pinned to their chests. These boys, obviously from the nearby Sheffield Avenue Station, looked tough and suspicious, and one of them hopped out, clutching a shotgun.

Zarkovich ran up to him before the cop had reached the sidewalk.

"This is a federal stakeout, mac," Zarkovich said. "On your way."

The Chicago cop didn't take kindly to that, but a more diplomatic Cowley interceded, showed the cop his ID, and affirmed that this was a federal stakeout.

"We'd appreciate it if you'd remove yourself from the vicinity," Cowley said, "before you blow our cover."

The cop made a face. "Yeah, right. They'll never spot you guys in those suits. Oh, brother!"

And he got in the squad car and they rolled away.

I went up to Cowley and said, "You might've told them it was Dillinger."

Cowley said, "Chief Purvis is insistent on no Chicago cops. Anna Sage is deathly afraid some insider with the police will tip Dillinger off."

"At this stage, how, exactly? Mental telepathy?"

Cowley glared at me, and I went over and leaned against the building by the barber pole. I was tempted to go across and get in my coupe and drive away. I was helpless to do anything about this situation; I could only hope my presence would be a reminder, a nagging one, to both Cowley and Purvis, of their responsibilities. That both of them would rein in on the East Chicago cops more, if I were around; that they'd both work a little harder at keeping their prisoner alive. I had told Cowley I wasn't his "conscience." Now I found myself somehow hoping I was.

The night wore on; I wasn't sweating much, but I didn't have a coat on like the rest of these jokers. Most of them looked drenched. Across the street sweat beads hung on Purvis' face like the tears of a bawling baby. He wiped his face now and then, with that monogrammed hanky, but the sweat popped right back. Every now and then he'd take his revolver out and see if it was loaded; every time, it was.

Then a little after ten-thirty, by my watch, people started to come out of the theater. They didn't stream out: Nobody was anxious to trade the cool interior of the Biograph for the sweltering Chicago night.

And through the milling crowd I could see Jimmy Lawrence emerge, with a woman on either arm. Polly and Anna. And he was hemmed in by the crowd, men, women and children. He seemed to be rather near Purvis and the display of movie stills. He seemed to glance at Purvis, and then glance away. I wondered if Melvin's shorts were dry, after that.

Then the crowd, getting reluctantly used to the heat again, began to disperse, some of them getting into autos parked along Lincoln Avenue, others crossing the street toward me (and Cowley and crew), some turning left, others turning right, down the sidewalk.

These people allowed the feds in their suitcoats to blend in better, simply because there was something to blend in with. But since Lawrence/Dillinger was back in the recessed area between the box office and the display case of movie stills, few of the agents had spotted him, and those of us across the street, with a relatively good vantage point, couldn't see all the agents, now. I did notice several who were giving some good-looking girls in the crowd the eye. They'd apparently had Biology, these college-boy feds.

Gradually the field cleared a bit and Jimmy Lawrence, arm in arm with his ladies, one of whom wore a dress that glowed red in the bath of marquee lighting, stepped out onto the sidewalk.

And a nervous Melvin Purvis tried three times to light his cigar with a match, by way of signal, and on the fourth succeeded.

From my vantage point I saw it all go down.

The agents closed in on him, like flies swarming on a single drop of honey. He didn't see them. He walked slowly, as if strolling on a Sunday afternoon (and this was Sunday, although later than that, particularly for him), past the tavern, past the grocery store, and just at the alley Zarkovich, who'd jumped from his parked car and run across the street, where traffic was at the moment nil, shoved Lawrence or Dillinger or whoever the hell he was face-first to the pavement, flinging him out of the grasp of the two women, who fell away immediately, or at least Anna did, pulling Polly back by the arm as Zarkovich fired and someone else, O'Neill I think, fired from the other side of the prone man, fired down into the man while he, whoever he was, lay half in the alley, headfirst in the alley, rest of him on the sidewalk, and took the shots in the back and in the back of the neck, his body jerking, flopping, like a fish on the beach.

I ran across the street; several cars screeched to a stop, not to avoid hitting me, but because they'd heard gunfire and screams.

The screams hadn't come from Lawrence, but from two women; in a bizarre piece of slapstick, both of them were holding their dresses up over their legs, where blood streamed from ricochet wounds. One of them collapsed near my coupe, by the time I crossed the street. A man bent to help her.

The body of the man who'd been shot was surrounded, too, by the agents and East Chicago cops; when they broke their circle, they had turned the body over and it held a .38 automatic in its slack dead hand. I pushed my way through the already building crowd ("Dillinger has been killed! They got John Dillinger!"). Got a closer look.

His face was gouged by two slashing bullet wounds; his eyes were open and empty. His shattered eyeglasses hung cockeyed across the bridge of his nose; his straw hat was still on his head, the brim bent back with a bullet hole angled through it. I leaned over him and touched the face, looked into the face.

A hand on my shoulder pulled me back. It belonged to Zarkovich.

"Get away from there, Heller!"

Another hand from behind me yanked me into the alley. People were coming down the alley toward the body; their feet clomped, echoing on the cobblestones.

But two others were running down that alley, away from the scene, hand in hand, like schoolgirls.

Anna and Polly.

I walked back toward the gathering crowd. *This was Dillinger*, they said; *they got Dillinger*. Women were kneeling, dipping their hankies and even the hems of their skirts into the pool of the man's blood. Souvenir hunters.

Then Purvis was in their midst; he was angry.

"Get away!" he said. "Get away!"

They scrambled away, like rats in dresses, clutching their bloody booty. Purvis had frightened them, because he had a gun in his hand, and his coat was open, the buttons torn away when he reached for the revolver, going after Dillinger. But he hadn't fired the gun.

Zarkovich and O'Neill had done all the shooting.

Cowley appeared from somewhere and was directing his men to cordon the body off.

"Keep these damn ghouls away!" Cowley ordered.

I approached the body again and looked down at it. Purvis and Cowley were there with me. They glanced at each other, then looked at me. They actually seemed embarrassed.

"I wanted to take him alive," Purvis said, "but he pulled a gun."

Cowley nodded, pointed down to the gun in the corpse's slack hand. "You can see it right there."

Purvis knelt over the body; with both him and the dead man wearing straw hats, Purvis seemed to be looking down at a ghastly mirror image. "It's Dillinger, all right. No doubt about it. But it's amazing the extent of plastic surgery he underwent. All the distinguishing marks on his features have been worked over. It was a good job the surgeon did."

"Check his pockets," Cowley said.

Purvis did. He found $7.80 and a gold watch.

Purvis held out the $7.80 in the palm of one hand, and said, "So much for the fruit of crime."

Cowley took the watch; popped it open. There was a picture inside. He showed it to Purvis.

Purvis said, "That's Dillinger's old sweetie, Evelyn Frechette. No doubt about it."

Cowley nodded.

I took a look at it. The picture was of Polly Hamilton. I didn't say anything.

A couple of Chicago uniform cops, in blue shirts with badges pinned on, pushed through the crowd.

"So this is John Dillinger," one of them said, looking down at the corpse.

Purvis said, "Yes it is. Uh . . . . what do we do now?"

The two cops looked at each other. Then they looked at Purvis.

"Who's in charge here?" one of the cops asked.

"I am," Purvis and Cowley said.

The Chicago cops shook their heads and one of them said, "I'll call a meat wagon."

In minutes it was there, and the dead man was put on a stretcher and slung in back of the wagon; Purvis rode with him, with several other feds. Cowley stayed behind. The crowd remained thick. I pushed through toward my parked Chevy.

In the midst of the crowd, by the tavern, I bumped up against a big guy in a fedora. The tavern's neon turned his face orange. He had a bandage across his nose. I gave him the hardest kidney punch I could muster.

"Ooooofff," he said, and hit the pavement. People were walking on him.

I kicked him in the ribs, while he was down there, and another East Chicago cop, a guy with a puffy face—courtesy Barney Ross— came pushing through the crowd, having seen what I did, and he swung at me and hit some woman in the side of the head. A barrel-chested man with her, her husband I guess, said, "Hey!" And smacked the East Chicago cop in the face a couple of times.

The crowd was such that it didn't go further than that—no fight ensued or anything; and I was to my coupe, with a small sense of satisfaction in having somewhat settled a score.

But as I pulled away from the Biograph theater, I felt sick to my stomach, and vaguely ashamed. I'd seen this happening, and I hadn't been able to stop it. Maybe I wasn't smart enough or brave enough or tough enough. I must've been lacking something.

Because a man had died tonight. A man I had, in a roundabout way at least, fingered.

I'd got my first good close-up look at Jimmy Lawrence tonight, when I'd held his dead head in my hands.

And he'd looked less like John Dillinger close up than at a distance.

But he had looked real dead.

POLLY—THE PHOTO IN THE WATCH

20

By a quarter till midnight, I was sitting at my desk in my office in the dark. Neon pulsed through the half-open windows in tempo with the rubber-hose aches and pains that had started in again, now that Sally's last round of aspirins had worn off. I'd considered stopping in at Barney's Cocktail Lounge for another sort of painkiller, but was in the sort of black mood that drinking would only turn blacker.

This was the first I'd been back to the office since I took that beating. Barney had cleaned the place up; everything was in order. What did I have to complain about? I had the world's lightweight champ for a personal valet.

My mouth was trying to remember how to smile when the phone rang.

"Yeah?" I said.

"Nate?"

It was Sally.

"Hi, Helen."

"I *thought* maybe you might've gone back to your office . . ."

"Where are you calling from? Didn't you have a show tonight?"

"Yes—I'm calling from backstage. I tried to get you at my suite, thinking you'd be back there by now . . . I *did* give you a key, didn't I?"

"You did. I just didn't think I'd be very good company the rest of the night."

"I understand."

"You do, Helen?"

"Yes." A pause. "People are saying John Dillinger was shot."

"Christ, word travels fast in this town."

"It's true, then."

"Somebody was shot, yeah."

"Were you there?"

"I was there. I saw it."

She didn't say anything right back, and I could hear the Café de la

Paix orchestra playing "Whoopee" in the background, Paul Whiteman style.

Then: "I'm going to take a taxi home in about fifteen minutes, Nate. Why don't you head over to the Drake and meet me?"

"I don't think I better."

"We could talk . . ."

"I don't think I have any talk left."

"I'd like to help."

"If anybody could, it's you. Tomorrow."

Another pause; another bride, another groom . . .

"Tomorrow," she said.

And hung up. Me too.

I sat in the dark a few minutes; the street sounds were subdued tonight, I was thinking—then the El rushed by. After that I got up to pull the Murphy bed down out of its box. I was reaching up to do that when there was a sharp insistent knock on the door—a three-beat tattoo. Then again.

There was just enough light out there in the hall for me to make out through the frosted glass the shape of the person knocking. It was a small person. Not two cops with a rubber hose.

I unlocked the door and peeked out.

"I'll be damned," I said.

She smiled nervously and long lashes fluttered over eyes as blue as Sally Rand's. But this girl in a white blouse and tan skirt and open-toe sandals was not Sally Rand.

"Hello, Nate," Polly Hamilton said.

"Hello."

"Can I come in?"

"Okay, but I'm not going to the movies with you, so don't bother asking."

Her lower lip quivered and she glanced down. "You must think I got that coming."

"Don't you?" I opened the door wide for her, and she slipped by me, her reddish-brown hair swinging in arcs alongside her face; she smelled like jasmine. I glanced out in the hall to see if anybody else was around. Nobody seemed to be.

I shut and locked the door, reached for the light switch and she touched my hand; her touch was as warm as the air coming in my open windows.

"No," she said, breathily. "Leave them off." For a minute I thought she was vamping me, but then I recognized the breathiness as fear. Fear and passion have similar symptoms, after all.

She had a little white purse with her, which she clasped fig-leaf style before her as she looked around the room. The light from the street let her do that.

"I didn't notice you had that purse at the Biograph," I said.

She looked at me sharply. "Were you there?"

"Are we going to kid each other, Polly?"

She got wide-eyed and sucked in air.

"No!" she said, as if insulted by the very idea she might be capable of less than truth.

"Yes, Polly, I was there. Across the street with my hands in my pockets, playing with myself. Just like the fed I was with."

She gave me a reproving look. "Do you have to be so crude?"

"Funny, that's what that fed's always asking me. Personally, I think getting shoved on your face and shot in the back a couple times is rather on the crude side."

She covered her mouth and looked down at the floor with the wide eyes; the hand was shaking. She was shaking. She seemed about to cry. But I didn't see any tears.

"Why don't you sit down, Polly?" I pointed to the chair opposite my desk.

She nodded and sat, clutching the little purse, her legs tight together like a virgin on her first real date. And trembling the same way.

I got behind the desk. Sat. Gestured to the lamp, and she nodded she didn't mind and I turned it on. It didn't make the room bright— just made a pool of light on the desk, not big enough for either of us to bathe in.

She glanced around the room some more. "Is that a Murphy bed?"

"I guess if anybody'd recognize one, it'd be you."

She gave me a sharp look and didn't seem to be trembling now. "What's that supposed to mean?"

"It was a crude remark. Forget it."

"All right. Aren't you . . . wondering why I'm here?"

I shrugged. "I know I should be, but I haven't been feeling good. Probably tomorrow I'll get around to wondering, if you haven't told me by then."

With what tried to be sarcasm but came off as pique, she said, "I'm sorry you don't feel so good."

"Some of your ex-husband's pals worked me over a couple nights ago."

"My ex-husband's pals?"

"Sure. He worked for the East Chicago police, didn't he?"

"I, uh . . . yes. So?"

"So you divorced him a couple months ago. Was it amicable?"

She looked at me blankly. I liked her mouth; couldn't help myself.

"Was it friendly? Your splitting up, I mean."

She shrugged. "I suppose."

"When did you meet him—while you were working at the Kostur Hotel?"

She nodded, then caught herself. "I thought you didn't feel so good."

"Having a pretty girl around seems to pep me up. In fact, I feel so much better, I *am* starting to wonder what you're doing here."

She looked at the pool of light on my desk, glumly. "So am I."

Suddenly I was sick of this game.

"If you don't know why you're here," I said, "you better go. I don't relish being seen with you."

That amazed her. "Why?"

"As it is now, I'm on the fringes of this mess. If I'm lucky I won't get noticed much, when the cops and newshounds start sniffing. But with you in my lap, I'm smack in the middle."

She leaned an elbow on the desk, cupped her hand and rested her forehead in it; she looked like a child who just heard about death for the first time.

She said, "I'll go, then."

But she made no move to. Just sat there looking like a tragic waif. Or trying to. She had too much sex to get by with it, exactly.

"Look, Polly, I was told by Frank Nitti not to get in this any deeper. And yet there I was tonight, out in front of the Biograph. It's time I dropped out of the picture. And I don't mean *Manhattan Melodrama.*"

Still with her head in her cupped hand, she shut her eyes and squeezed out a big tear that angled down her cheek and across her tilted face, her mouth, her chin, in a shiny line, before plopping on my desk like a solitary raindrop.

"I swear I didn't know," she said, wiping off her face with the back of her other hand. Her nails were as red as Anna Sage's dress under the marquee lights.

"Didn't know what?"

"That they'd kill him."

"What did you think they'd do?"

"I didn't think anything. I didn't even know he was Dillinger."

"Was he?"

She raised her head from her hand and looked at me, wondering what conversation I was in. "Was he what?"

"Was he Dillinger?"

Her eyes got even wider. Silent-movie wide. "Well, that's what they're saying . . ."

"Who? Who told you it was Dillinger, and when?"

"Well . . . I heard the federal men say it, just before Anna and me headed down the alley. I went back to the apartment with her for a while, and she admitted she knew he was Dillinger. She knew from the start."

"Did she admit she'd put him on the spot for the feds tonight?"

Polly shook her head. "She just said she knew he was Dillinger. And then she told me to go home and . . . lay low for a few days."

"So you came to see me."

She shook her head again. "I took the El to the restaurant, first."

"The S and S?"

"Yes. They were just closing. One of the girls there, Maxine, went across the street and had a beer with me. She didn't want to, though . . . not proper, two girls alone in a tavern, she said. But she could see I was upset. She could see I needed the company."

"What did you tell her?"

"Nothing much. I told her Dillinger was dead. She wanted to know how I knew, and I told her to look in the papers tomorrow. And I told her I didn't feel so good."

"There's a lot of that going around."

"Why do you talk that way?"

"Because it amuses me to. It helps me not think about how much I hurt from your ex-husband's pals feeding me the goldfish." "Goldfish" was Chicago for rubber hose.

"Why do you keep saying that? You act like I know something about it, and I don't."

"What *do* you know?"

She leaned back in the chair; back away from the light and her face was less distinct. But I could hear her voice just fine: "Anna just told me to . . . date this guy. Keep him occupied. Keep him . . ."

"Happy?"

She sighed. "Happy. You mind if I smoke?"

"No. Use the ashtray, though."

"Where is it?"

I pushed it towards her. It was a thick-rimmed little circle of glass that said Morrison Hotel in it.

She lit the cigarette and the orange tip was an eye in the darkness. She blew some smoke out and then started talking.

"He was a good-hearted guy. I got a thrill out of going around in cabs all the time. Twice he gave me money so Maxine and me could go to the fair. Once he gave me forty dollars and said I should go out and buy something with it. Another time he gave me fifty bucks to get my teeth fixed. I bought clothes with it, though. But he wasn't mad when he found out."

"He treated you right."

She nodded through trails of smoke. "We had a lot of fun."

"Who did you think this guy was?"

"Jimmy Lawrence. He said he was with the Board of Trade."

"Did you buy that?"

"Well, he had plastic surgery scars, behind his ears. So I figured he was a small-time con Anna was keeping on ice for the Boys."

"The Outfit, you mean."

"I guess. I don't know much about that sort of thing."

"But Anna does."

"Sure. She's a madam, right?"

"You're asking me?"

The blue eyes flared. "Does needling me make you feel like a big shot, Heller? Is that why you do it?"

"Sorry. Please continue."

She drew on the cigarette again. "There's not much more to say. He was a good dresser, clean and neat. He had a nice smile."

"So keeping him happy for Anna wasn't much of a chore."

"That's the hell of it. I got to like him, I really did. I was crazy about him, Heller. He had this terrific personality—he was kind and good to me. But he couldn't have *really* been kind and good, and been John Dillinger, too, could he?"

"I'd say not."

"I didn't count on that. Liking him. You know, there was one song he was crazy about, from a Joan Crawford picture we saw at the Marbro." She started to sing, in a pleasant little Betty Boop soprano: "'All

I do is dream of you the whole night through . . .'" Her lip was quivering. Another tear rolled down her cheek.

"Did he have a good voice?"

"He could carry a tune. You know, he was crazy about the movies. Couldn't get enough."

"Till tonight. You really did like him, didn't you?"

"I did."

"You didn't know they were going to hit him tonight?"

"No."

"But you knew he was going to get hit sooner or later."

"No! And I didn't know he was Dillinger!"

"Why'd you come see me, Polly?"

"I knew you were following me and Jimmy—or Dillinger—around, before. Anna told me you would be."

"Did she? Did she say why?"

"No. She just said if I noticed you following me, not to mention it to Jimmy."

"Did she explain any of this?"

She shook her head. "No she didn't."

"Yours was not to reason why."

"Mine was to do what I was paid to."

"At least you're honest about that much."

"Nate, I've been telling you the truth. You got to believe me."

"Then tell me why you're here."

She cleared her throat. "I wanted you to understand that I'm innocent in this."

I almost fell out of my chair. "Innocent?"

"I didn't know they'd kill him. I'm no—no finger man."

"You're no man, I'll grant you that. Why tell me?"

"I just wanted you to know. That night we were together, it was special, Nate."

"Bullshit! I was just another john. A drunk one, at that."

She leaned forward, stabbed out the cigarette, reached her soft warm hands out and touched the hand I was resting on the desk. She had a pretty smile. Part of me wanted to pitch a tent in those blue eyes, and stay there.

"You were nice to me," she said. "I liked you."

"Like you liked Jimmy Lawrence."

She drew back, pulled her hands away from mine, as if burned.

"You're a nasty man," she said.

"Maybe," I said. "I'm also a live one, and hanging around with you probably wouldn't do much toward my staying that way."

"You bastard—"

"My parents were married, lady. I don't know which side of the sheets you come from, and I don't care. I do know why you came here, more or less . . . you're trying to make yourself look 'innocent' in my eyes, so that when I tell my story to the cops and/or the papers you won't look like Judas in a dress."

"You son of a bitch!"

I stood. "Wrong again. My mother was kind and good. Like Jimmy Lawrence. Now, get the hell out of here."

She stood. "You fucker!"

"You finally got one right. But not tonight, and not with you. Get out."

Steaming, she turned to go and I followed her, to let her out. Just as we were approaching the door, a shape loomed behind the frosted glass and a loud knock accompanied it. I pushed her into the bathroom, at our immediate right, and raised a finger to my lips in a "shush" gesture, and she looked at me startled and scared, and I shut her in there.

Then I went to my desk, got my gun out and walked carefully to the door. Stood sideways against a wood portion of the wood-and-glass wall next to it. I didn't know if my shape would show through the frosted glass, but I couldn't see taking the chance.

Then somebody said, harshly, "Open up, Heller, or we'll bust it down."

I thought I recognized the male, gravelly, mid-pitched voice; I hoped I was wrong.

"Then *don't* open it! Give me an excuse to kick it in!"

I wasn't wrong.

I went back to the desk and put the gun away and glanced at the bathroom door and thought, *Oh, boy*, as I unlocked and opened my office door and a short stocky man with dark-rimmed glasses and white hair was standing there, fanning himself with his hat. That was the only sign the heat was getting to him, however: he wore a suit and tie and looked comfortable, not a bead of sweat on him. A heavy-set, taller man, also in a suit, sweating like sin, stood behind him in the hall against the wall, like a man in a line-up.

The stocky little man pushed by me and shut the door behind him, leaving his backup out in the hall.

"Make yourself at home, Captain Stege," I said.

21

Stege went over and sat in the chair, which was probably still warm from Polly Hamilton. I didn't turn on the overhead light; the desk lamp would be plenty. Stege found me distasteful enough to prefer the dark and, what the hell, looking at him did nothing for me, either.

He sniffed the air. Glanced at the smoldering lipstick-ringed cigarette butt in the ashtray. "Been entertaining a woman up here, Heller? I smell perfume amidst the tobacco fumes—and of course you don't smoke."

"I also don't wear lipstick, but I'm flattered you know so much about me, Captain."

He grunted. "Don't be. It's my business to know the enemy."

"I'm not the enemy, Captain."

He looked around the office. "Is that—"

"A Murphy bed? Yes."

He nodded. "You work *and* live here. Business must not be good."

"My business isn't any of yours."

"Don't get smart with me."

"You're here by my good leave, Captain. I didn't see a warrant."

He held out two small but powerful-looking hands, palms up; his fingers looked like thick sausages. "Am I searching the place?"

"Not yet."

"And I won't. This is a . . . friendly visit." He almost choked on the word "friendly."

"Your opinion of me is all wet, Captain. You think I'm a dirty cop, and—"

He pointed one of the thick sausages at me, blinked at me like a bird behind his round dark-rimmed glasses lenses. "I think you're an *ex*-dirty cop. Let's not get careless with our facts."

I sighed. I should've felt nervous, what with Polly Hamilton in the bathroom across the room; but mostly I was annoyed—and weary. I still ached—and not just from the recent physical beating. There was

CAPTAIN STEGE—WITH AL CAPONE

a man who had died tonight and I'd been part of it. And I'd tipped to what was going on and still hadn't been able to stop it.

And now here was pious Capt. John Stege, a Chicago cop so honest he made Eliot Ness look like Long John Silver. I needed this dose of conscience like Jimmy Lawrence needed a hole in the head.

"You know something, Captain . . . you pretend to hate me because I used to be a dirty cop. But that isn't the real reason. The real reason is I *exposed* some dirty cops, and embarrassed you and yours."

"Don't be impertinent, or I'll—"

"It's just you and me in here, Stege. Maybe you ought to watch your mouth."

He thought about that. Then said, "Are you threatening me?"

"No. I'm just prepared to tell you to go to hell anytime I feel like it. Understood?"

He took in a deep breath and something like a smile crossed his thin, tight mouth. I had the damnedest feeling he respected what I'd just said. Whatever the case, he said, "Understood," and took a folded sheet of paper out of his suit pocket and unfolded it and spread it out on the desk before me.

It was a Division of Investigation wanted poster for John H. Dillinger.

"Thought you might like this souvenir," Stege said. "I'll be cleaning out my desk, you know."

I nodded. "Not much for the Dillinger Squad to do with Dillinger dead."

"What were you doing there, Heller?"

He meant the Biograph, of course. I didn't pretend I didn't know that.

I said, "Trying to stop it."

"*What?*"

I wished I hadn't said it.

But I had, so I needed to elaborate. "It was a setup, designed to let the East Chicago cops execute their man without interference. I knew it, and tried to convince Cowley. I tried to convince Purvis, too. Actually, I think I convinced 'em both, but they weren't able to stop it. If indeed they wanted to."

"Damn!" Stege said, and slammed a hard tiny fist on my desk top. The ashtray jumped. And unless I missed my bet, so did Polly Hamilton in the toilet.

"Sorry, Captain—that's the way I see it."

He waved me off. Stood and paced. Then he came over and leaned one hand against the desk and gestured with the other.

"They came to my office, beginning of last week. Zarkovich and his captain. What's his name?"

"O'Neill," I said.

"O'Neill," Stege repeated, like he was uttering an oath. "You know what the sons of bitches said?"

"No."

"They told me they knew where Dillinger was. He was in Chicago, hiding out, and they could lead me to him. But there was one condition—one small proviso . . . we had to kill him."

He drew in a breath and looked at me, his eyes popping a little, a vein by one eye pulsing. Silence filled the room; a very loud silence.

Then he said, "We, the Chicago Police Department's Dillinger Squad, were to promise that we would ambush our man, execute him. Or no information from our brother officers from East Chicago would be forthcoming." And under his breath: "Bastards."

"And you threw 'em out on their butts."

He nodded slowly. "I told 'em I'd give even John Dillinger a chance to surrender."

"Over these last six months or so, you've said the opposite to the press."

He sat back down. "Not really. I picked the best marksmen on the force for our squad, simply because these outlaws are trigger-happy. Fight fire with fire."

"You said you wanted to either drive the Dillinger gang out of the state or bury 'em. And you said you preferred the latter."

Oddly, he seemed almost embarrassed. "Hyperbole."

"Captain, you should be a happy man. John Dillinger is dead. Your quarry's been bagged . . . even if you didn't bag him yourself."

He took a cigar out of his inside pocket, bit off the end, lit it up. "Your sarcasm isn't lost on me, Heller. If you're saying I'm jealous of the federal boys landing my man, you're as full of crap as a Christmas goose. I don't care who gets these lice, just so long as they get got."

"Then why aren't you a happy man?"

He put the cigar in the ashtray without puffing it past getting it going. With a bleak expression, he said, "Police executions make me sick."

"The guy on the receiving end doesn't feel any too well, either."

He ignored that. What he said next seemed more for his own benefit than mine. "I try to be a good cop in a town where it isn't easy being one. There's few towns more political, and there's no town as under the influence of gangsters. But I still take pride in my work, in my town, because once in a while we succeed. We fly in the face of what people expect from us. But when cops shoot fugitives in cold damn blood, without even a nod toward capture, well it makes me sick, Heller. It makes me wonder what the hell country I'm living in; we're no better than Hitler's bully boys, are we."

"It wasn't Chicago cops who killed the man at the Biograph."

"No, it was federal men, I know that."

"I told you before it wasn't federal men."

"Oh?"

"Take a wild stab at what two individuals fired the killing shots."

"Zarkovich and O'Neill did it *themselves?*"

"Bingo, Captain. I'd give you a cigar but you already got one."

"Damn. They were in with him, you know."

"What?"

"That whole East Chicago crowd. Cops and politicians and judges. In with Dillinger. That's what this is all about, really about. They wanted to silence him before he could spill the beans where Indiana corruption's concerned. It all goes back to Crown Point."

"The jail, you mean? Dillinger's wooden-gun crash-out?"

Stege smiled his thin little smile again. "That was no wooden gun. Somebody smuggled it in to him. Somebody on the inside."

"Who?"

"My sources say Zarkovich and a certain judge engineered it. I can't prove it. Did you know that not long ago two East Chicago cops, two *honest* East Chicago cops, were investigating that very case, and during the course of it turned up dead alongside the road in their car? Fifteen minutes from their station house? With their guns tucked inside their coats? Never even went for 'em."

"Cops killed by cops," I said.

"So it would seem. What a world."

I shook my head.

Stege wasn't saying anything; he was, in fact, eyeing me suspiciously.

Slowly, he said, "You were part of it, weren't you?"

"What do you mean?"

"There was money to be made in this. Graft money; mob money. Were you in bed with the East Chicago cops?"

"Please. Not on an empty stomach."

Stege's face was impassive, but his voice had an edge in it. "I know you, Heller. You were always for sale. You were always in it for yourself. You're smooth in your way. You have a crude sort of wit. You almost fooled me. But I'm a cop with a cop's instinct. And I think you and Zarkovich and O'Neill are bound up in this together. It doesn't take me giving you the third degree to find that out."

"You don't have to give me the third degree at all. Zarkovich and O'Neill beat you to it."

Stege laughed humorlessly. "Of course they did."

"Not personally. They sent two of their strong-arms, and *they* fed me the goldfish."

"Why?"

"Because I was trying to stop this from going down! And you can see how successful at it I was."

Stege sighed coldly. "I don't believe you. But I intend to investigate this matter thoroughly, and if I can nail those East Chicago cops to the wall, I will, so help me God."

"Expose crooked cops, Captain? That'll make the police look bad in the public's eye. Are you sure you want to do that?"

He stood. "Your irony is heavy-handed, Heller. I'm unimpressed."

I stood. "Did you ever see Sally Rand dance, Captain?"

"What? Uh, well . . . yes."

"Were you impressed?" I was unbuttoning my shirt.

"What the hell are you doing?"

I took the shirt off and shined the lamp on me.

Stege said, "My God . . . they did feed you the goldfish."

"Yes they did."

He sat back down. So did I, after I put my shirt on.

I told him most of it—with the exception of meeting Nitti face-to-face; I kept my thoughts about the Outfit's connections to Dillinger on a theoretical level. And, for the moment, I left out my notion that the dead man might not be Dillinger; one step at a time, after all.

He took out a small pad and wrote down the names Anna Sage and Polly Hamilton; he'd heard about two women being with Dillinger at the theater, but the feds had refused to give the names even to the Chicago cops.

I told him how I'd been chosen for my role at least partially because I would take my information to the feds, rather than the cops, since I was on the outs with the local P.D.—particularly the head of their Dillinger Squad, one Capt. John Stege.

"So even I played an unwitting role in this farce," Stege said.

"Just some more heavy-handed irony," I said, "only I can't claim it as mine."

He stood slowly; he seemed beaten down.

"There's something else," I said.

"Yes?"

"I don't think the dead man is Dillinger."

Stege gave me a look like I was a candidate for the loony bin. "Don't be ridiculous—one of my men has already been to the morgue and shook hands with the corpse. It's Dillinger all right."

"It doesn't look like Dillinger."

"Plastic surgery," Stege said, repeating the by-now-familiar litany.

"This whole elaborate setup might've been staged to put a patsy in Dillinger's place, and let the real Dillinger ride off into the sunset."

"Poppycock."

"Well, if you feel that strongly about it, Captain . . ."

"No," Stege said, shaking his head solemnly, "John Dillinger's dead. No getting around that. But I aim to find out who put him on the spot . . . and that includes those crooked East Chicago bastards and Anna Sage and Polly Hamilton."

"Be my guest."

He walked toward the door and I followed him. We stopped by the door to the bathroom.

"Is this the commode?" he asked.

"Yeah."

"Mind if I use it?"

"It's out of order. Best I can do is a chamber pot."

"Ah, never mind. It'll keep. Thanks for the information, Heller. Thanks for the names of the two women. Very helpful. We'll want to talk to them as soon as possible."

"Right."

I opened the door for him and, as an afterthought, he turned and offered me his hand. Surprised, I shook it.

Then he walked like a little general down the hall with the burly plainclothes man in attendance. Off to do battle with the East Chicago police; and to find a bathroom.

I closed and locked the door. Opened the bathroom door and Polly Hamilton, fists on her hips, was burning at me.

"You gave him my name!"

"Did you think it was going to be a secret? The dead man had your picture in his watch, you know."

"I—I forgot he had that picture . . ."

"Well, you were at the scene when he was killed. Lots of people saw you. Come on out of that bathroom, Polly."

She did. She looked forlorn. But pretty.

"I can't go home. They'll be waiting."

"Face the music, or better, go see the feds. They'll probably shield you."

She looked up and her eyes did a little dance, like maybe she was remembering something Anna Sage told her along the same lines.

Then she got angry with me, or mock-angry. There was some co-quettishness in it.

"Why did you tell him all that?" she wanted to know.

"He's a cop and he asked me."

"Oh, you're such a shit."

"I thought you had special memories of our night together?"

That made her smile; I still liked her smile.

"I need a place to stay," she said. "No one would think of looking for me here . . ."

I was tempted. I admit I was tempted.

But I said, "Try the YWCA," and pushed her out the door. Hoping Stege was long gone by now.

Before I shut the door she stuck her tongue out at me, and said, "Fuck you." A strange combination of childishness and adultness. Or is that adultery?

Then I went back to the desk and sat. Looked at the federal wanted poster for Dillinger spread out there, where Stege had left it. His irony was a little heavy-handed, too. Looked at my watch. It was after one.

I called her anyway.

"Helen," I said into the phone. "Did I wake you? Is that offer for me coming over tonight still open?"

"Yes," Sally said.

22

The next afternoon, around three, I was sitting in my shirt sleeves having a bagel and a glass of cold milk in the deli-restaurant below my office. Milk was almost never my drink of choice, but coffee was out of the question—the day was steaming hot, so who the hell needed coffee?

I hadn't been upstairs yet, having just got back from Sally's. She'd been good to me last night—we didn't talk at all; in fact, we didn't do anything except sleep together—just sleep. And it was exactly what I needed.

What I didn't need this afternoon was a reporter, but suddenly that's exactly what I had: Hal Davis, of the *Daily News*, a little guy with a big head—by which I don't mean he was conceited: he had a big head, literally, a size too big for his smallish frame. He stood grinning in front of me in shirt sleeves and bow tie and gray hat. He was one of those guys who would always seem to be about twenty-two years old. He was easily forty.

"I been looking for you," he said.

"Sit down, Davis, you're making me nervous."

He sat. "You're a hard man to find."

"You seem to've found me."

"Pretty wild carryings-on at the morgue last night."

"I saw the papers."

He told me about it anyway. "I don't know how the word got out so fast, but there they were, before the body was even cold, swarming like flies. Couple thousand sweaty souls crowdin' around the morgue like they were waiting for Sally Rand to go on."

He meant nothing personal by that; Sally and I hadn't made the gossip columns yet.

"And that son of a bitch Parker scooped us all," he said, shaking his head with admiration.

He meant Dr. Charles D. Parker, one of numerous assistants to the coroner's pathologist, J. J. Kearns. Parker, however, also hap-

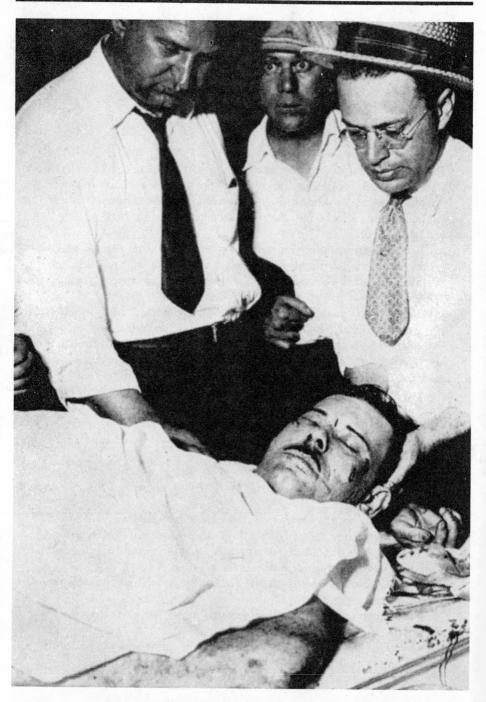

THE BODY AT THE MORGUE

pened to be a stringer for the *Trib*, covering hospitals and the morgue for 'em. Somehow Parker had got tipped to the shooting early enough on to be able to beat the body to the morgue, where he wheeled a receiving cart up to the door and waited for John Dillinger to arrive.

Soon the meat wagon delivered Dillinger—and exclusive *Trib* coverage of the morgue end of the story—to Parker.

"Got to hand it to that bastard," Davis conceded. "Hell of a piece of work."

I took a bite of bagel.

Davis cleared his throat. "I hear you were at the Biograph last night."

"So were a lot of people."

"Garage mechanics sitting on their stoop and old ladies hanging out their windows 'cause of the heat. Not trained observers like you, Heller. Your version of the shooting could be a corker."

"Gee whiz, aw shucks. I'm real flattered, Davis. Now can I finish my bagel?"

"Hell, I'll buy you another! How 'bout giving me your eyewitness account. For old times' sake."

"What old times are those? When you dredged up the Lingle case in your coverage of my part in the Nitti hit? Get fucked, Davis."

He smiled. "A newsman knows he's doing a good job when people resent him. You can't hurt my feelings, Heller, don't even bother trying."

"You're short."

He stopped smiling. "*You* get fucked, Heller."

I gulped my milk. "Every rag in town this morning, including yours, had a dozen eyewitness accounts of the Biograph shooting. This is old news. Why bother?"

Davis waved that off. "Dillinger dying's gonna be front-page fodder for days, maybe weeks. Besides, the bozos we got eyewitness stories from came in after the show started; you were there for the whole picture, and the featured attractions to boot."

"What's in it for me?"

He shrugged facially. "How 'bout a double sawbuck."

"I don't think so, Davis."

"What *do* you want?"

My curiosity got the better of me. "Were you at the inquest?"

"Yeah," he said, shrugging, with his body this time.

"Anything interesting come out?"

"What's interesting is what *didn't* come out. Excuse me." He went up to the deli counter and got a cup of coffee, and came back and told me about the inquest.

Coroner Walsh himself had presided, at the Cook County Morgue on Polk Street, and had gone first into the little formaldehyde-reeking basement room where the corpse was displayed on a tray draped with a towel, nude but for tags on his toes. The body, that is, not Walsh, who was a big man, sweating, beet-faced, posing stiffly with the stiff for press pictures. This was in the same room where, late last night, those thousands of "morbids" milling about the morgue had finally been allowed to file past their dead "hero."

Then Walsh moved to the inquest room where the noon sun blazed through the wire mesh on the windows and made checkerboard patterns on the spectators and witnesses and officials who baked their way through the perfunctory proceedings.

"The odd thing," Davis said, "is Melvin Purvis wasn't there. By all accounts, it was his operation—some of the witnesses say he's the one fired the shot—but instead his assistant Cowley takes the stand."

I didn't correct any of that, just nodded interestedly.

"And Cowley ducked the issue—when Walsh asked him who committed this 'homicide,' Cowley would only say that it was 'a government agent, properly authorized.' No names. And they never even broached the subject of who the informant was."

"Is that right."

"Do *you* know, Heller? Do you know who the 'lady in red' is? Or the other dame with Dillinger? What were you doing there, anyway?"

I sipped my milk; it was getting warm. "Did they introduce fingerprints into evidence?"

He shook his head. "Another government agent testified that the prints corresponded, is all. They didn't enter comparisons of the prints or anything—this guy just said the prints compared. A botched acid job, I hear."

Davis meant the corpse's fingertips had been dipped in acid, back when he was alive, in the usual (unsuccessful) underworld attempt to obliterate prints.

"And," he continued, "the pathologist, Kearns, read a summary of his autopsy. Four wounds, one of which caused death." He got a notebook out of his back pocket and flipped through some pages; read aloud: "'Medium developed white male, thirty-two years of age, five feet seven, one hundred and sixty pounds, eyes brown.'" He put the notebook away, shrugging again. "Pretty standard."

"I see."

He stirred his coffee absentmindedly. "Something else odd, though. The corpse only had seven dollars and eighty cents. Word was Dillinger always wore a money belt, with thousands of dollars. Think somebody stole it?"

"Maybe that money belt's just a myth."

"Yeah, maybe. But why would a guy like Dillinger, who might have to lam at any moment's notice, go out with little more than movie and popcorn money?"

"I wouldn't know."

"And another thing—why the hell'd he go out without a coat?"

"It was hot."

"Very funny, Heller. It's hot today, too. But where'd he tuck his gun, if he didn't have a coat to hide it under?"

"Good question."

"Did you see he had a gun at the scene?"

"There was a gun in his hand, by the time he was dead."

He thought that over. "It wasn't entered into the coroner's docket at the inquest, this gun Dillinger supposedly drew on Purvis."

I smiled. "Since when is a gun turning up in a dead suspect's hand news in Chicago?"

He sat forward and pointed at me like Uncle Sam. "Look, if you really know some inside dope, I can get you some *real* money. If you know the lady in red's name, for instance . . ."

"I'll give you my story for fifty bucks, but you got to mention my business by name and give the address."

"Done."

I sipped my milk. "That way Baby Face Nelson and Van Meter and the rest will know where to find me."

He grinned, then the grin faded. "You think Johnny's buddies might really seek revenge?"

"No. I think they got better things to do."

"Such as?"

"Such as read the writing on the wall. Such as rob a few more banks before going south. Things are closing in on them. The feds may be stupid, but they can cross state lines and carry guns. The

Wild West show will be closing down soon—after one last bloody act."

"Can I quote you on that?"

"Do, and I'll crucify you in Marshall Field's window. That sort of talk just *might* tempt the likes of Nelson into retaliating."

"I hear he's a fruitcake."

"Can I quote *you* on that?"

"Okay, okay. So what's your story, Heller?"

I told him my story. I told him that in the course of working in Uptown on a divorce case for a client, who would have to remain nameless, I'd stumbled upon a man who resembled John Dillinger. I'd reported this to Melvin Purvis and Samuel Cowley of the federal Division of Investigation. They had kept me informed as the inquiry developed, including the fact that two East Chicago, Indiana, police officers had corroborated my story through their own sources. For that reason, I'd been invited as an observer to the showdown at the Biograph.

I also gave him a detailed description of the way the stakeout had been conducted, and the manner in which the suspect had been taken down, though I did not mention that he'd been shoved to the pavement and shot in the back of the head. I said only that officers had swarmed toward him and shots had been fired.

No mention of Anna Sage, Polly Hamilton or Jimmy Lawrence.

I sipped my milk.

Frank Nitti would've been proud of me.

And Hal Davis gave me fifty bucks—two double sawbucks and two fins—and left.

I put the money in my pocket and walked outside. The heat was even worse today. I ought to go to the beach and find an umbrella to lie out under, and splash around in the lake when the shade got old.

Instead, I drove over to the morgue.

23

For a dreary-looking stone structure on a blistering hot July afternoon, the morgue was doing brisk business. About the only difference between it and the Biograph last night was the lack of a
marquee, and the melodrama attracting the crowds was Chicago, not
Manhattan.

The line to the front doors was a double one and, splitting off,
extended well down the sidewalk in both directions; a steady stream
was coming out the morgue doors, as well. Formal attire was not
required, at this mortuary—the dressiest "mourners," many carrying
cameras, were men in shirt sleeves and women in summery dresses,
and not a few females were in beach apparel, and many a male wore
his undershirt. There were plenty of kids in the crowd, mostly boys
with their thoughtful moms. The hot air was filled with hot air—a
constant chatter not limited to the dead subject at hand added to the
holiday mood. A guy in a big orange tie and orange cap was hawking
orange juice a dime a cup out of a tray full of ice slung over his
shoulder on a couple of straps, cigarette-girl style; the ice was melting
quickly, but not as quickly as the paper cups of orange juice were
going. Another guy, wearing a straw boater and no tie, was going
around waving two handfuls of blood-stained swatches of white cloth,
yelling, "Genuine guaranteed Dillinger's blood!" More bloody
swatches protruded from three of his four bulging pants pockets; apparently blood had been running down Lincoln Avenue like a flood,
last night.

All this humanity, if you want to call it that, was being overseen by
a handful of cops, uniformed guys still lacking their uniforms due to
the heat wave, badges on their light blue blouses; but the caps and
guns and nightsticks were still there. These were cops, no mistaking
'em.

I walked up to a burly Irish flatfoot in his forties, with red cheeks
and light blue eyes; I didn't know him, and hoped he didn't know

me—and would maybe take my reddish-brown hair as us having a bit
of the Blarney in common.

"What's the chance of getting in past this crowd?" I asked him.

He smiled and shook his head. "Slim and none."

"What if I just wanted to talk to a morgue attendant and didn't care
about getting a view of the stiff?"

He scratched his head, still smiling. "Might be done. But they're
greedy lads, those boys."

"Think you could pave the way for me?"

"Might be done."

"Thanks," I said, and shook his hand; mine had a buck in it. For a
while.

He led me through the crowd, saying, "Make way, make way," and
introduced me to a pasty-faced, pencil-mustached, skinny fellow
named Culhane. White-smocked Culhane had eyes like a gingerbread man and was about as animated. We were in a big reception
area on the first floor, where the lines of people coming through the
door turned into a mob, a vocal one, waiting to be let down the stairs
by a police guard, who was only letting ten or so at a time go. There
was no air conditioning and the place smelled stale and bad; body
odor was on a rampage. Culhane curled a finger and led me to a
corridor, where we were alone.

His voice was soft and oddly seductive. "I can take you downstairs
and inside the cubicle with him."

"Swell. How much?"

He pursed his lips and the tiny mustache went up at either end.
"There's a group down there right now that gave me fifty dollars."

This wasn't a morgue, it was a whorehouse.

I said, "How many in the group?"

That threw him momentarily; then he said, "Five."

"Then I'll give you ten."

Being a man of science, he could hardly argue with my logic. But
he was pouting as he led me back into the big reception area and
through the noisy, pushing-and-shoving crowd, where at his nod the
cop let us down the steps into the basement. We moved past and cut
through a single line of curiosity seekers that extended down the corridor. Culhane led me through a door into a larger room, where the
smell of formaldehyde sliced through the air and made me nostalgic
for the body odor upstairs. The smell was so overpowering you didn't
notice at first that the room was refrigerated. Or that along the walls

were rows of corpses, in open vaults, one atop the other. Most of the tenants—running to old folks and down-and-outers—had died of the heat; hell of a way to get into an air-conditioned room.

Culhane led me into a small adjacent chamber off the main room and there, with four men and a woman crowded around him, was the dead man, propped up at a forty-five-degree angle on the slab, his body partially covered with a sheet, his face completely covered by a damp white mass. The man applying the damp white mass, a heavy-set brown-haired man about forty, wearing a towel like a bib, looked up nervously and said, "We're from Northwestern University, officer. We got permission to do this."

The other four, including the rather pretty girl, who had a cute brunette bob, were young, in their early twenties; they looked at me apprehensively.

"I'm not a cop," I said, and Culhane whispered to me, "They're making a death mask for the Northwestern Museum of Crime."

I'd never heard of any such museum, but couldn't have cared less.

"I need a look at him," I said to the heavyset man, presumably the professor to these apparent students.

"Oh, but we can't remove the moulage yet," he said, still nervous.

"I don't need to see his face," I said. "I've seen his face."

I lifted the sheet back. Glanced at the body; noted various scars. I had company: through a glass panel just a few feet away from me, the openmouthed spectators were slowly filing by, pointing fingers, taking pictures. Their jabbering was faintly audible through the heavy plate glass; it sounded like swarming insects.

Before I left, I looked at the heavyset man and said, "If you're from Northwestern, why does your towel say Worsham College on it?"

He glanced down at the bib and swallowed. "We—we, uh, frequently exchange ideas with the Worsham faculty."

"And towels?"

He swallowed again, and I pulled a confused-looking Culhane by the arm out into the larger room, where stacked stiffs seemed to eavesdrop as I said, "Worsham's a trade school for morticians. Those people in there are having a little practice session at your expense."

"Oh my . . ."

"Better clear 'em out. Letting somebody from Northwestern play footsie with your prize corpse isn't going to get you in trouble; but some yo-yos from an embalming society using him to make practice death masks, that could lose you your job."

He nodded gravely, and I followed him out into the hall, away from the formaldehyde smell and the cool air, and up the stairs into body-odor heaven. He found a spare cop, told him to evict the embalming students and their prof, and the cop went off to do so. Then Culhane turned and looked at me, with some irritation, his little mustache twitching over a puckered mouth.

"Are you still here?" he said. It wasn't a question that wanted an answer.

"Least you could do is say thanks."

"Thank you. You've had your ten dollars' worth. Now go away. Shoo."

I put my arm around his shoulder and walked him toward that private corridor; he pouted, but seemed to like it.

"Mr. Culhane," I said, "I have another request. I also have another ten dollars. As a matter of fact, I have twenty dollars."

He began nodding. His puckered lips smiled.

I removed my arm from around his shoulder; enough's enough. I said, "I'd like a look at the autopsy report."

He thought that over. Then he said, "Why?"

"Why not?"

He thought some more. "Who are you? A reporter?"

"I'm a guy with twenty dollars."

He held out an open palm. "If you want it, it'll cost a lot more. There's only two carbons, you know."

I put a sawbuck in the open palm. "I don't want a copy. I won't even make notes. I just want to look at it, for a couple minutes."

He thought again, but not for long; closed his hand tight over the sawbuck, touched my sleeve with his free hand and said, "Don't move from this spot."

I didn't, and soon he was back with three sheets of paper. Handed them to me.

It was a carbon copy of the coroner's protocol, two pages of which were a form, the final page of which was a separate typed sheet, elaborating on the wounds and condition of the dead man's organs. Fairly detailed, it took me five minutes to read and absorb, while Culhane stood there like a skinny stone. Then I handed it back to him, gave him the other sawbuck and walked ahead of him out into the reception area, pushing through the noisy, smelly crowd.

A fat blonde in a polka-dot dress was scrunched beside me, putting on her lipstick, looking in her compact's mirror, as we moved through the sea of flesh; she managed to put the lipstick on without mishap, as well as make a comment.

"I'm disappointed," she told me. "He didn't look like his pictures in the paper. He looked like any other dead guy. But what the heck—I think I'll get back in line and go through just once more."

"Good idea," I said, and we burst out through the door into the hot, fresh air. The guy in the orange cap and orange tie was back with a fresh tray of ice and juice. I couldn't help myself: I bought a cup and swigged it down. It was cool and tasted good. Spending time in a morgue can make you appreciate the little things.

I was walking toward where my coupe was parked when a father, gesturing with one hand, the other on the shoulder of a weeping eleven-year-old boy, walked briskly by, saying, "Now I wanted you to see that as a moral lesson, Tim—it's like Melvin Purvis says: Crime don't pay, remember that!"

The father held one of the bloody swatches of handkerchief as he gestured.

I kept that in mind as I drove to the Banker's Building, where I hoped Purvis and Cowley would both still be on hand.

24

They seemed almost glad to see me.

Cowley, in a brown baggy suit, was standing over by nattily dressed Purvis, seated behind his big glass-topped desk, and they looked toward me as I came in, followed me with their eyes as I approached them. There was no college boy in the receptionist's slot this time to try to stop me—it was nearly six and most of the desks in the big office were empty, the windows half-open, letting in some warm but anyway fresh air and a glimpse of the day dying out there.

I stood across from Purvis and pushed my hat back on my head; I was still in shirt sleeves—sweaty ones, by now. I probably didn't smell any better than the rest of the crowd at the morgue.

I said, "Looks like things have settled down around this joint."

Cowley found an uneasy smile for me. "You should've seen it this morning. Real madhouse."

Purvis mustered an unconvincing smile, and stood. "Nice of you to stop by, Mr. Heller," he said in that faintly Southern drawl, as if he'd requested this visit. He gestured with an open hand back toward where I'd come in. "Let's step into the conference room down the hall, for a chat. . . ."

I didn't see why not.

We sat, the three of us, with me in the middle, at one side of a long table for twelve in a big room that had a few smaller tables, apparently used for interrogation, along the wall by the windows. Through the windows I could see the Rookery just across the alley, looking enigmatically on. The Rookery was an early near-skyscraper, whose eleven stories had an oddly moorish ornamentation that made it stand out among its newer, taller, sleeker neighbors and its older, more staid, stodgy ones, too.

Speaking of staid and stodgy, Cowley started in. "I haven't seen you quoted in the press as yet."

"You will."

Purvis, on the other side of me, spit out the words; his cordial pose hadn't lasted long. "What have you said?"

I scooted my chair back so that I could look at both of them, undercutting the double-teaming routine they were trying to pull. I gave them a brief rundown on what I'd told Davis, and they seemed relieved, and relieved was what they should be: it was a whitewash, after all.

Purvis said, "You didn't mention Anna Sage? Or Polly Hamilton?"

"No. But I did tell Stege their names, when he came to see me last night."

Cowley looked momentarily glum, but said, "We know. We've dealt with that."

"Oh really?"

Purvis said, "Stege was questioning Anna at the Sheffield Avenue Station this afternoon, but we sent our men to pick her up." A thin smile flitted across thin lips. "We told 'em it was a federal job and squelched the interrogation. She's in federal custody, now. Protective."

"She's in jail?"

"No," Cowley said. "We're just looking out for her."

"What about Polly?"

"Her too," Purvis said, nodding.

"I notice you've kept their names out of the papers. You think that's going to last?"

Purvis smirked. "Not since you gave the women's name to Stege. Once the Chicago cops have it, the papers soon will, too. Those louts would sell their grandmother for a cup of java."

I couldn't help smiling; when Purvis tried to talk tough, it was kind of pitiful. I said, "You shouldn't worry. You boys are getting good press on this."

Cowley was impassive, but Purvis had a smug, tight little smile.

I decided to wipe it off his face by saying, "You are aware by now that you killed the wrong man, aren't you?"

Purvis threw his hands in the air and said, "Jesus! Not that again!" Cowley just sat shaking his head, like I was a promising student who continually disappointed him.

"I don't plan to go to the papers with it," I said. "I plan to stick to the version I gave Davis. I was just curious if you guys finally copped to what you've done—which is do Dillinger and Nitti a favor and kill some ringer for 'em, and get the heat off."

Cowley brushed a comma of brown hair off his forehead, but it only fell back again. He said, "If you believe this to be true, why keep it to yourself? Why not go to the papers? You might make some tidy pocket change off it."

Purvis glared at Cowley for having suggested that.

I said, "I'm keeping it to myself because Frank Nitti might not like it if I didn't. And because whoever that poor shmuck in front of the Biograph is—or was—doesn't much matter, at this point. He's dead. I saw it coming, and would've liked to stop it from happening. But I wasn't up to the job. So be it. Best of luck to all concerned."

Purvis got up, paced for a moment, then went over to the open window and looked out at the Rookery, hands in pockets. "I don't get you, Heller. You're not a stupid man. Yet you seriously entertain such a stupid goddamn fantasy. We killed a 'ringer'! Utter rubbish." He turned and looked at me with a painfully earnest expression. "How in God's name could that have been anyone else *but* John Dillinger last night?"

Without malice, I said, "You were so eager for it to be him, it didn't have to be."

He strode over to me, hands still in pockets; he seemed a little boy playing man. "What the hell's your meaning?"

With malice, I said, "Listen to me the first time I say something, Little Mel—then you won't have to ask me to repeat it four times."

His marionette features took on a hurt, angry cast and he told me to go hell and walked briskly toward the door.

"I have a train to catch," he said. "I don't have time for your nonsense."

He was opening the door when I said, "I can prove it wasn't Dillinger, Melvin."

That caught his attention.

"I really can, Mel," I said. "But if you have a train to catch . . ."

He shut the door and walked back. Sat down next to Cowley. Both men looked at me with doubting, but troubled, expressions.

"I was just at the morgue," I said. "I got a good look at the body, and a good look at the autopsy report."

That angered Purvis. "How did you manage . . ."

I rubbed my thumb and fingers together, in the money gesture. Purvis fell silent and Cowley winced and nodded and I went on.

"The man Zarkovich and O'Neill shot was approximately Dillinger's height and weight. He was a little shorter and a little heavier than the real McCoy, but within an inch and ten pounds, so what the hell. Facially he doesn't resemble Dillinger much, but certain scars indicate a face-lift, so plastic surgery *might* explain that. But how do you explain the eyes?"

"The eyes?" Purvis said.

"Yeah—the eyes have it, you know. And the corpse has brown eyes. I saw it for myself, last night; and that's what the autopsy report says, too. Brown eyes."

"So?" Cowley said.

"Dillinger has gray eyes."

Purvis said, "If the corpse has brown eyes, Dillinger has brown eyes, because that corpse is Dillinger. This is ridiculous. I really do have a train to catch." He stood again. "You fill Cowley in on your fantasy, if you like, Heller—I have neither the stomach nor time for it."

"Sit down, Melvin," I said. "You're going to hear this, or I'll find somebody else to tell it to."

He sat.

"There was also a birthmark, a mole, missing on the body—right between the eyes—and several scars from bullet wounds and a scar on the lip were also not there."

"Plastic surgery," Cowley offered.

Cockily, Purvis said, "We know for a fact that Dillinger had plastic surgery just within this past month or so. This afternoon agents from this office picked up two of the ring involved in Dillinger's several face-lift operations—Louis Piquett's personal private investigator, and the doctor who performed the operation. And this office will be making more arrests in the days to come."

That sounded like a fucking press release. I said so.

"You're an annoying man," Purvis said, his Southern sense of manners apparently infringed.

"If Dillinger *did* have plastic surgery this past month or so," I said, "how could he be completely healed so soon? The skin on his upper lip would at least look pink, for instance. Nothing looked pink about that stiff, believe me."

Purvis was shaking his head, scowling. "Where are you getting your 'facts'? Newspaper files? What description are you going by? What's the basis of your comparison? Get serious, Heller."

I took a folded-up piece of paper out of my front right pants pocket and spread it out on the table.

"Division of Investigation identification order number twelve-seventeen," I said, pointing to the federal wanted poster for John Dillinger. "Given to me by my friend Captain John Stege as a souvenir of this little episode."

Both Purvis and Cowley just stared blankly at the poster. Purvis was swallowing, like his mouth was suddenly dry.

I said, "And as you well know, the physical description of the fugitive on this ID order is detailed and exact. Notice the eye color listed: gray."

Cowley gestured toward the paper, as if afraid to touch it. "This is what you compared the autopsy report to?"

"Yes, and if any reporter in town gets ahold of that report, and does the same thing, some very messy questions are likely to get asked."

Purvis looked at the poster with wide, empty eyes; he too didn't touch it. Just stared at it.

"You may be lucky," I said. "The newshounds seem satisfied with the abbreviated report Kearns read into the record at the inquest. So far, apparently, nobody has thought to bribe a peek at the actual report—except me."

Purvis started to say something dismissive, but I interrupted. "There's more, gentleman. Your corpse has some things Dillinger did not have—a tattoo on the right forearm; scars from bullet wounds in places Dillinger never got shot; black hair, not brown; thin, arching eyebrows instead of bushy straight ones; and a tooth—the top right incisor, to be exact."

Purvis was shaking his head again, but slowly, now. "This is ridiculous. Sheerly ridiculous. You're basing this on an autopsy conducted in a carnival atmosphere . . . and comparing that report to data gathered from hither and yon, over the years, on a *fugitive*."

Cowley, bleakly, said, "Mel, much of the ID order description comes from Dillinger's Navy records, remember?"

"Right," I said. "And the Navy physical he got was surely pretty accurate."

Defensive, Purvis said, "How can you know that? Were you there?"

"No I wasn't, and maybe you're right. Maybe the Navy doctor was drunk that day. But the coroner's pathologist, Kearns, isn't a drinking man. That autopsy was carefully handled, despite the ghoulish goings-on at the morgue. Kearns is a top doc; he's done every major murder in Chicago from Bobby Franks to the Saint Valentine's crowd. And he was assisted in this by another doctor, and a medical stenog was recording everything. This was not your typical Cook County foul-up."

"Ridiculous," Purvis said, softly.

"I'll tell you something else the dead man had that Dillinger didn't: a bum ticker."

Cowley sat up straight. "What?"

"A bum ticker. The corpse had a rheumatic heart condition. He'd had it a long time, since he was a kid. How could he have passed the Navy physical with that? How could he have played baseball like he did? Not to mention certain other strenuous activities he's been involved in this past year or so."

Cowley finally picked up the wanted poster and glanced at it.

"Maybe," he said, "his heart condition was something he knew about but kept to himself. Maybe it was what made him live the reckless way he did."

"It won't wash," I said. "That's some other guy on that slab down there at the morgue."

"*Who* then?" Purvis demanded.

I shrugged. "Maybe he *is* a guy named Jimmy Lawrence. One of Anna Sage's pimps from East Chicago or something. Most likely he's a small-timer on the run who had some plastic surgery a while back and was hiding out, with the help of some friends. Or some people he thought were friends. When Frank Nitti needed a patsy to stand in for Dillinger, this poor shmuck got elected."

Purvis stood again; paced with his hands in his pockets, checking his wristwatch now and again, nervously. He said, "Nitti. You see Nitti under every bed. I don't see him even *vaguely* figuring in this. Not vaguely . . ."

I ticked the points off on my fingers. "Anna Sage is a madam and connected to the mob. Zarkovich has Capone ties going way back, and probably engineered the Crown Point escape for Dillinger. Even the Biograph theater has Nitti's name on it—there's been a bookie joint over the theater for years and, hell, Nitti's got a lock on the movie projectionist's union, so what better place to rub out the patsy?"

Cowley, his face ashen, his eyes haunted, said, "Why did you do it,

Heller? Why'd you go to the morgue? Why are you stirring things up?"

"It's something you two wouldn't understand. It's called being a detective."

Purvis laughed humorlessly. "Very funny," he said, and stopped to look out at the Rookery, then at his watch.

Cowley said, "You had this theory, and you just had to see if it was right. You just had to know."

I shrugged, said, "Yeah, I suppose. I had to know."

"Did you ever go to college?"

"For a while."

"Did you take any science?"

What the hell was this about? "Some," I said.

Cowley leaned forward, hands folded, and tried to look fatherly, wise. "Did you learn anything about what happens when a scientist goes looking for a certain answer, when he should just be looking?"

"You're saying I was predisposed to finding out this guy wasn't Dillinger."

Cowley nodded.

"Hell, I wish the guy *was* Dillinger. I'd feel like less of a chump. It would mean a couple of corrupt East Chicago cops used me to help put public enemy number one on the spot, for the reward money. I wouldn't be nuts about that either, but it's better than helping set up some poor dope for a bullet or two so John Dillinger can drink tequila and lay Mexican broads into his old age in peace. No, Dillinger's eyes are gray, the dead guy's are brown. And so on. Better face up, boys."

Purvis whirled and pointed a finger at me, like I was a suspect he was interrogating; he was trying for a dramatic moment, but it didn't play. He said, "Suppose you're right. Suppose there was some grain of truth in this nonsense you're peddling. What do we do about it?"

I shrugged again. "Announce your mistake. It'd be embarrassing— the headlines are half 'Dillinger Dead,' half 'Purvis Hero.' It wouldn't be easy. It'd be embarrassing as hell. Little Bohemia was a spring picnic compared to this."

Purvis lifted his chin, looked down his nose at me. Small guys like to do that, sometimes, when you're sitting and they're standing. He said, "Why should I buck the tide? If the corpse has been identified as Dillinger, why should I think otherwise? The fingerprints match up, after all, and—"

"That does have me stumped," I admitted. "But I noticed the

prints didn't get entered as evidence at the inquest. Some agent just testified they matched up, right? So who took 'em?"

"Uh, took what?" Purvis said.

"The prints, man! Which of your men took the prints?"

Purvis and Cowley exchanged looks; I couldn't read the meaning. Cowley said, "It was done by some Chicago police officer, at the morgue last night."

"Chicago police officer?"

"Yes."

"You mean, East Chicago?"

"No. Chicago."

"Do you know the cop's name?"

Both men shrugged.

"Let me get this straight—there's been absolutely no Chicago police involvement in the case whatsoever up till this point, then suddenly it's not one of your men, but a Chicago cop who takes the prints. A nameless Chicago cop, at that."

This time only Cowley shrugged. "It was at the Cook County Morgue. What can I say?"

"Why don't you go down and take another set of prints while you still can?"

"What for?" Purvis said, irritably.

Cowley shook his head. "I think it's too late. I think Dillinger's father has come from Indiana for the body. They're supposed to've shut down that show at the morgue by now, and turned Dillinger over to—"

"Well, hell, go to Indiana, then. Catch up with Dillinger Senior before the burial. Save yourself exhumation expense. Check the prints."

"Why bother?" Purvis said.

"Why bother? Because as somebody said—I think it was you, a couple of hundred times—the Chicago cops would sell their grandmother out for a cigar. Or words to that effect."

Purvis looked at his watch. Then, suddenly civil again, he said, "I have to stop back at my apartment for my luggage, before I get that train. I'll have to leave you gentleman, now." He walked to the door, turned and said, "See you in a few days, Sam. Mr. Heller, thanks for sharing your theories with us. Interesting if farfetched, but we do appreciate that you're otherwise keeping them to yourself. Good evening."

"Oh, Melvin," I said.

He stopped momentarily, the door open.

I said, "You may catch your train, but you are definitely missing the boat."

He snorted and went out.

Cowley and I just sat there awhile.

Then I asked, "Where's he off to?"

"Washington, D.C.," he said, quietly.

"Going to shake his boss's hand, I take it."

"Yes. He'll be meeting with the director, and the attorney general as well."

"Lots of publicity shots, I suppose."

Cowley shrugged, then nodded.

I said, "Melvin Purvis is building a big reputation on this dead man's back. I wonder how Little Mel's going to sleep, over the next twenty or thirty years, knowing the man he's supposed to have killed might turn up, any minute?"

Cowley said nothing.

I got up. "I wish you guys luck. At least I wish *you* luck, Cowley. You seem decent enough."

He stood, shook my hand. "You're all right yourself, Heller. I don't really think there's anything much to what you've said here today . . ." He didn't sound quite convinced of that. ". . . but I do appreciate that you, out of some sense of civic duty or honor or whatever, chose to come to us with this."

I laughed. "That's a new one. I never had civic duty or honor laid on me before. By the way, I got a piece of that reward money coming, don't I?"

Cowley seemed surprised by that. He said, "I would assume so."

"Well, if this sweater don't come unraveled in the next few days, and that stiff manages to get planted under a gravestone that says Dillinger, you know where to send the check."

He nodded.

The check came in a few weeks. Five hundred dollars was all I got. Word was Anna Sage got five grand, though some said ten. Zarkovich got around five gees, too, word was. That's what the government paid 'em. Who knows how much they got from John Dillinger. And/or Nitti.

What followed, in the aftermath of the Biograph shooting, I viewed from the sidelines, reading the papers, listening to the radio, and hearing small talk in bars and such.

During the next day or so, more morbids thronged the small funeral home in Mooresville, Indiana, Dillinger's hometown. The papers reported another five thousand people (one for every dollar the feds paid Anna Sage) viewed the corpse, laid out on a brocade spread in the visitation parlor. The papers reported that most of the people who had known Johnnie over the years had "difficulty" recognizing him, he'd changed so. This included the corpse's sister Audrey, who'd all but raised him; she never did identify the body exactly— she only said, "There's no question in my mind—just bury him."

When Dillinger's father had come to Chicago to pick up his son's remains, the early interviews had the father bemoaning the lack of funds for burial; but by late the same afternoon, after a meeting with attorney Louis Piquett, a more cheerful elder Dillinger said it turned out there was money enough after all. Maybe he found somebody's wallet on LaSalle Street.

Among the other interesting events of the days that followed was Anna Sage coming out in the open, for newspaper interviews and such, basking in her "lady in red" celebrity. Early stories circulated by Purvis and Cowley—complete falsehoods designed to shield Anna and Polly—were soon forgotten, and Anna held court with the press—until Cowley and Purvis sent her on a paid vacation.

A discovery the Chicago police made, at Anna's apartment in the early days, was that somebody had been staying with her, rooming with her—a man. According to the papers, the cops believed Dillinger to have been that man. Nothing ever came out, though, as to what might or might not have been found in the fancy apartment near the lake, on Pine Grove Avenue.

On the Friday after the Biograph shooting, one James Probasco (the papers said) fell nineteen stories from a window in the Banker's Building to the alley below; he splattered headfirst, getting some of himself on a passing pedestrian. He had fallen from that same interrogation room where Purvis and Cowley and I talked; he'd been left alone there, by Cowley and some other agents who'd been questioning him (Purvis was still picking up accolades in Washington at the time), and jumped to his death, reportedly. Cowley said the man had seemed "despondent"; nobody in the building across the way, the Rookery, saw the man leap. One of the reasons for Probasco's despondency, besides a fear of his underworld associates thinking he may have "talked," was a nerve infection called herpes, for which he was under medication.

Probasco, whom I'd heard of but never met, was said to be a "hot-money" fence, and his connections to both the mob and the likes of Dillinger were well known. He even had some political connections, being related by marriage to an old Cermak crony, former alderman Thomas J. Bowler, currently president of the Sanitary district.

A man in his mid-sixties who'd be facing at most a year or so in jail on harboring a fugitive and conspiracy charges, Probasco seemed an unlikely candidate for suicide. Something that didn't get much coverage in the papers was the word among cops and crooks in town that the feds regularly hung suspects out the windows by the feet to try to make 'em talk. In Probasco's case, they were probably trying to make him comply with the face-lift story they were trying to make float.

Probasco, a former veterinarian, apparently had, in addition to his fencing activities, been running a face-lift shop for some time—the feds found rubber gloves, ether, bandages, adhesive tape, iodine and guns in his apartment. He was, they said, part of a conspiracy that included Piquett's personal investigator and two other doctors and Piquett himself, in giving Dillinger (and his pal Homer Van Meter) face-lifts.

Eventually the story did float (just as Probasco's "suicide" did) and virtually everybody turned state's evidence in return for probation, with only Piquett actually standing trial, and he was found not guilty, since the jury felt he was just an attorney trying to help a client, Dillinger.

Whoever it was that was murdered at the Biograph that hot Sunday night ended up being buried at Crown Hill Cemetery in Indianapolis on the Wednesday after. This time the crowd of morbids was chased away by God—a thunderstorm beat down on the graveside ceremony, lightning and thunderclaps overseeing the casket's entry into ground that also held the remains of President Benjamin Harrison, several U.S. vice presidents, several Indiana governors, novelist Booth Tarkington, poet James Whitcomb Riley and the inventor of the machine gun, R. J. Gatling.

A few days later, the elder Dillinger, that dirt-poor farmer, paid to have the casket uncovered. Over the casket was poured concrete mixed with scrap metal; when that had set, some earth was shoveled in. Then four concrete slabs reinforced with chicken wire were buried, in staggered intervals, over the concrete-entombed casket.

Dillinger's father did this, he said, to prevent "ghouls" from disturbing his son's rest.

"If they want to get him out of there," the father said, a smile cracking his weather-beaten face, "they'll have to blast him out."

The old man needn't have worried.

Nobody wanted him out of there.

2
THE FARMER'S DAUGHTER
AUGUST 24–SEPT. 1, 1934

25

A month later I was starting to wonder if Sally might not be right about my chosen profession. My name had been in the papers—including my address, in the *News*—but no business had been generated by this notoriety, not even a death threat or two from Baby Face Nelson or Homer Van Meter. All I had to show for my trouble was a few hundred bucks and the growing suspicion I was a horse's ass.

"What good am I?" I asked her, as we lay in her soft bed, the silk sheets draped around us, Sally snuggled against me in the dark.

"You're very good," she said, smiling up at me.

"Don't change the subject."

"Do you have to be so gloomy, Heller?"

"Am I getting you down with this talk?"

She shrugged. "Not really."

She was a better dancer than actress; I told her so.

"Go to hell, Heller," she said. Good-naturedly. Sadly.

"I was right on top of this," I said, "and it didn't do a damn bit of good."

"Why don't you get right on top of this," she said, snuggling closer.

"I quit the cops 'cause I was sick of being used. I quit and went in business for myself because people kill people in this town as casual as flushing a toilet, which is fine, which is great, that's their goddamn business. Just leave me out of it."

She pulled away from me and sat on the edge of her side of the bed, her back to me.

"What the hell kind of detective am I, if I can't stop something like this from happening when I see it the hell coming?"

She was lighting a cigarette.

"Not that I give a damn about Jimmy Lawrence, whoever the hell *he* was. I never even met the son of a bitch. What's it to me if Indiana and Frank Nitti want him dead. Just don't make *me* part of it! Damnit!"

She sighed and blew smoke out at the same time.

"Helen . . . you okay?"

I touched her shoulder and she flinched and I took my hand away.

"I've been going on about this too much, haven't I?"

Without turning to me, she said, "It has been a month, Nate."

"I know. I didn't mean to get going again."

"I thought maybe you were over it," she said, wistfully. "It's been almost a week since you last went into this song and dance."

That made me bristle a little. "It isn't a goddamn song and dance. It's something that's eating me. Sorry!"

She turned and smiled over her shoulder at me; breathed smoke out her nostrils like Dietrich. "Whatever happened to the strong and silent type? I didn't think you tough detectives ever wore shirts made outa hair."

That made me smile and I touched her shoulder again; this time she didn't flinch.

In fact she was in my arms after that and I kissed her on the mouth and remembered why being alive was worthwhile.

I kissed her neck, whispered into her ear. "Sorry. Sorry. I won't go on about it anymore. I'll let go of it . . ."

She pulled back to look at me and smile, just a little.

"I don't mind that what you were caught up in bothers you," she said. "That quality in you is probably why I love you so damn much. . . ."

In our time together, this was the first love had ever come up; in words, anyway. Hearing her say that was like getting struck a blow. Pleasantly struck. But struck.

She put a hand in my hair, roughed it up, smiled her sad wry little half-smile. "I just hate seeing it eating you up like this."

"I love you, too, Helen."

"I know. Quit the business."

"What?"

"I'll be leaving in a few months to go on the road with my show. Starting in November."

"Please, Helen. Not this again . . ."

"I listened to your song and dance, now you listen to mine."

"Helen . . ."

"I need somebody smart and tough to handle the sharks in my business."

"Your business."

"Show business. I want you to be my personal manager."

"What I know about show business you could store in a flea's navel."

"You know people."

"I know crooks."

Little wry half-smile. "Perfect."

"We've been through this before . . ."

"Nate. We'd be together. Work together. Live together."

"You'd marry me, you mean."

"Sure."

"What about kids?"

She shrugged. "Anything's possible."

"You'd need a bigger bubble."

"I wish you'd take this seriously. I really want you to consider what I'm offering."

"You make this sound like a business proposition; before it was love."

"It's both. You're in a business that's making you very little money and has given you a good deal of heartache. I'm giving you the opportunity of getting into a business that'll make you a lot of money and warm your heart, among other things."

"Helen, this Dillinger thing was . . ."

"Just a fluke. Not the sort of thing that happens every day in your business. Yes, I know. I've heard you say that over and over. I've also heard your stories about the Lingle killing and the Frank Nitti shooting and the Cermak assassination and Nate, give it up. Come live with me."

"And be your love?"

She laughed. "Poetry, huh? You're full of surprises, aren't you, Heller."

"My father ran a bookshop. A little of it rubbed off."

"My father had a farm. A little of that rubbed off on me—enough to make me long for some of the traditional virtues, like having a man who loves me around."

"A bookshop and a farm. Neither one of us seems to have gone into the family business. Though we each have our own cockeyed idea of how to go about making a living, don't we?"

She stroked my face with the back of her cool long-nailed hand. "Let's merge."

"Yeah," I said, "let's," and kissed her again.

Now, the next day, a balmly Friday afternoon, I sat behind my desk in my dreary little office thinking about life with Sally Rand and show business and how any guy in his right mind would jump at this chance.

If I was so goddamn set in my ways, where the A-I Detective Agency was concerned, I should've been doing my fucking job instead of sitting staring at my new office furniture. I had an afternoon's worth of phone calls I was supposed to be making; credit checks. But I couldn't seem to do anything but sit there and stare and wonder about my future. Would I be in this same office, a year from now? Five years from now? Ten years from now? Would I ever have a secretary? Operatives under me? How 'bout a wife and kiddies? Or was I destined to plod along making just enough money to deceive myself into thinking I had a "growing" business. Never getting far enough ahead to feel secure enough to make a home and family. Just sitting in this office till hell froze over.

I'd used up part of the six hundred-some dollars I'd cleared off the Dillinger fiasco to improve my office. I'd got rid of the patched brown-leather couch and put in a modern one, artificial-leather maroon cushions on the left and right and cream cushions in the middle, sitting on a swooping chrome-tube frame. I'd picked up a matching chair with maroon seat and cream back cushion; it looked like an electric chair out of Buck Rogers, and the couch was like something in the drinking car on the Silver Streak. A little steel smoking stand with an ebony Formica top was to one side of the couch, and in front of it was a steel, ebony-Formica-topped coffee table. The woman at Sears said the stuff was "as modern as tomorrow." And on sale today.

Sally had helped me pick it out, and her thinking had been to make my office look more like an office, and in the showroom she seemed to make sense—this streamlined modern furniture seemed just the ticket to pull me up into the twentieth century. Today it all seemed silly to me, absurd in the same room as my Murphy bed and scarred old desk and cracked plaster walls.

On a more practical note I'd put in a water cooler, which was humming over against the wall near the washroom. No use carrying that bottle too far to fill it back up. I'd picked it up used from a small import-export business down the hall, that went under a few weeks before. The heat wave had let up a bit but wasn't exactly gone, and the little paper cups of refrigerated water made life slightly more bearable.

I was filling one of the cups and the water cooler was saying, "Glug glug," when somebody knocked on my door.

"It's open," I said, and drank my water.

The door opened slowly and a thin man of about forty stepped one foot tentatively inside and peeked in around as if looking to see if the coast was clear.

"Mr. Heller?"

"Yes. Can I help you?"

"Might I step in, sir?"

"Certainly." I gestured with the now-empty paper cup toward the maroon-and-cream, chrome-tube throne I was now providing for clients, opposite my desk.

He came all the way in, a man about my height but twenty pounds lighter; his face was gaunt, weathered, lined with work, with eyes of that odd light blue color like the sky on certain washed-out summer days. He held his straw hat—not a boater—in his hands, and smiled one of those polite smiles that barely qualifies as smiling and nodded as I walked behind my desk and made his way uncertainly toward the chair of tomorrow.

He clearly was a man of yesterday. He slouched a bit—not from the weight of the world, but from something much heavier: he wore a sense of personal tragedy like a topcoat. A snug-fitting one. His clothes didn't make as close a fit: his dark brown suit wasn't cheap but wasn't tailored (like my furniture, it might've been gotten at Sears— though in his case surely by mail-order catalog) and shiny brown shoes and his light brown bow tie were obviously Sunday-go-to-meeting clothes, and he was less than comfortable in them. If he'd ever been comfortable in his life.

Certainly he wasn't in the modern chair; he looked at it suspiciously before sitting, then did, as if he had no choice, like Zangara taking the electric cure. He smiled again—it was just a crease in his face—and patted the ebony armrests atop the tubing at either side of him and said, "Seen some things like this at the Century of Progress last year."

I ventured a smile. "Nobody said the future was going to be a picnic."

He tilted his head; it was like a hound dog trying to understand an abstract concept.

"I'm afraid I don't follow you, sir," he said.

"Skip it. And let's skip the 'sir,' too—you can put a 'mister' in front of the Heller, if you like. Or not. I don't stand on ceremony." I ventured another smile. "Not as long as you're a paying customer."

His face creased in the sort of smile again, but he still didn't get my drift. Humor was as foreign to him as the chair he was sitting in.

"Now," I said, getting a yellow pad and a pencil out of a desk drawer, "if you'll give me your name and the nature of your business . . ."

"I'm a farmer. Or used to be."

I'd meant his business with me, but never mind. He was too young to be retired—despite his lined face, his hair was thick and black with just a salt-and-peppering around his ears. Maybe he wasn't a paying customer after all.

I said, "Did they foreclose on you?"

"No!" he said, as if offended. Then thinking it over, softened his tone and repeated, "No. Plenty folks I know did get their notice. It's better, now."

"Thanks to FDR and Henry Wallace, you mean."

He rested the hat on my desk, off to one side, near the edge. "No," he said, flatly. "Just folks sticking together. When the banks were holding farm sales, not so long ago, those of us with any money a'tall would go and bid a nickel for a plow, dime for a horse, quarter for a tractor, and then just give it all back to the real owner, afterwards. We spread word anybody was to bid against us would be dealt with severe. And there'd be a couple hundred of us at the auction, so . . ."

"But you still have your farm."

"No. I sold out. Took a loss, but I sold."

"Excuse me, mister, uh . . . ?"

"Petersen," he said, rising, stretching his hand across my desk for me to shake, "Joshua Petersen."

I shook his hand. "Pleased to make your acquaintance, Mr. Petersen."

He sat back down. "I live in De Kalb, these days. Used to live just outside of there. But now I'm in town. And I took the train this morning to come in here just to see you, Mr. Heller." Taking the train was clearly a major decision in his life.

"Was I recommended to you?"

He shook his head. "I seen your name in the paper. When they killed Dillinger."

So—it *did* pay to advertise. I said, "Why are you here, Mr. Petersen?"

He seemed momentarily confused, as if the answer to that was self-evident.

"Why, Mr. Heller—the only detectives in De Kalb are the police kind. I need somebody private." He cleared his throat, and formally made his intentions clear: "I come by train seeking the help of a big-city detective."

I didn't know whether to laugh or cry. Instead I just scribbled circles with my pencil and asked, "Why are you seeking a detective's help?"

He leaned forward; there was no self-pity in his gaunt face, just tragedy.

The reason for which was now explained: "My daughter," he said. "She's missing."

"I see."

"She'd be . . . nineteen, now."

"Has she been missing for some time?"

He nodded. Kept nodding as he went on: "Last I knew she was running with a bad crowd."

"A bad crowd."

He looked at me with those empty light blue eyes; they were as barren as an unplanted field.

"I better tell you the story," he said.

He told me the story. At seventeen his daughter Louise had married another farmer, only a few years her father's junior. Her father, a widower since the girl's childhood and a rigidly religious man, admitted having been a strict disciplinarian with his only child.

"By that," I said, "you mean you beat her."

Nodding, head gazing down, blue empty eyes finally filling with tears, he said, "I make that admission freely."

"Mr. Petersen, this isn't a court, and it isn't church, either. You don't have to punish yourself, here. And I'm certainly not going to judge you. But you do have to tell me the facts, so I can help you."

He nodded some more. Said, "No need to punish myself."

"That's right."

"The Lord will take care of that."

I sighed. "I suppose he will. Please continue your story."

He went on in a voice as hollow as his eyes; his words had a formal,

practiced sound—as if he'd said these words to himself every night,
over and over again, when he should have been sleeping.

"It was my cruel treatment of Louise that drove her from me," he
said. "Into his arms. But he was worse than I was. More cruel, more
jealous than ever I was. His punishment exceeded the crimes."

"Mr. Petersen, I'm not following you. What man are you taking
about? Her husband?"

He looked at me sharply. "Yes. Her husband."

"And he was a farmer, too?"

"Yes. And she'd go off to town without asking him. And do Lord
knows what. Men. Drink." He covered his face with one weathered
hand and wept. Tears found their way through the cracks of his fingers and fell on his lap. I'd never had a client cry in the office before—not even when I handed 'em my list of expenses—and it made
me uncomfortable. This man was devastated by the road his daughter
had gone down. His moral and religious convictions must've been
strong, I thought, for him to take having a loose daughter so hard.

I got up and began filling a cup of water for him from the cooler,
which said, "Glug glug." I said, "So her husband beat her, and she
skipped."

He took a handkerchief out of his pocket, dried his eyes, blew his
nose. "Yes. She ran off."

I handed him the cup of water; he drank it greedily, then didn't
know what to do with the cup. I took it from him and wadded and
dropped it in the wastebasket behind the desk. Sat again.

"Did she come home to you?" I said. "After she left her husband?"

He shook his head. "She never thought to. She never even thought
to. She lumped me in with Seth—I must've seemed just as bad as he
was, in her mind."

"Seth is her husband."

One quick curt nod.

"How's he feel about getting Louise back?"

"Ain't interested. He's took up with several other 'ladies,' hear
tell."

"I see."

"But I want her back. I want to do right by her. Make it up to her.
She'll like livin' in town. . . ."

"I'm sure. You mentioned something about her running with a 'bad
crowd.' How bad?"

The blood drained out of his face.

"That bad?" I said.

"Ever hear of a man called 'Candy' Walker?"

"Jesus."

He sighed heavily. "I take it you heard of him."

I had. I'd never met him, but Clarence "Candy" Walker was a small-time hood from the North Side, a handsome ladies' man of about thirty, a wheel man who drove beer trucks for Bugs Moran in the old days and had been in Nitti's stable till maybe a year ago. Since then—like Baby Face Nelson and a few other graduates of the Capone mob who'd been laid off after Repeal—he'd been seen driving for the Barkers. The bank-robbing Barkers.

He'd also driven for Dillinger a few times in the last six months, if I wasn't mistaken. Small world.

I said, "I take it from your tone you know who Candy Walker is."

"He drives what they call in the papers the 'getaway car' in robberies. He's a bank robber."

"He drives getaway cars, and he's a bank robber. Yes."

He dug in his left suitcoat pocket. Took out a folded newspaper clipping; as he did, he said, "She ran off to Chicago about a year ago. She was seen with him here. She was living with him, as a matter of fact."

"How did you find this out?"

"Seth reported her as a missing person. He left it pretty much drop, after that. But I kept after the sheriff's office, and the sheriff's office said the Chicago police knew she was in Chicago living with this Candy Walker feller."

"If you're thinking Walker is still around Chicago, I'd doubt it . . ."

"That's what the sheriff's office's been tellin' me. And I can figure that for myself. Melvin Purvis has made your town too hot for them gangsters. This Walker's living out on the road somewheres. Going from here to there. Stealing. May the Good Lord damn him to hell for eternity."

"Good odds on that," I said, taking the clipping he was holding out. It was an interior page from a *Daily News* from July 2 of this year, detailing the robbery of the Merchants National Bank in South Bend, Indiana.

At 11:30 A.M. on Saturday, June 30, five men (later identified as John Dillinger, Homer Van Meter, Baby Face Nelson, Charles "Pretty Boy" Floyd and Clarence "Candy" Walker) parked their Hudson in front of the bank. Walker remained at the wheel, and Nelson,

his machine gun under his coat, took up position near the rear of the
car. Van Meter, with a rifle, took position just down the street, in
front of a shoe store. Inside the bank Dillinger and Floyd made a
withdrawal—only when the tellers weren't filling their sacks up
quickly enough, Floyd fired a burst from his machine gun into the
ceiling, to perk up the proceedings. Outside, a traffic cop heard the
commotion and came running. Van Meter fired his rifle and the cop
fell in the street, stopping traffic. The owner of a jewelry shop down
the way ran out of his shop and shot at Nelson, whose bulletproof
vest saved him as he spun and began firing wildly. Only the cop was
killed, but several pedestrians were wounded, including the hostages
who were made to ride the running boards as Candy Walker wheeled
out of town, with around twenty-five thousand of the bank's money in
tow. On the west side of South Bend, the hostages were set free; the
group split in two and climbed into separate cars.

This was, as far as anybody knew, Dillinger's last caper.

Of course that wasn't what made this clipping noteworthy: it was
the other story, the sidebar. A Pontiac with Indiana license plates
stopped at a filling station near Aurora, Illinois, later that same afternoon. Two men and two women were in the car. The men seemed to
be Candy Walker and Homer Van Meter; police sketches of them
were reproduced, as well as of the "unidentified molls" who'd been
with them.

Petersen stood and pointed at one of the molls pictured. From an
inside coat pocket he produced a snapshot of himself and a pretty
teenage girl with blond bobbed hair, a farmhouse glimpsed behind
them. He had his arm around her and was smiling—a real smile, not
a crease—and she had a glazed smile, behind which unhappiness
clearly lurked. Still, these were happier times (at least for him).

And, of course, the girl in the snapshot closely resembled the police sketch of one of the women seen with Candy Walker and Homer
Van Meter.

"Mr. Petersen, this police sketch resembles your daughter, but
she's a pretty woman, a young woman, and a lot of pretty young
women look pretty much like this. . . ."

"It's her," he said, flatly. "Now let me show you something else."

This guy had something in every pocket; he reached into his right
suitcoat pocket and produced another clipping. He spread it before
me.

"This was in this morning's paper," he said. "I read it and went and got on the train—I knew I'd waited long enough. Maybe too long."

I'd already seen this: a story from this morning's *Trib*. But it took on a new significance, now.

The St. Paul police had shot about fifty bullets into Homer Van Meter yesterday. Not surprisingly, it killed him.

Petersen, trembling, sat back down.

"I've been reading the papers," he said, "reading the blood in the headlines. Clyde Barrow and Bonnie Parker . . . John Dillinger . . . now Van Meter . . . the outlaws, they're all going to die like that, aren't they? In hails of bullets?"

I shrugged. "More or less."

"I'm afraid for my daughter, Mr. Heller."

"I don't blame you."

He sat forward; earnestness engulfed his face. "Retrieve her for me."

"What?"

"Get her back for me." He pointed to the Van Meter clipping. "Before she meets a similar fate." He sat back, as if to say, I rest my case.

I looked at this gaunt Midwestern ghost sitting holding onto the ebony armrests on the chrome tubes of my silly goddamn chair, and I wanted to laugh. Or cry.

Instead I simply said, "Mr. Petersen, surely you understand what you're asking is, well . . . a tall order. Maybe an impossible one."

He said nothing, just leaned forward, with anticipation. Waiting for me to say yes. Or even no. Something.

His daughter would go to jail, upon capture—if she was lucky. She could just as easily die—go down "in a hail of bullets," as he had said. But since she was just another faceless moll (but for one police artist's sketch), a name that hadn't got into the papers as yet, it was vaguely possible it wasn't too late, that she *could* be rescued, that she *might* be pulled from out of the fire before the fat fell in. . . .

"Okay, Mr. Petersen," I said. "I tell you what. I'll snoop around a bit. Walker used to live in Chicago, so maybe through some of his old contacts I can find out if your daughter's still with him. If so, maybe I can get a message to her that her father would welcome her home, with open arms."

He shook his head no. "That wouldn't be enough. You have to *find* her. You have to bring her back. Whether she wants to come or not, Mr. Heller."

"How can I promise to bring her back, if she doesn't want to come? Be reasonable, Mr. Petersen. After all, that'd be kidnapping. . . ."

"Is it kidnapping to return a daughter to her father?"

He had me there.

And knew it. He stood and dug in another pocket; right pants pocket this time. He took out a thick fold of bills, money-clipped. Counted out five hundred dollars in twenties.

I watched this, amazed. With probably about the same look he'd given my modern chair, coming in.

I picked the stack of money up in one hand; it felt heavy.

"Mr. Petersen—why five hundred dollars?"

He got oddly formal again: "Because you will take risks. You will need to go among the wolves."

He had a point; it would be dangerous to go around asking questions about the girlfriend of a wanted man, a public enemy. But five hundred dollars was five hundred dollars.

"What do you expect for your money, Mr. Petersen?"

"I want you to look for Louise, Mr. Heller."

"For—for how long?"

"For five hundred dollars' worth."

"At ten bucks a day, that's a long time."

"Find her, and you can keep what you don't use. If you use it up, call me . . ." He reached in his left pants pocket and removed a slip of paper with his name and phone number and address written on it, and gave it to me. ". . . I will probably authorize you to continue."

Petersen picked his hat up off my desk.

"And," he said, putting on the hat, "there's a thousand more if you deliver her to me."

That knocked the breath out of me. I was stunned by the kind of money this simple retired farmer was throwing around. "Mr. Petersen, excuse me for asking this—I don't mean to pry, or look a gift horse in the mouth. But how can you possibly afford this, in times like these? Or *any* time?"

His crease of a smile seemed weary, now, and somehow worldly. "My health is bad, Mr. Heller," he said. "I'm a lunger. Picked it up in the war. I got my pension to get me by and then some. That's how I was able to sell my farm, and get this money together—to find my girl. I got my little house in De Kalb, where we can live together. On

my pension. She can make a new start. Find herself a nice little job,
and find a good new man, to take care of her after her daddy's gone.
Which will be soon, Lord's will be done."

He extended his hand across the desk and I stood and shook it.

"Tell her that when you find her," he said. "Maybe then she'll
come home of her own volition."

I nodded.

"But *find* her," he said, and slammed the desk with his fist with
sudden force on the "find"; the lamp shook. Then more quietly, and a
little embarrassed, he said, "Please find her. Bring her home."

And he left me alone in the office with my modern furniture and
his old-fashioned money.

26

When Frank Nitti wasn't holding court at the Capri Restaurant, or meeting with the inner circle of the Outfit at his home in suburban Riverside, he would occupy a suite in various Loop hotels. This was standard operating practice, for meeting with politicians and labor leaders and the like. It made a safer, more neutral ground.

So it was no surprise to me, after I called the Capri and sought an audience with Nitti, that the return phone call I received was a male voice that did not identify itself telling me to be in the lobby of the Bismarck Hotel, two o'clock Monday afternoon.

The Bismarck was on the corner of LaSalle and Randolph, across the street from City Hall—making it a natural place for Nitti to hold meetings. The recently rebuilt hotel dominated German Square, the group of German clubs, steamship offices and shops at the west end of the Rialto Theatre district. But my meeting that Monday afternoon would have a distinctly Italian cast.

I went past the uniformed Bismarck doorman and through the revolving door and up the wide, red-carpeted stairway and my footsteps echoed across the marble floor of the high-ceilinged, elaborate lobby, where I found an overstuffed sofa and sat. Pretty soon a rather short man in a gray suit approached me; his shortness meant nothing: this was a big man. He had shoulders broad enough to balance a midget on either side of his oblong head. His hair was dark and starting to thin; his dark eyes were colder and harder than the marble floor beneath us.

He was Louis "Little New York" Campagna, Frank Nitti's personal bodyguard.

He didn't speak. He just stood in front of me and had a faintly disgusted look—and Little New York Campagna looking faintly disgusted was scarier than Bela Lugosi and Boris Karloff put together, I might add—and jerked his head, indicating I was to get up. I got up.

I followed him onto an elevator, and the uniformed operator didn't ask for our floor; he just took us up to the seventh, where Campagna waited for me to get out first.

As we were walking down the hallway, I said, "I hope there's no hard feelings about that other time."

I'd knocked Campagna out once; it's a long story.

Without glancing at me, just walking alongside me, he said, "As long as Frank says there's no hard feelings, there's no hard feelings."

I left it at that.

At the end of the hallway was a little vestibule; the door within the vestibule said 737, with a little gold plaque that said *Presidential Suite* below it. I stood to one side of the door, within the vestibule, and cold-eyed Campagna stood to the other. He stood with his arms loose at his sides, big hands free.

"Wish I could find a suit like that," I said. "I can't find one a gun won't bulge under."

He said, "You couldn't afford my tailor."

I shrugged. "Probably not."

It occurred to me then that he hadn't patted me down for a gun; he could tell just looking at me I wasn't armed—the suit I had on wasn't tailored well enough to conceal one. Grooming hints from the underworld.

The door opened and a fat little man with wire-frame glasses, a loud tie and a black silk suit came out, smiling, calling back behind him, "Always a pleasure, Frank!"

Campagna reached over and shut the door for the fat little man, who put his hat on and was going past me when I said, "How you doing, Willie?"

Willie Bioff squinted behind his wire-frames, then said, "Heller?"

"That's right."

He smirked. "How's it feel to be an ex-cop?"

"How's it feel to be an ex-pimp?"

The smirk shifted to a sneer. "Once a smart-ass always a smart-ass."

"Once a pimp always a pimp."

Bioff thought about doing something about my mouth. I knew he wouldn't. He was a former union slugger, but known for doing his slugging with a blackjack from behind. And in his pimp days he was famous for slapping his whores around. I'd arrested him, back in my plainclothes days, for that very act. Right before I was assigned to the pickpocket detail, I'd accompanied one of Chicago's honest detectives, William Shoemaker, "Old Shoes" himself, on a brothel raid. We'd caught Willie going down the backstairs with a tally sheet, and when we hauled him back upstairs and one of his girls admitted Willie was her pimp, he'd hauled off and slugged her. We got a six-month conviction on the little bastard, but he never served it. Chicago.

Bioff was still standing there, trying to decide if he should get tough—maybe thinking Campagna would back him up. But then Bioff had no way of knowing why I was present; maybe I was on Nitti's team, too, and he better not risk messing with me. He was nothing if not a coward.

Bioff said, "We should let bygones be bygones," and waddled quickly off.

"I hate that little pimp," I said.

Campagna looked at me impassively, then his tight mouth turned up at one corner. I took that to be a sign of agreement, and a possible softening of the tension between us. Still, if Nitti ever wanted me dead, Campagna would probably push to the front of the line to get the job.

For now he pointed one of his shotgun-barrel fingers at me and said, "Wait here—I'll see how Frank's doing."

I waited; it was just a matter of seconds and Campagna was back, saying, "Frank wants to know if your business is private."

"Pardon?"

Campagna looked faintly disgusted again. "Can you talk in front of anybody, or is it for Frank's ears only?"

"Frank's ears only," I said.

Campagna nodded and went back in, came right out, said, "It'll be just a few minutes. Frank's getting a haircut."

"Oh," I said.

We stood there for a while, on either side of the door.

Suddenly Campagna said, "Me, too."

"What?"

"I hate that little pimp, too. Bioff. You want a cigar?"

"Uh, no thanks."

Campagna took out a cigar as thick as one of his fingers and lit it. It smelled pretty good, as cigars go. There were guys all over town who'd give their soul for a job that paid per day what that cigar cost.

Not that I blamed Campagna for enjoying himself; in his business, life was sometimes short—why not enjoy it while you had it? And I

was grateful for the gesture he'd made—some human contact between me and him, however slight, might be good for my health. At
least now I didn't figure he'd be wanting to be first in line to bump
me off.

The door opened suddenly and a white-smocked, skinny, swarthy
man with a pencil-thin mustache and slick hair came rushing out,
saying "'Cusa, 'cusa," and shutting the door quickly behind him.
Something smashed against that door—something glass, shattering.

The man, a barber apparently, seemed frightened but Campagna
stopped him before he could run away and gave him a fin, saying,
"You're lucky to get it."

The barber nodded, his eyes wide, terrified, and scurried off down
the hall.

Campagna, his mouth turned up at either corner, genuinely
amused now, pointed a thumb at the door and said, "Frank said you
could go in as soon as his barber came out. So you can go on in,
Heller."

I swallowed. "You're too good to me, Campagna."

Campagna actually grinned for a moment—the first indication I'd
had since knowing him that he had teeth—and opened the door and I
went inside.

Glass shards from a small hand mirror crunched under my feet as I
entered the plushly carpeted living room of the suite. Nitti was standing looking in a wall mirror, a white barber's gown tucked in his
collar; he was touching his hair, looking at himself with disapproval.

"Come in, Heller," he said, not looking at me. "Find a seat."

There was a high-backed chair near a sofa in this white-appointed,
gold-trimmed, rather Victorian-looking suite. Black hair trimmings
peppered the white carpet near the chair, so I sat on the sofa.

Nitti yanked the white gown from under his neck and pitched it
behind him as he walked over to the chair and sat, placing his hands
on his knees. He was in gray pants and a white shirt. His suitcoat and
tie were on a coffee table nearby, but he didn't put them on. He was
shaking his head.

"They don't make 'em like they used to," he said.

"Uh, what's that, Frank?"

"Barbers. That little cocksucker makes more money off me in fifteen minutes than I got in a week, when I was in the business, and
look what he does to me!" He gestured to his immaculately cut black
hair, slicked back, parted at the left, perfect.

"It looks pretty good to me, Frank."

"Does it? Well, maybe I'm too fussy. That's the fifth barber I tried this year. And they all got the same goddamn problem."

"What's that?"

"Their goddamn hands are shaking! Look—" He bent over and tipped his head to one side, folded his ear back; a little red showed. "I'm fuckin' bleeding! They ain't barbers, they're butchers! In my day, a barber had hands like *this*—" And he held his hands out straight in front of him and demonstrated how rock-steady they were.

"Maybe they're intimidated, Frank."

That seemed to confound him. "What the hell for?"

"Well," I said. "They're cutting Frank Nitti's hair. There's a certain amount of pressure in that, don't you think?"

He thought about that, nodded. "I never thought of it. But you're right, Heller. It could make a barber nervous, knowin' he's cuttin' another barber's hair. You may be right. Now." He slapped his knees. "What's this about?"

"I'm here for a favor—if you're willing to grant one."

He shrugged expansively. "You know I owe you, kid. From way back."

"Well, I don't figure you owe me. But if you'd do this for me, I could maybe owe you."

"You don't sound nuts about owing me, kid."

I admitted I wasn't. "I would like to ask that if you ever call my marker in," I said, "you'll restrict it to more or less legal services. Maybe sometime you could use some investigating and wouldn't want to use your own people—something on the q.t. I could be your man. No fee, no questions asked."

He nodded, smiling rather absently, almost to himself. "Maybe I ought to quit thinking of you as a kid, Heller. You seem to've grown up on me, when I wasn't lookin'."

I smiled at him. "You're always looking, Frank."

He laughed, the haircut forgotten. "You got that right. Look, I am grateful to you for that last little job you did for me."

I didn't know what he meant; I didn't say so, but he could see it in my face.

"You know," he said, gesturing with one open hand. "When I gave you that C to mind your own business."

He meant Dillinger; I was wearing the suit I'd used part of the money on.

"That's okay, Frank."

"You coulda gone to the papers, coulda found some newshound who'd paid you good dough for your story. I ain't sure anybody woulda believed you, but it's nice that story never got told. Coulda made a ripple or two in the lake. And ripples can turn into waves, if you ain't careful."

"Lake's real calm these days, Frank."

"I know. Let's keep it that way. Now. What favor you need?"

"Remember a guy named Candy Walker?"

Nitti nodded, and I told him my story. Told him Walker's current moll was a client's daughter and that client wanted me to try to retrieve her before she got caught in a crossfire somewhere.

I said, "Walker's running with the Barkers, I understand."

Nitti confirmed that. "That little penny-ante outfit's come a long way. They're in real tight with some of our friends in St. Paul."

By "our," he meant the Outfit's friends, not his and mine. And those friends were the Twin Cities branch of the Syndicate and various corrupt politicians on the municipal and even the state level.

"I, uh, figured you might've had some dealings with the Barkers."

He eyed me shrewdly. "How'd you figure that?"

"Can I speak frankly?"

He nodded.

"Well, when Shotgun Ziegler bought it in Cicero, I figured the Boys either did it or approved it."

Ziegler, a Capone gunman said to be one of the bogus "cops" who gunned down Bugs Moran's boys in a North Side garage on Saint Valentine's Day back in '29, had been cut in half, his head blasted into fragments, by four shotguns outside his favorite Cicero café this past March. Like Baby Face Nelson and Candy Walker, Ziegler had been a Capone soldier who defected in post-Repeal days to the army of outlaws, specifically the Barker–Karpis gang. Word was he had engineered the Hamm kidnapping for the Barkers—one of several crimes Melvin Purvis tried to pin on the Touhy mob, incidentally— but in the kidnapping's aftermath the Barkers had soured on Ziegler.

Nitti smiled humorlessly and leaned forward, his legs apart, his hands loosely clasped together, dangling between his knees. "Let me tell you about Mr. Ziegler. A lesson can be learned, there. He drank too much. You ever see me drink too much, Heller?"

"I can't recall seeing you drink at all, Frank."

"Right! I'm a businessman, Heller, mine is a business like any other. And businessmen don't get in their fuckin' cups and tell tales out of school."

"Ziegler told tales out of school."

Nitti nodded, still smiling, still without humor. "He was hangin' out at saloons and braggin' about his accomplishments. Startin' with a certain accomplishment that dates back to February of '29, if you get my drift. Right up to a couple of more recent accomplishments—namely, snatches. And I don't mean he was braggin' about gettin' laid."

He meant the Hamm and Bremer kidnappings, said to be the work of the Barber–Karpis gang (said by everybody but Melvin Purvis and his "G-men," that is).

"Frank, I think you know I can keep my mouth shut. So if you're willing to put me in touch with Candy Walker—or put me in touch with somebody who *could* put me in touch with Candy Walker—I sure wouldn't go spreading your Barker connection around."

"I know you wouldn't, Heller. I trust you. Besides, if you did, you'd wind up in an alley."

I breathed out heavily. "Fair enough. Will you help me out?"

He stood. He walked across the room to the bar and poured himself some soda water on ice; he offered me some and I said no thanks. He came back and sat and sipped the soda water, which bubbled in his glass like the thoughts in my brain.

Nitti was thinking too. Finally he said, "I could help you. But the best favor I could do you is not to."

I sat up. "Why's that, Frank?"

"Haven't you thought this through, kid?"

So now I was a "kid" again.

"Well, yes . . ."

"Don't you realize your name was in the papers, associated with the Dillinger kill. As far as some of these dumb-ass farmer-outlaws are concerned, you helped set their pal up for the feds. You helped kill Johnny Dillinger."

"I realize that . . ."

"How were you plannin' to go about lookin' for this girl, then?"

"You're saying if I go around asking questions of Candy Walker and his associates under my own name, I'll run into somebody who might want to do me in."

"No," Nitti said, shaking a finger at me like a disappointed school-teacher, "you'll run into *everybody* who might wanna do you in."

"I figured if I could restrict my investigating to Chicago . . ."

"Candy Walker ain't in Chicago."

I sighed. "I didn't figure there'd be much chance of that."

"You're probably gonna have to go out among them apple-knockers to find that girl. And you can't go out as, what's your first name again?"

"Nathan."

"You can't go out as Nathan Heller, private cop that helped get Dillinger. Not without comin' back in one or more boxes."

"I guess I knew that."

"Got any ideas?"

I sighed again. "I could go out under a phony name. You know—undercover."

Nitti lifted an eyebrow, nodded. "Like that fed your pal Ness sent around to suck up to Al. That guy sure looked, talked and acted like a real wop."

I nodded too. "Yeah—and his testimony had a lot to do with putting Capone away."

Nitti smiled, a little. "Maybe I should thank that guy—he made me what I am today."

"Some people think Capone is still running things from behind bars."

"He's in Alcatraz now. You don't run shit from Alcatraz."

"Anyway, it can be done. Going undercover."

"Yeah, but it'd be good and goddamn dangerous. I'd have to hand it to you, kid, if you pulled that off."

"Would you be willing to help me do it?"

Not smiling, he tipped his head back, narrowed his eyes. "How?"

"Give me a name I can use, and a background. Somebody who's out of circulation, in jail or whatever, who I can say I am, without risk of Candy Walker or anybody he runs with ever having met the guy. Somebody they might've heard of. Somebody they could call around and check up on. So I could get in and get this girl and get out again. In one piece."

About halfway through that, he started nodding. He was still nodding as he said, "Possible. Let me make a phone call."

He got up and went out of the room. I could hear his muffled voice, but not make out any of the words. Then he came back in, smiled meaninglessly and sat back down.

"It's fixed. I got a name for you to use."

"Good. Somebody in jail?"

"Better. Somebody dead."

"Oh . . ."

"This guy worked out East till about a year ago, when he come to work for us."

"Candy Walker never met him?"

Nitti shook his head. "No, but he's heard of him. That's the beauty part. There's a chance he was pointed out to Walker once or twice, but they never met."

"Well, if Walker saw him . . ."

"The guy had plastic surgery. That's your explanation, if it comes up—it also happens to be true."

"Oh—okay. How can I prove I'm this guy?"

"I'll fill you in some more—I'm going to have a driver's license in his name dropped off at your office tomorrow morning. We can make it work. A cinch."

"Well, uh. Thanks. I appreciate this, Frank."

"Actually, you're doing me a favor."

"How's that?"

"This guy you'll be playin'—he's dead, but nobody knows it. Or, not many people know it. And it makes things sweeter if he's seen walking around. It confuses the issue, see? Makes him not dead."

I didn't follow this exactly, but I nodded.

"Now," Nitti said, writing on a white pad on the coffee table before him, "here's an address. It's an apartment house. You'll go see this old hillbilly woman who lives on the ground floor. Her name's Kate Barker."

"Kate Barker. Is she related to the Barker boys?"

Nitti nodded curtly. "She's their ma."

No mention of an old woman being connected to the Barker–Karpis gang had been in any of the newspaper write-ups.

I said, "Is she aware of her boys' business?"

"Oh, yes."

"Does she approve of it?"

"They can do no wrong in her eyes. She goes on the road with 'em sometimes, I'm told. But sometimes she tires of that kind of life and goes and lives in an apartment in the 'big city.' She'll know where they are. Just tell her you want to connect up with her boys and Walker; she won't care why, she'll just do it. If she has any doubts about who you are, you have her check with one of my people, whose name I'm gonna give you."

He tore the sheet with the address on it off the pad; handed it to me.

I glanced at the address.

3967 Pine Grove.

"Jesus—Frank, this is the apartment building where Jimmy Lawrence lived . . ."

"I know," Nitti nodded. "I own it. Or one of my companies owns it."

I was finding out more about Frank Nitti and his business than I wanted to; I could see me, dead in an alley.

"She's living in Lawrence's apartment, by the way," Nitti said.

"Jesus," I said, just staring at the white piece of paper, the address starting to blur.

"That's only because the previous tenant vacated," Nitti said, smiling like a priest. "She never met Lawrence."

"She—she never met Lawrence?"

"No," Nitti said. "And that's to your benefit. Because that's who you're posing as."

"Jimmy Lawrence?" I said.

"Pleased to meet you," Nitti said, still smiling.

KATE BARKER

27

The next afternoon, Tuesday, I parked across from the big brick three-story on Pine Grove and just sat there for a while, collecting my thoughts.

In my billfold, where my Illinois state driver's license should be, was an Illinois state driver's license in the name of James L. Lawrence. I was wearing my white suit and a straw boater and gold-rim glasses with window glass in them. I felt faintly ridiculous. I probably was faintly ridiculous.

I was calling on the mother of the Barker boys.

Frank Nitti had spent another half hour with me, in his Bismarck suite yesterday, filling me in on Lawrence's background.

He—or I—had been born in Canada, moved with his—or my (our?)—parents to New York as a boy; the parents were both dead— the mother in childbirth, the father in a factory accident—and I'd been raised by my uncle and aunt. My uncle had worked in the garment district in the West Thirties, and I'd ended up a union slugger there, for Lepke—as Lucky Luciano's chief lieutenant Louis Buchalter was inexplicably called—and eventually became one of Lepke's top aides in the protection racket. But I had a New York murder rap hanging over me, now, and had been shipped out by the New York boys to their friends in Chicago about a year ago, who put me to work, after some plastic surgery.

That much I'd learned yesterday afternoon. This morning around ten Campagna had dropped off the driver's license and suggested I call a certain phone number, before noon. I did, and Nitti himself answered.

"I got just the ticket," Nitti said.

We'd discussed the need, yesterday, for me to have a cover story, in addition to the Lawrence name and background—that is, a reason for getting in touch with Candy Walker and the Barkers apart from my *real* reason for being there, specifically, to spirit Walker's moll away, which of course was nothing I dared advertise.

"There's a guy named Doc Moran," Nitti said. "Ever hear of him?"

"Yeah—isn't he a pin artist?"

"Abortions ain't all he does, Heller, but yeah, I suppose that's his specialty. He's got a practice over on Irving Park Boulevard, and he's done good work for us over the years. Lots of union work."

Underworld doctors like Moran came in handy, not just for providing abortions to Syndicate whores, but for dealing with the aftermath of union-busting activities, and any incidental gunplay Outfit troops might get involved in—the latter having declined since the rise of Frank Nitti, under whom less and less overt Syndicate violence was taking place.

I said, "Would I be wrong in supposing Moran's clientele the last year or so has been primarily of the outlaw variety?"

"You'd be on the money, kid. Matter of fact, right as we speak, he's in the Barker–Karpis camp . . . makin' an extended house call."

So now I was crossing the street and walking up to the relatively ritzy apartment house where the real Jimmy Lawrence had lived, not so long ago. I'd been his shadow, then; now I was his ghost.

In the entryway there were mailboxes with name cards; one of the ground-floor flats was occupied by the woman going under the name Alice Hunter. I knocked on her door.

A voice from behind the door, a melodious if quavering voice, feminine with a hint of a drawl, said, "Who is it, please?"

"Jimmy Lawrence," I heard myself saying. "I'm a friend of your landlord's."

"Pleasure to meet you," the door said, sincerely. "Why'd you drop by, Mr. Lawrence?"

"I need to contact Doc Moran. Can you help?"

"Why, I certainly would like to," the door said. "Would you mind waitin' out there a mite, while I make a telephone call?"

"Not at all, ma'am."

I stood facing the door, straw hat in one hand.

A few minutes later the door cracked open and two bright, dark eyes peered out at me from behind gold-rim glasses, in the midst of a fleshy face highlighted by a witchlike pointed nose and chin, and a forehead where little ringlets dropped out of a skullcap mass of curly hair borrowed from Shirley Temple.

She was the oddest old lady I'd ever seen, and all I could see was her face, sideways, as she peeked around the door.

She smiled; her teeth were false, but the smile wasn't. "You're a right handsome young feller. Where'd you get that suit?"

"New York," I said.

"That's one place I never been." She was still just peering around the door. "Would you mind holding open your coat?"

"Not at all," I said, and did.

She smiled some more, as she noted my lack of hardware. Then the face momentarily disappeared as she opened the door wide and gestured sweepingly with a plump hand on the end of a plump, stubby arm.

I stepped inside. Just beyond the entryway where we were standing was a large living room, where a pastel-green mohair sofa with floral cushions shared the central space with several pastel-green lounge chairs, on a parquet floor somewhat covered by a fringed rug with a pastel-green-and-orange geometric design. Against one wall was a fireplace with a mirror with ivory-and-orange flowers superimposed on it. The apartment must've come furnished; this plump Ozark granny hadn't decorated it. The place must've looked about the same when Jimmy Lawrence lived here.

There were touches of the current tenant, however. In front of the straighter backed of the two lounge chairs was a card table on which a jigsaw puzzle was perhaps two-thirds completed: a country church on a fall afternoon, orange and red leaves, blue sky with fluffy clouds—a bunch of the sky was yet to be filled in. In front of the sofa was a round glass-top coffee table with a fat scrapbook on it; clippings stuck out of it like clothes from a hastily shut suitcase. Against one wall in a standing cabinet was a combination radio and phonograph, the cabinet lid propped up and open; the radio was on and a hillbilly song was blaring out.

The fat little woman—she couldn't have been over five feet two but must've tipped the scales at 170—moved gracelessly across the room and turned the hillbilly music down, but not off. She turned and smiled apologetically, girlishly. She took off her gold-rim glasses and tucked them away in a pocket. Her dress was a floral tent but she had what appeared to be a string of real pearls about her neck. Her stomach protruded enough to make the hem of her dress ride up and reveal the rolled tops of her stockings. She was a cross between an old flapper and a new tank.

She gestured for me to sit on the couch and I sat. She sat next to

me. She had lipstick on and smelled of lilac water and too much face
powder. The oddest thing about her was, despite the false teeth and
the jowly face and pointed features and absurd Shirley Temple curls,
how nice a smile she had.

"Can I get you some coffee?" she asked. The place was air-conditioned, so the request didn't seem absurd, despite the August heat
outside.

"That's generous of you, Mrs. Hunter, but no thanks."

She waved at the air and turned her head coquettishly. "That
name's just for outsiders."

"We'll make it 'Mrs. Barker,' then."

She was looking off absently. "Though I *do* like the name Alice . . .
wish my folks had called me that instead of Arizona."

"Pardon?"

She touched her massive bosom with a splayed hand; her fingernails, though short (possibly through biting), were painted red as her
lipsticked mouth. "Isn't that the most awful name? Arizona? Who can
picture callin' a little girl that!"

In the background somebody—Gene Autry?—was singing plain-
tively about his horse.

"I like 'Kate' better," I said.

"So do I. But you can call me Ma. All the boys call me Ma."

I suppose I should've been honored or at least flattered at being
admitted to the club so easily, so rapidly; but all I felt was a little
queasy.

I said, "You're too kind . . . Ma. And why don't you call me
Jimmy?"

"Jimmy. That's a good name. I like it."

"I'm glad."

"Well, Jimmy. How can ol' Ma be of help?" One of her plump arms
was brushing against me.

"I wonder if you could put me in touch with Doc Moran—a mutual
friend of ours has requested I find him, and bring him back."

She pursed her lips in what was meant to be a facial shrug but
came off more like a grimace. She said, "Might be I could take a
message for you."

"Are you going to be seeing the doctor?"

"Might be. If I can find me a ride."

"A ride?"

"The doctor's with my boys Freddie and Arthur right now. They're with that nice boy Alvin Karpis. Do you know Alvin?"

"Never had the pleasure."

"He's a right nice boy. Anyway, I got to get to 'em, soon as I can." Her fleshy face tightened. "They *need* me."

"You're in regular touch with them?"

She shrugged again, with her shoulders this time; the earth moved. "They don't have a phone where they's stayin'. But they call from in town now and then."

That sounded like they were in the country somewhere.

"And you're planning to join them, soon?" I asked.

She nodded, said, "But I don't drive. I have to find me a driver."

You never know when opportunity's going to knock; it might even knock in the form of a fat little old lady from the Ozarks . . . Gene Autry, if that's who that was, was suddenly singing something more upbeat, about the prairie.

"I could drive you," I said. Not too eagerly, I hoped. "My instructions are to see the doctor personally. No go-betweens."

She nodded sagely. "You gotta bring him back yourself. That's your orders."

"Right."

"And orders is orders."

"Yes they are."

She put her hand on mine; it was cold, clammy—hers, I mean. Hell, mine too.

She said, "Well, why don't you drive me there, then. But I gotta warn you. Somethin' big's in the wind."

"Oh?"

"Felt I should warn you. You might get caught up in it."

"In what?"

"Somethin' big."

"Well. Would that be bad?"

She smiled enigmatically. Still a nice smile, despite the otherwise physically grotesque person it belonged to. "Not if you like money."

"I like money."

"Well, wherever my boys go, there's money to be had. I got good boys who work hard, Jimmy. You looking to make an extra dollar?"

"Sure."

She winked at me. "You'll do no better than to stick with my boys."

"You seem proud of them."

"Couldn't be prouder. So—do I have me a chauffeur?" She said it like 'show fer.'

"It'd be my honor. I even have a car . . ."

"What kind?"

That stopped me.

"Chevy coupe," I said.

She shook her head. "Won't do, won't do." She got up and clomped over to a chest of drawers against one wall. She pulled open a drawer and it was brimming with cash. She counted out a stack and trundled over and handed it to me.

"There's six hundred," she said. "See if you can't get a nice used twelve-cylinder Auburn. With a radio. I'm partial to twelve-cylinder Auburns with radios."

I put the fat wad of cash in my suitcoat pocket as she went back and closed the drawer.

I said, "When would you like to leave?"

"Tomorrow afternoon soon enough? Like to pack my bags, and take in a movie s'evenin'—I just love the movies, and when I'm out on the road with my boys I sometimes go *weeks* without a movie. Or bingo, or anything civilized. But a mother's got to make sacrifices for her boys, don't you know?"

I said I knew, and told her I'd pick her up the next day at one.

She walked me to the door, her arm linked in mine; gave me a pat on the cheek. Her fingers were cold and soft.

"You seem like a nice boy," she said. "You gone always to be good to your ol' Ma, now, ain't you?"

I said I'd do my best.

Then I went out and bought a used twelve-cylinder Auburn. With a radio.

The next afternoon I was tooling up Highway 19 through McHenry County—its green rolling hills interspersed with rich farmland, lakes and the occasional gravel pit—behind the wheel of the nicest automobile I ever sat in. Though only a '32, the Auburn had quite a few miles on her, which had helped me land the sporty two-seater (we were keeping the top up today) at a reasonable price. It was just the kind of automobile every man dreams of owning, to impress the girl riding next to him. Unfortunately the "girl" next to me had more miles on her than the Auburn.

She was wearing a hat that fit snugly on her skull, like something an aviator might wear, only floral. Her baggy dress was an off-white with light purple flowers that clashed with the hat and the snow-white seat cushions. Of course, she was sitting on a cushion of her own, an air cushion that boosted her up so she could peer out the windows; even with the air cushion, she was so squat she barely rose above the dash. Right now she was leaning forward, turning the tuning dial of the Motorola radio built under the dash, the needle on its little round face spinning like a hand on an out-of-control clock, as she desperately searched for hillbilly music.

"The music this radio gets is just plain lousy," she said, turning off Bing Crosby singing "Where the Blue of the Night Meets the Gold of the Day." There was an accusatory note in Kate Barker's voice, as if had I been more careful in picking out this particular vehicle, I might have been able to get one that played "That Silver-Haired Daddy of Mine" continuously.

But we'd been through all that when I picked her up, around 1:00 P.M., at the Pine Grove apartment. She'd taken a look at the Auburn coupe I'd arrived in and made a face like a displeased five-year-old.

"You bought a two-seater!" she said, standing on the sidewalk, a bag in either hand, romance and movie magazines stuffed under one arm, oversize purse under the other. "I wanted a touring sedan!"

I was standing alongside the car, leaning against the fender; it was as supple as a pretty girl's hip. Shrugging, I said, "You said a twelve-cylinder Auburn. With a radio, which this has. I had to call all over town to find a used one, and had to pitch an extra hundred bucks in at that."

She frowned at me, then frowned at the Auburn. "We got a big family. We need more than two seats."

"You also need more than one car. Look, I was just trying to get what you asked me to get, Ma."

She shook her head vigorously. "And I like black. That's blue."

She was right: it was as blue as Sally Rand's eyes.

I said, "I can't take it back—it's a used car: 'All Sales Final.'"

"Well . . . it is an Auburn V-Twelve. I do like my Auburn V-Twelves."

"With a radio, don't forget. I was lucky to find one that way."

"Well, all right."

I put her suitcases in the trunk. "Could I have that extra hundred I had to give?"

"You'll get it," she snapped, and went around to the driver's side and waited for me to open the door for her. I did.

Once we'd got outside of Chicago a ways, into the farm country, her spirits perked up, even if she couldn't find any hillbilly music on the radio.

"Goodie goodie!" she said, clapping her fat little hands together, a romance magazine open on her lap.

"What?" I said. I was concentrating on my driving; despite being a two-seater, the Auburn was a big car, much bigger than my Chevy coupe, and it drove a little like a barge. On the other hand, it was fast. I had to work to keep it down at fifty. My Chevy shimmied like your sister Kate when I went a mile over fifty.

She was saying, "He had the ring . . ."

"What?"

"He had the flat . . ."

"Huh?"

"But she felt his chin . . ."

"You okay?"

"And that was that!" She turned her face toward me and that ungodly flabby pan split in a smile. "Burma Shave!"

"Oh," I said, and went back to my driving.

From then on she was on the lookout. There must've been an industrious Burma Shave advance man working this territory, because the little signs, spaced a hundred feet or so apart, seemed to pop up every few miles, like wooden weeds.

And it kept Ma busy.

"Your beauty boys . . . is just skin deep . . . what skin you got . . . you ought to keep. Haw haw! Burma Shave!"

She did have a faint mustache on her upper lip; maybe she was a potential customer . . .

I was still wearing the window-glass wire-rim spectacles and straw hat, but today I had on a brown suit, as well as my automatic in a shoulder holster. I hadn't carried the gun in a while, and it felt heavy under my arm; made me uncomfortable. For one thing, if I got stopped by a state cop for speeding (and with this Auburn under me, with a mind of its own toward how fast it wanted to go, that was possible) I would have some embarrassing questions to answer—like why I was carrying a driver's license under James Lawrence's name, when this gun was registered to somebody called Nathan Heller. And for another thing, I just plain didn't like carrying guns.

Barney had noticed the gun this morning; I hadn't been wearing the straw hat and eyeglasses, but I was in the brown suit and the gun in the shoulder sling bulged a little. Like Little New York said, I couldn't afford a tailor as good as his.

"Is that what I think it is?" he said, frowning, nodding toward my left arm. He was waiting for his turn, shooting pool with a couple of his sparring partners. I'd gone looking for Barney in the small gym in the traveler's lounge at the Morrison Hotel, and when I hadn't found him, had gone next door to Mussey's, and had.

Mussey's was a pool, billards and bowling hall next door to the Morrison and was a major meeting place for the sporting fraternity. Theatrical celebrities mingled with those of the boxing, baseball and racing world, as well as a certain number of con men and racketeers. The second floor was where billiards and pool ruled the day, and that was where I'd found Barney.

I admitted to him that I was heeled.

He shook his head, taking his turn; missed his shot. His sparring partners chuckled—they had to grab the occasional victory over Barney here, because in the ring they didn't have a prayer.

"I don't like it when you pack that thing," he said, uneasily, nodding toward the bulge under my arm. "Pallbearin' ain't my idea of a good time, you know."

"If you feel that way about it," I said, smiling gently, "don't come to my goddamn funeral."

"Jesus, Nate, can't you find a better business to get in?"

"I hate it when Jews say 'Jesus.' It confuses me."

"Nobody likes a wise guy," he said, grinning in spite of himself, and took his turn. Made the first shot, missed the second. One of the sparring partners elbowed the other one and they traded sideways grins.

"Seriously," he said, "why don't you find some other business? I could probably use you on my staff—"

"Christ, you and Sally! Nobody likes my trade, everybody wants to put me to work as their fuckin' maid or something."

Barney put an arm around me. "I hate it when half-Jews say 'Christ.' It confuses me. But you can say 'fuck' all you want. That don't confuse me in the least."

"Is that what I am, half a Jew?"

"Yeah, and half a Mick, and full of shit. That's Nate Heller. Now, get outa here while I try to catch up with these guys."

"Before you blow your next shot, let me tell you why I looked you up this morning."

"Tell."

"I'm going to be out of town awhile, and you're going to have to cover for me, where my night watchman duty's concerned. Okay?"

"Sure," he nodded. "How long you be gone?"

"Not sure," I said.

"What's up, exactly?"

"Looking for a girl," I said.

One of the sparring partners said, "Who ain't?"

Barney said, "Don't get killed or anything, okay, shmuck?"

"Okay, pal. Don't you have a fight in a few weeks?"

"More like a month," he said, bending to shoot.

"That's a unique way of training you got there," I said, and he missed his shot.

"The game laws ought . . . to let you shoot . . . the bird that hands you . . . a substitute! Haw haw!" Ma Barker grinned at me. "Burma Shave!"

There wasn't much to say to that; I just kept driving. We were well into the afternoon, now, and Wisconsin. Taking Highway 89, which had just turned from nice spanking-new pavement into gravel. I kept the Auburn at forty-five. Somehow, even though this wasn't my car (except for a hundred bucks' worth of it, anyway), I hated to think of those shapely blue fenders getting nicked by those wicked little rocks.

I hadn't done much cross-country driving, and, on these two-lane highways, each oncoming car we encountered made for a nerve-racking experience. The Auburn was wide enough, and the roads narrow enough, to make meeting the occasional road hog border on meeting your Maker. This was heightened by Kate Barker's humming hymns, something she did whenever she couldn't find hillbilly music on the radio or a Burma Shave sign to read.

"On a hill far away," she bellowed suddenly, "stood an old rugged cross . . ."

"Burma Shave," I said.

She glared at me; we weren't getting along as well today as yesterday. "That's disreligious," she said.

"I suppose it is."

"What church do you go to?"

"None to speak of, Ma."

She tsk-tsked. "That's very sad. Very sad."

"I suppose it is, Ma."

"You're sure to fry in eternal hell, you know."

"I'll have company."

"What do you mean by that?"

"Nothing. Look up ahead."

"Oooooh!" she squealed. "The bearded lady . . . tried a jar . . . she's now a famous . . . movie star! Burma Shave! Haw haw!"

Sally hadn't been crazy about my leaving on this little jaunt. In fact, she'd been downright angry.

"You really disappoint me, Nate. Really disappoint me!"

We were sitting at her breakfast table having coffee.

"Why is that, Helen?"

"I just thought you were smarter than—than to behave in such a *suicidal* fashion!"

"Suicidal."

"Going out among those . . . crazy maniacs!"

"Most maniacs are a little crazy."

"Right—like you!"

I'd made a big mistake: with the exception of Frank Nitti's role and the Jimmy Lawrence cover, I'd told Sally the whole story—the farmer's daughter in the clutches of the Barker gang, and how I was going undercover to bring her back alive, as Frank Buck would say.

"Don't you see what you're doing?"

"Yeah, I think so. A job."

"You're trying to . . . redeem yourself, in some childish way. You've been feeling so goddamn sorry for yourself, for the way you were used in the Dillinger shooting, that you're looking for some way to build your self-respect back up. So you take on this ridiculous case! You go out among killers and thieves and risk your life for a few dollars, just to play knight and save the fair damsel-in-distress! Shit, you've gone *simple* on me."

"Helen, it's not just a few dollars. It's the first real money I've seen all year, outside of that reward money."

"I don't see you denying you've gone simple."

"I've always been just a simple soul. That's what's so adorable about me."

"Don't butter me up, you louse. *Damn*, this makes me mad! You ought to go running back to that—that little actress of yours in Holly-wood—this is just her style . . . this is just the sort of romantic bull-shit she'd fall for. Why don't you call her on the phone, Heller—my treat! Long distance, person to person, Hollywood. My treat—my pleasure!"

I didn't say anything.

Sally sighed; stirred her coffee absently. Then she looked up with wet eyes. "I'm sorry I said that."

I sipped my coffee.

"I shouldn't have mentioned her, should I?"

I shook my head no.

"It still hurts you, doesn't it? Losing her."

"Ever talk to an amputee?"

That startled her.

She said, "Not really."

"Well, they say the worst thing about losing an arm, a leg, is that sometimes you can still feel it there. Even though it's been cut off. In the night, for example, it itches sometimes. The limb that's been cut off."

"You are a sentimental dope, aren't you, Heller?"

"Takes one to know one, Helen."

A tear was gliding down her smooth, round right cheek. "Well, then, you sentimental dope, why don't you mount your white horse and go riding off after your damn damsel. Shit! Why don't you mount the nearest damsel instead . . . let's go back to bed . . ."

"Let's," I said.

Later, she touched my shoulder and said, "I don't know if I want to see you, when you get back."

"Oh?"

"Maybe I want to let go of you now, so that . . . if something happens to you, it won't hurt so bad."

"It's up to you, Sally."

She looked hurt. "You called me Sally."

"So I did. I'll call you Helen again, if you let me back in, when this is over."

She wept as I held her; when I left, later that morning, she was mad again. Not speaking.

"Beneath this stone . . . lies Elmer Gush . . . tickled to death . . . by a shavin' brush! Haw haw! Burma Shave."

"Beaver Falls," I said.

"Huh?" Kate Barker said.

"That's Beaver Falls, up ahead."

We were on U.S. Highway 151, now, and it entered the little town along a shady street where two-story clapboard houses with front porches with pillars and swings, wide windows and pointed roofs, sat on big lawns, looking prosperous unless you noticed how many of them needed painting. We glided through the downtown, where the trees disappeared in favor of electric posts, and two-story brick buildings stared each other down on either side of Front Street—hardware store, boot shop, floral shop, tavern, J. C. Penney, movie house.

Ma turned around in her seat, as we passed, straining to look back. "What's playin'? What's playin'?"

"Huh?"

"At the movie house!"

"Oh." I looked back; winced when I saw what it was. "*Manhattan Melodrama*," I said.

"Oh," she said, disappointed. "I seen that. I like Clark Gable, but not when he dies at the end."

About four miles outside of Beaver Falls was a farm, the mailbox prominently marked GILLIS. I slowed and turned in the gravel drive. Chickens scooted out of my way. Over to the right was the two-story farmhouse, pretty good size, a swing on the pillared front porch, wide curtained windows, pointed gabled roof, much like the houses in

Beaver Falls, only no curling paint. At the left and curving back behind the house were several other structures, among them an un-
painted tool shed, a pump with windmill tower, a faded red barn, a
silo.

There were no other autos around; I got out of the Auburn, went
around and opened the door for Kate Barker. The lawn and house
were fenced in with unbarbed wire, and a few pine trees were spread
about the lawn in an undiscernible pattern, providing shade. Up on
the porch of the house, the door opened and a small man in a
rumpled white shirt and equally rumpled brown pants came down
the steps quickly and Ma moved toward him.

"Arthur, Arthur," Ma said hugging him to her; he was sort of stocky
himself, but she still seemed to smother him, slapping him on the
back. His hands clung loosely to her back, but he was glad to see her,
too, saying, "Ma, gee, Ma, it's good to see you . . ."

I was getting her bags out of the back when another small figure, in
a white shirt and a bow tie and a dark unbuttoned vest and gray
baggy pants, came bolting down the steps, feet making a clapping
sound. The chickens on the lawn scattered. He had a tommy gun
slung over his arm and I swallowed as he approached and pointed it
at me. I felt like joining the other chickens.

"Who the hell are you?" he said. He sounded like Jimmy Cagney
and I wondered if it was on purpose, maybe to offset his boyish features.

"I'm Jimmy Lawrence," I said.

"Oh yeah?"

"Yeah. Who are you?"

"Don't you know?" He laughed, like I was the dumbest shit he
ever saw. He pointed a thumb back at himself. "I'm Big George."

"Big George?"

"Nelson!" he said.

Baby Face Nelson said.

29

Ma let loose of her boy Arthur long enough to call out to Nelson: "He's from Chicago."

Nelson manufactured a sneer, over which the faint beginnings of a mustache were more threat than promise. "So am I. So what?"

"I'm here on an errand," I said, "for Frank Nitti."

The sneer faded, and he blinked. "Am I supposed to be impressed?"

"No," I said.

Ma and Arthur wandered over. Arm in arm. She said, "I called and checked on him."

Without taking his pale blue eyes off me, Nelson said to her, "Did you check with Nitti?"

"No. I called Slim."

"Slim Gray?"

"Yeah, and he said this guy was jake."

He thumped my chest three times with the side of the tommy-gun barrel. "I don't care if he's jake—I just want to know if he's Jimmy whosis."

"Lawrence," I said, stopping the barrel of the tommy gun with my palm, before it could thump me a fourth time.

Nelson's eyes flared. "Don't touch my gun."

"Then don't poke me with it."

"Yeah? Well, fuck you."

"I got no beef with you, Nelson. But I'm not going to stand here and be bullied and just take it, understand?"

The tommy-gun nose lowered; chickens were making noise in the background. He said, "I got no beef with you, either, Lawrence—if you're from Nitti. If you're a goddamn fed, you're fuckin' dead."

Arthur stepped forward and put a hand on Nelson's arm; both men were about the same size, but Arthur "Doc" Barker had haunted brown eyes and rather sunken cheeks in a baby face of his own, black

ARTHUR "DOC" BARKER

widow's peaked hair starting high on his forehead, and my instinct
was he was more dangerous than Nelson.

"Watch your language around my ma," Doc Barker said, in a flat
monotone that, unlike Nelson's Cagney impression, was menacing
without trying to be.

Nelson shook the hand off irritably, but said, "Yeah—okay. Okay."

I said, "You really think a fed would be smart enough to get this
far?"

Nelson thought about that, while Doc grinned and said, "Hell no!"

Ma was trundling across the lawn toward the porch, stacks of movie
and romance magazines under her flabby arms, leaving the bags for
the boys to carry.

"Somebody want to help me with Ma's things?" I asked.

They both did, Nelson still lugging his tommy gun; it was like an
appendage.

Inside the front door we faced the second-floor stairs; a hallway
alongside the stairs ended in a closed door. To our left was a sitting
room, with a piano and a fireplace and some overstuffed furniture but
no people. To our right an archway where floral drapes stood open
and fluttered with the summer breeze coming in open windows in
the living room beyond. Doc Barker nodded for me to set the bags by
the stairs—"We'll work out sleepin' quarters later," he said—and I
followed him into the living room, which was larger than the sitting
room and just as nicely furnished—but well-populated.

At the left, against the wall with a mirror hanging over it, was an
overstuffed bristly cream-color mohair sofa on which sat three
women, all of them rather attractive. On the near end of the sofa a
cute brunette with wavy hair falling to her shoulders and bright dark
perky eyes was smiling up at Nelson, who stood next to her, putting a
possessive hand on her shoulder, letting me know this one was his. I
could hardly blame him—even though she was sitting down, it was
easy to see she had a nice little shape on her, under the thin beige
frock, legs crossed under the pleated skirt. On the other end of the
sofa was another brunette, with eyes the color of the dark liquid in
the glass she held in one hand and a slightly puffy face that indicated
the dark liquid wasn't Dr. Pepper; still, look of the alky about her or
not, this one was a looker too, with startling curves under the navy
dress with its white polka dots and white collar and white trim.

Between them was a blonde. She wore a pink dress and a little pink beret and she was the best-looking dame of the bunch, her hair bobbed and her eyes big and brown and so far apart you almost had to look at them one at a time. She had beestung lips and rosy cheeks and a complexion like a glass of milk—pasteurized.

The whites of her big brown eyes, however, seemed at the moment to match the pink of her outfit, and she was clutching a hanky in a tight little fist. She'd been crying, and the other two women— the one with the drink in her hand especially—seemed to be giving her some support, some comfort.

The pretty blonde with the bobbed hair and the big brown eyes was Joshua Petersen's Louise, incidentally. The girl I'd come to fetch.

While I was taking in these good-looking apparent molls, Ma Barker was hugging another of her boys, who'd been sitting on the window seat over by the open windows, but had jumped up upon his beloved mother's entry.

"Freddie, Freddie," she was saying, "my good little Freddie."

"Aw, Ma," he was saying. "Don't embarrass me!"

But he clearly loved her attention, grinning with a mouthful of gold, his head on her shoulder as she pressed him to her.

He pushed his mother aside, however, when he caught a glimpse of me.

He was wearing a white shirt and brown pants, was in his early thirties, short, shorter even than Nelson, sandy-haired, shifty-eyed, sunken-cheeked. He looked a lot like his brother Doc, but not as stocky.

"Who's this?" he said, nodding at me, his cheerfulness dropping away so completely it was hard to remember it'd ever been there.

Doc, standing beside me, pointed a thumb at me; we were just inside the doorway, the archway drapes whispering behind us. He said, "He drove Ma here from Chicago. She says he's here to see Doc Moran, for the Boys."

Fred frowned, said, "We don't like tyin' in with rackets guys."

I said, "That's not what they say in St. Paul."

The frown eased into something approaching a faint smile. "We don't like tyin' in with Chicago rackets guys. How long you intend stayin'?"

"Overnight okay? I could stay in town—"

"No!" Nelson said. He was still standing by the wall, next to the sofa and the perky brunette. "You'll stay *right here* till I say different."

I decided not to push Nelson in front of his girl. I said, "I'm your guest, so it'd be bad manners to do it any other way than yours."

Nelson smiled at that, smugly, and the little brunette beamed up at him; she was nuts about him. Maybe that perky look in her eyes meant she was a little nuts period.

Then Doc started introducing me around. "That's Helen, Big George's wife," he said, indicating Nelson and his brunette, "and the little lady with the big drink is my brother Fred's girl, Paula. That's Fred of course."

Fred nodded to me and I nodded back. Paula saluted me with her drink and gave me a sly, sexy smile and Fred frowned at her and she stuck her tongue out at him. I made like Buster Keaton.

I moved tentatively toward the sofa and Nelson lifted his head warily; but I wasn't approaching his wife. I stood in front of Louise and asked, "Who might you be?"

The big brown eyes blinked; pink tongue flicked out nervously over red beestung lips. She looked to each side of her, at each of the two women, as if asking if she should answer. As if she needed permission.

"This is Lulu," Doc answered for her. "Candy Walker's girl." He took me by the arm and pulled me gently away, buttonholed me. "She's out of sorts at the moment," he whispered, "'cause her boyfriend's getting carved up in the kitchen."

"Huh?"

He gestured to his face. "Plastic surgery. Her boyfriend's Candy Walker, and Candy's got pretty hot lately. Pictures in the paper, wanted circulars. You know. So he's getting his face done over. And Lulu's nervous about it. She don't like docs. Except me, of course. And I don't operate on anything but banks."

"I hear you're a regular surgeon," I said.

He liked that; when he smiled his lip curled up, like he was smelling something unpleasant. "I open 'em up and remove the money," he said. "Yeah. I'm a regular bank surgeon."

Fred wasn't listening to any of this, nor was Ma. She and her younger son were sitting on the window seat like a courting couple, Fred holding her hand and her looking moon-eyed at him, as they spoke in hushed tones.

Doc gestured to an overstuffed lounge chair opposite the sofa and bid me sit. I sat. He pulled a straight-back chair from someplace and sat near me.

"You been with the Boys long?"

"Just a year or so."

"Oh, yeah? Where you from, originally?"

Piece by piece, I fed him the Jimmy Lawrence background story: born in Canada, raised in NYC, union slugger, Lepke's boy, murder rap, plastic surgery, cooling off in Chicago.

From across the room, Nelson—sitting on the arm of the sofa next to his wife Helen—was sneering. He called out, "I'm checkin' up on you, Lawrence. Understand? I used to work for the Boys, you know. I'm going to make some calls."

I shrugged. "Fine."

He hopped off the arm of the sofa. "Maybe I should do that right now. Maybe I should drive into town and make those calls. . . ."

"Sure," I said.

Nelson stood there for a moment, then sat back on the arm of the sofa, one hand on his tommy gun, other on his wife's shoulder.

"This is a nice farmhouse," I said to Doc Barker. The furniture was all relatively new, and the walls seemed to have been papered recently, a pleasant pink-and-yellow floral pattern; the carpet that pretty much covered the oak floor was oriental. It clashed, but it wasn't cheap.

"It's a nice farmhouse," Doc agreed.

"Where are the owners?"

"Verle's out farming, where else? His wife and the two little boys are off at the store. We sort of sent them out, for while Doc Moran operated on Candy."

"I see. Why no phone? They can obviously afford one . . ."

"Party line," he said. "The Gillises do a lot of business here at the farm." By "business" he meant the place was used as a cooling-off joint, a hotel for outlaws on the run. He went on: "Can't do that kind of business over the phone—not when half the county's listening in."

"I see."

Suddenly, through the draped archway at left, emerged yet another attractive brunette, with a heart-shaped face, brown eyes and a generous figure filling out a stylish sand-color dress with a lace collar, her plump tummy pushing at the sheer fabric. The most distinctive thing about her right now, however, was her ashen face.

All eyes were on her.

Louise—Lulu—sat forward, but reared her head back, biting her knuckles; she was like a teenager watching a Dracula picture.

Doc stood. "Dolores—what is it? What's wrong?"

She swallowed. Covered her mouth with one hand, lowering her head. Then she raised her eyes and said, softly, "The bastard's killed him."

Louise screamed.

Doc walked over to Dolores. "Candy's . . . ?"

"Dead," she said.

Doc moved quickly through the archway.

I thought for a moment, then followed; nobody tried to stop me. Louise, however, was being held back by the two women beside her.

In the kitchen—a big country kitchen with enormous cabinet and sink with pump and old-fashioned stove and an oak icebox—spread out on the long kitchen table like an enormous Christmas turkey, was a man, naked to his waist; his face was rather handsome and very blue.

On the stove in the background a teakettle whistled, as if scolding somebody.

That somebody just might have been the tall, rather distinguished-looking man of about forty, dark hair streaked with gray, who stood near the corpse with forceps in a trembling hand. Eyes under shaggy, twisting eyebrows looked right at me—they were dark and rheumy—and, as if he'd known me all his life, he said to me, "Poor beggar swallowed his tongue. I pulled it up with these"—he meant the forceps—"and tried artificial respiration on him, but he died. He just died."

"Shit," Doc Barker said. "I tried to talk him out of this, you goddamn quack. Face-lift my ass. What good did you do Old Creepy and Freddie?"

Snootily, as if forgetting the dead man stretched out before him, Moran said, "They seem satisfied."

"You'll never put the knife to me, quack. Shit! You killed him."

Moran put the forceps away, in the standard medical black bag which was on the table next to the corpse. "An unfortunate, an unavoidable . . . mishap."

Then, behind me, a woman was in the doorway, screaming. Louise.

"Candy!" She pushed past me and flung herself across the half-naked corpse. "My candyman . . . oh my candyman . . ." Tears streamed down her face.

"You bloody butcher!"

It was Nelson pushing past me this time, tommy gun still slung over one arm.

The little man grabbed the doctor by the shirtfront and lifted him off the floor and tossed him bodily into the icebox, with a clatter. Moran slid to the floor, sat there for a moment, then stood and brushed himself off, raised his head, dignity preserved.

"My good man," he said to Nelson, "I did not even *touch* Mr. Walker. I merely adminstered the ether"—he pointed to a wadded towel on the table—"I did not begin cutting. You will notice not a single drop of blood in this room."

"Not yet," Nelson said.

"Your threats fail to concern me," the doctor said. "My services to you—you *people*, in so many ways, are I should think invaluable. The occasional . . . slip-up, well. That can't be helped."

There was a back door, a kitchen door, and Dr. Joseph P. Moran walked to it rather grandly, and exited. Nelson looked out the window.

"He's getting in his car," he said.

Doc Barker said, "Going into town to drink and chase the skirts, no doubt."

Fred Barker, who'd entered after Nelson, said, "He already smells like a brewery. I think he went into this operation soused."

"I'm going after him." Nelson patted the machine gun.

Doc thought about that, then nodded. "You can make those phone calls and check up on our friend Lawrence here, while you're at it."

Nelson glanced at me. "Good idea. Why don't you ride along with me, Lawrence. Maybe we can get to know each other better."

"Why not?" I said.

Dolores was moving Louise away from the corpse; Louise was sobbing, the little pink beret dangling at an odd angle, about to fall off any second. Fred Barker's girl Paula came in with the sheet she'd got from somewhere and covered Candy Walker up.

"Who's going to take care of me now?" Louise asked. "Who's going to take care of Lulu now?"

She was looking right at me when she asked it, but I didn't answer. Her little pink beret fell off and I bent and handed it to her.

Then Ma Barker was standing in the kitchen doorway, hands on her hips.

"Wrap him up and put him somewheres," she said. "It's after six and I want to start supper."

Louise shrieked, but while Paula comforted her, Fred and Helen and Dolores, as detached as meat-packers, wrapped the blue-faced body in the sheet and carried him out of the house, into the barn.

Ma Barker was scrubbing the kitchen table down, humming a hymn, when I went out the back door to go into town with Baby Face Nelson.

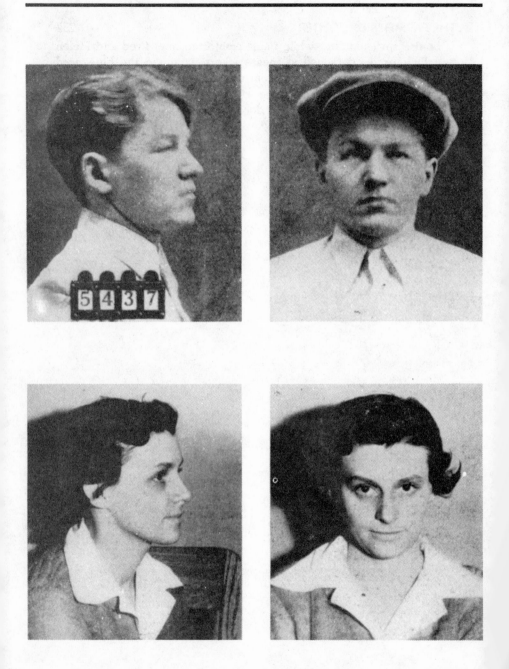

"BABY FACE" NELSON AND HIS WIFE HELEN

30

Something odd happened on the four-mile drive into Beaver Falls. Nelson acted civil toward me.

I have no explanation, other than possibly the lack of an audience, prompting him to abandon, at least temporarily, his Cagney pose. Or perhaps it was his having to leave the tommy-gun appendage behind, settling for a modest .45 Army Colt stuck in his waistband. But as we rode in the Auburn, with me at the wheel, top down, he smoked a cigar, leaned back, relaxed, and shared his insights into Doc Moran with me.

"You know," he said, blowing smoke out easily, sun low in the sky and streaming through the cornfields as we whisked by, "Candy Walker was a fuckin' chump to let that drunken sawbones near 'im in the first place."

"Really?" I said. I took one hand off the wheel and pushed the window-glass wire-frames up on my nose.

"Sure. When you get back, get a load of Freddie Barker's fingertips. The doc did a scraping on them last spring. You know how this genius surgeon goes about that?" He grinned, cigar atilt, gesturing with both hands, relishing the gore he was about to describe. "He loops rubber bands around their fingers, at the first joint. Then he sticks a hypo of morphine in each fingertip—how's that for laughs? Then starts scraping. With a scapel, like he's sharpening a pencil." Nelson laughed, a high-pitched giggle like a kid. "Really carves the ol' meat off. Ha ha ha!"

"Did the operation take?"

Nelson smirked, the wispy beginnings of his mustache riffling in the breeze like fringe on a curtain. "A couple of Freddie's fingers got infected—one thumb swelled up like a blimp. They took him to a vet and got 'im some medicine, but he was burning up with fever for about a week."

"But did the operation take?"

Nelson laughed again, same high-pitched giggle, blew out cigar smoke in a fat circle. "Take a look at his fingertips when we get back. You'll see."

I knew what I'd see. I'd never seen a fingerprint job that *had* taken; in every case I knew of, the telltale whorls stubbornly returned, forming patterns still discernible, if streaked with scar tissue.

"He's got a big mouth, too, the doc. Comes in town and boozes and chases the local gash. Of course he knows better than to even *look* at one of *our* women." He gave me a sideways glance that let me know that was a warning partially directed at me. "But Verle and Mildred got a nice thing going, usin' the farmhouse as a cooling-off joint and all, so we got to be careful around the locals. Don't need no drunken sawbones spillin' his guts to every hunk of quiff he meets."

"Why do the Barkers put up with him?"

The wind blowing as we sped along put Nelson's cigar out; he relit it, shrugging. "Like the old bastard himself said, he's useful. He did do some face-lifts that turned out, well . . . okay. Like on O.C."

"O.C.?"

"Old Creepy. Karpis. Oh, yeah, you ain't met him yet. He went to town with Mildred and her boys. Dolores is his broad. Hell of a guy. He's from Chicago, too, from the back o' the yards, like me. Hell, you're from Chicago. Maybe you met him?"

"I only been in Chicago a year or so."

"Oh yeah—you're from out East."

Was he trying to be cute, fishing like that? Or just making conversation? Maybe Nelson was more complex—and more intelligent—than I'd first given him credit for.

I said, "So Moran gave Karpis a face-lift?"

"Yeah—a pretty good one. O.C. didn't have no earlobes, and that's the kind of thing that sticks out on a wanted circular. And Moran did manage to fix him up with something that's more or less like lobes. And O.C. had a busted nose since he was a kid and Moran straightened that. And tightened his face up. But his face is real scarred along his cheek by his ear. Both cheeks, I mean."

"But it served its purpose, the face-lift."

Nelson shrugged again. "I guess. I think O.C.'s changed his looks more from combing his hair straight back and wearing glasses than from what Moran done, but he seems satisfied. Enough that Walker wanted a face-lift, too. Big sacrifice for a ladies' man like Walker to let that doc carve on his puss." He laughed again, one short guttural laugh, but still high-pitched. "Well, he's a ladies' man in hell, now."

We were coming up on Beaver Falls, now. Maple trees and two-story clapboards.

"I still don't get it," I said. "Why does Moran act like he's so invaluable? There's plenty of underworld docs around, doing first-rate face-lifts." I took a hand off the wheel to gesture alongside my right ear. "See any scars on my face?"

"No," Nelson admitted. "But Moran's been valuable to the Barkers and Karpis in a lot of ways. I shouldn't have to tell you he's connected to the Chicago Boys, which can come in handy. And other ways."

"Such as?"

Another shrug, another cocky puff of the cigar. "He was fencing hot money for 'em. He handled the Bremer ransom."

"I thought that was Boss McLaughlin's piece of work."

"Him and Moran."

"But the feds got McLaughlin, didn't they?"

Like that other hot-money fence, James Probasco, ward-heeler McLaughlin had been hung by his heels from the Banker's Building by the feds, seeking a third-degree confession; he hadn't talked, but he was facing five years in Leavenworth anyway. He was still better off than Probasco, who as you may recall when similarly dangled did a dive into the cement court of the Rookery Building nineteen stories below.

Nelson continued. "The feds got McLaughlin, yeah—but he didn't talk. And Moran still has fencing connections. Plus, like he's always remindin' us—he knows where the bodies are buried."

"I see."

"Pull in there," Nelson said, motioning to a parking place in front of a store called Hubbell's.

We left the Auburn at the curb and Nelson, his coat buttoned over his waistband, where the .45 was tucked, smiled and tipped his hat at a fat farm housewife with a faded brownish-blond marcel and a pretty little girl with corn-yellow hair in tow. The fat farm housewife and the little girl both smiled and the housewife said, "You're Verle's relation, aren't you?"

"Yes ma'am."

"We could all use some rain for the corn."

"We surely could, ma'am."

The mother and daughter walked on by, and we went into Hubbell's, whose store window was a display of fishing rods, and the narrow, yellow-painted interior proved to be a hardware store of sorts in

front—hammers and nails, fishing rods, a wall display of jackknives—
and a bar in back, with three side booths.

"This is where Verle picks up his messages," Nelson said, sotto
voce, behind a hand.

"Interesting place."

Nelson smirked. "Half hardware store, half bar. Ever seen the
like?"

"Nothing better, if you're in the mood for a claw hammer and a
shot of whiskey."

Moran was down at the far end of the bar, bending over a bottle of
bourbon and a tall glass, giving what was left of his attention, after
the bourbon got done with it, to a busty corn-fed barmaid of twenty-
five or so with short curly strawberry-blond hair, wearing a white
apron over a red-and-white checked housedress, looking very homey,
wiping the bar with a rag while she smiled and listened to Moran's
smoothest line of bull. He was selling her a shopworn matinee-idol
smile, gesturing with the hand that wasn't wrapped around the tall
glass. If this was a movie, John Barrymore would play him and Joan
Blondell her.

A man of about fifty was working the counter in the front, hardware
half of the store; he had thinning blond hair and a shovel jaw and a
disgusted look.

"Can't you keep your friend away from my daughter?" he asked
Nelson.

Nelson said, "Sorry, Kurt. You shouldn't oughta let her tend bar, if
you don't want her meetin' men."

With tight anger, Kurt said, "Just because she's divorced don't
mean she's loose."

"Did I say that? Anything for Verle?"

"Nothin'."

"Can I use the phone?"

Still disgusted, Kurt nodded, and Nelson went behind the counter;
he nodded to me, then toward Moran. I got the picture.

I went down and sat by Moran.

He turned and cast his rheumy gaze upon me. He was wearing a
dark suit with a dark tie and a dark vest; it wasn't as hot a day as we'd
been having, and there were fans going in here, so he wasn't sweating, and looked very professional, very proper. If a little tanked.

"Do I know you, young man?"

"I'm staying out at the Gillises. I walked in on the last act of your latest operation."

He lifted an eyebrow, placing me, then nodded gravely, but I could tell Candy Walker's death didn't mean a damn to him; he'd seen too many outlaw and gangster patients die to be too concerned. And, in his defense, they were lucky to have him, often working under unsanitary conditions in cellars and hotel rooms, patching up hoodlums who could go nowhere else but to a "right croaker" like him for the tending of a bullet wound that would *not* get reported to the police, or to bring him a knocked-up moll or prostie so he could "pull a rabbit," or to fix a too-familiar face, or what-have-you. The underworld needed its Doc Morans.

He offered his hand. "Joseph P. Moran. Doctor."

"I know. I'm Jimmy Lawrence."

He had a strong grip, but his hand was trembling. Whether from drink, fear or palsy, I couldn't tell you.

The strawberry-blond strudel behind the counter started moving down the bar with the rag, and Moran called out to her, "Don't leave, my dear! We've so much else to discuss."

She smiled at him, a pixie smile in a prettily plump face, and said, "There's always later, Doctor."

"A misnomer, my dear. As my former patient, Candy Walker, may now realize . . . 'later' is a commodity that can prove rare indeed."

She didn't understand that, so she giggled at it, and moved on down the bar, where a scruffy, apparently unemployed gentleman in coveralls had found a quarter to spend.

I suggested we move to a booth, and Dr. Moran agreed, taking glass and bottle along.

"Why are you here, young man?" he asked, pouring himself some bourbon, though his tall glass was already half full. "Getting hot for you elsewhere? Perhaps you've heard of my services. Not cheap, but well worth the price, I assure you. Now, don't be put off by that unfortunate mishap with Mr. Walker. A one-in-a-thousand occurrence, a freak happenstance, a medical misfortune of the rarest order."

"No. No thanks . . ."

"What you need," he said, narrowing his eyes, holding his thumb up to his eye like an artist measuring distance, "is a good surgeon. I, myself, was an honor student, a young physician with a distinguished career ahead of me, when I ran afoul of fate. But that's my story, and what we're concerned with here is *yours*. Afraid of the authorities, are you? Well, you can go *anywhere* without worrying, after I've done a lift job on that face of yours. I'll alter that nose—some Jewish blood in the line? Not to worry—change the shape of it entirely. And lift those cheeks, pull 'em up tight, even in a young fella like you it makes a difference . . ."

"Doctor . . ."

"I can change the expression of your eyes. I can raise those eyebrows . . ."

They were already raised.

" . . . take the sag out of your mouth. Your family, your best friends? They'll never know you. And let's see those hands—I can get rid of those bothersome fingerprints with the easiest, nearly painless little operation . . ."

"I already had a lift, Doctor."

He drew his head back; reached in an inside coat pocket and took out some wire-rim glasses and looked at me close. "I say. Outstanding job. Who did it?"

"None of your business."

He smiled, looking as sophisticated as a John Held, Jr., drawing. "Quite the proper answer, in your line of work. I have no difficulty with that answer whatsoever. Say! You have nothing to drink—we'll remedy that—my dear! I prescribe alcohol for this young gentleman!"

The nicely chubby strawberry blonde walked over like an advertisement for making babies. I ordered a beer.

"Healthy lass," he said, watching her go, almost licking his lips. "Good bone structure, beneath that well-placed beef. Ah—farm country. A rest in the country is just what I've needed, of late. By the way, what *does* bring you into the company of such notables as our friend Baby Face Nelson? An appellation, I might add, one might best refrain from using to the little weasel's face."

"Actually, Doctor," I said, "I'm here to see you."

"Me? Why, I'm honored, Mr. Lawrence. What brings you here to see me?"

"Frank Nitti."

He swallowed, and he didn't have a mouthful of liquor, either. The blood drained out of his face.

"He'd like you to come back to Chicago," I said.

"Young man, I'm afraid that's impossible."

"Why?"

"Because I'm in the process of . . . relocating."

"I heard you were well-connected."

"Perhaps you're aware of my dealings with one 'Boss' McLaughlin?"

"Just vaguely."

"He suggested I dispose of certain funds—certain *warm* funds—by doling it out, a few dollars at time, to some of my patrons . . . if you follow me."

"You mean, some of Nitti's people were passed hot money?"

"Indelicately put, but true. In small amounts, Mr. McLaughlin thought the bills would cause little trouble. For his efforts he's facing a penitentiary term. As for me, well . . . an emissary from Mr. Nitti passed me an envelope, shortly before I left the city. Do you know what was in that envelope, Mr. Lawrence?"

I said I didn't.

"Nothing much," he said, sipping his tall glass of bourbon. "Simply a single unfired round. A bullet. Do you understand that? Do you derive a meaning from that?"

It was a death sentence.

I said, "Perhaps Nitti would like to work it out with you."

"Did he say as much?"

"Not really. He just said to tell you that he wanted you to come back to Chicago. He had work for you."

"I see. Then I hardly understand why he bothered sending you—he'd know I wouldn't return with so little assurance of my safety." He looked at me as if he hadn't looked at me before. "Unless, of course, you're here to . . . but you don't look like a gunman. Then looks at times deceive. Take, for example, the childlike countenance of the gentleman approaching . . ."

I turned and saw Nelson swaggering toward us, a big grin riding his face. He scooted in on my side of the booth.

"I made a couple calls," he said to me. "You're okay, Lawrence." He put his hand out. "No hard feelins for the hard time I give you at the house?"

I shook the hand, said, "None."

"Good." He looked across at Moran. "I talked to some of your pals in Chicago. I talked to Slim Gray, for one."

"Alias Russell Gibson. I know him well. And how is Slim?"

"He says Frank Nitti wants you back in Chicago."

"People in hell want ice water," Moran said, and gulped the bourbon.

"Maybe you can serve it to 'em," Nelson said.

"You don't scare me, little man."

Nelson smiled at him; the muscle on his jaw was jumping. "That's fine. Finish your drink—time to go home."

"I'll return in my own good time. I have my own transportation."

"Fine. Drive your own car. But finish your drink, and do it now."

The blood flowed back into Moran's face till it was crimson. He half-stood in the booth, leaned forward and waved the glass, the bourbon sloshing around in it, all but shouting as he said, "Don't threaten *me*, Baby Face. Who do you think you're crowding? Think I'm afraid of you—or any of that mob?" He stretched his free hand out and held it palm open, cupped. "I have you—all of your crowd— in the hollow of my hand. Right here! In the hollow of my hand."

Back behind the bar, the plump strawberry blonde looked scared; her father, Kurt, was standing near her, expressionless, but looking our way.

Moran sat back down. "One word from me, Baby Face—and your goose is *cooked*. Understand? Cooked."

Nelson, jaw muscle throbbing, leaned forward and patted Moran on the arm, soothingly, while the doctor stared into the blackness of the bourbon.

"There, there, Doc," Nelson said, "don't talk that way about your pals. We're on your side. Aren't we, Jimmy?"

I nodded.

"You're a great guy, Doc. Just a little tight right now. Now, can you drive back yourself? Or would you like one of us to drive you?"

"I can drive myself."

"Okay. When you're ready, come on back to the farmhouse."

"Well. I'm ready, now."

"Good. Come along, then."

"I'll drive myself."

"Fine."

The doctor stood, moved slowly away from the booth. We followed him out onto the street. It was dusk, now.

Nelson smiled at him as we went toward the Auburn. From the sidewalk he called out to us.

"Don't forget!" Moran said, walking unsteadily, pointing a shaky finger at us. "I know where the bodies are buried. I know where the bodies are buried. . . ."

31

When we got back just after sundown, everybody (almost) was eating at the kitchen table. The table was covered with an oilcloth, and the oilcloth was covered with bowls of food. Fried chicken. Mashed potatoes. Gravy. Corn on the cob. Cottage cheese. Freshly chopped cabbage. Stacks of white bread. Pitchers of milk; slabs of butter. Biscuits the size of saucers. The smells in the room were warm and good. Around the table sat various public enemies and their molls, chowing down.

"Find a chair!" Ma said to us as we came in. In a calico apron that was too small for her, stocky Ma was milling around, refilling the bowls of food, keeping the chicken frying over at the stove, running the whole damn show. "Get it while it's hot!" She sounded like a newsie.

Nelson, Moran and I took three of the four empty places at the long table. The remaining place was for Louise, or Lulu as they called her here; she was, I thought, understandably absent.

No one bothered to make introductions, though there were several people at the table I hadn't seen before. Despite the fact that I'd seen a blue-faced corpse on this table an hour and a half ago or so, I found myself digging right in. I was hungry, the food smelled good, tasted better, and what can I say? Ma Barker was a hell of a cook.

As the meal wore on, I began finding out who the various people were. Quite obviously the lanky man of about forty in coveralls was Verle Gillis, owner of the place, pale blue eyes set in his weathered face like stones; and next to him, a few years younger, a heavyset woman with a sweet face and dark hair in a bun and sad dark eyes was his wife Mildred. Next to Mildred were two boys, one about eight, the other ten or eleven. But for the years between them, they could've been twins and had the father's lanky build and the mother's almost angelic face—without the sad eyes. The boys were well-behaved; the only talking they did was some whispering back and forth.

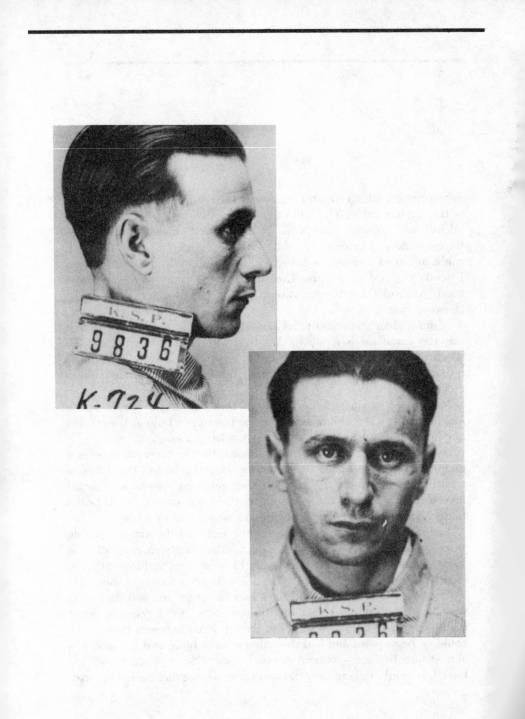

FRED BARKER

"I appreciate your hospitality, Mr. Gillis," I offered, after a while. I was working on a breast of chicken.

"Our pleasure, Mr. Lawrence. There'll be no charge for your stay, by the by."

"Well, that's very kind."

"Just remember us to Chicago."

"Well, uh, sure. Glad to."

Verle leaned toward his wife and whispered; she nodded, then said, "Mrs. Barker—I want to thank you kindly for preparing dinner."

"I enjoyed it," Ma said. She was finally sitting down and eating, starting her first plate when most of us were on our second or third. Doc Moran, however, seemed morose and was picking at his first.

Ma went on: "I apologize for taking over your kitchen like I done while you was gone. I just figured it was gettin' late and I should start 'er up."

Mildred said she was "happy" Ma had taken over; but I didn't think Mildred meant it.

Ma did, however, saying, "Well, I hope you'll let me pitch in again while I'm here. I just love cookin' for my boys."

Fred, sitting to one side of her (she was at the head of the table, of course), spoke through a mouthful of potatoes; what he seemed to say was, "Nice to have your good home cookin' again, Ma." Or something.

One by one everybody complimented Ma, and meant it—hurting Mildred's feelings, I thought—though Fred's girl Paula seemed to like the glass of liquor she had brought to the table more than the meal.

In the brightly lit kitchen I noticed for the first time just how hard the faces of the women were. These women—all of them naturally attractive, and well-groomed, if occasionally overly made up—were in their early twenties; but they had a hard, worn look that made them seem ten years older. But it was an oldness age didn't have anything to do with. A sixteen-year-old prostitute is old that way.

With the exception of Helen Nelson: She had a smooth, young face. Worry seemed never to have crossed her consciousness.

She and her husband flirted, giggling with each other, throughout the meal. It was as though they were newlyweds. Later I learned they had two kids and had been married for years.

Down at the other end of the table, opposite Ma, was a slight man in glasses with his hair combed back, with a tight mouth and gray, dead eyes. I'd been in the room fifteen minutes before he introduced himself, suddenly.

"I'm Karpis," he said.

I'd guessed that.

"The folks around here call me Old Creepy," he said. "I don't know why." And he smiled. It was a ghostly, ghastly smile. It was a smile a mean kid wore when pulling the wings off a bug. He was pulling part of the wing of a chicken off, at the moment.

"Or O.C.," Nelson corrected.

"Or O.C.," Karpis allowed. "I'll answer to that."

I nodded to him. "Glad to meet you, Karpis."

He held up a greasy hand. "We can shake hands later. I understand your name is Lawrence."

"That's right."

"From Chicago."

"As of now."

"And connected."

"Well, yeah."

"I've had dealings with the Chicago Boys before."

"Really."

"I'm not crazy about Chicago. A plain Kansas boy like me, I prefer the wide-open spaces. I like to be able to make a getaway through a field or a farmyard, down a dirt road, across a dry creek bed. In Chicago, the city—it's all asphalt and traffic and big buildings. Who needs it."

I swallowed a bite of mashed potatoes and gravy. "It's nice out here. I could be a convert to this country life."

Karpis nodded; the glasses and slicked-back hair made him look like a math teacher. But that smile would give Lon Chaney the willies.

He said, "You'll find the company better, too, I think. We work for a living, unlike your hoodlum pals."

He returned to eating his chicken. I didn't understand what he meant, but I didn't feel like following up on it.

Ma said, "Somebody ought to go up and drag that girl down here. She needs to eat."

She meant Louise.

Dolores, sitting next to her man Karpis, said, "I don't think so, Ma.

She's had quite a shock. She's crying her fool head off. I don't think she could keep anything down."

Ma shook her head, looking at the remaining food on the table. "It'd be criminal to waste this good food," she said. "The poor little thing ought to come down and eat."

Paula smiled as some whiskey went smoothly down, then said, "Maybe I could take a plate up to her."

Ma was adamant. "She should get right back in the swing of things. Best thing in the world for her."

I couldn't help myself. I said, "Ma, don't you think it's asking a little much of her to sit down and eat at the table she just saw her boyfriend stretched out dead on?"

That should have killed a few appetites, but everybody's appetite was alive and well at this table—except for Moran, who was looking at Paula's glass with glum envy.

Ma didn't get my point. She said, "It's just a table."

Doc Barker, who'd been silently (and dedicatedly) eating, lowered his ear of corn and smiled messily and said, "Ma, sometimes you're a riot."

"Don't sass!"

Across the table from his brother, Fred grinned his mostly gold grin, and said, "You're a cold-blooded old Ozark gal, Ma, no gettin' around it!"

"Well," Ma said, her feelings a little hurt, "there's apple pie for them that wants it."

Everybody wanted it except Moran, who sat at the table, slumped. Paula finally took pity on him and went out in the other room to get her pint; she filled a water glass half full for Moran, and freshened her own glass, too.

But he drank it quickly down, and most of us were hardly started on our pie when he stood and announced, "And so to bed."

Ma said, "So early, Doctor?"

He touched a hand to his chest with mock-drama. "I've had a long, tiring and quite difficult day, madam. I lost a patient, in this very room, mere hours ago. There are times when I seek refuge in a bottle; but there are times when sleep can serve that function just as well."

The two farm boys nudged each other with elbows and laughed. The old doc talked funny.

"Sit down, Doc," Nelson said, quietly, cutting a small bite of pie with his fork.

"Are you addressing me . . . Baby Face?"

A pall fell over the room.

Nelson smiled as he forked the bite of pie; lifted fork to lips, ate. "Yes. Sit down."

"I'm tired. And I will take no orders from—"

"Sit down."

There'd been no menace in Nelson's voice.

But Moran thought it best to sit down.

Saying, "Why is my presence required here?"

Nelson said, "Ain't good manners not to clean up after yourself."

Moran seemed puzzled, glanced at the area near his plate where he'd been sitting, which was rather tidy actually.

Like a stage magician, Nelson made a sweeping gesture with one hand that summoned to my mind's eye, and I'd wager to that of anyone else who'd been in this room not long ago, the blue-faced corpse that had been stretched out on this very table.

Finally my appetite deserted me. I pushed the plate of pie away and suddenly the food in my stomach was churning.

"He's still in the barn," Nelson said. He looked at Fred. "Right? You haven't moved him?"

The youngest farm boy whispered to his mother, "Who?" and she shushed him.

Fred said, "He's out there. Not going anywhere."

"Well," Nelson said, rising, wiping his hands with a napkin, "it's time he did."

Moran was wide-eyed, indignant, but a little afraid. "This is preposterous."

Doc Barker rose. "I agree. You botched the operation, Doc. Least you can do is help dispose of the remains. Besides—like you always like to tell us—you know where the bodies are buried. Why should this time be any different?"

Soon five of us were moving through the darkness. Six, counting the sheet-wrapped body of Candy Walker. Doc and Fred Barker carried him, one at either end of him, and he sagged in the middle. Nelson, who knew his way around the farm (I was beginning to gather that he really was related to Verle and Mildred), led the way, with a flashlight in hand. The flashlight was hardly necessary: it was a clear night, stars scattered across the sky like diamonds across a dark tapestry (stolen diamonds, in this company) and part of the moon was up there, working for us, too. The night air was almost cool and the smell of grass and wheat and such was strange and strangely soothing to these city nostrils. I had the shovels over my shoulder, three of them. Moran, muttering to himself, was carrying a heavy bag of quicklime.

We moved past a shocked field, then down into a hollow. We stopped near a clump of trees. Near the trees, but not so near as for the roots to be a problem, we began to dig.

Everybody had a turn, even Nelson, but first up was me and Moran. The body, for the moment, had been rested beneath the nearby trees, out of the way of the dirt.

With everybody having a turn, it didn't take long, despite being six feet deep. Two people going at it at a time made for a hole larger than need be, but we got the job done. For some reason the physical labor felt good to me. The night had a clarity that made the event seem very real, and yet completely dreamlike.

The two Barker brothers, having hauled the body here and apparently feeling it therefore their province to do so, carried the body of Candy Walker over and rolled it out of the sheet into the hole. They stood looking down in there dumbly, the empty sheet in their hands, like a husk.

Nelson stood there, no tommy gun, but vest open and .45 sticking threateningly up out of his waistband, hands on hips, and ordered Moran: "Get down in there—you're gonna dump some lye on his hands and face."

"I will not!"

"Do it," Nelson said.

Moran, quite sober now, the outburst at the hardware store/saloon well behind him, said, "If you're considering killing me, keep this in mind: my attorney has an envelope in which much that I know has been recorded. Upon my death, that envelope will—"

"Yeah, yeah," Nelson said. "Get in there and use the lye. Hands and face. It'll be the best plastic surgery job you ever did."

Moran snorted at that, but he climbed down into the hole. Doc Barker handed him down a can of lye, already opened; the strong odor rose up out of the grave like a chemical ghost.

"It's done," Moran said hollowly, looking up out of the hole. Wondering if he'd be allowed to emerge.

Nobody said or did anything for the next few seconds, so I reached my hand down to him and pulled him up and out.

Then Nelson said to him, "Now dump some quicklime on him. Half a bag will do. You can do that from up here."

Moran sighed, irritated but still apprehensive, and took the bag of quicklime from Doc Barker, ripped it open; Freddie stood casually nearby, shovel over his shoulder.

The doctor poured the lime down into the hole, over the body, like he was planting seed; then he set the half-empty bag on the ground near the hole and, standing at one end, looked across the hole where Nelson was and said, "Now what?" and Fred Barker hit him in the back of the head with the shovel.

The sound was something I'll never forget, yet I can't describe it. Two sounds, actually, all the result of Fred Barker's roundhouse swing: metallic at first, almost a clang, echoing across the night; followed by a smack, a sickening smack, like a melon hitting the pavement from a high building. That's as close as I can come to the sound. But I can hear it to this day.

Dr. Joseph Moran wasn't hearing anything. He fell facedown into the hole, sprawled on top of dead Candy Walker; the back of Moran's head was caved in and his brains showed. Doc Barker, without climbing in, poured lye down on the doc's hands, not bothering with getting in to do his face, then poured the rest of the quicklime over him. And dropped the sheet into the hole; it fluttered in like a wounded bird.

"Come on, come on," Nelson said to me. "Grab a shovel and start filling in that hole!"

Fred, Doc and I filled in the hole; Fred used the same shovel he'd used on Moran.

We headed back, each of us but Nelson with a shovel over his shoulder, like Snow White's dwarfs, our footsteps on the grassy ground the only sound in the clear, dead night. Not a cricket nor a farm animal had a thing to say in the immediate aftermath of Doc Moran's murder.

Nearing the lights of the house, I somehow managed to ask Nelson about that envelope Moran had claimed his attorney had.

"That's where *you* fit in," Nelson grinned.

"What do you mean?"

"Those phone calls I made. One of 'em, I checked with Nitti. Nitti himself."

"And?"

"They got to Moran's lawyer."

"Killed him?"

"No! Bought him. Chicago, remember?"

"So Nitti told you Moran could be killed without any worry of . . ."

"Right. And Nitti *wanted* him dead."

"Because he passed hot money . . . ?"

"That, and Nitti was just as nervous about how the doc's drinking was going to his mouth as we was."

"Oh."

"Didn't you know that's why you was here? To hand Doc Moran his passport to the next life? D'you really think Nitti wanted him back in Chicago just to pull a rabbit outa some bimbo or something?"

That was one little thing Nitti hadn't told me, in generously providing me with Jimmy Lawrence's identity and the accompanying cover story: that I'd been sent here to set Doc Moran up.

And now here I was, right in the middle of a nest of public enemies and who could say I wasn't one of them?

I was an accomplice, now. In my way, I'd helped kill Moran. I hadn't seen it coming. I couldn't have stopped it. But I was there; here. I filled in the hole.

I knew where the bodies were buried.

IDENTIFICATION	DIVISION OF INVESTIGATION	Fingerprint Classification
ORDER NO. 1218	U. S. DEPARTMENT OF JUSTICE	$\frac{13\ \ 1\ \ Rr\ \ 5}{1\ \ U\ \ 7}$
March 22, 1934	WASHINGTON, D. C.	

WANTED

ALVIN KARPIS, with aliases,
A. CARTER, RAYMOND HADLEY, GEORGE HALLER, ALVIN KORPIS,
EARL PEEL, GEORGE DUNN, R. E. HAMILTON, RAY HUNTER.

KIDNAPING

DESCRIPTION

Age, 25 years (1934); Weight, 5 feet,
9-3/4 inches; Weight, 130 pounds;
Build, slender; Hair, brown; Eyes,
blue; Complexion, fair;
Marks, 1 inch cut scar lower knuckle
left index finger.

RELATIVES:

Mr. John Karpis, father, 2842 North
Francisco Avenue, Chicago, Illinois.
Mrs. Anna Karpis, mother, 2842 North
Francisco Avenue, Chicago, Illinois.
Mrs. Emily Newwold, sister, 2840 North
Francisco Avenue, Chicago, Illinois.
Mrs. Robert (Clara) Kokota, sister,
1829 West Erie Street, Chicago,
Illinois.
Mrs. Albert (Amelia) Grooms, sister,
1234 North Monroe Street,
Topeka, Kansas.

Photograph taken May 19, 1930.

Alvin Karpis

CRIMINAL RECORD

As Alvin Karpis, #7071, received State
Industrial Reformatory, Hutchinson, Kansas,
February 25, 1926; crime, burglary-2nd
degree; sentence, 10 years; escaped March
9, 1929; returned March 25, 1930.

As Raymond Hadley, #17902, arrested
Police Department, Kansas City, Missouri,
March 23, 1930; charge, larceny-auto and
safe blower; released to State Industrial
Reformatory, Hutchinson, Kansas, as an
escape.

As Alvin Karpis, #1533, received State
Penitentiary, Lansing, Kansas, May 19, 1930 -
transferred from State Industrial Reformatory;
crime, burglary-2nd degree; sentence, 5 to 10
years.

As George Haller, #6006, arrested Police
Department, Tulsa, Oklahoma, June 10, 1931;
charge, investigation-burglary; delivered
Police Department, Okmulgee, Oklahoma.

As A. Korpis, #1609, arrested Police Department, Okmulgee, Oklahoma, June 10, 1931; charge, burglary;
sentenced September 11, 1931, 4 years, State Penitentiary, McAlester, Oklahoma; paroled.

Alvin Karpis is wanted for questioning in connection with the kidnaping of Edward G. Bremer at St. Paul, Minnesota, on
January 17, 1934.
Law enforcement agencies kindly transmit any additional information or criminal record to the nearest office of the Division
of Investigation, U. S. Department of Justice.
If apprehended, please notify the Director, Division of Investigation, U. S. Department of Justice, Washington, D. C., or
the Special Agent in Charge of the office of the Division of Investigation listed on the back hereof which is nearest your city.

(over)

Issued by: J. EDGAR HOOVER, DIRECTOR.

"OLD CREEPY" KARPIS

32

By eight o'clock that evening, the farmhouse was humming with lei-
sure activity: Dolores and Helen were sitting on the sofa listening to
Burns and Allen on the radio (Gracie was still looking for that missing
brother of hers) and Ma had found a little table to work one of her
jigsaw puzzles on, sitting on the window seat as she did, feet not
touching the floor; Mildred Gillis was doing needlepoint in the sitting
room with the piano, her boys spread-eagled in the middle of the
floor, playing a board game, getting loud occasionally and getting
shushed accordingly; a penny-ante poker game was going on in the
kitchen, the players crowded down at one end of the banquetlike
table—Fred and Doc Barker, Verle Gillis and Baby Face Nelson
were playing. Despite the stakes, everybody seemed to be taking the
game quite seriously, especially Nelson, whose displeasure and glee
seemed disproportionate to the nickels and dimes he was alternately
losing and raking in. I played a few hands myself, stopped when I was
thirty cents ahead—and Nelson glared at me like I was leaving with
everybody's money.

You would never have guessed two men died tonight. Certainly
not one of them on this card-and-change-strewn table. And cheerful
Fred Barker, with his ready-to-smile mouthful of gold teeth, did not
seem like somebody who'd killed a man with a shovel recently.

I, on the other hand, felt exactly like a man who'd help dig—and
fill—a grave.

I went out into the almost cool night, walking around the farmyard,
getting a feeling of where the buildings were. This was made easy by
several electric lights on tall posts. Some of the cars were parked out
back, but others (I surmised) must've been in the barn. The hayloft
door stood open. Crickets were chirping and there was manure in the
air. I found Karpis sitting on the porch, in the swing, gently rocking.
The porch light wasn't on, but I could see him fine. He looked small,
slight. Which he was.

He smiled at me and nodded; the smile was meant to be friendly but it was just unsettling.

I leaned against one of the porch pillars.

"It was bound to happen," Karpis said matter-of-factly.

"What's that?"

"Doc Moran." He lifted his shoulders, set them back down. "Just a matter of time."

"I guess."

"You look like killing don't agree with you."

"It's not my favorite thing."

"Me either. Oh, I don't mind putting a little muscle into a stickup, waving a gun around. Don't even mind winging a guy. But I don't look to killing for my fun."

From the living room, laughter came from the radio; Gracie had said something funny again.

"Now, you take Freddie," Karpis said, amused, smiling his ghastly smile, "he's a born killer. Sometimes it shocks me a little to see how free and easy he is with a gun. He don't mind gunning down somebody that gets in his way—cop or hood or ordinary joe, it's all the same to him."

I didn't know what to say to that.

Karpis went on: "Maybe it's being raised in the Ozarks; maybe all those hillbillies are like that. I don't know. Could be it runs in the family—their older brother Herman died shooting it out with the cops, and Doc, hell, he's got quite the itchy trigger finger himself."

"Ma seems harmless enough."

The swing made a creaking sound as he rocked; it seemed louder than the crickets and other night sounds, and the muffled radio from within the house.

"Yeah, Ma's harmless all right. She's quite a character, though."

"She doesn't seem to mind what her boys do for a living."

Karpis smiled some more and moved his head side to side. "Anything her boys do is okeydoke with Ma. They can do no wrong."

"They seem to feel the same about her."

"Well, look how she sticks by them. Sometimes she travels with us, and Freddie and Doc and me are just three brothers taking care of our widowed momma, should anybody ask. Foolproof cover. What could look more innocent?"

The swing creaked; laughter from the radio.

I said, "I didn't know Nelson ran with your gang."

"Usually don't, but I've known him for years and he's sharp and loyal and there's nobody braver. We're hooking up for something big." He gave me a long sideways appraising look. "You strictly a rackets guy, or do you ever work for a living?"

I sat in the swing next to him; Karpis stopped rocking, but it rocked on a little anyway, on its own steam.

I said, "I don't get you. You said something like that at supper, and I didn't get you then, either."

He sighed, and started gently rocking again; I joined in.

"Now look," he said, as if explaining the obvious to a small child, "we're strictly heist guys. We done some branching out into kidnapping, but that's just another kind of stealing. Plus, our gang's on the fluid side. . . ."

"Fluid?"

"Yeah—people come and go. Me and the Barker boys have been together a long time, but we worked with dozens of guys, from time to time. Not tight and organized like you rackets guys."

"What've you got against rackets guys?"

He made a face. "They're too picky about what they'll let you steal. They don't like the kind of stealing that gets the heat turned on 'em; they're in more public-service-type business."

"Public service?"

"Yeah—pussy, drugs, bookmaking. That ain't crime. That's business. True crime's when you get out and work for a living, like robbing a bank, or breaking into a place, or kidnapping somebody. Really give some effort to it. The rackets guys aren't up for that. Yet at the same time, when those guys get *mad* at you, well, Jesus . . . anything can happen."

"Yeah. Ask Doc Moran."

Karpis raised a lecturing finger; he looked even more like a math teacher, now. "Okay, so maybe Chicago did okay Moran's exit—maybe even requested it—but they didn't pay for it. Killing people for money don't appeal to me, or anybody connected with me. I'll leave that to the rackets guys."

"Why are you telling me this?"

"Because you're no Chicago hoodlum."

The Auburn keys were in my pocket.

"I'm not?"

I edged my hand near the gun under my arm.

"No," Karpis smiled, "you're from out East. You're a fish out of water, in Chicago. You looking for some honest work?"

I sighed relief. To myself, that is.

"Maybe," I said.

"Something real big's coming up, soon."

"How soon?"

"Friday."

"This Friday?"

"This Friday."

"Day after tomorrow, you mean?"

"Right."

"What is it?"

"A snatch."

Fine. Now I was mixed up in a kidnapping; I could see myself, being strapped into the chair, telling the reporters in the gallery how I was a private detective gone undercover to retrieve a farm girl.

"Interested?" Karpis asked.

"I might be," I said.

"Decide by tomorrow. We'll be driving back to Illinois, to a tourist court near Aurora. We're meeting some people there, to go over the plans."

"I appreciate the offer."

"We can use you. We were counting on having Candy Walker, you know. And we don't really have time to go pull somebody else in."

"How could Walker have helped you, if he was recovering from plastic surgery?"

Karpis shifted his smile to one side of his face; it didn't look any better there. "We just need someone to stick by the women. While we pull the snatch, and for a time, after. Easy work. Candy could've cut it, even with bandages on his puss."

"I see. Well . . ."

"You'd only get half a cut—half of which goes to Candy. Or to Lulu, that is. We look after our own."

"That's only right."

"Still, it should run five grand. What do you say?"

Five grand!

"I'll, uh, sleep on it."

"Good. Maybe you can get to know Lulu while you're at it."

"You got to be kidding . . . she just lost her man . . ."

"She's going to need comforting. She needs somebody to look after her."

"Well, uh . . ."

He put a fatherly hand on my shoulder; he was younger than me, and I owned suits that weighed more than he did—but his words carried weight just the same.

He said, "Guys like us got to pick our girls from the circles we move in. My first real girl was Herman Barker's widow. Took up with her before Herman's body was cool. It's nothing to be ashamed of—just the facts of life in this game."

"I do feel sorry for the kid," I said, referring to Louise. This was perfect, actually: Karpis was trying to fix me up with the girl I'd come here after.

He slipped his arm around my shoulder. "Don't feel like you're getting sloppy seconds, Jimmy. Mind if I call you Jimmy? For example. I took up with a lot of whores in my time, but I never had any complaints about their personalities or their morals or brains or what-have-you. You can always trust a whore."

That might make a nice needlepoint for Mildred Gillis to hang on her farmhouse wall.

"Now, Dolores, she was the sister-in-law of a guy I used to do jobs with; she's been with me since she was sixteen. Don't get the idea she's fat, either—she's just knocked up. Second time. We decided to have this one—what the hell."

"Uh, congratulations, Karpis."

"Thanks, Jimmy."

I noticed a small figure walking across the farmyard toward the barn; he had a bottle of liquor in one hand, tommy gun slung over one arm.

Nelson.

"What's he up to?" I asked.

"Oh—just taking his friend Chase some refreshment."

"His friend who?"

"Chase. John Paul Chase. Guy worships Nelson; adores him." He let out a nasty snicker that went well with his smile. "If Helen weren't around, I think they'd be an item."

"What's Chase doing in the barn?"

"Staying there."

"What do you mean?"

Karpis shrugged. "Staying there. He sits up in the loft with a rifle and keeps watch out that little window or door or whatever it is. See?"

I looked over toward the barn, and saw the open loft door, but nothing else.

I said, "Doesn't anybody take turns with him?"

"No," Karpis said. "Nelson told him to take that post, and he didn't even blink. Just does whatever Nelson says. Sits up there and reads Western pulp magazines and keeps watch. Three days, now. Sleeps there, too—but I never knew a man to sleep lighter. Nice to have him around."

"Hell, he didn't even have supper with us."

"Nelson took some out to him. He treats Chase fine—like a faithful dog."

"Is there anybody else here I haven't met yet?"

Karpis flashed that awful smile. "Not that I can think of, offhand."

He went inside and I followed him; he joined the poker game, taking Nelson's empty chair. I watched for a few moments, then went into the living room, where Burns and Allen were just getting over. When George had said "say good night, Gracie," I asked Karpis' girl Dolores about sleeping arrangements.

"You could take Doc Moran's bed," she suggested. "It's free."

"No kidding."

"There's a lot of bedrooms in this house, but they're all taken. The Nelsons sleep upstairs, and Alvin and me have an upstairs bedroom, and so do Paula and Fred, and Candy and Lulu too, or anyway they did."

"Where did Moran sleep?"

She pointed behind her. "There's a sewing room back by the kitchen, and the two Docs each had beds back there. Cots, actually."

"Where do the farmer and his wife sleep?"

"There's a Murphy bed in the sitting room."

This was turning into home away from home.

"The boys sleep in there, too," she continued, "in pallets."

"Sounds like a full house."

"Sure is. Could be a topsy-turvy one tonight, though. Last I knew Paula was upstairs in her and Fred's bedroom nursin' Lulu."

"Oh?"

"Yeah, and Lulu don't want to sleep in her and Candy's bed tonight. She wants to sleep with Paula."

"Think Fred'll go along with that?"

She grinned; she had a much better smile than her boyfriend Karpis. "He would if he was included. But he'll have to go sleep alone in that other bedroom, I guess."

I decided to go up and see how Louise was doing. I found brunette Paula standing out in the hall, smoking, ever-present glass of whiskey in one hand.

"Hi," I said.

"Hi," she said. Smiling. Sultry.

"How's the kid?"

"Lulu? Busted up about it."

"It's a tough one."

"She's asleep, now. Poor thing."

"Best thing for her."

Paula brightened. "You want to do me a favor?"

I shrugged. "Sure."

"Go in and look after her for me. Keep her company."

"She doesn't even know me . . ."

Paula swatted the air with her cigarette in hand. "She won't wake up till September. But if she does, somebody should be with her."

"I guess I could sit in there awhile."

"That's not what I mean. You need a place to sleep, right? Bunk in with her."

"Don't be foolish."

She crooked her finger, like she was summoning a child. I complied. She leaned in with me in the doorway, where I could see Lulu, curled up in a fetal ball, pink dress way up over pretty white legs. She was sleeping deeply on one of two twin beds that were pushed close together. The bedroom was regularly the boys' room, obviously. There was a balsa wood model plane hanging from the slanted ceiling, which was papered in dark blue with silver stars, a child's idea of the nighttime sky.

Standing away from the open doorway, now, Paula said, "Freddie'll be tickled to death to get the bed Lulu and Candy been sleeping in—we ain't had a double bed in a week. You'd be doing us a favor, and she isn't going to mind, you in your separate bed and all. She shouldn't be left alone, you know."

I thought about that.

Paula put a hand on my shoulder; her breath was whiskey-scented, but she was sexy just the same. She said, "Let me tell you something.

My husband Charlie was knocked off on a bank score, a year ago spring. Freddie picked me up on the rebound, within the week. It's not that I'm such a floozie, understand. It's just I needed a strong shoulder. And Freddie didn't come out so bad on the deal, d'you think?" She smiled wryly and gestured to her navy dress with the white polka dots and the curves.

I smiled back at her. "I think he did just fine."

She patted my cheek, sipped her glass. "You could get lucky, too, friend. Lulu's a hell of a girl. What's your name again?"

"Jimmy."

"Nice name. Nice guy. Maybe Lulu's the one who might strike it lucky. Who knows?"

Soon I'd moved myself into the little bedroom—all I had was one small overnight bag with a change of underwear and socks, and some toilet articles (the toilet was out back, incidentally—like the Auburn, a two-seater); but I decided it best to sleep in my pants and my undershirt on top of the covers. There was an open window by a small desk on which some Big Little Books were confined by horse-head bookends twice their size. On one wall were some shelves with a baseball glove or two and some toy guns and such. Despite the trappings being male, I couldn't help but feel this child's room was appropriate for the slip of a thing next to me, the farmer's daughter who slept so deeply beside me.

I lay on my back, staring at the slanted ceiling, its starry sky visible above me; light from outside—not just the moon, but that well-lit farmyard—made that possible. The girl beside me seemed bathed in blue ivory.

I thought about waiting till everyone was asleep and spiriting her out to the Auburn. But how could I do that and get past this fellow Chase, in the barn? And surely somebody in the house kept a sort of guard; I hadn't heard the details, but that seemed a safe assumption to make. And how was I to take this girl with me, without her making a fuss? Her emotions were on edge already, let alone a stranger grab her and try making off with her.

My thoughts careened from dead Dr. Moran to the pending kid-napping that I hoped to avoid being drawn into—though I knew I already was. Maybe if it had been a bank they were planning to rob, I could've let it pass. But kidnapping? No. Like every other red-blooded bozo in this country, the Lindbergh tragedy had got to me, and made the idea of kidnapping seem something abhorrent. It had me thinking in terms of children, too, which was ridiculous, because the Karpis–Barker specialty was a rich banker or brewer. Still, stealing money was one thing—stealing a person was quite another. . . .

I should have been frightened, and I suppose I was, but too much was going on, too much was whirling through my brain, for me to feel the full impact of what I was caught up in.

More than anything, I missed Sally. Missed her and her silk sheets—how I wished this dinky kids' bedroom was her white bedroom at the Drake—and I regretted our parting angry.

Angry. That was something else working at me: anger. Anger and my old friend frustration were knocking around with everything else in my head, vying for attention. I'd been suckered, I'd been used—Frank Nitti had made me pay for my trip to Outlaw Land with the Moran setup. And what could I do about it? Being angry with Nitti was like getting pissed off at God. You could do it, but it wouldn't get you anywhere. Except hell maybe.

My fault—my own damn fault for dealing with Nitti, and expecting a fair shake. From his point of view this no doubt *was* a fair shake: tit for tat. He'd done a lot for me—he gave me a name and cover and backed it up, and now here I was, the girl I'd come to find lying right beside me.

I just had no idea how to get her the hell out of here.

That was the thought Louise—Lulu, if you will—interrupted when she woke up and saw me and screamed.

33

I placed a hand over her mouth as gently as I could; she continued to scream into it, but I'd stifled her enough for her to be able to hear me.

"Please," I said. "Please don't. I'm just here to keep you company."

Her wide, wide-set brown eyes seemed to consider that, and beneath my palm she stopped screaming.

I took it away. That had been one hell of a piercing cry she'd let out, worthy of Fay Wray, but I didn't hear footsteps rushing up the steps or down the hall—no one was hollering out, wondering what was wrong. Maybe women screaming in the night was standard stuff around these parts.

She looked at me, mouth open, lips trembling, eyes still wide, nostrils flared, like the distressed damsel on a pulp-magazine cover.

"Who—who are you?" she finally managed.

"You met me before," I said. "Jimmy Lawrence. I drove Ma here from Chicago."

The eyes narrowed a bit. "Oh."

"They didn't have a bed for me, and your friend Paula asked me to sleep in here, so somebody'd be with you through the night."

The door cracked open and Paula, cigarette dangling from her red lips, said, "That's right, sugar. Didn't want you to be alone in your hour of need."

Somebody'd heard the scream, after all.

I said to Louise, "I'll leave if you like."

She looked toward Paula. "Can't *you* stay with me? You're my *friend*."

"I'm your pal," Paula said. "But I'm Freddie's girl, and he wants the pleasure of my company, tonight. You understand, sugar. You going to be all right?"

I got off the bed, stood. "I'll leave."

Louise looked at me; she was a small thing, but she had eyes you could dive into and swim around in for a lifetime or two.

Paula said, "Why don't you let him keep you company? You don't want to be alone tonight."

Louise thought about that for a moment, shook her head no, meaning she didn't want to be alone, and Paula smiled and said, "That's a good girl," and shut the door on us.

I stood there looking down at the girl, in the blue-ivory semi-light. She looked up at me. She looked pretty pitiful.

I said, "Is it all right if I lay back down, there?"

She swallowed. Nodded. Then quickly added, "But keep your pants on."

I smiled at her. "I don't do anything in a hurry."

Despite herself, despite her situation, she found a tiny smile for me. Said, "Well, keep 'em on, anyway."

"I can pull these beds apart a ways, if you like."

"No. No, that's okay."

I lay back down.

She turned her back to me.

A few minutes ticked by, and then I heard her sobbing. I thought about touching her shoulder, but let it go.

Then she turned to me and, a hanky clenched in her fist, face slick with tears, said, "This is all wet." She meant the hanky. "You wouldn't happen to . . . ?"

"Sure," I said, and dug out a handkerchief for her.

She patted her face dry; no new tears seemed on the way, at least not immediately. She said, "I must look a mess."

"You look fine. But you got a right to feel that way."

She shook her head despairingly. "He was alive one minute, and the next . . ." Her chin crinkled in anger; she looked like a little girl about to throw a tantrum. "I'd like to kill that damn doctor!"

"It's been taken care of."

That shocked her. The angry look turned blank and she said, rather hollowly, "They . . . killed him?"

I nodded.

"Good," she said. But I didn't quite buy it.

"You don't have to pretend for me," I said.

"What?"

"That you like it. The cheap way life and death is traded in around here."

She swallowed again. "I didn't really mean I wanted Doc Moran dead. He's a . . . he was a lush and always crowing about himself. But . . ."

"But he didn't deserve to die for it. That what you're saying?"

She shrugged a little; leaned on her elbow and looked at me. Those eyes. Those goddamn eyes.

"He didn't mean to kill Candy," she said. "I hate him for not being a better doctor. But I'm not glad they killed him."

I didn't say anything.

"Just don't expect me to cry for him," she said, with an edge of bitterness. "I don't have any tears left for that damn old drunk."

I nodded.

"You're nice to stay in here with me, Mr. Lawrence."

"Call me Jimmy. Should I call you Lulu?"

"If you like . . . Jimmy."

"What's Lulu short for?"

"Louise. Nobody around here calls me that."

"Would it be okay if I call you that?"

That surprised her; but she nodded, three little nods.

"Why don't you get some sleep, Louise."

"All right," she said.

She turned on her stomach, facing away from me.

I lay looking up at the stars in the ceiling-paper sky.

After a while she said, "Jimmy?"

"Yes, Louise?"

"Would you do me a favor?"

"Sure."

"Slide over onto my bed, with me."

"Well . . ."

"Not for that. I need . . . held. You won't try anything. You don't have that sort of face. I can trust you. Can't I?"

"You can trust me, Louise." Taking into consideration I was pretending to be somebody I wasn't, I figured she could do worse than trust me, among this company.

"I'm going to turn on my side," she said.

She did.

"Now could you cuddle up to me? Maybe slip your arm around my waist?"

I did.

"That's . . . that's how Candy and me slept. Like spoons."

"I got a girl back in Chicago," I said. "We sleep like this some-times."

"It's nice, isn't it? Kinda . . . comforting."

"It is nice."

I was right up against her; she was soft and smelled like perfume. Dime-store perfume maybe, but I liked it anyway. I felt a stirring in me and had to pull back away from her rounded little rump; but she pushed back against me and said, ingenuously, "Candy was so sweet."

Soon she began sobbing quietly; into my hanky. My erection re-ceded. I kept my arm around her waist and hugged her to me.

"What am I going to do without him? What am going to do?"

I stroked her head, said, "There, there."

And pretty soon she fell asleep.

So did I, and then I heard an unearthly sound, a screech out of a nightmare, and bolted upright in bed.

"What the hell was that?" I said.

Louise was sitting over at the child's desk, combing her bobbed blond hair out with a brush; she was wearing that same pink dress I'd seen her in yesterday—like me, she'd slept in her clothes. She smiled over at me. She had no makeup on and looked about thirteen years old. The kind of thirteen-year-old that makes boys reconsider how they feel about girls, however.

She made a crinkly smile. "A rooster, silly. Haven't you ever been on a farm before?"

I rubbed my face with a hand; I needed a shave. Sun was begin-ning to find its way in the open window next to her, but it still seemed pretty dark out to me.

"No," I said. "This is a first for me."

Still brushing her hair, she said, "I was raised on a farm. My daddy's a farmer."

"Do you miss your daddy?"

She looked sad, kept brushing. "Sometimes. I don't imagine he misses me, though."

"Why's that?"

"He thinks I'm a bad girl. A sinner."

"He's a religious man, your daddy?"

"Too religious. He used to beat me with a belt because I wasn't devout enough."

"I'm sorry."

She shrugged. "At least when he beat me I knew he cared."

"Pardon?"

She put the brush down and came and sat on the side of the bed next to me. "Sometimes that's how people show you they care about you."

"Hitting you?"

She nodded. "I don't say it's the best way. I wouldn't ever hit anybody myself. And Candy—he hardly ever hit me. I guess that's why I loved him so much."

She seemed better this morning, seemed already to have accepted the finality of Candy's death. Maybe in this fast crowd she ran with, fast death was commonplace. I asked her.

"You ever see anybody die before?" I said.

"Sure. Two times."

"Guys working with Candy, you mean?"

She nodded. "They got shot on jobs."

"I see."

"And Candy killed some people. I never went on any jobs with him, so I never saw it. And I don't like to think of it. But it's true."

"What kind of people?"

"Did he kill? A bank guard and a sheriff's deputy. It bothered Candy."

"It did?"

"Yes—he was afraid of the electric chair."

I said nothing.

"He doesn't have to be afraid anymore," she said, and then tears gushed forth, and she was burying her face in my chest.

I held her for a while; by the time she came up for air, the sun was pouring through the windows like fresh buttermilk.

I wiped her tears with the bedspread. She smiled at me bravely. I got lost in her eyes, brown, brown eyes.

She said, "You didn't take advantage of me last night."

I swallowed.

"Most men would've."

"I don't know about that."

"You could've. I was helpless."

"You look like you've got some spunk left. You let out a pretty good scream when you saw me, for example."

She shrugged. "That doesn't matter. You could've taken me. A man can have a woman if he wants her."

"You mean he can rape her."

She nodded.

"Where I come from," I said, "that's not an acceptable way of getting to know a girl."

"Where do you come from?"

"Back East."

"Is that why you're such a gentleman?"

I smiled. "That's another first for me—being called a gentleman."

"I think that's what I'll call you. Gentleman Jim. A real gentleman in a lousy world."

"Let's just leave it at 'Jimmy.'"

"No—I like 'Gentleman Jim' better." She beamed at me; she was trying a little too hard to be cheerful, but I was glad she was making the effort.

"Whatever you say," I said.

She grabbed me by the hand and yanked me off the bed.

"Come on, Gentleman Jim . . . this old farm girl's going to show you around a farm. You got some learning to do."

I told her I had to go the bathroom, but she said that would be no problem.

I could stop at the outhouse on our way.

34

When we cut across the backyard, a dozen chickens were dancing around, scrounging for food. One with yellow legs and another with bluish-green legs were dancing in place, pecking at something that looked like an old beat-up leather glove.

Louise caught my curious expression and said, "That's a rat skin. That's about all the cat leaves behind, when she's done with it."

"Hens aren't real particular about their breakfast, are they?"

Deadpan, she said, "Those aren't hens. Not yet. They don't start laying eggs till they're seven months."

She led me by the hand beyond the barn and silo, down a dew-wet path, at the end of which half a dozen cows, black, brown, stood gazing at us with bored expressions. Then we cut over by a shocked field, each shock looking like a small rustic wigwam.

"Velvet barley," Louise explained. She pulled a stalk out of one of the shocks, crushed the head against her palm, lifted her palm to her lips and blew away the chaff. She held out her palm for me to see the seeds there. "You like beer?"

"Sure."

"That's the malting barley." She dropped the seeds to the earth and moved on. "Mr. Gillis has fifteen acres of barley. They plant this stuff quick, soon as the ground's fit."

"How many acres does Gillis have here?"

"Eighty."

"Is that big?"

"Not really. Not small, though."

Birds were singing. I wasn't used to seeing this much sky; in Chicago, in the Loop, you have to raise your head to see any sky. And the last bird I heard sing in the city was Anna Sage's parakeet.

I asked, "Can he make a living at it?"

"He could if the prices were right. The livestock'll get that barley. He can't afford to sell it for what it's going."

"You ought to be able to make a living with land like this. Crops like these."

She shrugged, walking ahead of me now. Not holding my hand— leading the way.

"Mr. Gillis does all right with his sideline," she said.

"You mean taking in house guests."

She nodded.

"You ever stay here before?" I asked her.

She nodded again. "A few times."

We were at the edge of the barley field, now. Some stones were scattered about, some of them nearly boulders, big cold seeds not worth planting. She pointed.

"That grass is Mr. Gillis' hay. He's got about six acres in grass. For the cows and horses."

We walked along, skirting a patch given to more stones and nettles. "Always a patch or two a farmer can't tame," she explained. "There's the corn."

I walked behind her, like an Indian, down green rows of corn only a few feet high. Silo corn, she said; planted late to keep it green. It would go eight feet. Up ahead, she said, was some corn Gillis had planted around the end of May.

I followed her down these rows, too, but they were damn near as tall as I was. The air here smelled sweet; up ahead Louise was breathing it in, smiling. At home.

We passed a field of yellow sweet clover, on our way to a field of (she said) alfalfa. She picked off a few tiny purple flowers, saying, "Relish for the cows." Gillis only had a couple acres of alfalfa, not enough by her way of thinking. We walked past another field (oats, she said) cut and shocked, which she dismissed as pig feed.

"Because of the price?" I asked.

"The price," she nodded. "My daddy got two dollars for an eighty-pound tin of milk, few years back. Now it's less than a dollar."

"That's rough."

"It's the banks. That's why I don't think it's so bad, what Candy and the others do."

"Rob banks, you mean."

She glanced at me, brown eyes wide. "Sure. All the banks ever do is foreclose on farmers."

We were to a big white-flowered field, riffling in the slight morning breeze. Buckwheat, she said.

"Just an acre," she went on. "Used for chicken and hog feed. You know what he could get selling it? Penny a pound." She shook her head. "Farmer's life."

"But you miss it, don't you?"

She was looking at the ground, watching her feet as she walked. "Maybe. A little."

I followed her down into a hollow and we sat under some trees. Another bird was singing. I asked her what kind it was.

"Robin," she said. "He doesn't know from the Depression."

"Why don't you go back home, Louise?"

"Home?"

"The farm."

"I can't do that."

"Why?"

She was sitting with her knees bunched up, clutching her legs with clasped arms; she had nice legs, by the way. White. Smooth.

"I was married. Still am, really."

"I see."

"He was bad to me. Worse than my daddy, even. He was a lot like my daddy, really. Maybe that's why I took up with him."

That seemed a pretty fair insight for a girl who was part farm girl, part moll. Louise was somebody who had the promise of being her own person, if she could just break away from the sordid world Candy Walker had introduced her to.

"Couldn't you go back to your daddy?" I asked.

"Would he take me back?"

A rhetorical question, but I thought about answering it, anyway.

Before I could, she answered it herself: "He wouldn't want me back. I'm a sinner. A fallen woman. And as for Seth, he'd probably shoot me. He said as much."

"He did?"

She hugged her legs, as if chilled. And it wasn't chilly.

"He said if I ever took up with another man, he'd see me dead."

I thought about telling her what her father had told me—that her husband Seth had already taken up with another woman (or two), and could care less about getting her back, at this point; it had been a year, after all.

"And even if Seth *wasn't* a problem, I don't know if I'd want to go back to my daddy even if he'd have me. Go back to some stupid little farm after the life I've seen?"

I didn't point out that we seemed to be on a stupid little farm at the moment, and that the life she'd seen with Candy Walker was a squalid nightmare.

But I did say, "Maybe you should start over. Just go to a big city and find a job."

She released her legs and stretched them out in front of her; the pink dress was up around her knees. Nice calves, as we say down on the farm.

She said, "I did have some typing in school. I had almost two years of high school, you know."

"You speak well. Express yourself well."

She liked hearing that; she gave me a broad, toothy smile that was as refreshing as that sweet smell back in the corn rows. She said, "I read a lot, you know. I like the movies, too. I always thought I'd be . . . you'll laugh."

"No I won't."

"An actress. There, I said it, go ahead, laugh. Every dumb little farm girl wants to run off to the big city and be a star."

"Sometimes it works out," I said, thinking of Sally.

"Well, at least I ran off. I don't suppose my life is so different from being in show business."

"You're sure on the road a lot."

"But even a typist. A secretary. That wouldn't be so bad, would it? That'd be a step up, and in a big city. I can't stay on with the Barkers and all. With Candy gone, I just don't see why I'd stay."

I touched her shoulder. "Why not go home, at least give your father a chance? Then you can go to the big city, if you like. I got friends in Chicago, for instance. Maybe I could help out."

She touched my face with a hand that smelled nicely of grain; the hand she'd cracked the barley stalk with. She said, "You really are sweet, my Gentleman Jim."

She really did read, didn't she? The romance magazines, that is.

She was saying, "How can anybody be so good and honest as you?"

Since I was a liar trying to manipulate her into doing my client's bidding, I couldn't wholeheartedly agree with her.

So I just said, "I'm not, really. I just think a girl as pretty as you doesn't need a life as shabby as this."

I thought she might take offense, but she didn't.

She raised her skirt. Lifted it slowly, up over her thighs. Up to a yellow fringe between her legs. No underthings.

She wasn't bashful, this girl.

"I know Candy is fresh in his grave," she said, "but it doesn't matter. He's gone, and you're here—and I want you. I need you. You could make me feel better."

This would go over real big with my client.

I said, "I don't think I should, Louise."

She reached behind her and was unbuttoning the dress; then she was easing it down to her waist and her breasts were round and her nipples were pink and I unbuttoned my trousers.

I was getting a Sheik out of my billfold when she said, "No. You don't need that."

"You want me to . . . ?"

"Pull out when it's time? No. Don't worry. I can't have kids."

A more sensitive man might've had his ardor dampened by that remark; but I was still caught up in the sweet smell of corn and the fringe between her legs and pink nipples and I had her on the grass, under the trees, her bottom small and firm and yet soft in my hands, as I slid in and out of her, went round and round in her, as she moved beneath me with a yearning that went beyond the moment, and she moaned and groaned and cried out when she came, and so did I. Then she was sitting up and in my arms, a bundle of flesh and undone clothes and sobbing.

Pretty soon I put my pants on.

That's when I noticed, not far from where we'd just got to know each other, biblically speaking, a patch of ground without any grass.

The grave where Candy Walker and Doc Moran lay entwined, much as Louise and I had been.

A wave of nausea hit me, as strong as the smell of ammonia. But there was nothing in my stomach, so nothing came up.

But Louise, standing now, hands behind her, buttoning, said, "What's wrong?"

"Nothing."

"We better get back for breakfast."

"Okay."

"Hmmm," she said. Noting the patch of grassless ground. "Wonder what's planted there."

Nothing that'll grow, I thought.

"Let's get back," I said.

Breakfast was under way, when we did, and Paula—having the alcoholic's standard plate of hardly any food (but no glass of whiskey yet)—smiled wickedly at Louise, recognizing what I can best if rudely describe as the freshly fucked look on Louise's face, and Louise blushed, and I frowned at Paula, but nobody else noticed anything. We sat and ate. Ma wasn't cooking, this time, but Mrs. Gillis did a pretty fair job of it herself. Scrambled eggs and bacon and fried potatoes with gravy and glasses of milk all around.

Ma seemed a little blue about it, actually—especially since her boys Fred and Doc were bent over their plates, inhaling the stuff.

Karpis was sitting next to me, his girl Dolores next to him. "You can freshen up in our room," he said. "Right across from yours."

"Thanks."

"Towels and a mirror and a basin. You'll have to come downstairs and get some fresh water, though. If you want to shave, anyway."

"Yeah, I guess I do look a little scruffy."

He pushed his glasses up on his nose. "We don't stand on ceremony, here."

Nelson was eating a plate of food that would've fed a man twice his size; sitting right across from me, next to his cute little brunette wife, he said, "I hear you're coming in with us. Taking Candy's place."

At the phrase "taking Candy's place," Paula laughed, and a few heads turned toward her with expressions that said they didn't get it. But the moment quickly passed, thank God.

"Yeah," I said. "And I'm pleased to be in such high-flying company."

Nelson smiled; his mustache looked both wispy and fake, like he was a kid who pasted on each strand with glue, one at a time. "Good to have you aboard. Sorry about the ridin' I give you yesterday. Chicago says you're aces, so there'll be no more complaints from me."

"Thanks, Nelson."

"You can call me B.G."

For Big George.

"Sure, B.G.," I said.

I was shaving in Karpis and Dolores' room when Karpis came in, his creepy smile on display.

"You forgot these," he said.

He was holding out my glasses. I had set them on a dresser last night before I went to bed, and had, frankly, forgot to put the damn things on this morning.

"Thanks," I said, gliding the razor across my throat.

"I notice they're window glass," he said.

I wondered if I had the nerve to use a razor to kill a man.

"So are mine," he said, tapping the side of his wire-frames.

"No kidding," I said. Shaving.

"Got to change our looks as best we can, in this business. I try to wear 'em all the time. You get used to 'em after a while."

I smiled at him in the mirror. "I still forget sometimes. The plastic surgery's a help, but glasses add to the basic change of appearance. Don't you agree?"

"Couldn't agree more," Karpis said. He put the glasses down next to me. "Now, we'll be leaving today, throughout the morning and early afternoon. In several cars, at staggered times."

I nodded. "Not a good idea to travel in a caravan."

"Nothing that attracts attention is a good idea."

This might work out. If I could just get Louise in the Auburn—the two-seater Auburn—I could drive away with her, and break off from this fun group before they were any the wiser.

I said, "I, uh . . . I'm getting attached to Louise."

Karpis flashed his sick grin again. "You're a fast worker."

"She's a nice kid."

"And lonely. You must peddle a pretty slick line to the ladies, Lawrence."

"I get by. You mind if she rides with me?"

"Not at all. I'll give you directions to the tourist court, before you leave."

"I'll take the Auburn, if that's okay."

"Sure. Why not."

Karpis nodded and went out.

I dried my face off, left the big bowl of soapy dirty water on the bureau and went across the hall to the farm boys' bedroom. Louise wasn't in there.

I found her in the room next door. A yellow-papered room with a big double bed with a bright yellow spread. She was packing.

She looked over her shoulder at me. "This was our room. Candy's and mine." She gave her attention back to packing.

"You okay, Louise?"

"I'm fine." But she didn't sound fine.

I went over to her, touched her shoulder. "What is it?"

"I'm an evil girl. Just like my daddy always said."

"What are you talking about?"

"We did it. You and me. Fornicated. And Candy not even dead a day. How could I be so bad?"

"It was my fault. I made you do it."

That wasn't true, and we both knew it, but it made her feel better to hear it. She turned to me and put her arms around me and pressed the side of her head to my chest.

"Don't think badly of me for it," she said.

"I wouldn't ever."

"I just needed to be loved. And you were so nice. I wanted you. I had to have you."

"You're a beautiful girl, Louise, and I'll never forget making love to you under the trees."

She liked the sound of that; it was sappy and romantic, like the romance magazines she was packing with her clothes. Her and Ma Barker.

She smiled up at me and went back to her packing.

I said, "I'm going to drive you today."

I'd decided not to spring my notion on her to flee our fellow outlaws and return her home to daddy. Not just yet.

She said, "We're going to that tourist camp near Aurora, aren't we?"

"Yes."

"It's kind of a nice place. Can we share a cabin there? I mean, do you want to?"

"I'd love to."

"Hand me my scrapbook, please. Over on the dresser."

I got it for her; it was a big fat book, bulging with clippings.

"What's in this?" I asked her.

She laid it in the suitcase, on top of her clothes, but opened it up to show me. I saw a headline: BANK GUARD SHOT.

"It's all Candy's press notices," she said, like she was talking about an actor. "I'm even in some of them."

I leafed through it. Bank robberies, a gas station stickup, jewelry store, the Bremer kidnapping. I even found the duplicate of the clipping her father had shown me, in which she (an "unidentified moll") was pictured, that is, sketched.

As I turned the pages, she was looking down at them with a fond, nostalgic little smile.

"Candy made his mark," she said. "They can't take that away from him. Or me."

She closed the book, and closed the suitcase.

"Excuse me." It was Karpis, peeking in.

"Change of plans," he said. "You're going to drive Ma. She says the Auburn's hers, and you're her driver, and that's that. No use arguing with Ma."

He smiled that smile and was gone.

"No use arguing with Ma," Louise said, smiling a little herself, but meaning it.

"I guess I'll see you later," I said. "At the tourist camp."

She put her arms around me and gave me a kiss. A long romance-magazine kiss.

And then I left.

Because there was no use arguing with Ma.

35

So Ma and I went back on the road, back pretty much the way we came—down Highway 19, turning onto 22, heading south toward Aurora. Ma couldn't find any hillbilly music on the radio, but she did discover a fresh batch of Burma Shave signs along the way, and read them to me, haw-hawing. In between she'd hum her hymns.

I didn't mind Ma. I was used to her. I wished she was Louise, so I could get the hell out of this, but I was used to her. I was getting used to this highway driving, too; passing slower moving traffic—the occasional slowpoke in a Model T, the farmer hauling a hayrack—with some confidence, now. The Auburn could overtake another vehicle with relative ease, despite these narrow two-lane highways.

Like Ma said: "Keep well to the right . . . of the oncoming car . . . get your close shaves . . . from the half-pound jar! Haw haw."

Burma Shave.

It was late morning when we reached the tourist camp, several miles north of Aurora on a curve of the highway outlined by whitewashed stones that parted midway like the Red Sea; there a gravel drive led in to a court where against a backdrop of lush trees half-a-dozen two-room white frame cabins were arranged in a gentle arc, with a larger cottage in the middle. As you pulled in the drive, a neon sign, burning pointlessly in the sun, said FOX VALLEY COURTS, and NO VACANCY. In case you couldn't make out that the sign was lit, a card in the window of the central, larger cabin repeated the NO VACANCY message in bold black letters. A lanky man in his forties in a Panama hat and a white shirt with sweat circles and tan baggy pants sat on a bench, one knee pointing north, the other pointing south; he was weathered and tan and licking an ice-cream cone.

I got out of the Auburn, leaving it running, and went over to him.

"No vacancy," he said, looking at the cone, not at me.

"We got a reservation," I said.

Now he looked at me. "Name?"

I glanced over at Ma. She leaned out the window and said,
"Hunter."

The man nodded; the cone dripped onto his lap. He didn't care.

"Little woman'll fix you up," he said, and pointed behind him with
a thumb to a screen door. I went in, and there was a check-in counter
and a dreary little reception area—the only color in this narrow outer
room was provided by a rack of postcards on the counter—but no
little woman. There was a metal bell, however, which I dinged.

The little woman came through an archway behind the counter, to
the left of the wall where a dozen room keys hung. The little woman
weighed about 210 and stood five nine. She could've put Baby Face
Nelson in her back pocket and sat on him—of course his tommy gun
might've goosed her some. She had a blue-and-white floral housedress on, very cheery, but she looked as depressed as the economy.

"I never seen you before," she said, looking at me wearily, warily.
She was in her thirties, I'd wager, but most people would've said
forties—her hair in a graying bun that seemed about to unravel, several chins stacked on each other. A pretty face was buried in there
somewhere. Green alert eyes.

"We never met, ma'am."

"But you're one of them." Accusingly.

"I guess I am."

Heavy sigh. "How many cabins you need?"

"Two."

She got a pair of keys off the board behind her. Handed them to
me. Looked at me slow and hard.

"Stay away from my Eddie and Clarice."

"Pardon?"

"I got two young ones—Eddie seven, Clarice eight. They already
think your friend Nelson's the cat's meow. I don't want 'em shining
up to any more of your kind."

Even though I wasn't an outlaw, really, I resented her attitude.
"Our money's good enough for you," I pointed out.

"That's my husband's doing. If he hadn't done time, he wouldn't be
so partial to you people." She shook her head side to side; her lower
lip trembled—like she was angry, or about to cry, or both. "You'll be
the death of him yet."

Or maybe he'd just do some more time. He had to be a greedy
type, her ice-cream-cone licker out on the bench; there were plenty
of tourists, this time of year, to fill a tourist camp like this, in the

heart of the Fox River valley. But they'd pay perhaps a buck and a half for a room for a night. The tourists about to descend on Fox Valley Courts would be paying twenty times that.

I drove Ma down to her cabin. Each white frame structure was divided into two numbered rooms. The half a cabin I'd be sharing with Louise was down a few doors. I began carrying Ma's things in for her; she immediately stretched out on one of the twin beds and began to read a *Photoplay* magazine with Claudette Colbert on the cover. It took me two trips to cart her stuff in, by which time she was asleep, snoring, the magazine folded over her generous bosom, Claudette's smiling face rising and falling.

I decided to have a nap myself. In my own room. There were twin beds here, too, several feet apart, and I hoped to keep it that way tonight. *Your client's daughter*, I reminded myself. The stiffening in my trousers at just the thought of her, however, indicated my client's best interests were probably not going to be served, in this little puce-papered room.

First order of business was to use the indoor plumbing each room seemed to have. As I stood there emptying my bladder I reflected on how nice it felt to be back in the twentieth century—even if there was a bug the size of your thumb in the bathtub at my right. I didn't bother to kill it. Live and let live. Took off my pants and took my nap.

A knocking at the door awoke me. I checked my watch and it was a little before two o'clock. I took the automatic out from under my pillow and went to the open window, where sheer curtains fluttered in a slight summer breeze. I peered out through them.

A big man—barrel-chested, six foot two, ruddy, round-faced, dark-haired, early thirties—was standing there in his shirt sleeves and suspenders. The butt of a .45 peeked out of his waistband.

It took me a few seconds, but then I realized who it was. I'd seen his picture in the papers often enough.

Charles Arthur Floyd.

Pretty Boy.

He knocked again. "Lawrence? Jimmy Lawrence?"

I cracked the door, gun in hand out of view. "That's right," I said. Doing my best to keep recognition out of my voice and face. "Who wants to know?"

"My name's Charlie Floyd," he said, and smiled. He had a small, cupid mouth, but a big smile, because when he smiled, his whole

round face lit up. Like Polly Hamilton, he had apple cheeks. "I been
hearin' some good things 'bout you from mutual acquaintances."

"Such as?"

His smile continued, but some strain was starting to show.
"Nelson, Karpis, so on. Open up. Let me in. You can see both my
hands and my gun. You surely got a gun on me, so what's the worry?"

I stood back, eased the door open, held the gun on him.

He came in, shut the door behind him. His hair was dark as an
Indian's and parted in the middle, slick with grease. He had tiny
brown eyes and a large nose.

"Put the shootin' iron away," he said. Still friendly. Still smiling—
but just barely.

"Nobody mentioned your name," I said.

"Well, you know who I am."

"You're Pretty Boy Floyd."

He flinched at the name. "Don't believe that newspaper shit. Nobody calls me that. Nobody but dumb-ass feds." He stuck out his
hand; it looked like a flesh-colored catcher's mitt. "My friend's call
me Chock. Short for Choctaw."

"Choctaw?"

"That's what they call my favorite home brew, back in the hills
where I come from." He drew back the hand to pat his generous
belly. "I got a weakness for it, as you can plainly see."

Then he stuck the hand back out, and I put the gun in my waistband and shook hands with him. He had a firm grip; he may have had
some fat on him, but he had more muscle.

He sat on the edge of one of the twin beds. "I'm the one who
should be suspicious, Jim. Care if I call you Jim?"

"Jim's fine. Why should you be suspicious?"

He shrugged. "I never heard of you before Nelson called me this
morning."

I shrugged. "I got pulled in on this at the last minute."

Floyd nodded, tsk-tsked. "Shame about Candy Walker. Worked
with him a few times. Nice feller. Nice of you to fill in, though. I hear
you're tied in with the Chicago crowd."

"Yeah. So to speak."

He pointed a finger at me. Gently. "You don't want to go calling
any of your friends, now, 'tween now and tomorrow."

"Oh?"

He shook his big head slowly side to side. "Frank Nitti wouldn't approve of what we're up to." Then he grinned like a mischievous kid with a private joke, that little mouth turning up at the corners and sending his apple cheeks into high gear. "No, sir!"

"Why wouldn't Nitti approve?"

"You don't know the lay of the land yet, do you, Jim? Well, what the hell—you will soon enough. Plenty of time for that." He glanced at a pocket watch. "We'll be having our meet, 'fore too long. You et yet?"

"I didn't have lunch. Slept through it."

"We're having barbecue tonight. The feller what runs the place stocked up on chickens and ol' Ma's gonna cook for us. I hear she's a *whale* of a cook."

"Ma Barker? Yes she is."

"Hey, Jim—sit down. There's a chair over there—use it. You're makin' me nervous." He said this with good humor, and he didn't seem to have a mean bone in his body; but, unlike certain smaller men who waved tommy guns around, this was a big bruiser of a man, who could hurt you slapping you on the back for luck.

So I sat down.

"Where you from?" he asked. "Before Chicago, I mean."

I gave him the standard Jimmy Lawrence spiel, a piece at a time; we talked for fifteen minutes. He seemed nice—I liked him. But he was obviously pumping me for information, checking me out, getting a feel for whether he could trust me or not.

Pretty soon he slapped his thighs with two catcher's mitt hands, stood. "I could use a Coke-Cola. How 'bout you? I'm buyin'."

I said okay, and followed him outside. We walked up to the central cabin, where the man in the Panama hat was no longer licking an ice-cream cone, though its tracks were evident on his trousers, his legs still pointing north and south. Near his bench, just under the NO VACANCY sign in the window, was a low-slung icebox of Coca-Cola, into which Floyd pumped a couple of nickels and withdrew two small, icy bottles.

We sat on the bench with the guy in the Panama; Floyd talked about the weather—how the heat wave seemed to have let up some—and the guy nodded while I just listened. We drank our Cokes, slowly. The little woman glanced out angrily through the screen door now and then. She didn't like Floyd any more than she liked me, apparently.

A big brown Buick touring sedan pulled in around three, and Baby

Face Nelson got out; he was wearing an unbuttoned vest and a snap-brim hat but no gun. Staying in the car were his wife Helen, in front, and Fred Barker and Paula in back.

Nelson strutted over to Floyd. "How are you doing, Chock?"

"Can't complain," Floyd said.

Nelson nodded to me. "Lawrence."

I nodded back to him.

The guy in the Panama hat jumped up like a jack-in-the-box, grinning the same way, and pumped Nelson's hand.

"Good to see you, Georgie," he said.

"You look good, Ben."

Ben turned his head to grin proudly at the still-seated Floyd, pointed with a thumb at Nelson. "We was in Joliet together," Ben said.

Nodding sagely, Floyd said, "It's good to have friends."

The screen door flew open and a boy and a girl came running out, pell-mell. The boy was towheaded and wearing a blue-and-red-striped shirt and denim pants; the girl was dark-haired and wore a blue-checked gingham dress. They both had the pretty face I'd suspected had once been their mother's.

They ran to Nelson immediately, crowded around him, bouncing up and down, laughing.

He tried not to smile as he said, "What makes you think I got anything for you?"

"Oh, I know you do, Uncle George!" the boy said; the little girl was just squealing.

Nelson's dark-haired wife hung out the car window with a goofy smile on her face, adoring her husband and his way with kids.

Holding his hands up like a traffic cop, Nelson said, "Okay, okay—maybe I did bring something for you. Maybe I did. You know how the game goes . . ."

He sat on the bench where his Joliet pal Ben had been sitting; Ben was standing by the screen door, now, wearing a big shit-eating grin, watching his kids being catered to by Baby Face Nelson.

The two kids stood and waited for the signal.

Nelson held his hands up in the air, like somebody had said, stick 'em up, and said, "Okay—search me!"

The kids, squealing, yelping, began to search, looking in his every pocket, and coming back with candy—Tootsie Rolls, mostly, but some jawbreakers and other hard colorful candy, too.

When the kids each had a fat handful of candy, Nelson stood and waved his hands, saying, "Okay, okay—you got me. Now promise you won't eat any of that till you had your supper?" And he winked elaborately at them, and they squealed some more and ran off God knows where.

The little woman had been standing watching all this out the screen door. Nelson noticed her, smiled her way, said, "I stocked up on candy 'fore I left Beaver Falls. Didn't want to disappoint the little rascals."

She looked out at him coldly, then receded back into the house.

Nelson shrugged, asked Ben for some room keys. Ben dutifully went inside and came back out with them.

Before he got back in the car to drive to his cabin, Nelson said to Floyd, "We never worked together. Looking forward to it."

"Likewise," Floyd nodded, smiling.

But the men didn't shake hands. There was mutual respect, here, but this was an uneasy truce, just the same. Babe Ruth and Lou Gehrig sizing each other up.

Nelson grinned at me, wolfishly; the mustache still looked fake. "You don't even know what this is about yet, do you, Lawrence? Ha ha ha! You're in for a surprise."

Then he got in the Buick with his wife and the others and drove a few doors down.

"Let's walk," Floyd said.

Hands in our pockets, we strolled aimlessly around back, through the trees, down to the riverbank. Trees on both sides of the river reflected off it; the sun looked at itself on the peaceful shimmer of the water.

We sat on the sloping ground, looking down at the river; there wasn't any beach to speak of, right here. Floyd plucked a weed and chewed on the end of it.

"Ever think about getting out of it?" Floyd asked.

"Out of what?"

He smiled; cheeks seemed about to burst, and they were a burning red. "This life of crime, friend. This ol' life of crime." He looked out toward the trees across the river. "Wouldn't you like to cross over there, and just be done with it?"

"Sometimes," I said.

"You probably better off with those Chicago Boys." He said "Boys" like "bow-ahs."

"Why's that?"

"They's business men."

"Well, aren't you?"

He grunted a laugh. "We's small fry. Kind gets gobbled up by the bigger fish."

I knew what he meant. There would always be room for the Capones and the Nittis; like Karpis said, the Syndicate was in "public-service-type business." The outlaws were a dying breed. And some of them seemed to know it.

"Take this 'Pretty Boy' shit. And 'Baby Face.' Those ain't names nobody who knows us calls us. That's newspaper shit. Only I don't think it starts with the newspapers."

"You don't?"

"I think it's Cummings and Hoover trying to make saps out of us."

Cummings was the U.S. attorney general, the man who was spearheading FDR's war on crime.

"Why?" I said.

"Why? They make us sound like mad dogs so they look like big heroes when they catch us."

"They haven't caught you yet."

He shook his head. "Matter of time. Matter of time."

"My experience with the feds is they're pretty goddamn lame."

Floyd nodded, chewing on the weed. "But they's so many of 'em."

"Yeah. And they got guns now. They can cross state lines, and they got guns now."

"I got so little to show."

"Huh?"

"I been at this since I was in my twenties. Just a kid. And I got so little stored away. This life is expensive, you know."

"They say you gave a lot of your money away."

He smiled, almost shyly this time. "I did some of that. I ain't no Robin Hood, like some'd have you think. Took care of my friends, in the hills, is all. And they took care of me. And mine."

He sat and stared at the river.

Then he said, "I got a boy, nine. Just a tad older than that boy of Ben's. And I got a pretty wife." He chewed the end of the weed; then turned eagerly and said, "Want to see?"

"Sure."

Grinning, he dug his wallet out of his back pocket. He showed me a snapshot of his wife—a lovely dark-haired woman in a white dress and hat; standing near her, putting a supportive arm around her, was a beaming kid in a white shirt and slacks.

"Good-looking kid," I said. "Honey of a wife, too."

He smiled, looking at the picture; after a while the smile faded, but he kept looking.

Then he put it away in the wallet; stuffed the wallet in his pocket.

I said, "They were dressed nice—look healthy, well-fed."

Floyd nodded. "I been providin' for 'em. But in the long run, what? This life can't last. I'm gettin' too old for it. And the times is passin' me by. It's time to get across the river."

I didn't follow him. I said so.

He smiled. "Sometimes you got to do something that common sense says not."

"Like what?"

"Like a impossible job. Like a score so big, you can make a new life."

My mouth felt dry.

I said, "Is that the kind of job going down tomorrow?"

He nodded—just the trace of a smile on the cupid lips.

I said, "All *I* know is it's a kidnapping."

"Did you know it's a big shot? A national figger, like the damn papers put it?"

I felt something cold at the base of my spine.

"No," I said.

"Well, it is, Jim." He rose.

He began to walk up the slope.

I followed.

"Who?" I asked.

"How much did they say you'd be getting?"

"My cut? Something like five gees."

"It'll be more. I promise you that."

We were through the trees, now.

"Who, Chock?"

"I don't want to tell you, unless I know you're in. In all the way. In for sure."

"I'm in. Who?"

"One of them that's out to end us."

"Who."

"Not 'who.' Hoover. John Edgar Hoover. Attorney general's right-hand man. Better hurry, Jim—it's gettin' time for Ma's barbecue. . . ."

"PRETTY BOY" FLOYD

36

Shortly after Floyd and I came back around the front of the tourist camp, a Ford sedan pulled in, driven by Doc Barker. Karpis rode in front with him, and Dolores and Louise were in back. The guy in the Panama hat, Ben, fetched their cabin keys. Louise saw me through her window, beamed and climbed out of the sedan and all but ran to my side. I'd known her less than twenty-four hours and there she was, clinging to my arm like life was a sinking ship and I was a piece of floating wood.

I walked her down to the room, carrying her bag.

"Twin beds," she said. "Too bad."

"Louise," I said. "I'm not so sure what happened this morning is something we ought to repeat. . . ."

She pretended to be hurt by that; the wide-set brown eyes looked comically woeful. God, she looked cute—the bobbed blond hair, the rosy cheeks, pouty lips, slight but rounded figure well displayed in a form-fitting pink-and-white-print cotton dress with a shoelace bow at the neck. She sat on the edge of one of the beds and hiked her skirt up to where the milk of her thighs said hello above her rolled stocking tops.

"You're too *much* of a gentleman sometimes, Jimmy—don't you think?"

Then there I was with my pants down around my legs and her skirt up and I never said I was perfect, did I?

She went into the bathroom for a while, came out looking fresh and sparkly, and we lay together, clothes more or less buttoned up and back in place, and she had a smoke. I hadn't seen her smoke before.

"You want a drag?" she asked, offering the ciggie.

"No thanks. Never picked up the habit."

"My daddy'd whip me sure, if he saw these lips touching tobacco. Candy got me started."

She spoke Candy's name with a sense of history; he'd retreated into the past. Dead a day.

It wasn't that she was cold, or heartless; she was a warm little thing, in about every way you could imagine. She'd just learned the facts of life on the outlaw road.

She said, "Should be suppertime soon, shouldn't it?"

"Real soon. Ma's cooking out back."

"She's a good cook." Puffed the cig. "This is a nice room."

"No outhouse tonight."

"Yeah, and a bath and everything. That's ugly wallpaper, though. Is that purple or brown or what? It makes the room seem small—why would they pick something so dark?"

"To keep us from noticing the cockroaches."

"Oh," she said, nodding. She didn't seem to be inhaling her smoke.

Bedsprings making their unmistakable music came through the thin wall.

She giggled. "Somebody else is being naughty."

"Who's next door?"

"I think it's the Nelsons."

"Well, then they're not being naughty. They're married, so it's okay with God and everybody."

She nodded; she had a disconcerting way of taking my wisecracks at face value.

From next door, a woman's voice said, "Less . . . less . . . oh, less!"

I said, "Doesn't she mean 'more'?"

"She's saying Les—the name, Les. Short for Lester? That's Nelson's real name. Lester Gillis."

That was news to me.

"Louise, honey. Can I be serious for a second?"

She shrugged. "Sure."

"You said this morning you couldn't have kids. You're a young woman. Are you sure about that? Have you checked with a doctor, or . . . ?"

She tried to be nonchalant, puffed her cigarette. She definitely wasn't inhaling. She said, "A doctor made me this way. Candy knocked me up one time, and the doc that took care of it didn't do me right."

Next door, Baby Face Nelson's wife was moaning.

"I'm sorry," I said.

She shrugged facially. "A real doctor looked at me later. He told me I couldn't have kids. It's okay. I don't think I want kids anyways. They're just a bother."

The bedsprings sang next door; Nelson's wife said, "Les! Les!"

I hugged the girl to me. "Don't you worry about anything," I said. "Everything's going to be okay."

She looked at me; the big brown eyes were wet. "Really?"

"I promise."

She hugged me. Hard. Desperately hard.

Silence next door.

A few minutes later somebody knocked and hollered, "Soup's on!" Nelson.

"Time to chow down, lovebirds! Ha ha ha."

Behind the central cabin, in which Ben and the little woman and their two kids lived, was a little brick patio, surrounded by a stone wall about waist-high. A slatted brown-stained picnic table, large enough for a dozen or so people, was in the middle. At the left was one of those white swings that looked like an inverted wooden V with the top squared off, in which two people could sit facing each other. At the moment Baby Face and his wife Helen were doing that very thing. To the right was a brick barbecue oven, the lower part as tall as a man and wide as his reach, with two openings, wood burning in the bottom, smaller one, and iron grids in the larger arched opening above that, at which point it narrowed into a chimney. Ma, wearing her calico apron over one of her familiar floral tents, was poking at various halfed chickens spread out on the lower of two grills, basting them occasionally from a bowl of thin red sauce; a pot of baked beans was biding its time on the upper grid.

The picnic table began to fill up, and soon the whole gang—if you'll pardon the expression—was having at the platters of barbecue chicken and the several bowls of coleslaw and the pot of baked beans; beers, Cokes, glasses of milk were scattered about, as were plenty of paper napkins. Baby Face Nelson and Helen, Pretty Boy Floyd, the Barker brothers and Fred's girl Paula, Old Creepy Karpis and Dolores, chowing down like this was a family picnic. Speaking of family, Ben, the little woman and their two kids were down at one end of the table. The little woman had, in fact, made the slaw, which was very good, and had got the fire going earlier in the afternoon that had made the chicken possible. But that was the extent of her being sociable, and she wasn't eating much, just picking at her paper plate.

Her kids would look down the table toward Nelson, who would wink at them, and the kids would grin at him, and each other. I'd seen this at the farm, too—Nelson got along famously with Verle and Mildred's two boys, as well—and wondered if somehow I was seeing the real George Nelson. Or anyway, Lester Gillis.

His wife Helen picked up on the byplay between him and the kids, and said to him, "I miss our two."

Nelson looked momentarily sad—the only time I ever saw sadness touch his face—and said, "We got to find a way to get to Mom's and see 'em. We just got to."

Louise whispered to me, "That's sweet," without sarcasm. I don't think she and sarcasm were acquainted, actually.

Next to Nelson was a dark-haired, dark-eyed man, eating quietly, holding the messy chicken in his hands almost daintly, like the dead barbecued bird was a teacup. He was handsome, a lady-killer type, but on the cadaverous side, with a little Ronald Colman mustache, and even sitting down you could see he was tall, much taller than Nelson. This was John Paul Chase, Nelson's dog-loyal sidekick, who'd been posted in the barn back at the Gillises'. I hadn't seen him arrive, so he'd apparently come later in a car of his own.

He said, "Pass the salt, please."

It was the only thing I ever heard him say.

Nelson would speak to him occasionally, and Chase would just nod. Nelson called him J.P. Using initials for nicknames was a trend Nelson was trying to set in these circles, with no apparent success.

There was no talk of crime at the table. The subjects at hand were baseball (did the St. Louis Cardinals, a.k.a. the "Gashouse Gang," have the pennant sewn up or not?) and boxing (would Ross take McLarnin in their rematch next month?) and how good Ma's cooking was (better 'n Betty Crocker's).

Doc Barker, who'd taken little part in the small talk, did at one point say, "Where's your friend Sullivan?"

Floyd, hands red with barbecue sauce, glanced above the half-eaten half a chicken he was eating (his second) and said, "He don't feel so good. We tied one on last night."

Fred Barker paused mid-chicken to grin, gold teeth flashing. "Hung over, huh?"

Floyd smiled; he had sauce all over his lips and teeth. "*Way* over."

Doc said, "Is he going to be up for it?"

"Sure," Floyd said, matter-of-factly.

"I never worked with the guy."

"I have," Floyd said. Friendly but with a hard edge.

"I never even heard of him."

Floyd put the chicken down. "I don't work with just anybody, Doc."

"I never said you did, Chock."

Nelson, working on a bite of baked beans, said, "Yeah, why isn't your pal Richetti in on this one? I thought *he* was your right-hand man."

"He's on the mend. Caught a bullet while back."

"Sorry to hear it," Nelson said. "Suppose he's holed up in the Cookson Hills, huh?"

Floyd shook his head no. "We been havin' to avoid the hills. Ever since the feds and the state militia did that sweep through there February last, we been stayin' out."

Karpis, who was sharing half a chicken with Dolores, said, "I heard they only nailed a dozen or so crooks, all of 'em small-timers, with that search party." Small laugh. "A thousand men combing the hills for small change."

Floyd nodded. "Still, with the governor willin' to turn up the heat that high, we been keeping out of there. We been holing up 'round Toledo way."

Doc said, "Licavoli mob's helping you out, I suppose."

"Yeah," Floyd said. "For a price."

Doc sighed, nodded. "Yeah. This ol' life ain't cheap, is it?"

"Life's cheap enough," Floyd said. "It's livin' that gets expensive."

Louise, who was an even daintier eater than John Paul Chase (she was the only one at the table cutting the meat off the chicken with her knife and fork, instead of just using her hands—her daddy must've beat some manners in her), had finished her meal and was starting to complain of getting eaten up by mosquitoes. The sun was going down and the bugs were coming out.

Floyd stood. "You nice gals can clear the table, if you would, and get in away from the skeeters. Us men got work to do."

Karpis wiped his face and hands with a napkin and stood as well. "Yes we do. Let's go down to my cabin."

The men went down to his cabin.

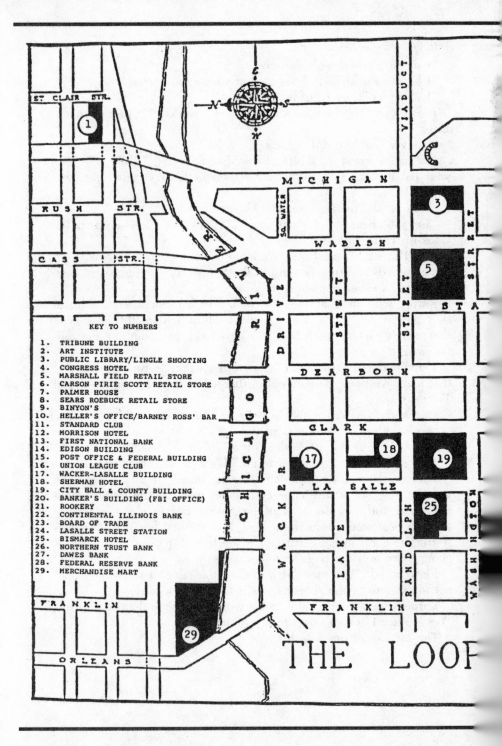

KEY TO NUMBERS

1. TRIBUNE BUILDING
2. ART INSTITUTE
3. PUBLIC LIBRARY/LINGLE SHOOTING
4. CONGRESS HOTEL
5. MARSHALL FIELD RETAIL STORE
6. CARSON PIRIE SCOTT RETAIL STORE
7. PALMER HOUSE
8. SEARS ROEBUCK RETAIL STORE
9. BINYON'S
10. HELLER'S OFFICE/BARNEY ROSS' BAR
11. STANDARD CLUB
12. MORRISON HOTEL
13. FIRST NATIONAL BANK
14. EDISON BUILDING
15. POST OFFICE & FEDERAL BUILDING
16. UNION LEAGUE CLUB
17. WACKER-LASALLE BUILDING
18. SHERMAN HOTEL
19. CITY HALL & COUNTY BUILDING
20. BANKER'S BUILDING (FBI OFFICE)
21. ROOKERY
22. CONTINENTAL ILLINOIS BANK
23. BOARD OF TRADE
24. LASALLE STREET STATION
25. BISMARCK HOTEL
26. NORTHERN TRUST BANK
27. DAWES BANK
28. FEDERAL RESERVE BANK
29. MERCHANDISE MART

THE LOOP

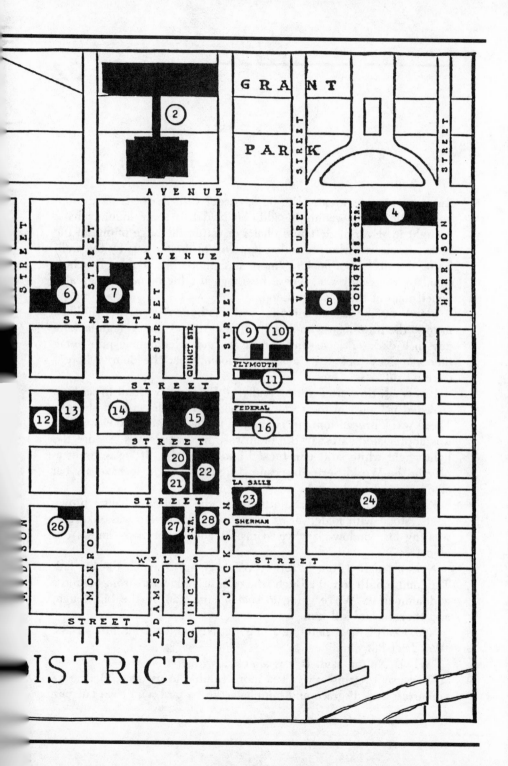

37

Karpis' cabin was identical to ours, except with the beds on the opposite side of the room. In addition he'd had some folding chairs brought in. Everybody found chairs or sat on the edge of one of the beds, which was where I ended up, over to the far left, by the wall, facing Karpis, who, looking more and more like a schoolteacher, stood by the facing wall where he'd tacked a big homemade grease-pencil map of the Chicago Loop.

Floyd was the last to come in, with his hungover partner Sullivan in tow, the little-man-who-wasn't-there at dinner, an average-looking guy in a dark suit, wearing sunglasses and a fedora, despite being indoors. They took seats across the room, near the door, where I couldn't quite see 'em.

It was a little warm, a little stuffy in the room, with all these men crowded in, most of them smoking; no cigars in the crowd, at least. There was a breeze tonight, coming in the half-open windows, and it was appreciated. Most of the men were in shirt sleeves; I wore the lightweight white suit, gun tucked under my arm. If I was going to play in the World Series of crime, I figured I ought to have my bat along.

Karpis, in a white shirt buttoned to the neck and baggy brown pants, stood with folded arms, slouching a little. He was, like me, wearing his window-glass wire-rims. "I guess everybody knows our objective."

Nelson laughed, but bitterly. "We're going to snatch the big fed. The loud-mouth son of a bitch who calls us yellow rats from behind a goddamn desk. We're going to snatch him, haul in the big dough, and then fuckin' kill him."

"*No*," Karpis said, pointing a finger at Nelson like a kid in his class. "We *don't* kill him."

"Why?" Nelson said. It was almost a whine.

"Because," Karpis said, "he's more trouble to us dead. Better we embarrass and disgrace and humiliate the bastard, and *then* cut him loose, than have him be a dead hero for the feds and press to rally 'round."

From across the smoky room came Floyd's voice. "I agree. The son of a bitch likes to call us 'vile' and 'vicious' and 'mad dogs' and that. Kill him and we make him look right."

"I don't give a shit," Nelson said evenly.

Floyd said, "That's just handin' Hoover's attorney general boss more ammunition against us. Then he just sticks another son of a bitch in Hoover's chair, and what's to gain? The days ahead is gonna be hot enough."

Karpis took over. "George, listen. Sure, picking Hoover for our mark comes partly out of wanting to even scores with the son of a bitch. Make him look bad, make him look stupid, put him on the spot. Of course. But the real point of this, the main point, is to grab a public figure so important the government'll cough up some real dough to get him back. The fact it also makes the feds look sick is just frosting on the cake."

Doc Barker was sitting next to me; he seemed impatient as he said, "Quit chasing your tails, fellas. I ain't convinced yet this is even gonna come off. I'm not in unless somebody can show me how this fool thing can really work."

Fred Barker nodded, said, "Yeah. Yeah, me too!"

Karpis said, "That's why we're here, Doc."

Doc said, "From what you told me before, I take it you're planning to snatch Hoover right on the street, right in front of the feds' own office building."

Jesus.

"Last time we tried something in the Loop we damn near got our asses shot off," Barker was saying.

"That's not fair, Doc," Karpis said. "If we hadn't got in that accident, we'd been in the clear."

"Bull*shit*. You got in a accident 'cause of traffic, and then them cops swarmed on us like flies on shit."

"The basic plan was sound, Doc. We can make it work this time."

"You're going to use the *same* plan as for the post-office heist?"

Karpis smiled a mildly embarrassed version of his ghastly smile. "Well, yes, sort of, as a stepping-off point anyway—the Banker's Building is right across from the post office, where we made the other hit. Direct across. We can build on that same plan, and learn from our mistakes."

Doc was shaking his head. "Learn from our mistakes? What you should learn from that post-office flop is not to pull jobs in the Loop. City jobs are a bitch in general. Now, in the country, shit, you can hit a place, drive like hell, know your back roads and you're home free. But in the city, fuck."

Karpis was getting worried. "Come on, Doc, keep an open mind. . . ."

"You got traffic to deal with, cops on every block, one call and the word's out to hundreds of radio cars . . . shit. And a plan that went bust one other time. Creepy, I'm surprised at you."

Nelson said, "Doc, you knew what this was about coming in—why bitch now?"

Doc said, "I'm all for snatching Hoover. It's a sweet way to get even and get rich. Understood? But why not snatch him at the track—he likes the ponies, you know—or at the train station, when he comes to town, or leaves."

Karpis said, "Those are city jobs, too, Doc."

"Yeah, sure, but they're easier to deal with than the goddamn heart o' the *Loop*. Don't forget—I was *there*, on that post-office heist. I saw the fuckin' bullets fly."

"Doc," Nelson said, an edge in his voice. "Why don't you let Karpis lay it out for us?"

Karpis laid it out.

He pointed to the map as he spoke, using a grease pencil to trace various routes.

They had inside word that Hoover was coming in tomorrow morning to spend a day at the Division of Investigation's Chicago bureau, giving the boys in the trenches pep talks and confabbing with Purvis and Cowley. Of more interest to Karpis, however, was Hoover's evening dinner date with State Attorney Courtney and the Chicago police commissioner. This was a pass-the-peace-pipe powwow initiated by Hoover, seeking to build more cooperation between the feds and the local cops; my guess was the state attorney and the police commissioner were going along with the meeting in order to ask for Purvis' ouster. The cops had covered the feds' trail any number of times (the Probasco "suicide" fall, for one thing) and all they'd got in return was bad-mouthing in the press by self-aggrandizing Little Mel. So a meeting was in order.

None of this was anything Karpis went into; these were simply thoughts that flitted through my brain as he stated that Hoover was planning dinner with Courtney and the commissioner at seven o'clock at the Bismarck Hotel. Shortly before seven, a car from the state attorney's office was to pick up Hoover at the Banker's Building and escort him to the Bismarck.

"Where'd you get that kind of inside dope?" a smiling Nelson asked.

Karpis smiled his awful smile. "Friends in high places," he said, and let it go at that.

My guess was attorney Louis Piquett had sniffed this piece of news out; he had plenty of lines into Courtney's office.

Karpis' basic plan was simple if cunning. The state attorney's car was distinctively decorated: a black Hudson with one red and one green headlight, and a red star on the spotlight. Karpis had arranged with "our favorite underworld garage, in Cicero" to have another Hudson similarly decorated—and, in addition to police siren, equipped with such accessories as bulletproofing, shortwave radio and a sliding panel in the doors through which guns could be fired.

Karpis planned to have this car pick up Hoover.

The real state attorney's car, in a city parking garage near City Hall, would have a convenient flat tire, delaying the Hoover pickup a few minutes—long enough for the ringer to make the pickup instead.

Karpis was drawing on the map, saying, "If the pickup goes smooth, our Hudson just continues on down Clark to Jackson and turns west—like we were heading back to the Bismarck. After that we switch cars."

Nelson said, "We'll have a extra car stashed? Where?"

"In a loading dock in this alley," Karpis said, pointing to the map. "It's after work; deserted. We stuff Hoover in the trunk of the second car, and drive away, nice and easy."

Doc said, "Fine and dandy, if the snatch goes smooth. What if it's queered at the scene? What if some fed recognizes somebody, or wants to look at ID, or they send a different car? What if the shit hits the fan, right there in front of the Banker's Building?"

Karpis just smiled patiently through all this. He said, "We got all that covered. There'll be a backup car with extra firepower parked across the way, in front of the Edison Building—on Adams, kiddy-corner from the Banker's Building. If shooting starts, they cover the escape by opening fire from another direction. And if the snatch goes smooth, they cruise down Adams—dumping tacks behind 'em like bread crumbs, making flat tires and jamming traffic. At LaSalle, the backup car'll head north, dropping more tacks, to throw the laws off the trail—and ditch their car and switch in an alley off Franklin and Monroe to a new car. And drive away."

Doc was smirking, skeptical as hell. "All of this in the Loop. Creepy, you're dreaming."

Karpis said, "No, Doc—you're sleeping. *Think*. Between six and seven, the LaSalle Street district is deader than a doornail. The market shuts down at three—everybody'll be out by six, easy. On our way in, both the backup and the Hudson'll take different routes—and if on the way in we see a lot of cops or anything else out of the ordinary, we'll fold it up. Either car'll have the right to fold it—if the Hudson gets there and the backup isn't in position, that means they chose to fold. If the Hudson wants to fold, they just drive on by the Banker's Building, east on Adams, without stopping."

Then Karpis went through the escape route—the one that would be taken should the job go sour. The Hudson would turn hard down Quincy, and take a very tight turn down the alley, Rookery Court. Then would pull west on Adams, and once there, if traffic's heavy, use the siren, crossing LaSalle and Wells, going under the El. After another block on Adams, the Hudson would take a left and go south on Franklin Street. If the siren had been in use, it would be turned off here. Two short blocks later, the Hudson would cut across Jackson and dodge into a narrow, barely noticeable alley behind the fifteen-story building on the northeast corner. This alley led into a system of several alleys, the main, widest one of which was where the loading dock was, with the extra car.

"It's a two-bay loading dock," Karpis said, "nice and deep—a car can enter it and not stick out in the alley at all."

Whether the snatch went smooth or soured, the Hudson would end up here, pulling into the bay next to the second car; everybody would tumble out, putting Hoover (gagged by now) in the trunk of the second car. Of the three men who picked up Hoover, two would be in Chicago police uniforms; they would quickly strip out of those with street clothes underneath—and drive out of the bay and onto Van Buren, going west.

Doc was starting to look less skeptical; but he still asked, "What about *real* cops? Two to a block, in the Loop, you know."

Karpis shrugged like Jack Benny. "Supper hour, Doc. Streets are good and empty of uniforms 'tween six and seven."

Doc nodded slowly. Then said, "Streetcars? Traffic?"

"Both'll be slow at that hour, that part of the Loop."

Nelson was nodding, too, saying, "And what traffic there is'll mostly be people coming *into* the Loop, for dinner and an evening's fun 'n' games—not going *out*, like we'd be doing."

Doc said, "But State and Wabash and the streets around there will be hopping."

Karpis shrugged again. "That's in our favor. If an alarm *is* sounded, the cops'll have to break through that traffic to get to us. By the time they reach the Banker's Building at the southwest tip of the Loop, we'll've switched cars."

Doc thought about that.

Karpis went on. "The Hudson'll only be on the street for about four blocks, remember. A few minutes at most."

Karpis then went into the deployment of men: three in the fake state attorney's car; two in the backup car; one at the loading dock waiting with the second car; another to disable the real state attorney's car at the city garage near City Hall.

And me—I'd be baby-sitting the ladies, in Ma Barker's apartment on Pine Grove Avenue. I might be there for weeks—as long as it took for Hoover to be ransomed, plus some cooling-off time. The men didn't want to hook back up with their ladies till they were sure the Hoover grab was a success. Nobody wanted his girl serving time on this one.

Also, the guy who'd disable the state attorney's car had a bigger job than just kicking the nail in the toe of his shoe into the tire on a Hudson. First he'd have to go up a fire escape to get into the garage (which was serviced by carhops); then he'd have to hang around on the street and watch the state attorney's real delivery boys go after their car and, when it turned out they were delayed by a flat tire, try to delay whoever it was from calling the office.

"That's your job, Chase," Karpis told Nelson's lapdog John Paul. Chase nodded.

"Just sap him or something," Nelson said, offhandedly. "Don't kill him or nothin'."

Karpis underscored that. "*No* killing—if you can help it. We're going to be *hot enough*. If they don't believe they'll get him back alive, they won't pay the freight. We leave a trail of bodies, they'll figure us to kill him for sure. Got that?"

Heads nodded.

"Now, we got a problem in possibly being recognized," Karpis said.

"I don't think it's much of one, 'cause Hoover and his people aren't going to be looking for the likes of us to be picking him up for supper. But it's a problem. So me and Chock and Chock's pal Sullivan will do the pickup in the Hudson."

Doc said, "Chock's picture's been plastered to hell and gone."

"I know—but he'll be in a police uniform, driving; he's a big guy— he'll look like your typical well-fed Chicago cop—won't you, Chock?"

"Damn tootin'," Floyd laughed.

Karpis pointed to himself with a thumb. "My face-lift and glasses and such makes me a good candidate for not being made. And Chock's friend Sullivan doesn't have a famous puss like some of the rest of us; he'll be the other cop, the one in back. I'll be in a nice suit and look like a state attorney's assistant. And then the three of us'll give J. Edgar a ride."

Nelson pointed toward the map and said, "I want the backup car, parked on Adams there."

Karpis nodded. "My thoughts exactly. You and Freddie."

Freddie grinned, goldly, and nodded. "I'll be wheel man."

"Doc," Karpis said, "you got the dock. The loading dock. All you got to do is baby-sit the switch car."

Doc didn't seem thrilled about it, but he nodded.

Karpis said, "Chock and Sullivan and me'll baby-sit Mr. Hoover, incidentally. We got a place waitin'. Nobody else in this room needs know where that place is. Just rest assured it's safe. Once the ransom's delivered, I'll find everybody and distribute the wealth."

As an outsider to the ways of the outlaw, I was surprised to find that no one objected to this arrangement; the thought of a double cross never arose. They trusted each other. Or at least they trusted Karpis.

Then Doc nodded toward me. "What about Lawrence?"

"He baby-sits the girls."

There was some laughter.

"Nice work if you can get it!" Floyd hooted, still out of view.

Even Doc smiled. "Where do I sign up to get *my* harem?" he said.

Nelson didn't find it funny. "You got a job to do, Lawrence—do it! And no funny business."

Fred grinned and said, "Don't you worry about your better half, George—Lawrence's already got his hands full with Lulu."

That wasn't a particularly witty remark, but there was more laughter, nonetheless, some of it from Nelson this time. Nobody seemed to mind that I'd taken over for Candy Walker with "Lulu" so quickly; it was just part of their world.

Floyd's voice said, "Seriously, fellers—I think we oughta talk money. Jim mentioned he'd been promised five grand—and that sounds kinda low to me, even if his job is on the soft side."

Doc said, "I'm for that. Lawrence'll fall just as far as the rest of us, if it all comes down around us. Kidnapping's kidnapping."

Nelson jumped up. "He don't get a full share. No way he gets a full share."

Fred said, "Some of his share's got to go to Candy."

"Candy's got no kin," Doc said. "So it goes to Lulu."

Nelson laughed, sat back down. "So it goes to Lawrence after all."

There was some more general good-natured laughter, and Karpis pushed the smoky air with his palms, the teacher quieting his class. "We come to money, then. Fine. You might as well know an extra cut comes off the top."

"Fuck!" Nelson said. "What for?"

Karpis said, "There's a silent partner."

"Who?" Nelson demanded.

Karpis shook his head no. "No name. That's why they call it 'silent,' B.G."

There were some smiles at the use of the initials; Nelson didn't pick up on it, but Karpis was gently deriding him.

Karpis went on. "Our silent partner is bankrolling the job, out of his share. If it queers, he takes the loss. Also, he provided the inside dope on Hoover's activities." He nodded toward the map. "And he helped me put together this whole shootin' match."

Floyd's voice: "It's fair, George. It's only fair."

Doc Barker was nodding, and Fred said, "It is fair."

Nelson, disgruntled, said, "Yeah, yeah. Okay."

Karpis smiled benignly. "We got a big pie to cut up, George. We *are* talking about five hundred thousand dollars."

Five hundred thousand dollars!

Suddenly I heard myself talking.

"You really think the government is going to meet that?" I asked.

Karpis said, "Yeah, I think so. I can't guarantee it. But I think they'll meet the ransom demand, yeah."

I didn't, but held back further comment.

Nelson was putting his two cents in. "Uncle Sam can just print us up some money," he said, "and if he don't—then we *will* kill Hoover, and won't that be sweet."

Doc, not liking the sound of that particularly, said, "Then what?"

Nelson grinned; he was shifting into high-gear Cagney. "Then we grab Cummings or the president or somebody, and let's see 'em fuck with us *then*."

Nobody countered that. Just no arguing with logic, I guess.

Karpis said, "Here's the way the money shakes down. We're going to pay Lawrence twenty grand off the top, and give Lulu five, out of respect to Candy. Any argument?"

No argument.

"That gives each of us fifty grand and pocket change."

The room was quiet as church, while everybody contemplated the new start that could mean. That could indeed get Chock Floyd "across the river," in style.

"Get some rest, boys," Karpis said. "Drink and be merry if you like—if you ain't alone, show her a good time. And sleep till noon. But at one, meet back in this room, for a final run-through. Because tomorrow's opening night, already."

People stood up, started moving out.

That was when I got my first good look at Chock Floyd's friend Sullivan, and he got his first good look at me.

We both recognized each other, and why not?

He was the man who'd called himself John Howard, when he came to my office last month—the traveling salesman who hired me to follow his "wife," Polly Hamilton.

38

It was the longest few moments of my life, standing there in Karpis'
room near the door, about to go out, heart in my throat as I looked in
the face of a man who knew I wasn't Jimmy Lawrence.

Slowly he removed the dark glasses and there my name was, in his
eyes: "Heller," they said, narrowing. Hell, he was as shocked as I
was.

And there we stood, blocking the way.

"Move along, gents," Nelson said. "We baked in this oven long
enough."

I swallowed; said, "Sure."

My onetime client swallowed, nodded, put the dark glasses back
on, moved out the door and I followed him out into the breezily
warm summer evening, my hand drifting toward the automatic under
my jacket as I walked.

The men were milling about, out in front of Karpis' cabin, some of
them having further smokes. Nelson tapped Sullivan on the shoulder
and Sullivan looked at him from behind the dark glasses, with a tight,
blank expression.

Nelson said, "You sure we ain't worked together before?"

Sullivan smiled politely, shook his head no.

Nelson looked confused, momentarily, said, "You seem familiar.
Huh. Well, what the hell."

And he walked over to Chase and began talking, smoking.

I smiled at Sullivan.

Because I knew.

I knew why he hadn't given me away to the others. And I knew
he'd had just as long and sweaty a last few minutes as I had.

He was lighting a cigarette; his hand was shaking—it was barely
perceptible, but I caught it.

I stood close to him, put a comradely hand on his shoulder. Spoke
so low he could barely hear me.

But he heard me.

I said, "Let's talk, Johnny."

And John Dillinger nodded, and we began to walk.

"I'm surprised to see you, John," I told him.

"Let's leave names aside, Heller, here on out, okay? Some people got big ears."

"But neither one of us better have big mouths, right? We can't afford to give each other away, can we?"

We stopped in front of the central cabin; Karpis and Dolores were sitting on the bench, having Cokes. I put a nickel in the low-riding icebox and opened the lid and slid a bottle out for myself. Dillinger stood and watched me through the dark circles of the glasses, fedora brim pulled down. He was smoking, looking relaxed, calm; but I could feel his nervousness in the air, like electricity crackling between us.

We strolled around back; found a tree to stand under. No one else was around. It was a clear, moonlit night; we could see each other fine. Not that he wanted to see me.

Dillinger didn't like this at all. On the other hand, I was getting a perverse sort of charge out of it. I'd thought the house was coming down on my head, minutes ago; now I knew I was sitting on top.

"What are you doing here?" he asked me. Clipped words. He took off the dark glasses, slid them in his shirt pocket behind his pack of smokes. He didn't have a gun.

I took a sip of the Coke. "Let's start with you," I said. "Who knows you here? Knows who you really are, I mean."

He exhaled smoke. "Just Floyd."

"Not Karpis?"

He shook his head no.

"But you're the silent partner Karpis was talking about," I said.

He nodded.

"And Karpis seems to've been in on the planning, all the way . . ."

He shrugged. "He is," he said. "But he thinks I'm just some friend of Chock's. I'm supposed to be a guy from Oklahoma wanted for murder, who had a face job."

"That isn't far wrong."

He gave out a short, humorless laugh. "Anyway, I never worked with Karpis. I met him once or twice. But not so's he could recognize me."

"But Nelson and the others are a different story."

He exhaled some more smoke; it made a sort of question mark in

the air. "Yeah," he said. "They might pick up on my voice, or my
eyes. Plastic surgery don't change you as one hundred percent as
people think."

"Yours ain't bad," I said.

He sighed heavily; a weight-of-the-world sigh. "It cost me. And it
wasn't just one operation. It was a whole series of 'em, out West. No
hack like Doc Moran."

"He's dead, you know."

"Lot of that going around."

This time I was the one who laughed humorlessly. "Threatening
me, John? Or referring to your own greatly exaggerated demise?"

He sneered. "What do you think?"

"I think you went to a hell of a lot of trouble to get officially dead.
You should've dropped off the face of the earth by now. Why get back
in the game again, so soon, or at all—when you went through so
much trouble getting out?"

The sneer got nastier. "Guess."

"I'll take a wild one—money. Death is free, but only if you really
die, right? Take Piquett—he wouldn't come cheap, not for a scam
this size. He's risking disbarment, after all."

Another laugh. "He risks that every day. But, no, he didn't come
cheap."

"Or Zarkovich and O'Neill, either."

"No."

"Or Anna Sage."

"Or Anna Sage," he admitted.

The muffled sound of hillbilly music could be heard from the tourist camp, behind us; Ma had finally found her station.

"Does Polly Hamilton know?"

"That I'm alive? No. You're part of a select group, Heller."

"No names, remember? It does explain why you came to my office
personally, to put me in motion where Polly Hamilton was concerned. I came to think you were just some con man Piquett hired.
You did it yourself, though, to keep the circle nice and tight. A secret
like this isn't easily kept. Fewer conspirators the better."

He said nothing.

I swigged the Coke; finished it. Tossed the bottle into the trees.
"Yeah, it must've cost you, really cost you—or you wouldn't be risking your new face out in the open like this . . . not to mention this

lunatic plot to kidnap Hoover. Jesus! You really believe the government'll pay you people off?"

"Yeah," he said, testily. "I think they'll pay. And I don't think
they'll even tell the public it ever happened."

That hadn't occurred to me.

I said, "You figure they'll put on a press blackout till they get
Hoover back."

"I do. And after. They got a lot of press and prestige tied up in that
fat little bastard. He's riding my 'death' like a rodeo pony."

Ma's hillbilly music in the background lent some color to his remark.

I grunted a laugh. "Must frustrate you—here you are 'dead,' and
the fuck-ups you fooled, you used, are using you to make themselves
look like Saturday afternoon heroes."

"G-men," he said, derisively. "They're going to kill us all, you
know. That's why I went out my own way, on my own terms. The
feds, they're dopes, they're fuck-ups, they're boobs—but they got
money and time on their side. It's over. This whole damn game is
over. Even a chowderhead like Nelson can see that."

Male laughter came from up by the cabins; they were taking Karpis' advice and making merry.

I said, "Well, Floyd sees the writing on the wall, all right. He said
much the same thing as you, this afternoon. He said it was just a
matter of time."

"Well, it's true, and this snatch is risky but it stands to stake every
man one of us to a ticket out of this outlaw life."

"Yeah, and you get a double share."

He nodded, smiling; under the mustache, I could see the famous
wry wise-guy Dillinger smile, pushing through the tight, new face.
"Over a hundred grand. That ought to buy me a farm."

"If this job doesn't buy all of you the farm."

He put a hand against my chest, flat; there was more menace in the
gesture than in all of Nelson's tommy-gun waving. "Why?" he asked.
"You planning to pull the plug on us, Heller? You the undercover
man in the woodpile?"

"No names, remember?" I said, suddenly a little scared. "I'm not
here to pull anybody's plug."

"Why *are* you here? And why the hell are you calling yourself
Jimmy Lawrence? When I heard that name kicked around, I had to
wonder. It's common enough, but . . ."

"Nitti gave it to me to use. I'm helping *you*, really. He figured it'd be good having somebody named Jimmy Lawrence wandering around, *after* the Biograph."

Dillinger flicked the stub of his cigarette away, smiled mildly, said, "Nitti's smart. Too fuckin' smart for his own good. He's gonna die of being smart someday."

"He plays people like a hand of cards, I'll give you that. As for why I'm here, it's strictly a mission of mercy—and it's with Nitti's full okay."

"Make me believe that."

I told him, in enough detail to convince him, that I was here to retrieve Candy Walker's moll Lulu for her ailing farmer father.

He seemed to buy it, farmer's kid that he was himself; but he said, "I can check on this with a phone call."

"I know you can. But do you really want Nitti to know you're in the neighborhood? He's not exactly going to be tickled pink about what you're planning for tomorrow, you know."

Dillinger got out a new cigarette, lit it up; in the orange glow of the flame, his mask of a face gave little away. "He's not going to know I was involved—unless you tell him."

"Why should I tell him?"

He didn't answer me. Instead he said, reflectively, "I suppose you'd like to just take the girl and scram. Just hop in one of these cars and rescue the fair maiden, and not get caught up in tomorrow's business."

My answer to that flatly posed question would be crucial; I could see it in his face, hear it in his voice, if just barely—he was doing his best not to tip his hand.

But I could tell what he wanted to hear—and what he didn't want to hear.

So I said, "Hell, no. I'm in."

He studied me. "You're in?"

"Hell, yes. twenty-five gees worth, I am."

"You're supposed to be a stand-up guy, Heller. So honest you quit the force and all. Why all of a sudden are you willing to get in the kidnapping racket?"

I put on my best smirk; inside I wasn't smiling. "Hoover's nothing to me. The feds gave me nothing but grief, when you were staging that ballet at the Biograph. Make 'em look as stupid as you like, and squeeze as much dough out as you can."

He studied me.

"Look, I can use twenty-five gees, friend. I had two clients in the last month and a half—and you were one of 'em."

He drew on the cigarette.

I said, "But I'm not in for murder, understand. I want your word Hoover won't be killed. Even if they don't fork over the dough."

He said nothing for a while. Fiddles were playing on Ma's radio station.

Then he said, "You got my word," and held his hand out for me to shake.

I shook it.

"Hell," I said, "all I got to do is bunk in with some good-looking women for a few weeks. I had worse jobs."

Dillinger laughed; a genuine laugh. "Yeah. There's worse ways to score twenty-five grand. And when it's over, you can take the skirt and blow."

"Fair enough," I said.

"But Heller—if you're stringing me along—if you fuck this up for me—you're dead. Got that? Plain old dead."

"Understood."

He threw the latest cigarette away; it sizzled in the grass, and we walked back around front of the tourist cabins.

As we walked, I said, "You were some actor, back in my office that time. You really had me going."

He smiled. "I always have had a smooth line of bull."

Me, too, John. Me, too.

39

We were gathered much as the night before, in the same smoky room, only now sun was filtering through the sheer curtains, dust motes floating, as Doc Barker said, "Ever hear of a guy named Nate Heller?"

He was sitting right next to me when he said it; I felt myself starting to shake. The gun was under my arm, but my hand was on my knee, a world away.

They'd been talking about the possibility of the feds marking the bills. It had happened in the Bremer snatch, and the dough had been so hot no fence wanted to touch it at first, though they finally sold most of it at a ten percent discount. Karpis said in this case they'd insist on used, non-consecutive bills, and set up for a fast ransom exchange—too fast, Karpis hoped, for the feds to get serial numbers recorded.

Floyd had suggested they sit on the money awhile, but float a few bills out just to see what happened. Karpis suggested the way to do that was remove some bills from Hoover's wallet and substitute ransom money.

"If the bills are hot," Karpis had said, "then Hoover'll be the first to pass 'em. The papers'll report the bills turning up, in whatever city he passes 'em in—Washington, D.C., most likely—and we'll know right away if we need to fence the cash."

Nelson said, "Anybody know a good hot-money fence? I hear Doc Moran's gone out of business."

A few smiles greeted this slice of gallows humor, and then Doc Barker made his remark about Nate Heller.

I glanced across the room at Dillinger, playing Sullivan, in fedora and dark glasses; below the mustache there seemed to be a trace of a smile.

"Yeah, I know him," Karpis said. "He runs the Parkview Hotel in Havana. That's a good thought. Heller's a good prospect for moving the cash, if it turns out the feds marked it."

I let some air out, and Doc glanced at me. "You okay, Lawrence? You sound like some old geezer gaspin' his last."

I managed a grin. "You should've seen me before I gave up smokin'," I said.

He smiled briefly, and with his sunken cheeks it was like a skull smiling; then he turned his attention back to Karpis, who was asking for the group's permission to sit on the money till they'd determined whether the feds had marked it or not; and, if so, to go ahead and fence the dough before the split. There was a general agreement on the subject.

After the final briefing, we drifted outside. Dillinger, or Sullivan— take your pick—strolled up to me, unable to suppress his wry smile. He glanced around to see if anybody was within earshot, and then quietly said, "You went white as a ghost in there, pal. What's wrong—d'you think you were the only Nate Heller in the world?"

"I guess if there can be two of you, there can be two of me."

He shrugged. "Anything's possible."

We were about an hour from Chicago. Karpis, Floyd and "Sullivan" left around two o'clock in one car; at three, Nelson, Chase, and the Barker brothers took off in another. I was to leave at four, driving Ma in the Auburn, followed by the Ford sedan, driven by Dolores, with Louise and Paula and Nelson's wife Helen riding.

Not long after the Nelson car had taken off, I found myself back in the puce-papered room, in bed with Louise. There were worse ways to kill an hour, but she was starting to wear me down. I don't mean to make like she was a real hot tomato or something, a regular sex fiend—no. She seemed to enjoy the act, all right, only she liked the attention, more. She liked being held. She liked being close to me. And I liked being close to her.

Maybe having been with a woman as strong as Sally made me appreciate this more dependent girl. I liked being looked up to; leaned on. The role of protector was attractive to me, just as attractive as her big brown eyes and blond bobbed hair and pale skin and . . .

And now and then it occurred to me how short a time I'd known her. That in those two days or so, I'd had her half a dozen times. I felt funny about it, though I didn't quite know why—I just knew it was more than some kind of guilt over sleeping with my client's daughter.

Now we lay between the sheets, naked, my arm around her. She had her head nestled in the crook of my arm, cheek against my chest,

a pink-nailed hand against my chest as well, playing with the hair
there.

"How'd you like to be free of all this?" I asked her.

She cocked her head and the brown eyes blinked. "Free of all
what?"

"This. This life—on the road. On the run. Living with crooks,
Louise."

She smiled, put her head back on my chest. "You're no crook to
me. You're just my Gentleman Jim. . . ."

"Remember what we talked about yesterday? The big city, and you
finding a job?"

"Y—yes. But that was just talk."

"It wasn't just talk. You know, there's nothing binding you to this
life, anymore."

"But I been with Candy ever since—"

"Candy's dead."

She still had her head against my chest, as if listening to my heart.
"But I'm with you, now—aren't I?"

"Right now you are, yes. But I'm not Candy Walker. I'm not an
outlaw."

"You aren't?"

"No. I don't live in tourist cabins and farmhouses and the back
seats of cars. I live in Chicago, Louise."

"That doesn't make you not an outlaw."

She had me there.

"Well," I said, "I'm not."

"What are you, then? A gangster?"

She'd apparently heard of Chicago.

"No. Louise, listen to what I'm saying. I'm saying I can help you go
straight."

She lifted her head again; the brown eyes narrowed—I'd hurt her
feelings. "I'm not a criminal. I may've sinned, but I'm not a criminal."

"I know you aren't. But wouldn't you like to have a fresh start? In
Chicago, maybe?"

"Sure. But you make it sound so . . . easy."

"It is easy. Besides, I'll be there to help you."

She lifted her head to smile at me, pursing the beestung lips.
"Good, 'cause I'd need help."

"Of course, the first thing I think you should do is go home."

The smile faded. "Home?"

"To see your father."

"Oh. Oh, I don't know about that . . ."

"You ought to set things straight with him. You owe him that much. And you owe it to yourself."

"I wouldn't want to see him alone."

"Who says you'd be alone?"

"You'd go with me?"

"Sure. Right there by your side."

"Then I'll think about it," she said. Snuggling closer.

I was helping her; I knew I was helping her. But I still felt like a dyed-in-the-wool bastard. For all my soft soap about setting things straight with her father, I knew damn well she'd do just fine never seeing the old boy again; I just wanted to deliver her and collect that thousand bucks.

It wasn't that I didn't want to tell her the truth—but what if I did, only to have her take a powder? That would be that grand her father promised me, you'd see going out the door with her.

And/or she might spill to Ma Barker and Helen Nelson and the rest of the mamas, some of whom were pistol-packing, and that wouldn't fit in with my plans.

So at four I was on the road with Ma Barker, one last time, for one final round of Burma Shave readings, hymn humming and the eternal quest to find hillbilly music on the Auburn's radio.

Ma, with a freshly curled head of Shirley Temple hair, interrupted those three favorite pastimes of hers now and again for some actual conversation.

"Big responsibility," she said, kidding me, "havin' a whole houseful of women to look after. . . ."

"I figure they can look after me, Ma," I said, smiling at her.

She smiled back, that oddly attractive smile that found its occasional way out of her homely countenance, saying, "You're gonna treat that little gal right, aren't you?"

"Lulu, you mean? Sure."

"Got a good little gal, there. Don't let 'er get away."

"I'll try not, Ma."

But conversation was the exception not the rule, as most of the time she devoted herself to her usual interests, and I was grateful. Because my mind was going faster than the Auburn. Racing ahead to things I had to do . . .

I parked the Auburn in an open space in front of the big brick three-story on Pine Grove, where the real Jimmy Lawrence once lived. Shortly after, Dolores pulled in half a block down. I glanced at my watch: five-fifteen. The Hoover pickup was set for ten till seven. Plenty of time.

I carried the girls' bags in for them, and they all pitched in (except for Ma, of course) and it was around five-thirty when everybody's things had been deposited in an appropriate bedroom.

The last of these was one Ma showed Louise and me into, a small room decorated in shades of blue; there was a double bed with a baby-blue spread. Sounds romantic, but there was also a picture of Jesus over a doily-strewn dresser.

"You kids can bunk in here," she said.

Louise said, "Thanks, Ma—you're a saint."

I thanked Ma, too; I couldn't quite go the rest of the way, Jesus picture or not.

Ma said, "Jimmy, I know you're supposed to stick by us, 'specially this afternoon . . . but I need some things."

"Oh?"

"Yes. Come with me."

I followed her, Louise in tow.

We ended up in a big white modern kitchen. Ma opened the Frigidaire for me to see mostly empty shelves.

Ma spread her arms like an angel its wings. "What am I going to cook for supper, if you don't go to the store for me?"

What, indeed.

"If you make me out a list, Ma," I said, "I'll go shopping before the stores close."

She sat and scribbled a list.

I'd been planning to make my own excuse to leave, saying I needed to go to my apartment to pick up a few things for the duration of my stay; but she was saving me the trouble. Karpis had asked that I stay close to the phone all afternoon and evening, just in case the need for some sort of backup developed. But now I had Ma, who this very moment was handing me her grocery list, to cover for me.

"Come on, Louise," I said, holding my arm out to her, "keep me company."

"Sure," she said, taking the arm.

Ma wasn't sure about that. "Now, Alvin and Arthur said the girls was to stay around home, today."

"Maybe so," I said, "but you wouldn't want to send a man to the store *alone*, would you?"

That she gave some serious thought.

"You're right," she said. "I'll get my hat and go with you, m'self."

"I'll take Louise," I insisted. "You can't leave here. If Alvin or Doc, uh, Arthur should call, they won't want to talk to one of these silly girls. They'll want to talk you, Ma."

She nodded sagely.

Then she smiled her oddly nice smile and made two limp wrists and brushed the air with them, saying, "Shoo, then, you two, shoo!"

We walked through the living room on our way out. Paula was lounging on the green mohair sofa in Ma's generous living room, ever-present drink in hand. She smiled and winked and lifted her glass in a one-sided toast, saying, "Ya make a damn cute couple, you two," smug in her matchmaking abilities. Nearby, Helen Nelson seemed melancholy, sitting by a window, obviously worrying about her husband. Dolores was in her room, unpacking her things. Ma, with nothing to do in the kitchen, sat back down to her unfinished puzzle of the country church.

That was where I came in.

And soon Louise and I were in the Auburn, heading for the Loop.

"Just what store are you going to, anyway?" Louise asked, after a while.

We were tooling up Lake Shore Drive, the Gold Coast whizzing by on our right, the lake shimmering at our left. Up ahead the Drake stared me down, like a stern scolding face; sorry, Helen.

"No store," I said.

"No store?"

"I'm just getting you away from that place."

"You are?"

"I am."

"But I—I left all my things back there! My clothes . . . my brush . . . my scrapbook . . ."

I looked at her. "You're leaving everything behind, Louise. Understand? Everything."

She didn't understand, but she didn't say anything.

It was almost six when I pulled the Auburn in the alley behind my building and squeezed it in the recessed space next to my Chevy coupe where Barney's Hupmobile sometimes was but right now wasn't. I took her by the hand like a child and moved right along and she had to work to keep up. Past the deli on the corner, the El a looming reminder we were back in the city, to the door between Barney's Cocktail Lounge and the pawnshop, and up the stairs, four flights, her feet echoing mine as she followed me up.

I unlocked the office door.

"But this is a detective's office," she said, looking at the lettering on the door's frosted glass.

"That's right."

I shut the door behind her. She stood clutching her purse to her, looking around.

"Isn't that a Murphy bed?" she said.

"Yes," I said. Back behind the desk, pulling the phone book out of a drawer.

"Gee. I saw furniture like this at the world's fair."

"Everybody did," I said, looking for the number.

"Whose place is this?"

"A friend," I said, dialing.

"Wonder if he needs a secretary."

"Who knows," I said, getting a busy signal.

I sat behind the desk. Yanked the window-glass wire-frames off and flung 'em in a drawer. So, the line was busy over at the Banker's Building. It was just five after six. The pickup wasn't to be made till six-fifty. Plenty of time.

She sat across from me in the chair her father had sat in not long ago.

"Why are we here?" she asked. Her eyes wide and brown and confused.

"It's a safe place," I said. Drumming my fingers on my desk.

"What about Ma, and Paula and everybody?"

"They're in the past, sugar."

"The past."

"That's right. And you're leaving the past behind you, under-stand?"

"No. Not really . . ."

"Do you know what's happening today? What's set to happen in about forty-five minutes?"

"No," she said, shaking her head.

"A kidnapping. Do you want to be part of that?"

"No," she said. But she didn't seem sure, as if I was posing some abstract problem that went way over her head.

"Forget Ma and Paula and all of them. Got it?"

"Why?"

"Because those people are going to be in trouble. You don't want to be in trouble, do you?"

Her face fell, her eyes got even wider. "Why . . . you're not going to *rat* on them . . ."

"Never mind what I'm going to do," I said, dialing again.

Busy signal.

"I don't want you to rat on them," she said. "Jim. Please don't."

"You're with me, now, remember?"

"Jim . . ."

"Are you with me now?"

"Yes . . ."

"Then you've got to go along with me. You went along with Candy Walker, you can go along with me, for Christ's sake."

"Please don't yell at me, Jim. Please don't yell."

I didn't know I was.

"Sorry," I said.

She stood; leaned her hands against the desk, and those big brown eyes I loved so much begged me. "Jim, if you call the police, leave Ma and Paula and Dolores and Helen out of it. Please. You got to promise."

"Okay. I promise." But I was thinking about the police she'd mentioned. Maybe I *should* call them. But I figured Cowley and Purvis would want to handle this themselves; it would mean the difference to them between a feather in the cap or a major embarrassment. Squelching the kidnapping themselves beat hell out of having the local cops pull their director's butt off the burner.

And I could use Purvis and Cowley's goodwill—I was involved in this just deep enough to need to explain myself, and better them than the Chicago cops, Christ! I was an accomplice in the murder of Dr. Joseph Moran, if you got right down to it. You could make a case—a convincing one—for me being part of the kidnap ring. But time was slipping away—if the snatch went down, I wouldn't just be up shit creek, I'd be drowning in it. Maybe I should call the cops anyway; take my chances with Chicago's finest—hell, I hadn't been fed the goldfish in weeks.

The number at the Banker's Building was still busy.

It was six-ten.

I got up and pulled the Murphy bed down.

"Jim! What are you doing?"

Now she thought *I* was a sex fiend.

"Are you sure this is all right with your *friend* . . . ?"

"It's fine with him. And it ain't whoopee time, so relax. You're just going to take a rest. I have to step out for a while."

"Where are you going?"

"Just a few blocks over. I got an appointment."

"But what if your friend comes back?"

"It'll be okay." I sat her on the edge of the bed. "Just catch a nap. Okay?"

"Jim, I'm so confused . . . what's going on? What's this about?" She had tears in her eyes.

Shit.

Without knowing it, without meaning to, I'd joined the club: joined the ranks of men who'd abused this girl, pushed her around, hurt her. Damnit. Fuck. Shit.

I sat down on the bed next to her. Slipped an arm around her. "I won't be gone long. Just stay here and take it easy. Tomorrow, I'm going to take you to see your daddy."

"Do you think that's for the best?"

"I do."

"But you said I should leave the past behind me, Jim."

"Some things you simply got to face before you can put 'em behind you. Now, I'm going to be with you, all the way. Right at your side. And then we're coming back to the big city and find you some honest work. In fact, my friend who runs this office just might be able to use a secretary, at that. Would that suit you?"

She smiled, but it was forced. "Sure, Jim. Any friend of yours . . ."

I kissed her cheek, and she grabbed me, clutched at me. Kissed me hard on the mouth. There was more desperation than passion in it, and I held her close to me, hugged her close, and whispered in her ear, "I'm not going to hurt you, Louise—nobody's going to hurt you anymore."

I tucked her under the covers and smiled at her and she smiled at me, a brave-little-soldier smile, and turned on her side and shut her eyes.

I locked the office behind me, and got the hell out of there. It was six-fifteen. I was only a few blocks away from the Banker's Building; three or four minutes by foot, five tops.

All I had to do, I thought as I walked briskly by Binyon's, was head

over there and take the elevator up to the nineteenth floor and tell
'em the tale. It was late enough that most, maybe all, their agents
would be gone for the day—but at least the call to the cops could be
placed by Purvis or Cowley—at least they could initiate and coordi-
nate the effort to stop the kidnapping and nab the kidnappers. Somehow I didn't think Hoover would grab a gun, though.

I was walking by the Federal Building, now; sidewalks were all but
empty, this time of day, and I could move right along. It felt good to
be home, where the buildings were taller than the corn, where the
cattle was lined up in the stockyards where it belonged. It would be
over soon—already, I was out of the outlaw's world and back in my
own; and the girl I'd come to get was tucked safely away in my office.
I almost smiled.

But around the next corner there was one last street to cross.

Maybe the feds, maybe Cowley anyway, could keep this thing from
turning into a bloodbath. Just as I couldn't allow myself to be party to
Hoover's kidnapping—even for twenty-five goddamn grand—a
massacre of Floyd and Nelson and the others was nothing I cared to
be part of, either.

As I rounded the corner of Jackson, just before six-twenty, with
half an hour to spare, moving to the crosswalk, I glanced down the
street and there, in front of the Edison Building, was the backup car
with Baby Face Nelson and Fred Barker sitting in it.

And if the backup car was in place, the Hudson—and Karpis and
Floyd and Dillinger—wouldn't be far behind.

40

I slowed my pace.

I couldn't get lost in the crowd: there wasn't one. The sidewalks weren't empty, though—there were a few people around, so I didn't stick out like a sore thumb, either. I pulled the brim of my hat down, lowered my head, waited for the light and crossed Clark Street and walked toward the Banker's Building. The backup car in front of the Edison Building was almost a block away. Far enough that I'd had to look hard to recognize Fred Barker behind the wheel of the car, a black Ford roadster.

So maybe they wouldn't notice me. They certainly wouldn't be looking for me.

Then again, I hadn't been looking for them and I spotted 'em, easy enough.

I glanced at my watch: six-twenty.

Hoover's powwow with Courtney and the police commissioner had been moved up, obviously, and the same inside source who'd leaked the original information had passed the change of plans along to Karpis and company. It had been a seven o'clock dinner, with the pickup to be made at ten till; my guess was it'd been moved up to six-thirty, in which case the next pickup time was *right now*.

The Hudson should be making its appearance, any time.

I walked by the Clark Street edge of the Continental Illinois Bank Building, and strolled down Quincy. Once the Banker's Building was blocking me from the parked backup car's view, I ran to the side door and found my way to the bank of elevators and punched the UP button.

I gave the uniformed operator, a tall red-haired guy of about twenty-five, a buck and said, "Nineteenth floor and step on it."

He yanked the handle so hard the box lurched, but he earned his dollar: within a minute we were on the nineteenth floor. I gave him another buck and told him to wait for me; he questioned that with his

eyes, and I gave him another buck hurriedly and said there'd be a sawbuck for him if he kept his end up.

Then I was off the elevator and running down the hall to the Division of Investigation field office.

The door was shut.

Locked.

I banged on it.

"Hey, in there! Come on—somebody!"

Seconds that seemed an eternity passed and the door opened, and there was Cowley, his moon face somber as ever, then he squinted at me, which was his way of registering surprise.

"Heller?" he said. Like he couldn't believe I was standing there; I was something he thought he'd put behind him.

"Is Hoover in there?"

He sighed through his nose and his mouth made a tight line, barely opening to say, "Is that any concern of yours?"

I pushed him out of the way, pushed inside the room.

"Hey! What do you—"

The room was full of desks and no people.

"Where's Hoover?" I demanded.

"What business is it of yours?" He was indignant and condescending at the same time.

I liked Cowley, far as it went, but it didn't go that far. I grabbed him by his coat and vest with two hands and said, "Where the hell is he?"

Cowley was bigger than me, and probably tougher, and armed, and a fed; but he forgot all about that and sputtered, "He and Purvis . . . they just went down in the elevator."

I let go of him. "Shit!"

"You must've been coming up as they were going down. *Why*? What's this about, Heller?"

"Grab a tommy gun and come with me—I'll explain in the elevator."

"Are you serious?"

"Baby Face Nelson and Pretty Boy Floyd and the rest of your public enemies' list are in two cars down on the street, waiting for your precious goddamn director. Get a gun!"

He went to a closet and unlocked it quickly and grabbed a tommy gun from a rack and an extra magazine and didn't ask any more questions, just followed me out in the hall.

My red-haired elevator guy was waiting; he grinned when he saw me coming, then the grin faded as he saw Cowley bringing up the rear with the Thompson.

We got on, and went down.

I filled him in quick: "There's a fake state attorney's car in front, to pick Hoover up. It's a snatch. Three men in the car, including Alvin Karpis and Pretty Boy Floyd—two of 'em dressed as cops. There's a backup car parked across the way, in front of the Edison Building, with extra firepower. Baby Face Nelson and Fred Barker are in that."

The elevator guy was glancing over at me, swallowing.

Cowley said, "How'd you happen onto this?"

"Time for that later. When did they move Hoover's dinner party up?"

Cowley squinted again, wondering how the hell I was so on top of all this. "They called before noon," he said. "Courtney and the commissioner wanted it earlier. So they could just go over after work and not have to wait around."

I was getting my gun out from under my arm.

Cowley touched my arm. "You just stay back. I'll appreciate having you covering my butt, but you stay the hell back, understand?"

I grinned at him. "I wish you wouldn't swear like that. I hate to hear it, coming from a good Mormon."

He smiled, nervously, and the elevator guy set 'er down and opened the cage and Cowley took the lead, his footsteps slapping the marble floor as he headed toward the front door.

Where a short, slightly stocky man in a dark suit had his back to us—Hoover—with another short man in a straw hat and white pants and blue coat—Purvis—just about to go out the inner doors into the vestibule and out onto the sidewalk.

"Stop!" Cowley called, running, tommy gun in one hand, pointing up.

But they were through the doors, now, and moving across the vestibule, and Cowley sprinted, and I was right behind him.

He must've gone through the inner doors just seconds after Hoover and Purvis; I caught up a second or so later, and heard Cowley yell, "Hit the deck!"

And saw Hoover, a dark little man whose eyes were as white in his face as a minstrel's, look back, and Purvis, reacting faster, reach for one of his arms to pull him down.

In a cop's uniform, Dillinger, a.k.a. Sullivan, was holding open the back door of the black Hudson with the red and green headlights, for Hoover to get in.

All this I took in in a split second, 'cause that's all it took for Purvis to yank the startled Hoover by the arm and flatten him unceremoniously on the pavement while Cowley opened up with the chopper.

The burst of bullets put a row of puckers across the heavily plated Hudson, kissed little spider webs into its bulletproof glass, and Dillinger caught at least one of the slugs, as he reared back from the impact, with a yowl, but tumbled in the back of the Hudson and the rider in front, Karpis, reached back and pulled the door shut and the Hudson pulled away, while Cowley moved forward, spraying it with slugs.

Purvis was up and his revolver out and he took some potshots at the fleeing car; Hoover, on his belly, looked up with wide, wild eyes and then got on his knees and, keeping low, scrambled for the doors, and shouldered them open and he cowered against the wall. I was standing there with my gun out, keeping an eye on Cowley's butt, like I'd been told to. I looked at the shaking, sweating director of the Division of Investigation and he glared at me, said, "What are you looking at?"

I looked back outside.

Traffic was light, but what few cars there were were slamming on brakes, and running up onto sidewalks. A Model A drove up on Cowley's side of the street, on the walk, and Cowley had to let up fire. He moved out into the middle of the street, and started back in firing, as the Hudson narrowly missed some of the confused, frightened motorists who'd stumbled onto this.

The Hudson, despite its portholes in the doors for gunplay, hadn't fired a shot. It had, according to plan, ducked down Quincy, which was just a glorified alley, down the mouth of which was where Cowley now stood with his machine gun spewing.

That was when I saw the backup, a roadster, come careening around onto Clark.

I pushed open the glass door and yelled, "Cowley! Your flank!"

Purvis, who was backing Cowley up, saw the car coming and hit the pavement.

Barker was driving and Baby Face Nelson was hanging out the rider's side, half-standing on the running board, with a tommy gun of his own in his hand. He had a crazed look on his face. He loved his work.

"*Sons of fucking bitches!*" was his war cry, or one of them anyway—he said more, but you couldn't hear it over his chopper.

I fired a few shots over the roadster—I couldn't make myself fire at Nelson, and to this day I can't tell you why—but it was enough of a distraction to make him pull the Thompson and fire into the street, and that gave Cowley the split second he needed. He dove in the alley, and ducked in a recessed doorway, and the roadster did a screeching U-turn on two wheels and raced back toward Adams, disappearing around the corner.

Then they were gone—both the Hudson and the backup.

And there was nothing left but some startled pedestrians and shaken-up motorists, and two special agents whose suits and faces were dirty and rumpled from rolling around on the pavement.

Cowley came around the corner; the tommy gun was pointing down now, but smoke was still curling out its barrel. He'd gone through both magazines. He looked tired, washed out. Purvis was just standing there, gun in hand, like a kid who just ran out of imaginary Indians to shoot.

I was still standing there holding the glass door open with one hand, the automatic in the other. Nelson and the others hadn't got a look at me—at least not enough of one to recognize me, I didn't think. That was a break.

Hoover was plastered against the wall, within the vestibule. Shaking. Eyes open wide. He really seemed terrified.

"It's nothing to be ashamed of," I said.

He swallowed. "What?"

"Being afraid in a situation like this."

His eyes flared; he stepped away from the wall. "What's your name, mister?"

"My name's Heller."

"If you prize your job, you'd better watch your tongue."

He thought I was one of theirs; a fed. That was a laugh.

"And I've never seen such pathetic shooting," he said. "You seemed to aim deliberately high—"

"Mr. Hoover?"

"What?"

"Fuck you."

I went out onto the street and joined Cowley.

Who said, "How's the director doing?"

Purvis was over talking to a couple of the motorists whose cars
were up on the sidewalk, calming them down. A crowd was gathering; not a large one.

"A change of diaper, and he'll be a new man."

Cowley ignored that. "What's this about, Heller? How'd you happen onto this?"

"I didn't. I been undercover looking for a runaway daughter. I fell
in with a nest of thieves, you might say. I just shook loose from 'em
this afternoon, and was on my way here to warn you, when I saw it
was coming down early."

Cowley brushed a comma of brown hair back in place, and gave me
a tight, one-sided smile. "Thanks, Heller. I'm glad you were here."

"It's swell to be wanted."

Two beat cops, pulled away from their supper at a nearby restaurant no doubt, came running up.

"What happened here?" one of them said.

"We're not sure just yet, officer," Cowley said. "Possibly a kidnap
attempt. There was some shooting—no one hurt on this end. I
winged one of them. One car cut down Quincy, here, a Hudson
dressed up like a state attorney's car; the other, a black roadster,
headed west on Adams. Three men in the Hudson, two dressed as
cops. Two in the roadster. Several are public enemies. My associate,
Agent Purvis, has the license plate numbers. Could one of you call
that in to your radio cars? And the other maybe help us see if any of
these citizens were injured?"

The two cops nodded.

Hoover came out of the building; his shakes were gone. He moved
like a little Napoleon.

He came up to me and demanded my resignation.

I laughed in his face, as Cowley said, "He doesn't work for the
division, sir. He's a private detective who happened upon this situation while undercover. You may owe him your life, Mr. Hoover. At
the very least he prevented your kidnapping."

You might think that would've embarrassed him. Or that he'd be
grateful. Or respond in some human manner.

But he just gave me a cold fish look and then said to Cowley, "Are we pursuing them?"

"We don't have any men on hand, sir," Cowley said. "Police radio cars have got it by now."

"Damn," Hoover said. "Who were they?"

Cowley let some air out. "Sir, just about everybody we'd like for breakfast. Pretty Boy Floyd and Creepy Karpis . . ."

Hoover's dark pupils lit up in the yolks of his eyes. "Do you know what we could make of that? If we could score a grand slam like that?"

"I sure do," Cowley said, wearily. "And wasn't that Baby Face Nelson hanging out of the roadster?"

That last was posed to me; I nodded.

"And I think Fred Barker was driving," Cowley continued. "I don't know who the other one in the Hudson was . . . the one I winged. Do you, Heller?"

I put a hand on his shoulder. "You're going to love this, Cowley. Maybe we should get Purvis over here to have a piece of this."

Cowley squinted again. "What are you talking about?"

"The guy you winged was a ghost. Ghost of a guy who got killed at the Biograph Theater not so long ago."

Hoover sneered. "This man is a lunatic!"

Cowley wasn't sure. He didn't say anything, just looked at me.

I said, "This time he really does have a new face."

Cowley's mouth hung open; then he looked down at the pavement. He still had the tommy gun in his hand, but now it looked heavy.

Hoover was pacing, rubbing his chin, thinking.

Cowley looked up and, all business, said, "Keep that, uh . . . ghost to yourself for the time being, Heller. All right?"

"Sure," I shrugged.

Hoover, not following any of that apparently, was giving me a long cold look.

"If you were undercover," he said, biting off each word, pointing a stubby finger at me, "and knew in advance of this scheme, it follows that you must know the getaway route, as well."

I glanced at my watch; they'd made their switch at the loading dock by now. They were probably heading down Van Buren. Not far from my office.

"I haven't a clue," I said to Hoover.

That was when the state attorney's car pulled up and a confused-looking little man in a mustache and gray suit got out and said, "Sorry we're late, Mr. Hoover. Uh, has there been some problem here?"

Sam Cowley hid his smile behind his hand.

I didn't bother.

41

She was asleep when I got back to the office. She was still in her pink dress, on top of the covers. Sleeping on her side, knees up, dress too, milky underneath of thigh showing, hands clasped as if in prayer; her lips apart, looking soft, pliant, like a baby's.

I sat on the edge of the bed and stroked her hair; she stirred, smiling. Gradually she opened her eyes, just partway, but you could still get lost in 'em.

"What—what time is it?" she asked.

The office was dark but for the pulse of orange neon.

"A little after eight," I said.

"Where have you been?"

"That's not important."

"What is?"

"Supper."

That got a big smile out of her, a farm-girl smile those beestung lips seemed incapable of, only there she was doing it.

She sat up, wide awake. "I don't have any clothes—just what I've had on all day. And slept in."

"We'll get you some things tomorrow. Smooth your dress out and bring your appetite."

"Well," she said, and shrugged, and smiled, "okay."

She freshened up in my bathroom (the last girl in there was Polly Hamilton), and we walked downstairs, out into a cool summer night, the heat wave finally a memory, strolling hand in hand and around the corner to Binyon's, where I bought her a T-bone steak with all the trimmings, which she gobbled down greedily. She hadn't eaten in eight hours.

Nor had I, but I didn't have much of an appetite. I ordered coffee and ate a roll or two, to keep my stomach at bay. We didn't talk much at dinner; she was busy eating, and I was busy wondering what the hell to do about her.

Actually, I'd already done something about her, and that's what was nagging me.

After I gave him a statement at the division field office, Cowley had let me use the phone. I'd reversed the charges to call Joshua Petersen in De Kalb, at the number he'd provided. To tell him I had found his daughter.

He'd shown no surprise, or joy; just relief, as he said, "That's good news, Mr. Heller."

"She isn't with Candy Walker anymore. He's dead."

"Good," he said.

His voice had a flat, dry sound, like his soul needed rain.

I said, "I've got her away from the 'bad crowd' she was running with, and she's ready to make a new start. I just can't guarantee you she's going to be willing to do it your way."

Silence.

"Mr. Petersen, I'm saying I'll bring your daughter to you—I think she'll be willing to meet with you at least. But whether she'll come home to stay or not is going to be up to her."

More silence; I waited, making him fill it.

Finally he did, stoically: "I understand."

"She's a big girl now, Mr. Petersen. She has a right to make her own way in the world. She needs to learn how, but that's another story. Anyway, I'm going to be right there with her, and I don't want you badgering her. I won't abide any show of force on your part. If you can mend fences with her, fine. But if she doesn't want to stay with you, she doesn't stay. It's that simple."

"All right."

"Okay. I just wanted that understood."

"It's understood."

"And that bonus you promised me, I expect it whether she stays with you, or not."

"The thousand dollars is yours, Mr. Heller."

"I earned that money, Mr. Petersen. Like you said, I had to go among the wolves."

"The money's yours, no argument. I'm grateful to you."

"Well, okay then," I said. "Where shall we meet?"

And we'd agreed on a time and place, the next afternoon; but this was tonight, and the girl across from me eating Mr. Binyon's cheesecake was still calling me Jim.

Somehow I just couldn't seem to level with her. Somehow I couldn't make myself risk seeing disappointment, perhaps even loathing, in those wide-set big brown eyes.

So by nine we were in my Murphy bed, just cuddling in the dark; I had pulled the shades so even the neon couldn't get in.

That way I wouldn't have to see her eyes when I told her.

"Sugar, remember when I told you I thought you ought to go home, and see your daddy?"

"Yes. Aren't we going tomorrow?"

"I have to tell you something first. I wasn't necessarily thinking about what was best for you, when I said that."

"Who were you thinking of?"

"Me."

I waited for her to say something, but she didn't.

So I went on. "There's no easy way to tell you this. I'm not Jimmy Lawrence."

She still didn't say anything; but she didn't pull away from me, either. Stayed cuddled right up next to me. Her breathing easy, calm, regular.

I said, "I'm the guy whose name is on the door. I'm Nathan Heller."

"I know," she said.

"You *know*?"

"I may be from the farm, Jim. Sorry—Nathan? But I wasn't born in a barn."

"How . . . ?"

"When you were gone, I looked through the drawers in your desk and your file. I found snapshots of you and a pretty girl at the fair. And some clippings about a trial with your picture and your name under it."

"Hell. Why aren't you mad?"

"I am mad." She said this like, pass the salt.

"You don't *sound* mad . . ."

"I forgive you, Jim. Nathan."

"Nate, actually, but—"

"I asked you before . . . Nate. I'll ask you again. I'm with *you*, now—aren't I?"

"You're with me. I'm right beside you, all the way."

"Then what does it matter what your name is, or why you came looking for me?"

"You—you know I came looking for you? How did you figure that out?"

"You had my picture in your desk. Did my husband hire you to find me?"

"No, your father."

"Daddy gave you that picture?"

"That's right."

"He really wants to see me again?"

"He does. He says his health is bad . . ."

"He's a lunger. Since the war."

"That's what he told me. He says he's got enough of a pension to get by on. He sold his farm, has a house in De Kalb—where you can stay if you want."

"My father sold his farm? I thought he'd never do that."

"Louise, he's coming to the end of his road. He says all he wants in life at this stage is to have a second chance with you. Make it up to you, for how rough he treated you, growing up."

"He used to beat me with a belt."

"I know. And if you don't want to go see him, you don't have to."

"I don't think I want to live with him. No matter what."

"You don't have to. It's like I told you before—we'll get you set up in the city, here."

"As your secretary?"

"If we can't find you something better, why not? It wouldn't pay much, but I hear the boss is a soft touch."

She snuggled to me. "I love the boss."

We made love.

And the next afternoon I was back on the road in the Auburn, gratefully free of Burma Shave signs and hymns and the threat of hillbilly music. This time the female next to me was perky and fresh and young and not wearing a floral tent: first thing this morning I'd taken her to Marshall Field's, and bought her a yellow-and-white frock with lace trim on the short sleeves and a little white collar. She'd have a whole new wardrobe tomorrow, after I got that grand from her old man.

That was the only thing I'd kept from her: that I'd be getting a bonus today for delivering her. It probably wouldn't have mattered to her, but who could tell? She wasn't from Chicago.

We took Highway 30 west for about an hour and then a sign said, WELCOME TO DE KALB—BARBED WIRE CAPITAL OF THE WORLD.

Every place is the capital of something, I suppose. We drove through the quiet little town, a brick oasis in the desert of corn we'd been driving through, and on the northern edge, there it was: Hopkins Park, lushly wooded, rolling. Saturday afternoon, and crowded: picnic benches packed with families chowing down, like Ma Barker and the boys, some having to settle for their picnic basket on a checkered cloth on the ground, ants and all; a swimming pool with a diving board and bathhouse brimming with people, particularly kids, darting about in their bright-colored bathing trunks, making up one big erratically waving flag of summer. This was August, after all, school looming up head. Desperate days. Time running out.

There was a band shell, and Louise and I walked around it; I slipped my hand in hers. If her father saw that, it might irritate him—the man he hired getting fresh with his daughter and so on. But she needed the support, and I gave it to her. Petersen was nothing to me except a thousand bucks, and a guy who used to beat his little girl.

We were a little early. I bought some popcorn from an old man at a stand; we shared a bag, she and I, sitting on benches before the band shell, an audience of two, as if waiting for some show to start. You could hear the kids splashing, yelling, in the pool, though we were well away from it. Over at the left, under a tree, a young mother sat on the grass reading a romance magazine and keeping one eye on her little boy who was tossing a stick for his little terrier to retrieve.

Louise said, "I hope I can make things right with my daddy. I'd like that. But I can tell you right now I want to go back to the city with you. I hope to make peace with my daddy—but I want *you*, Jim."

I smiled at her. "I'm not Jim, remember."

She smiled back. "You're no gentleman, either."

It was the closest I ever heard her come to making a joke.

Then she said, "You'll always be Jim to me."

We sat on the bench, not holding hands now, but sitting close enough to touch, just barely, enjoying the sounds of the kids splashing and families picnicking and a dog barking and I was just checking my watch when a voice from behind us said, "Louise! Louise."

I glanced back and Petersen was standing there, in the grassy aisle, in the midst of all those empty benches; his eyes were sunken in his weathered face, red, from crying, and crazed, from . . . craziness?

"Jesus," I said.

He was standing there in those same Sunday-go-to-meeting clothes he'd worn to my office, dark brown suit, light brown bow tie, shiny brown shoes, hands behind his back, leaning forward like a man about to fall on his face; the benches were on a gentle slope down to the band shell, which added to the effect. He had a whisper of a smile on his face. It made Karpis' smile seem like the Mona Lisa.

And Louise was screaming.

Just like that night she woke up and saw me in bed next to her and screamed. Exactly like that.

I tried to touch her shoulder, to calm her, but she slid off the bench, cutting her scream short, and stepped out in the aisle and faced him. They were maybe ten feet apart, and she pointed up at him, as if pointing at an animal in a cage, and said, "What are you *doing* here? You stay away from me. . . ."

"You shouldn't have run off, Louise." His voice as dry and cracked as parched earth.

I got up and stood in the aisle next to her. "Mr. Petersen, you promised me . . ."

She looked at me with her eyes so wide I could see the red lining them. *"What did you call him?"*

"Mr. Petersen. Louise, your father's obviously upset, so maybe we should just—"

"My *father*! This isn't my *father*!"

Petersen's smile was a wound in his face that wouldn't heal. "I love you, Louise. I still love you."

"He's my *husband*! That's *Seth*!"

He said, "But you shouldn't have been bad."

"He lied to you! He knew I'd never come back if I knew it was *him* who hired you!"

"I'm getting you out of here," I said, and took her by the hand, as Seth said, "I'll always love you, Louise," and a big black pistol came out from behind his back and blew a hole through her.

She swung in my arm like a rag doll, flung back by the impact. It pulled me down with her, my ears ringing from the gunshot; hit my head on the edge of a bench.

I wasn't out long but when I looked up Seth hovered over me, and her; I didn't have my gun, but I'm not sure I'd have had the presence of mind to use it if I had.

No matter. I looked up and Seth receded above me, his legs miles long, his head a tiny thing he was pointing the gun at, an old Army

.45 revolver it must've been, and the muzzle flashed orange and my ears rang and his tiny head came apart in a red burst; then he fell like a tree, away from us, leaving a scarlet mist in the air where he'd stood.

I heard screaming. Not Louise's. She had a blossom of red below the white collar of her new yellow dress, and lay silent, staring. It was the mother under the nearby tree doing the screaming, on her feet now, holding her little boy to her, shielding her little boy from the sight, but not able to keep her own eyes off it. The terrier was yapping.

I was just sitting there, spattered with their blood, the dead girl's hand in mine.

Just sitting right there beside her for a long time, looking at her. Her eyes staring up at the sky. Her eyes. As big and brown as ever; so wide-set you almost had to look at them one at a time. But they weren't beautiful anymore. I didn't want to dive in there anymore. She was no longer in them.

So I closed them for her.

3
WHERE THE BODIES ARE BURIED
SEPTEMBER 9, 1934

VIEW FROM SALLY RAND'S SUITE

42

When I got to her suite, she was standing in the doorway, leaning against the jamb in white lounging pajamas, a cigarette in one too-casual hand. Her light brown hair was marcelled, her mouth startlingly red, her eyes startlingly blue under those long, long lashes.

"Hi, stranger," Sally said.

"Hello, Helen," I said sheepishly.

"I was beginning to think you'd never call."

"I wasn't sure you'd want me to."

She unstruck her pose and gestured with a red-nailed hand. "Come in and set a spell."

"Thanks." I took off my hat and went in, still feeling sheepish somehow. She closed the door behind me.

We sat on the sofa in her white living room; she kept her distance, but reached over and put her hand on my hand. I sat there looking ahead blankly. I couldn't remember how to talk to her. I couldn't remember how to talk to anybody.

"You look lousy," she said.

"I feel lousy."

"There could be a connection."

I tried to smile; my lips couldn't quite make it.

She said, "When's the last time you slept?"

"I been sleeping a lot, really."

"You mean you been passing out a lot."

I swallowed. My mouth was dry, my tongue thick and furry. "You been talking to Barney?"

She nodded. "He's got a fight to train for. You shouldn't be distracting him like this."

"Nobody asked him to."

"To what? Sit with you while you drink yourself into a stupor? Carry you up the stairs and toss you in bed? Why'd you call me, Nate?"

Now I could find the smile; just barely, but it was there. "Barney talked me into it."

She shook her head, smiled wryly. "You don't deserve friends like us."

"I know I don't," I said, and started to weep.

She had an arm around me. I was hunched forward cupping my hands over my face. She was offering me a handkerchief that she'd had in her hand, at the ready; she'd been talking to Barney, all right.

"Ain't very dignified for a tough copper," I said, swallowing snot. "I been on this crying jag for so long my goddamn eyes burn."

"Is that why you're drinking, Nate? Does the flow of booze stop the flow of tears?"

I grunted something like a laugh.. "You don't drink much, do you, Helen? Getting drunk is the one socially pardonable way a man can cry in public. Nobody blames a drunk for crying in his beer."

"I hear you've been hitting something a little stronger."

"Yeah. But not today. Today I'm stone-cold sober. And it scares hell out of me."

She looped her arm in mine, moving closer. "Let's go to bed."

I shook my head, violently. "No! No. That won't solve anything . . . that won't solve anything."

"We don't have to do anything, Nate. We'll just get under the sheets and be together. What do you say?"

"I'm so goddamn tired I'd fall asleep in a second."

"That's okay. What else is Sunday afternoon good for?"

The satin sheets felt good; for a moment it was like I'd never left this room. Like I'd been here with Sally forever. For a moment I felt like myself again.

For a moment.

"Did you love her, Nate?"

She really had talked to Barney; I'd spilled my guts to the little palooka, and he'd spilled his to her. Damn him. Bless him.

"I don't know," I said. "It was too rushed. She wasn't . . . she wasn't like you, Sally. She was just this dumb little farm girl."

"I'm just an intelligent little farm girl, Nate."

I found myself almost managing to smile again. "She *was* like you, a little. She could've been like you, if she'd had a break or two in her goddamn life. She wasn't as smart as you, Helen. She wasn't stupid, but she didn't have your brains, your drive, your luck. You both found a way out, a way off of the farm. You just found a better way."

"Did you love her, Nate?"

"I don't know. It hadn't got that far, really."

"Did you sleep with her?"

I wondered how much Barney had told her.

"No," I said.

She smiled like a wicked madonna. "You don't lie worth a damn, Heller."

Somebody laughed. Me?

I said, "It probably wouldn't've lasted. But that isn't the point. She was this sweet naïve thing who had a father who beat her and a husband who beat her some more. And then she fell in with . . . a bad crowd, and I came along, and she trusted me, and I killed her. I fucking killed her."

She stroked my arm. "You didn't kill anybody."

"As good as. I took her right to the son of a bitch who did. For a thousand dollars."

It had come in an envelope, with a bunch of stamps stuck on it, the Monday after. A fat envelope full of twenties. I'd hurled it against the wall, and the money spilled out like green confetti. Later, in one of my rare recent sober moments, I'd picked it up and stacked it and put it in a new envelope. It was in my bank deposit box, now. Money was money; it didn't know where it came from. And even though I did know, I kept it. Out of perversity in a way. Because I had earned that money. Brother had I earned it.

"Why demand the impossible of yourself, Nate?" Sally asked. "There was no way you could have known that man wasn't really her father."

"I should have checked up on him. That's twice lately somebody's come in off the street and told me a story and I swallowed hook, line and sinker. I'm supposed to be a guy with some street savvy. Stick around—some guy'll sell me the Wrigley Building, before the summer's out."

Smiling, she said, "You're starting to sound like Nate Heller again, whether you like it or not."

I sighed. "It'd be all right with me to come out of this. And I will. Being here's a good sign."

"I think you're right."

"I'm getting off the rum, that much I promise you. I seen too many guys sitting in doorways in rags sucking a bottle in a bag. I'll eat my piece before I go that route."

"You're no suicide, Heller. You're not the type."

"My father was."

"Maybe that's why you aren't."

Seth Pearson had been. Louise's husband. I'd sat in the De Kalb County Sheriff's Office that Saturday afternoon, for hours, giving a statement, and gathered that everybody in town knew Seth was crazy with jealousy, rage and sorrow over his runaway wife, though the sheriff's people, at least, were surprised it had gone this far. I didn't tell them anything about retrieving Louise from the outlaw life; just that Pearson, posing as Joshua Petersen, had come to me so I'd find his "daughter." The real Joshua Petersen, I was told, had died several months ago.

The story got little play in the Chicago papers, just an item buried on the inside—any crime of passion in the state was bound to get at least that much ink. Louise's outlaw past did not catch up with her, or it'd have got more, much more.

"She *almost* told me," I said, shaking my head. "She was surprised that the photo I had of her came from her father—it was a picture of her and the husband, you see. But I didn't pick up on it. I was too thick, too eager to make that grand."

"You got to quit punishing yourself! That girl was a lost cause before you met her. Her fate, as we say in the theater, was sealed. You couldn't have prevented it. Some things you can't prevent, Nate. Some things you can't control, or stop. You're just a man."

"I'm a cop. A detective."

"Yes, right, and that's why you *are* a detective—you want to put this messy world in some kind of recognizable order. And that's of course impossible. But you do seem to manage to tidy up an occasional corner, now and again, you know. Give yourself a little credit. You saved J. Edgar Hoover's life, didn't you? Or at least his dignity."

"Barney told you about that, too, did he?"

"Yeah. You managed that one pretty well, wouldn't you say, Heller?"

"Ten of Hoover isn't worth one of her."

"Well, it doesn't work that way, that isn't the way life plays, is it?" She got out of bed and went over to the window and pointed. "Before you know it, winter'll be here, and those rich Gold Coast bastards'll wear mink coats while a couple blocks away people'll be freezing to death in the street. Is that fair?"

"No. But wouldn't you like to change it?"

"Sure. In my small way, I try. But I'm not going to fling myself out the window. I'm not going to throw my mink coat out, either, or give it to a peddler. Or cry in my beer."

"What are you going to do?"

"Survive. Best I can. Do my job. Best I can. Remember telling me that?"

I was smiling. Just a little; but it didn't feel unnatural, anyway.

She came back and got in bed, sitting up. "Why don't you quit depressing yourself with the what-ifs and the why-didn't-Is. Why don't you tell me about meeting Dillinger."

Barney really *did* tell her everything.

"I swore that little SOB to secrecy!"

"You're keeping secrets from *me*, Heller? Don't even bother trying."

So I told her about meeting Dillinger.

And I told her about how Cowley pretended to think the man named Sullivan I'd met was only bullshitting about being Dillinger— since Dillinger was obviously dead. The headlines had made Dillinger's death at the Biograph true. What was really going on in Cowley's mind, and Purvis', and even Hoover's, was then and is now beyond me. They had to know, or strongly suspect, that I was right. That Dillinger was alive.

But they stuck to the party line. Hoping Dillinger would stay underground and dead; or, if he went back on the outlaw trail, turn up dead with a new face and end up in some potter's field unidentified. Underground or under the ground—either way was fine.

Their odds weren't bad, actually. Dillinger struck me as cagey enough to stay dead. If he survived that tommy-gun burst in front of the Banker's Building, he'd be careful as hell before sticking his neck out again—attached as it was to that new face of his.

Cowley also agreed to keep my name out of it; the press never heard about my role in the action, and the kidnapping aspect was quashed, as well. The way it was given to the press (and they bought it) had Hoover, Purvis and Cowley stumbling onto the Continental Bank being cased for a heist. Rumors of the heavyweight public enemies involved did make the papers, but the Division of Investigation wouldn't confirm them. Losing a catch that included Nelson, the Barkers, Floyd and Karpis would've made the division guys look like saps, so they withheld the names. The "gang" members were unidentified, the official release went.

The papers ate the story up (G-MEN IN LOOP GUN BATTLE) an Hoover was portrayed as the hero of the piece.

I didn't care. My concern was keeping out of the papers, so Di linger/Sullivan, if he had survived, wouldn't think I betrayed him; h might strongly suspect, but he wouldn't *know*. Nobody had seen m there, despite my having leaned out the door to fire a few shots ove Nelson's head, late in the fray. All Dillinger could know for sure wa what the rest of them knew: that I skipped with the girl. The onl difference was he knew why.

And to Nelson and the others, of course, I wasn't Nate Heller: was Jimmy Lawrence.

And Jimmy Lawrence was, effectively, dead. Frank Nitti had a sured me of that. He had sent for me Monday afternoon, to ask m what really went down at the Banker's Building. When I told him I' defused that situation, he was pleased with me, and furious wit everybody else.

"Kidnap Hoover! Crazy bastards. The heat that'd bring dow woulda made this summer look like the North Pole. I owe you one Heller."

"No, Frank—you don't owe me anything. No more debts eithe way, between you and me."

"What d'you mean, kid?"

"I mean, I asked for a favor, and you did me one—but at the sam time you used me to finger Doc Moran. I was there when he wa killed, Frank. I was part of it—just like when Cermak's boys tried t gun you down. Remember?"

"Only when I breathe. Look, Moran was already dead. He wa walking around, but he was long dead. You had nothin' to do with it.

"Sure. Fine. Just I don't owe you anything, and you don't owe m anything. Clean slate. Okay?"

"Sure, kid. Except for one last favor I'm gonna do you."

"What's that?"

"I'm gonna spread the word Jimmy Lawrence went swimming i cement shoes. Just to keep those crazy bastards from comin' lookir for you."

"That I would appreciate, Frank."

"My pleasure. And you don't owe me nothin'. And, Heller?"

"Yeah?"

"Get a shave. Take a bath—you smell like a brewery."

Sound advice, touching as it did on two of Nitti's fields of endeavor.

And today, almost a week later, I'd taken it. Bathed. Shaved. Stopped the sauce. And come to see Sally.

"It'll pass, Heller."

"I keep seeing her eyes, Helen. In my dreams. That's why I kept drinking; when I was passed out, I didn't dream. Not that I can remember, anyway. But if I sleep, I see her eyes. The dead way."

"Shhh. Shhh."

"Helen."

"Yes?"

"Why don't you hold me."

"Why don't I."

She held me, and I slept. No dreams.

No Sally, after November.

She left soon after the fair closed; it had disturbed her, what happened then. It was our last night together—that is, the last night of our long summer together. She'd looked out the window at the Gold Coast and said, "Today they completely demolished the Century of Progress. They tore down flags, they tore down streetlights, they tore down walls. It started out being souvenir hunters, but it turned into mass vandalism. It was terribly frightening, Nate . . . Nate? Nate, this time why don't you hold *me?*"

I had, that one last time. It disturbed Sally, and I think it disturbed Chicago, to realize the fair was finally over. The illusion of a streamlined future was just so much scrap lumber now, in this city mired in a dreary present.

We never got back together, Sally and me, after our summer. We remained friends over the years, but she married (several times) and she wasn't the kind to fool around. She was a very moral girl, Sally Rand.

But she stayed in show business. She never made it in the movies, really, but she kept on fan-and-bubble dancing throughout her life. That wasn't all, of course—through the thirties she lectured on intellectual and political topics, speaking out for republican forces in the Spanish Civil War; she even went to college, earned a degree. Shortly before she died in 1979, I spoke with her on the phone; I asked her why she was still doing her fan dance after all these years.

"Don't be so up-tight, Heller!" she'd said. "I do it because I still like doing it. Better than doing needlepoint on the patio."

I sent a wreath that said, "Good-bye, Helen." I didn't go the funeral; it was in California, and I was in Florida, and try to avoid funerals, particularly my own, which at my age is a good trick.

As for the rest of them, well, I kept track of some; others just faded into a well-deserved obscurity.

Still others found a place in history, at least the sort of history "true crime" buffs thrive on.

I remember feeling strangely numb, reading the write-up in the paper, when Inspector Sam Cowley and Baby Face Nelson met for the second time.

November 1934. Cowley and another agent stumbled onto Nelson, his wife and John Paul Chase, their car stalled, spouting steam from a bullet caught in a wild gunfight with several other feds down the road. Helen dove for cover, as Cowley, in a ditch, traded tommy-gun fire with Nelson, who strode slowly, inexorably toward Cowley, machine gun spraying slugs. Cowley hit Nelson several times, but Nelson came on, his tommy gun blazing, sweeping the gun in flaming arcs across the ditch, bullets tearing across Cowley, killing him. A nearby construction worker said later, "It was just like Jimmy Cagney."

Soon Lester Gillis got in the car and asked his wife to drive. "I've been hit," he said. He had seventeen bullets in him. Helen and Chase abandoned his naked corpse in a drainage ditch.

Helen testified against Chase and got a reduced sentence; Chase went to Alcatraz, mellowed, and painted oils.

Doc Barker was captured in Chicago in January 1935; he was living in the Pine Grove apartment at the time, out having an evening stroll when Purvis captured him; Doc was unarmed, and when Purvis asked him where his gun was, he said, "Home—and ain't that a hell of a place for it!"

Ma and Fred had taken a two-story white cottage on Lake Weir in Florida when the feds surrounded the place and demanded their surrender. Someone within the house opened fire, and the agents riddled the cottage with slugs. Fred was found with eleven bullets in him; Ma with three. Both were dead.

Nobody had ever heard of Ma Barker, at this point; but the Division of Investigation had a dead old lady on their hands. So J. Edgar's publicity boys turned her into the brains of the gang and created the legend of the "bloody mama," avoiding the public embarrassment of having murdered a little-old-lady nonentity—at the same time, giving the newly rechristened Federal Bureau of Investigation that much further glory. Ma was never on a public enemies' list, nor was she ever charged with a crime, let alone indicted. She was just an Ozark ma who loved her boys, if not wisely.

In June 1939 Doc attempted to escape from Alcatraz and was hastily assembling a raft when the rifles from the guard towers cut him down.

George Barker, Ma's long-deserted husband, buried his boys and his wife in an open field near his small-town filling station in Oklahoma, in front of which he would sit in a chair leaned up against the building, listening to hillbilly music on the radio.

In October 1934, Pretty Boy Floyd, fleeing across an open field in Ohio, was cut down by Purvis and a squad of special agents in a hail of rifle and machine-gun fire. Purvis leaned over the dying man and asked him if he was Pretty Boy Floyd.

"I'm Charles Arthur Floyd," he said. Then he denied being part of the Kansas City Massacre, cursed Purvis, and, finally, got across the river.

I don't know what became of the "molls": Helen Nelson (Gillis), Fred's girl Paula, Karpis' girl Dolores. She had his kid, I heard, a boy.

Karpis himself became a special target of Hoover's. Hoover held Karpis responsible for the attempted kidnap in front of the Banker's Building, and—sensitive to criticism that he had no real police background, that he'd never been on a real case, made a real arrest—Hoover arranged to be present at Karpis' bloodless capture in New Orleans, in May 1936. Dozens of agents swooped down on Karpis, and once he was secured, Hoover was brought in to slap on the cuffs. But nobody had remembered to bring any, and an agent took off his tie and that was used instead. Karpis went to Alcatraz, was a docile prisoner, and upon his release was deported to Canada; he died in 1979.

As for the cops, Captain Stege retired and passed away a few years later. O'Neill the same. Zarkovich, however, became chief of detectives in East Chicago and then chief of police, surviving various grand jury investigations and reform administrations, working till his death in 1969. He never bragged about his role in the Dillinger shooting; he would only modestly say, "I just did my job."

Polly Hamilton dropped out of sight for several years, but she turned up in Chicago in the forties, working at the Ambassador East Hotel in room service. Rumor had it she was doing more than providing late-night snacks and club soda, as she had a fancy Gold Coast apartment at the time. She was living in Old Town, married, still working for a hotel, when she died in 1969 of cancer of the tongue.

Anna Sage, despite Purvis' pledge, was deported. In 1938 an angry Anna got on a train at LaSalle Street Station, destination Ellis Island; Hal Davis told me he saw a man see her off, and give her a package, whispering to her, calming her down. The man was Zarkovich. But before she sailed, she told reporters, "I will one day reveal startling new facts about the Dillinger slaying! They cannot keep me from coming back—I'll be back someday!" She never did. After running a nightclub in Romania for some years, she began talking about going onstage to tell the "real story" of the Dillinger shooting. She was found dead along a Romanian roadside in April 1947. Cause of death remains a mystery.

Louis Piquett finally was disbarred, and went to Leavenworth in 1936, for a two-year sentence. He returned to bartending in 1938, but did a lot of legal work on the side, and still had friends in high places: President Truman, in January 1951, gave him a full pardon, and his reinstatement to the Illinois bar was imminent when he died that December.

The publicity the Biograph shooting brought to Melvin Purvis made him, and the G-man in general, a public hero. He resigned the division in 1935, after an apparently jealous Hoover crossed him, failing to back Purvis' promise to Anna Sage of nondeportation, and (worse yet) pressuring Attorney General Cummings into denying permission for a Hollywood movie about Purvis' adventures. Little Mel, "the most famous operative of the most famous law-enforcement agency in the United States," hired on as spokesman for the Post Toasties Junior G-man Corps, appearing in comic-strip ads in the Sunday funnies. He worked on radio, as an announcer for FBI-oriented programs, and as a screenwriter; he even practiced law occasionally. During World War II he was a colonel and worked out of the War Crimes Office. But he ended up back home in South Carolina, running a radio station.

Then in 1959 one of Purvis' most famous cases belatedly, publicly, unraveled. A judge released Roger Touhy, saying the kidnapping charges Purvis had brought years before were a fabrication devised organized crime; twenty-three days after his release, Touhy was urdered by mob hit men.

Melvin Purvis, it was later said, read with morbid interest every wspaper and magazine piece he could assemble on the incident. At e same time he was suffering from mental depression, for which he ɔk electroshock therapy. On February 29, 1960, he shot himself in e head with a .45 automatic.

Some reporters were quick to say this was the gun Purvis had car-·d the night he "shot" Dillinger. Of course, Melvin hadn't fired a ɔt that night; nor did he or anyone else kill Dillinger.

No, gun buff that he was, Purvis selected something from his vast llection, specifically a chrome-plated .45, that he knew would do ιat he wanted it to: kill him.

I noted Purvis' passing with interest and a little sadness. I didn't ;like Purvis, really. He was no coward, certainly—he'd gone head-·head with Baby Face Nelson, Pretty Boy Floyd, Volney Davis, ɔc Barker and others, and come out on top. He'd even done some ɔd investigative work, in the year following the Biograph. But he'd en used by the Outfit, unwittingly, and seeing one of his most nous cases come publicly undone, as it had with Touhy, must've en the straw.

Or one of them.

In October 1959, a letter arrived at A-1 Detective Agency ad-essed to Jimmy Lawrence, care of Nathan Heller.

It said: "Sleep easy. I'm not much for grudges—decided not to en the score. Wish you were here."

It was signed "JD," and had no address; just a California postmark. Later I learned a longer letter had been sent to the Indianapolis ιr, with a picture of a white-haired man who might be "Dillinger, enty-five years later"; and yet another letter with picture to Emil anatka, the owner of the Little Bohemia Lodge, for the Dillinger useum there. Both letters included information about Anna Sage, nmy Lawrence and Dillinger that was not common public knowl-ge.

I don't know if my letter came from the same old guy who sent ters to the Star and Wanatka. But maybe Melvin Purvis received a nilar letter, in early 1960.

And maybe J. Edgar did, as well. It makes me smile to think so, yway. By the time such a letter might have arrived, the director's nous displays of ghoulish memorabilia were not just to be found in the FBI Museum, but in the very anteroom where visitors waited for admission to Hoover's office. Hoover would pass each day glass-cased enshrined mementos of that triumphant night at the Biograph: a straw hat, Polly Hamilton's picture, gold-rimmed glasses, a cellophane-wrapped La Corona–Belvedere cigar. And of course facsimiles of the famous death mask.

The mask those student morticians made back at the Cook County Morgue.

I OWE THEM ONE

Despite its extensive basis in history, this book is a work of fiction, and a few liberties have been taken with the facts, though as few as possible—and any blame for inaccuracies is my own, reflecting, I hope, the limitations of my conflicting source material, and the need to telescope certain minor events to make for a more smoothly flowing narrative. When fictional events have been included, an attempt has been made to graft them logically onto history, without contradicting known facts or the behavior patterns of the parties involved.

Several books consulted in the researching of this novel deserve singling out—notably *Dillinger Days* by John Toland (1963) and *Dillinger: A Short and Violent Life* (1962) by Robert Cromie and Joseph Pinkston. I am particularly indebted to Jay Robert Nash, whose persistence and research turned the legend of Dillinger's survival into a bona fide theory; his *Dillinger—Dead or Alive?* (1970) was most useful, and is highly recommended to readers who would like to dig into that theory further (Nash published a revised, expanded version, *The Dillinger Dossier*, in 1983). Nash further explores the theory in *Citizen Hoover* (1972), and in his extensive *Bloodletters and Badmen* (1973), which served as a general reference for this book. Others have explored the theory, including Toland and Cromie/Pinkston, and in particular Carl Sifakis in *The Encyclopedia of American Crime* (1982). I should note that I do not draw exactly the same conclusions from the evidence at hand as does Nash, so he should not be held accountable for the version of Dillinger's "death" as told in these pages; and I do not share with Nash any faith in the reliability of the reminiscences of Blackie Audett, a minor, self-aggrandizing contemporary of John Dillinger—Audett, in his autobiography *Rap Sheet* (1954) and in interviews given Nash, strikes me as a singularly unconvincing teller of tall tales. On the other hand, my own independent research has tended to substantiate Nash's findings, and reveal him to have been accurate and thorough in his writings on the subject.

The characterization of Sally Rand is a fictionalized one, though based upon numerous newspaper and magazine articles, and especially drawing from Studs Terkel's oral history, *Hard Times* (1970), which was a general reference for this book, as well. I know of no historic parallel in Sally Rand's life for her relationship with Nate Heller, and (though Miss Rand is treated with great affection in these pages) wish to stress that no unflattering reflection upon this historical figure is intended.

The death of Dr. Joseph Moran, while consistently reported in various sources in a fashion in keeping with its depiction here, varies widely from source to source as to location; so I have taken the liberty of burying Dr. Moran where I please.

The "other" Nate Heller mentioned briefly herein, as a "hot-money" fence, is a historical figure.

Several hardworking people helped me research this book, primarily George Hagenauer, whose contributions include helping develop the plan to kidnap J. Edgar Hoover (as George came to say, after initial skepticism about staging a kidnapping in the Loop, "I think we could pull it off!"). George, a life-long Chicagoan, is a Chicago history buff with an eye for detail; he provided invaluable help, and support. My friend and frequent collaborator, cartoonist Terry Beatty, also lent his support and help to this project, including adapting the map of the Loop printed herein. A tip of the fedora to Catherine Yronwode, for sharing with me the anecdote about a certain distant relation of hers ("Uncle" Lester Gillis) who played the game of "search me" with his young nephew. Thanks are also due Mike Gold; Ann DeLarye; Ray Gotto; Mickey Spillane; and the late Dave Gerrity. And I'd like to thank Dominick Abel, my agent; Tom Dunne, my editor; and Tom's associate, Susannah Driver.

Photos selected by the author for use in this edition are courtesy UPI/Bettman Archives. Melvin Purvis photo is courtesy Tom Tumbusch, *Illustrated Radio Premium Price Guide*. Remaining photos have been selected from the personal collections of George Hagenauer and the author. Efforts to track the sources of certain photos have been unsuccessful; upon notification these sources will be listed in subsequent editions.

Hundreds of books, magazine articles (including many true-detectives magazines from the thirties), and newspaper stories (from the *Tribune, Herald and Examiner, Daily News* and other Chicago papers of the day) have been consulted in researching *True Crime*, the companion volume to my earlier novel *True Detective* (1983). I am particularly indebted to the anonymous authors of the Federal Writers Project volumes on the states of Illinois (1939) and Wisconsin (1941). Also, a few other books deserve singling out: *The People Talk* (1940), Benjamin Appel; *The FBI Nobody Knows* (1964), Fred J. Cook; *Ten Thousand Public Enemies* (1935), Courtney Ryley Cooper; *Daddy Danced the Charleston* (1970), Ruth Corbett; *The Real Ma Barker* (1970), Mirian Allen deFord; *Captive City* (1969), Ovid Demaris; *The Director* (1975), Ovid Demaris; *Dining in Chicago* (1931), John Drury; *Tune in Yesterday* (1976), John Dunning; *Line Up Tough Guys* (1966), Ron Goulart; *Persons in Hiding* (1938), J. Edgar Hoover; *It's a Racket* (1929), Gordon L. Hostetter and Thomas Quinn Beesley; *The Alvin Karpis Story* (1971), Alvin Karpis with Bill Trent; *Chicago: Growth of a Metropolis* (1969), Harold M. Mayer and Richard C. Wade; *The Bad Ones* (1968), Lew Louderback; *The Legacy of Al Capone* (1975), George Murray; *G-Men, Hoover's FBI in American Popular Culture* (1983), Richard Gid Powers; *American Agent* (1936), Melvin H. Purvis; *The Devil's Emissaries* (1969), Myron J. Quimby; *No Man Stands Alone* (1957), Barney Ross and Martin Abramson; *The Verse by the Side of the Road* (1965), Frank Rowsome, Jr.; *Syndicate City* (1954), Alson J. Smith; *The Stolen Years* (1959), Roger Touhy; *Chicago Uncensored* (1965), Irle Waller.

When all the debts have been paid, or at least acknowledged, one remains: this book could not have been written without the love, help and support of my wife, Barbara Collins—Nate's mother.